The Low

Oceanside Height[s] [...] town. If you want[...] [...] [...] [...] somewhere else—somewhere your neighbors couldn't find you. Even the tourists were a wholesome bunch. With a population of 703, the "Christian seaside paradise" attracted young families and middle-aged matrons who came to enjoy the gorgeously clean beach and old-time preaching. Anne didn't mind being among strangers. They brought life to the Heights. And, unlike the all-year rounders, they didn't know the first thing about her past.

That was the problem with small towns. Everybody was familiar with everybody else's life history. Anne was thirty-six years old and every single resident of the Heights knew her as the Crazy Lady's daughter. It didn't matter that her mother had been dead for seven years. The stigma remained, like a permanent stamp imprinted on her skin. Oh, they were polite enough. Most of them, anyway. *"How you doing today, Anne?"* *"Write anything interesting today?"* But underneath the friendly patina, she sensed distrust and a thread of fear. It was as if they were waiting for Anne to change, to go crazy like her mother had. In the meantime, they kept a safe, civil distance . . .

DEAD MAN'S FLOAT

A JERSEY SHORE MYSTERY

BETH SHERMAN

AVON BOOKS  NEW YORK

AVON BOOKS, INC.
1350 Avenue of the Americas
New York, New York 10019

Copyright © 1998 by Beth Sherman
Published by arrangement with the author
Visit our website at http://www.AvonBooks.com
Library of Congress Catalog Card Number: 97-94866
ISBN: 0-380-73107-X

First Avon Books Printing: July 1998

AVON TRADEMARK REG. U.S. PAT. OFF. AND IN OTHER COUNTRIES, MARCA REGISTRADA, HECHO EN U.S.A.

Printed in the U.S.A.

WCD   10   9   8   7   6   5   4   3   2

For Andy

Chapter 1

Cleaning is like life. You've got to work at it if you want to see results.

Mary Lou Popper's Household Guide for People Who Hate to Clean

Tigger Mills never could shake trouble. It followed him around like a bunch of tin cans tied to the rear fender of a car. When he was younger, he seemed to welcome it. He had a reputation for being wild and would do just about anything on a dare: swing from the bell tower, lie down on the railroad tracks right before the train was coming around the bend, walk the cliffs blindfolded; whatever the challenge, he took it. That was before the fire. After, despite his claim that he had nothing to do with it, his reputation spread beyond the small town of Oceanside Heights to the surrounding Jersey shore, so if you happened to be in Bradley Beach or Point Pleasant or Spring Lake, and you let on that you knew Tigger (not mentioning, of course, that you knew him by sight, not personally), you became famous by association.

It was the fire that thrust the Heights into the spotlight

1

twenty years ago. All the local festivities—the tall ships, the lavish fireworks, the parade of floats—were a few miles away in Point Pleasant. But when the fire broke out on the Fourth of July, reporters rushed to cover it. In the days that followed, newspaper and TV accounts portrayed the Heights as more than just a religious enclave, the tiny square mile locals called "God's own acre." The news people photographed the splendid Victorian houses, with their wraparound porches and grand cupolas. They showed the boardwalk, and the gazebo, and the old-fashioned shops in town that date back to the nineteenth century, and that summer, for the first time, the tourists came. Each year, more people filled the faded hotels along the ocean, until the town had to build guest houses, taking care to make them look old, and the value of real estate started to soar.

So really, Tigger Mills was somehow linked to the growth of the summer tourist industry, Anne thought to herself, as she caught sight of him leaning against the railing of the boardwalk, looking out to sea. It was a hot humid morning, and the beach was packed because of the July Fourth holiday. Everywhere she looked she saw American flags—imprinted on bathing suits, planted in the sand, sticking out of picnic coolers. Independence Day was a big deal in the Heights, celebrated with gusto.

It must be strange for Tigger to be back here, she thought. It was exactly twenty years ago today that the fire broke out, and he hadn't returned until now. A few weeks after the Spray View Hotel burned to the ground, his parents shipped him off to live with relatives. She forgot where, exactly. Someplace in the Midwest. There wasn't enough evidence for a legal trial, but the people who lived in the Heights had convicted him anyway, and his parents thought it best that he leave.

The years had not treated him unkindly. He had a beard and mustache now, but his dark hair still fell across his forehead, just as it had when they were kids. And his eyes were still the incredible shade of green Anne remembered, the same jewel tone as those patches in the ocean where, when you swam through them, the water was surprisingly warmer. His jaw was set in the old, determined way, his lips parted to form the same sensual grin. His body had filled out, become more muscular, so that his white T-shirt and jeans appeared to cling to his skin.

Tigger Mills. Looking at him took her back to that fateful summer, when her crush, passion, call it what you will (she called it love) spread like fever, so that she only had to hear his name or catch a glimpse of his bike hurtling down the boardwalk for her face to prickle, turning as red as the roses in her mother's garden. Anne had never known anyone quite like Tigger Mills. No other boy was as handsome or athletic, no one else possessed his courage. She could still see him diving off the longest pier, just because the others said he couldn't, his body jackknifed in the air, plunging down, down toward the water, foam spilling over the rocks below. The moment when he disappeared beneath the waves, stretching out to two minutes, then three, until they all thought he had struck the rocks and was wedged between them, trapped, unconscious. The boys shuffled their feet, peered at the line separating sea from sky, as if the answer lay past the horizon. They started to blame one another for goading him into it, until Anne almost expected them to come to blows and pitch each other off the pier, as a form of retribution. One girl began to sob. And then, suddenly, someone saw his head bobbing above the water on the other side of the pier, and they all broke out laughing, chortling with relief, and no one laughed louder than Tigger. But that was nothing compared with the nights— all those nights she looked out her bedroom window and saw him on the boardwalk, holding hands with the prettiest girls in school, kissing them under the curved street lamps, bathed in white light, so that from a distance, he and the girl looked larger than life, incandescent as movie stars.

"Hey," he said now, turning toward her. "Hey, Anne, how've you been?" She walked over to where he was standing. Up close, his skin had a ruddy cast to it. From drinking, probably. Talk at the Mini-Mart was that he drank too much, which surprised no one.

"I'm fine," she answered. "How about you? I heard you were back."

"Yeah. My ma died last month, and left me her house. You know the place? The green house? Over on Embury?"

She knew it.

"My old man says it belongs to him. But Ma owned that house. And it's mine now. No matter what trash he's talking."

Anne looked at him closely. Troy Mills had been going around town threatening to disown his son if Tigger even set foot on the property. Odds at the Mini-Mart were running four to one that Troy would do it, if pressed. Troy had a bad temper. He didn't like being crossed. "Well, the house is legally yours though, isn't it?"

"Not according to the old man. He's contesting the will, claims a husband automatically inherits everything from his wife."

"Do you have a good lawyer?"

He threw his head back and laughed. "Lawyers cost money."

"Of course," Anne said, as if restating the obvious. "Where are you staying while you sort things out?" Maybe if they stood here long enough, she'd be able to ask him questions she didn't know the answer to. Like how it felt to be back here on the Fourth of July, the twentieth anniversary of little Ruthie Klemperer's death. She'd heard what they were saying about Tigger down at Moby's Hardware and the Pelican Café. Gossip ricocheted through the Heights like a stone skipping across a lake. They talked of nothing else at the Ladies' Auxiliary Book Sale and the Heights Kite Festival. Fishermen spoke of it as they set their lobster traps. So did shopkeepers sweeping the sidewalks on Main Street and the youth group who met each morning for devotions and donuts in Oceanside Chapel. Anne's neighbors talked about Tigger while weeding their gardens or fixing supper or hanging their wash out to dry. Everybody said the same thing: He should have been thrown in jail years ago for burning down the hotel and killing a three-year-old child who was trapped inside.

But Anne always believed he was innocent. Maybe because he said so, and the police could never prove otherwise. Or maybe because underneath his reckless charm, she'd sensed he had integrity. Or maybe because she knew firsthand how people in a small town liked acting as judge and jury.

From underneath the boardwalk, she heard the pop of illegal firecrackers. "I'm over at Ravenswood," Tigger said.

"That must be . . . difficult for you."

The Ravenswood Inn was where the state housed nearly two dozen elderly former mental patients, along with a few intrepid guests who paid a flat rate of $29.99 per night. The old people sat on the porch all day, rocking back and forth, staring into space. But some roamed the streets, asking for handouts, muttering to themselves, bothering the tourists, until the mayor had formed a committee, petitioning the governor to have the "loonies" moved elsewhere.

"It's not too bad," Tigger said, grinning. "I keep to myself. Don't disturb the disturbed, if you get my drift. And the price is right."

"Then I guess it's worth it," she said slowly. But she wouldn't have spent one night under the inn's roof. The residents of Ravenswood scared her. She often thought her mother could have ended up there, if her father hadn't generously blown his life savings to keep them afloat financially. First he'd hired a home health care attendant, and later, when things got really bad, he installed his ex-wife in a quality nursing home in Red Bank. Otherwise, Evelyn Hardaway might have ended up like the "loonies"—wandering the streets, uprooting her neighbors' flower beds, talking to imaginary friends.

The elderly people on the porch of Ravenswood reminded Anne of the way her mother looked when she was sedated. It was hard to tell which was worse: Evelyn medicated to a level of docility or Evelyn in a rage, unable to identify the refrigerator by name or even remember who Anne was. At Ravenswood, people rocked on the porch for hours on end. Although they sat in rows, close enough to hold hands, each one seemed entirely alone. When Anne walked into town, she stayed on the other side of the street.

"Helluva day," Tigger Mills said, gesturing toward the water, the cloudless sky, the red, white, and blue umbrellas massed on the sand like brightly colored moons. "Nice and hot."

"Yeah," she said, standing up. "I'll probably get to the beach a little later on."

In the meantime, Anne thought to herself, ask him over for coffee. And what's left of the apple crumb pie. Ask him. Do it. Suddenly aware that he was studying her, as if seeing her for the first time. He was sizing her up: her long, wavy red hair, her blue eyes, the smattering of freckles splashed across her nose and cheeks. His eyes roamed over her trim figure, taking in her dark green midriff top and her cut-off denim shorts.

Could he tell what she was thinking, beneath her no-nonsense straw hat, the heat lapping between her thighs? "Your skin's so pale, you look like you'd best stay out of the sun," he said, smiling. She smiled back. God, he was still so sexy. She watched him stretch. When he flexed his arms above his head, the muscles beneath his shirt rippled.

"Well," he said. "I gotta be going. Places to go, people to see." His grin mocking the words, rendering them useless. "Later," he told her, as he walked away, in the direction of Ravenswood.

In the summer, the small town of Oceanside Heights swelled to three or four times its normal size. It was easy to tell the tourists from the people who lived there year round: tourists were always looking up, gawking at turrets and gingerbread trim on the old-fashioned pastel-colored houses, as if the Heights weren't a town at all, but a board game of architectural delights. At night, they strolled along the boardwalk or along the piers, which jutted into the ocean like fingers on a giant's hand, noting the salty breeze, the picture-perfect loveliness of the tiny beach resort.

The town had been founded as a camp meeting site in 1896, and religion was still its biggest attraction. At the huge Methodist church on Trinity Lane, known as the Church by the Sea, there were morning prayers, followed by Bible study, a gospel sing, a noon sermon, afternoon prayers, and finally an evening devotional. Religion had been good for the town. It helped keep rowdy college kids away, cleansed the boardwalk of beer bottles and in-line skates. The Heights was a clean town, a cheerful town. If you wanted to sin, you went somewhere else—somewhere your neighbors couldn't find you. Even the tourists were a wholesome bunch. With a population of 703, the "Christian seaside paradise" attracted young families and middle-aged matrons who came to enjoy the gorgeously clean beach and the old-time preaching. Anne didn't mind being among strangers. They brought life to the Heights. And unlike the all-year-rounders, they didn't know the first thing about her past.

That was the problem with small towns. Everybody was familiar with everybody else's life history. Anne was thirty-six years old, and every single resident of the Heights knew her as the Crazy Lady's daughter. It didn't matter that her mother had been dead for seven years. The stigma remained, like a permanent stamp imprinted on her skin. Oh, they were polite enough. Most of them, anyway. *How you doing today, Anne? Write anything interesting today?* But underneath the friendly patina, she sensed distrust and a thread of fear. It was as if they were waiting for Anne to change, to go crazy like her mother had. In the meantime, they kept a safe, civil distance.

For the last several months, she'd been toying with the idea of moving. She imagined herself working at a big magazine in New York, writing about quirky topics: people who swim with their dogs in the Hudson River, or what the inside of a water tower looks like. She daydreamed about what it would be like to live among strangers—safe in her anonymity, protected from narrow-minded biddies, painful memories, and the pitying, superior glances of her neighbors. She would sell the house, the furniture, even her '68 Mustang, which she rarely used. The Heights was so small, she walked everywhere she needed to go.

Now she walked around her house, trying to evaluate each room the way a real estate agent would, appraising the scuffed oak floors, the chipped walnut banister, the plaster peeling off the ceiling in the bathrooms. Realtors were always urging her to sell, slipping their cards under her front door, sending her flyers in the mail. *You've got prime ocean property,* they told her. *Right across the street from the beach, can't beat the view. The house is worth at least $300,000, maybe more.* But when it came right down to it, she didn't trust any of them. They had no idea how much this house meant to her. All they saw was a three-bedroom Victorian fixer-upper and a nice fat commission.

On an impulse, she went to the phone and called Jim Walser, the president of the Oceanside Heights Association. Mr. Walser would be able to tell her which agency was on the up and up. He had his own real estate firm for years, before retiring to become president of the association, a nonprofit organization dedicated to making sure everything in the Heights ran smoothly. Walser knew more about historic houses than anyone else in Monmouth County. When people needed a building permit, they came to Jim Walser. When they couldn't decide whether to redo their roofs in shingles or slate, they consulted him. When their gutters were clogged, when they needed new storm doors, when their plumbing didn't work or their porches needed repairing, they went straight to Jim Walser, the heart and soul of the Heights. And although he sounded harried on the phone, he promised Anne he'd come right over.

While she waited, she tried not to think about the promise she had made to her mother. It had been her mother's last wish that Anne hold on to the house, a request Anne had agreed to when her mother was dying. The rambling yellow cottage had become the repository of her mother's memories, a sieve holding what was left of the past. Even when Evelyn Hardaway was so disoriented that she couldn't tie a shoelace or operate the TV, Anne knew her mother could look around the cozy, quilt-strewn living room and remember the time Anne first learned to play the piano or the day she herself was carried across the threshold as a young bride. Evelyn had grown up in the house, and the ghosts of her long-dead relatives seemed to provide her with a shred of continuity and comfort.

After Evelyn died, Anne found an old recipe box stuffed with scraps of paper containing scribbled directions. By laying the papers end to end on the kitchen table, Anne was able to figure out what she was looking at: notes and maps Evelyn had drawn, to guide her home from the grocery store or the bank. At the age of forty-eight, Evelyn couldn't navigate the tiny town without the aid of written instructions. "Evelyn," Anne's father used to shout. "Where is your mind? Where is it located?" Her mother had no answer. But Anne did. It's lost, she would think. Lost somewhere in this house. If she looked hard enough and long enough, she told herself, she would eventually find it.

Because there was another woman Anne remembered: the mother who baked gingerbread men and made ice cream from snow, who spun wonderful tales about the squirrel living in the maple tree, and grew sunflowers tall as cars, who smoked cigarettes in a silver holder and built lavish mud pie castles by the ocean, complete with turrets and a moat. The house on Seaside Avenue, *her* house now, helped Anne stay connected to the real Evelyn Hardaway, the mother she'd had before illness struck. She couldn't just pick up and leave.

When Triple Star Publishing announced in January that the company was relocating to North Carolina, and Anne was given a choice of moving or losing her job, she made her boss an offer. She would work from home, telecommute, and continue to ghostwrite books for the company's stable of authors. That way, she'd be able to stay in the Heights, and still keep her job.

The arrangement had worked fairly well so far. In the past six months, she'd managed to churn out two books, and she was halfway through a third—*Mary Lou Popper's Household Guide for People Who Hate to Clean*. Still, she daydreamed about getting away. Moving to New York would be like shedding her old self and starting fresh. She was three and a half weeks late turning in chapter five of the book: "Fast 'n' Easy Floor Care." But she couldn't bring herself to start writing it. If she moved to Manhattan, she'd quit Triple Star, and Mary Lou Popper would be someone else's headache.

A knock on the door interrupted her reverie. She looked out the window and saw Jim Walser had arrived. In honor of Independence Day, he'd dressed entirely in patriotic colors: a red golf shirt, white slacks, and blue cap. She opened the door. "Hi, Mr. Walser. Thanks for coming over."

"My pleasure, Anne," he said, removing his cap and stepping inside. "Happy Fourth of July. What can I do for you?" Jim Walser was in his mid-sixties, with a slight paunch. His bald head, the Coke-bottle thickness of his glasses, and his slightly befuddled air had always reminded Anne of the Mr. Magoo cartoons she'd watched as a child.

"I'm sorry to drag you over here," she said. "But I wanted to talk in person. I'm . . . thinking of selling the house."

"Of course. Of course. No need to apologize. I know how much this old place means to you," Walser said soberly.

When her mother had gotten sick, Jim Walser had been one of the few people in town who'd been of any help. Instead of passing judgment or staying away, he'd helped Anne research various nursing homes, speaking to doctors and hospital administrators to learn which ones offered the best-quality care.

"I wasn't sure who I should contact," she said. "The agents have been besieging me more than usual lately."

Walser frowned. "Now, that's not right. We've had a boom year in terms of real estate, but to harass property owners like this . . ." He shook his head. "I'll put a stop to it."

"I mainly wanted to ask who you thought should represent me."

"Well, Lorraine Glick's not bad. Although she's getting a little long in the tooth for climbing folks' stairs to show off their attics. I'd steer clear of Surf Realty. Harvey loves the hard sell, but I don't cotton to him twisting the screws."

He paused to scratch his head. "You know who I'd call? Harriet Tuttle, over at the Seagull Group. She's fair. And she's honest. I expect you'd get your asking price—you're looking at $300,000 to $325,000 easy—minus the surcharge, of course."

Anne nodded. The land in Oceanside Heights was owned by the church, administered by the association, and leased to homeowners, in a complicated procedure designed to ensure that four percent of the price of each real estate transaction went toward strengthening the church and beautifying the town. The founding fathers had set things up this way so that religion would always be of central importance in the Heights. Property owners didn't mind. The money was used for things like landscaping Main Street or offering a needlework class over at the library or hiring a guest speaker to preach one Sunday a month. Better to mine religion than to wind up like Wildwood or Avalon, rowdy towns where drunken teenagers mobbed the beaches and every night was a carnival.

"Here's where to reach Harriet," Walser said, removing a card from his breast pocket and scribbling down the number. "Now, I've got to get back to the office. Remember, the fireworks start at nine sharp. We've got a doozy of a show this year."

After Walser left, Anne called the real estate agent. As the phone rang on the other end of the line, she felt a surge of guilt. Could she actually go through with it? Break a deathbed promise to her mother? She put the receiver back in its cradle. Harriet Tuttle could wait. Besides, it was a holiday. She'd only reach the answering machine at the real estate agency anyway.

She could spend the afternoon decoding Mary Lou Popper's notes on water-based wax strippers, but she really wasn't in the mood. After fixing herself some lunch, she donned a bathing suit and an old work shirt and headed across the street to the ocean.

The beach was even more crowded now, jammed with umbrellas and blankets. A teenager with sideburns and a tattoo smeared across his chest was doing a brisk business selling miniature flags. The tattoo said: *God Bless America*. Anne wondered if it was removable.

Laying her beach towel behind the lifeguard stand, she settled into a striped sand chair, with a brand-new mystery novel. She was just about to start reading when she realized she should have chosen another spot. Teri Curley was sitting nearby, developing the summer's most spectacular tan. Wearing a white one-piece suit designed for a nymphet, Teri didn't so much tan as pose. She was in constant motion: shifting her sunglasses from her nose to the top of her head, sipping designer water, spritzing her body with water from a plastic spray bottle. How many sessions with her personal trainer did it take to reduce her thighs? To swell the curve of her breasts so they rose like twin snow cones? To tone her stomach until it was washboard flat? Teri looked like she had paid through the nose.

Though the two women had known each other all their lives, they nearly always avoided eye contact. Before sixth grade, they had been best friends. But that year, Evelyn Hardaway had started getting worse—becoming more agitated and confused, becoming what Anne in her darkest, most private moments could only call insane. One day after school, Anne had made the mistake of inviting Teri and three other girls home to study. Her mother had asked Anne to do it, as a way of making up for burned dinners and lost keys. She had promised to bake her famous chocolate fudge brownies. And she kept her promise, too. But when she walked out on the porch, holding the plate of brownies, she was naked from the waist down, without a skirt or panties. Anne could never forget the horror on her friends' faces as they stared at her mother's milky white thighs, watching her mother's hand stroke the tuft of red pubic hair. A string of garbled obscenities escaped her mother's lips. The plate dropped and shattered. Her friends fled. Anne could hear them laughing in terror and disgust as they ran away.

The rest of the afternoon was a blur of adults—a stream of women flowing in and out of the house, followed by the minister and lastly, at the end of the day, by her father, his shame lingering in the air like stale cologne. One of her mother's friends, she forgot which one, berated him. "If you still lived here, George," the woman said, "Evvie wouldn't have to parade around half-nude. She has needs, too." Her father recoiled as if struck and disappeared upstairs, to consult with the doctor. Later, he would tell Anne that the worst part of it was that everybody knew. The whole town knew Evelyn Hardaway was crazy as a loon.

Anne didn't have to be told. Overnight, she found she had become a social outcast. Before, she had been marginally popular. After, her classmates made her feel dirty, as if *she* had been the one caught masturbating in broad daylight. Teri and her friends recreated the scene over and over for the rest of the school's amusement. When Anne walked down the hall, boys would point and grab their crotches, boys whose names she didn't even know.

Ever since then, Teri had perfected the "intentional ignore"—looking right through Anne as if she were a stranger, only acknowledging her existence when absolutely necessary. And now Teri was going to ignore her for the next two to three hours. Anne could tell she'd been spotted from the way Teri had started speaking, her voice grown louder, her diction more pronounced. Teri was with her three beautifully groomed children, whose names Anne always forgot, although she was fairly sure they all began with the letter T.

Small town neighborliness at its best, Anne thought, picking up her book and reading the first sentence four times because it was hard to concentrate and pretend she wasn't angry at the same time. In Oceanside Heights, she'd always be known as Crazy Evvie's daughter. Some things never changed.

Chapter 2

*After a trip to the beach,
vacuum the inside of your
washing machine to
remove loose, stubborn
grains of sand.*

Tigger Mills seemed to appear out of nowhere. She looked up and there he was, smiling his funny, crooked smile.

"You made it," he said, as if they had arranged to meet earlier. He sat down next to her on the sand.

"Just look at her," he said, gazing at the ocean, which was calm, like a sheet of colored glass. "Isn't she something? Makes me sorry I ever left."

"Where *have* you been living?"

"Indiana. You ever been?" She shook her head no. "Don't bother. There's no ocean. I used to swim at the local YMCA. Drove the members crazy."

She remembered that he was captain of the swimming team, captain of the sailing squad, too, the one year the JCs raised enough money to support a team. "So what were you doing out in Indiana?"

"Odd jobs. Some construction work, painting houses,

14

that sort of thing. I tell you what, though. It sure was different from here.'' He looked at her closely. "You ever wished you lived someplace normal?"

"What do you mean?" she asked defensively. Color rushed to her cheeks. She could feel her body tensing up.

"You know. Like Margate or Wildwood. The *real* Jersey shore, with Ferris wheels and taffy and those tacky no-tell motels they built back in the fifties."

"Oh," she said, feeling relief wash over her. He wasn't talking about her mother. He never had been one of the boys who teased her. "I thought you said you wanted to move back here."

"I do. But I could live without the fake charm—the horse-and-buggy aren't-we-old-fashioned crap. And big-time religion leaves me cold."

"I don't even notice the religious stuff anymore," Anne said. "Since my father died, I only go to church two or three times a year."

"Doesn't matter. Look over there." He pointed to a heavyset woman in an oversize T-shirt, which said: *God Is Like Scotch Tape. You Can't See Him, But He Holds Things Together!*

"God is watching," Tigger said, in a stage whisper. "But no one else gives a damn. You know we're not even on the map? I remember the first time I tried to find the Heights in an atlas and I couldn't. It was like, I dunno, like I didn't exist or something."

"But we do," Anne said lightly.

"Yup. I'm stuck here on earth for eternity. *My* soul's not going to heaven. Not if the townies have anything to say about it."

"I heard heaven's not so hot. You can't even get a decent cup of coffee."

"Then count me out. In the meantime, how'd you like to go for a swim?"

"The water's freezing. I went in the other day and nearly turned blue."

"Is that a no?"

"It's a maybe," she said, smiling.

Could this really be happening? Could she really be flirting with Tigger Mills after all these years? It seemed odd, unreal. Her feelings for him had once filled up two leather-bound diaries. Those beguiling green eyes had inspired some truly bad poetry, which was collecting dust in a cardboard box in her attic.

"I can't wait to get my house back," he said, changing the subject. "It needs a lot of work. New shingles on the roof. New windows and doors. I'm thinking of painting it red, to annoy the neighbors."

"Would you stay and live here year round?" she asked. Over his shoulder, she could see Teri Curley staring at them.

The last summer Tigger lived in the Heights, the summer of the fire, Teri had been his girlfriend, the one he kissed under the glow of the street lights, beneath a black velvet sky peppered with stars. Tigger had spotted Teri as well. For all Anne knew, he had been aware that she was sitting nearby the whole time. Life really is high school, she thought. No matter how old you got, nothing changed.

"Hey, Teri," he called out, waving. Anne steeled herself for the response, expecting the ex-prom queen to choose this moment to cool her polished toenails in the ocean. From what Anne had seen and heard in town, even Tigger's old friends had stayed away. Once, they had admired him. Once, they would have followed him anywhere. Now they kept their distance, as if he'd contracted some incurable disease.

But Teri actually waved back. Not only that, she deigned to rise from her blanket and walk over to where they were sitting, spritz bottle in hand so she wouldn't melt in the heat. "How you doing?" she said, addressing Tigger only.

"Terrific. Happy as a pig in a pen."

"Great . . . that's great," Teri said, opening wide to smile. Not much penetrated her irony-free zone, Anne thought.

Teri pulled her long black hair off her face, began gathering it into a ponytail, then let it fall, and immediately proceeded to gather it up again, a mannerism Anne recognized from high school. She had applied so much hair spray it looked as if there was air between every other strand. If you stuck a pencil in the middle, it would probably have stayed suspended. Teri Curley's Amazing Superglue Hair!

"I heard about your mother," Teri said to Tigger. "She was such a darling. Bobby and I were so sorry to hear she'd passed away."

Anne studied Tigger carefully. The mocking grin was back on his face, but he was looking at Teri with interest. Anne wondered whether the old attraction still existed between them. Teri's husband, Bobby, had been Tigger's best friend in high school, his second in command. Tigger couldn't have been happy to hear they got married.

"You and Bobby have how many kids now? Five? Six?" Tigger asked.

"Three gorgeous girls, right over there," Teri said, nodding toward the three Ts.

"They're beauties all right."

If I stood up right now and walked away, Anne thought, how long would it take for them to realize I was gone? She was tempted to do just that, before they began strolling down memory lane. But right then Tigger put his hand on her shoulder and said: "You remember Anne Hardaway, don't you, Teri?"

Teri's brow cleared, her eyes snapped into focus, as if a fog had suddenly lifted, enabling her to be interested in what moments ago wasn't worth spit. Anne had seen Teri undergo the transformation before—at the annual end-of-summer fund-raiser for the church, on the steps of her pink Victorian home the day of the historical house tour, nose to nose with a horde of camera-toting tourists. It was what she called Teri's "tea and socials" face, and generally it didn't appear when Anne was around.

"Why, hello, Annie," Teri gushed. "How've you been? I haven't seen you in absolutely ages."

"I've been just swell," Anne said, playing along. "We really should have lunch one of these days."

"That would be lovely," Teri purred. "I look forward to it."

Why did she even come over here? Anne wondered. To cause a scene? Extend a peace offering? Because she was annoyed that Tigger was with me and not with her?

"You know," Teri said to Tigger, "you have something I want."

"Is that right?"

"You remember that old letter you were awarded, the varsity one, from when you were on the swim team?" she continued. "Well, next year is the biggie—our twentieth class reunion. And I want to include the letter with some other sports memorabilia I've been collecting."

"Sorry. No can do. I lost it."

"Really?" Teri said, frowning. "Why don't you take another look? You may still have it lying around somewhere. I might even be able to pay you for it."

"Pay me, huh? I don't think so. You can't put a price on memories."

A look of annoyance flickered across Teri's face. But it was gone in a moment, replaced by her customary perky smile. She gathered her hair up and let it fall. "Look," she said brightly, "why don't we meet for a drink later or an early supper?"

"I can't. I'm having dinner with Anne tonight."

At this piece of news, Anne shot him a questioning look. But Tigger was staring up at Teri. The three of them looked at one another, smiles plastered to their faces, waiting for someone to speak. It seemed the conversation had run out of steam. "Sooooo," Teri said finally. "Are you both planning to be at the reunion?"

"That all depends," Tigger said, "on whether dropouts get to go."

Teri hooked her index finger into the bottom of her bathing suit and readjusted her tan line. "After you moved away, you graduated from somewhere, didn't you?" she asked disdainfully.

"Nah. Degrees are a dime a dozen. I'll go for experience any time."

"Well, there's always the GED. You'll have to come anyway. It'll be tons of fun."

"And you always were up for fun, weren't you, baby?" Tigger said softly.

Teri's face turned one shade darker. "Oh, shoot," she said, clapping her hands together. "I really must fly. Tammy has Brownies today, and I have to drop her off. Call me later. We have so much catching up to do."

Without waiting for a reply, she walked back toward her blanket and began packing up her things. Anne could hear the two older girls complaining that they didn't want to leave. It wasn't fair.

"She's a regular Jersey shore Barbie," Tigger sneered. "I don't know how Bobby puts up with her."

"You used to like her."

Tigger's eyes were fixed on the ocean. "I used to like a lot of things about this town."

Each year, shortly after Labor Day, the restaurant on the northernmost end of Oceanside Heights went out of business, only to be reborn the following summer with a different menu and a different name. This summer's incarnation was the Albatross, serving "continental cuisine," not all that different from the surf and turf of the previous year, when the place had been called Joey's.

Tonight, there was hardly anybody in the restaurant other than the staff. Most of the tourists had migrated to Bradley Beach, picking out a good spot to watch the fireworks. The waitress led Anne and Tigger to a window seat, overlooking the ocean, with a view of plastic palm trees planted in the sand. Anne ordered the lobster dinner. If she weren't planning to pay half, she might have chosen something else, but at $14.99, it wasn't all that expensive. When the waitress walked away, Tigger pulled out the bottle of wine he'd been carrying in a brown paper bag.

"Isn't it stupid," he said, pouring the wine into their water glasses, "that the Heights is a dry town but they let you bring the stuff in?"

"That just started this summer. The town council voted.

They said it would hurt tourism if people couldn't drink.''

"So 'Thou shalt not drink' goes right out the window when there's big bucks at stake?'' He fidgeted with the silverware and looked around the restaurant. He seemed jittery, on edge.

"Well, no. I think they figured the people who were going to drink would do it anyway, even if there aren't any liquor stores here and the restaurants don't serve alcohol.''

"Remember when we were kids? The list of things you couldn't do on Sunday? No bike riding. No wash on the line. No parking on the street.''

"I remember you broke some of the rules.''

"Because there were so goddamn many.''

After swallowing half his wine, he poured himself a re-fill. So the rumors about his drinking were true, not made up for spite. She took a sip from her own glass. The wine was warm and tasted acidic, burning the back of her throat.

She couldn't shake the feeling that she'd been asked to the junior prom. That was what this night felt like, as though the air around her crackled with expectation. She had taken more than an hour choosing what she'd wear— a pale blue knit skirt and matching top that showed off her slim arms. The neckline was cut low, revealing the ivory skin on her chest. Her hair, set with hot rollers, bounced below her shoulders each time she moved her head.

Stop it, she scolded herself, taking another sip. It's not like you've never been on a date before, not like you've never slept with anyone or been through the whole drill— drinks, dinner, pillow talk.

Her last relationship had ended five months ago when Dr. David Chilton decided in a fit of remorse and con-science that he wasn't going to leave his wife just yet. Five months wasn't long at all. Anne had gone through dry spells between men that lasted up to a year. So why was she behaving as if she were sixteen again? Why was tonight so important?

"Tell me what's been happening in the Heights,'' Tigger commanded suddenly.

"You mean the gossip? Who's having an affair? Who's

not speaking? Which teenagers are knocked up?''

"You got it.''

"Hmm. I'm not sure if I can. Most of the dirt I know about has to do with stain removal and household cleansers.''

"Huh?''

So Anne told him about the book she was writing for Mary Lou Popper, the syndicated radio talk show host and celebrated household hints authority, who couldn't string two sentences together unless someone else spelled out the words and typed them into the computer. "Half the time,'' Anne complained, "even her advice is wrong. There's this one chapter on making your own detergent. And if you followed the directions, you'd get first-degree burns. So now I double-check everything she tells me.''

"How'd she get to be Suzy Homemaker?''

"S&M.''

"What?''

"Sales and marketing. She's a real self-promoter.''

The waitress brought their lobsters, crowded next to giant baked potatoes and barely thawed-out frozen vegetables. Outside, the sky was turning a deep electric blue, a surreal color that thickened and intensified before giving way to night.

The lobster tasted faintly of iodine. Anne dipped chunks of it in butter to drown out the flavor. The wine was nearly gone, and Tigger looked more relaxed. "So,'' he said, cracking open a lobster claw and digging the meat out. "You've lived here your whole life?''

"Uh huh.''

"What's it like now? Is it different from when we were kids?''

"Yes and no. I guess the main thing is that after a while, you get used to certain things.''

"What things?''

"Oh, the way the town is in winter. The quiet. Being . . . alone a lot. Things like that.''

He stared out the window, at the palm trees that swayed unsteadily in the evening breeze. His voice, when he spoke, was tinged with bitterness. "You can be alone anywhere, even in cities. Especially in cities. I'm good at it. You know, you're about the only one who's been decent to me since I've been back."

"Really?"

"You should see the way people look at me. Like I'm a monster or something. You wouldn't believe the hate in their eyes."

"Don't pay any attention. Their bark is worse than their bite."

"Is that right? You know Joe Vance?"

Anne nodded. Joe Vance owned Advance Pharmacy, at the corner of Main and Beechwood.

"When I was coming to pick you up before," Tigger continued, "I passed him and his wife on the boardwalk. He called me the most vile names under the sun. And she spit on my shoe. Lucky for me her aim was bad."

Anne stared at him in surprise. Just the other day, she'd spent fifteen minutes with Mr. Vance, discussing the merits of cold medicine, with and without sleep activators. His wife, Mary, baked Rice Krispies cakes for the church picnics and tutored Korean orphans every other Sunday. It was hard to imagine either of them having the nerve to swat a mosquito.

"It's not just Vance. It's this whole town." Tigger's brow was creased with worry. "Anne, I'm in big trouble here. I need your help."

"What's wrong?"

"Someone sent me a death threat."

"What!"

"Somebody ripped apart a magazine and cut out letters from the different articles. Know what it spelled?" She shook her head. "*DIE*, up and down the page. It had all these quotes from the Bible in it, too, about how sinners wind up dead." He poured more wine in his glass. "You live here. You know these folks pretty well. Who could have sent me something like that?"

"It must have been a prank," Anne said. "What happened to you before, well, that was years ago. People talk a good game, but when you come right down to it, all they might do is write a letter to the local newspaper or something.''

''You're wrong. Somebody wants me dead.''

''That's crazy.''

''They're still out for blood,'' Tigger said, as if he hadn't heard her. ''They still blame me. Not,'' he added quickly, ''that there's anything to blame me for.''

She looked at him closely. He sounded sincere. He'd always claimed he was innocent, even at the inquest, when four people testified they saw him running from the hotel, moments before it burst into flames.

She watched him crack open the other lobster claw and pry the meat loose with his fork. There were so many questions she wanted to ask him—about that night twenty years ago, about his life since then, about what he was doing here with her now. She picked the last bits of her lobster from the fiery red shell and said: ''So if you don't get the house back, what will you do?''

He looked surprised, as if he hadn't considered this possibility. ''I'm gonna get my house. It's just a matter of time.''

When the check came, Anne put her share on the small plastic tray shaped like a crab. Tigger threw down two bills and stood up.

''Where to?'' he said.

''Well, how'd you like a grand tour of your hometown?''

Chapter 3

*To remove fresh alcohol
stains, soak fabric in cold
water with a few
tablespoons of glycerin.
Then rinse in a sink full of
water to which you've
added a half-cup of vinegar.
Act fast! Stains turn brown
as they age.*

Out on Route 35, the entrance to the Heights was
marked with a wrought-iron gate, flanked by two
stone portals. On top of the gate, the founding fathers had spelled out a welcome in five-foot tall letters:
Enter Into the Kingdom of Heaven on Earth.

"I always thought it should say: *Ye of Little Faith, Keep
Out,*" Tigger joked.

They walked down quiet streets shaded by giant ma-
ples and pin oaks, past houses embellished with striped
awnings and lacy white fretwork. Many of the windows
were open, and peering through to the bright interiors,
Anne caught sight of her neighbors' antique-filled front
parlors. The rooms formed homey tableaus, like squares
sewn onto the same quilt.

24

Being with Tigger Mills disturbed the picture somehow by striking a forbidden chord. She thought back to when she was seven and had sneaked into the hall closet and unwrapped all her Christmas presents, examining the pink Drowsy Doll and the wool scarf embroidered with snowflakes. Cradling her presents, touching them, smelling their newness, was almost too wonderful to bear. By the time Christmas morning rolled around, and she had to open the gifts for real, feigning surprise, they already looked old and worn, cast-offs from toyland. Being with Tigger elicited the feeling she had all those years ago when she found the hidden presents—something scary and delectable was about to happen, and it had to do with not being caught. He was dressed all in black, and as he loped down the street, moving lightly on the balls of his feet, he looked to Anne like a dark spirit come to visit his favorite earthly haunts.

Through the trees, she caught sight of the half-empty marina. Most people who owned boats had sailed over to Bradley Beach to see the fireworks. The Heights was practically deserted. On each lamppost was a white sign, shining ghostlike. There must have been hundreds of the posters around town, urging people to contribute to the restoration of the Church by the Sea.

She had purposely steered Tigger away from Liberty Park, with its statue of little Ruthie Klemperer, festooned this week with bunting and flowers. Although surely he'd seen it. The Klemperers had erected the bronze statue the year after their daughter died, and it was starting to turn green in spots. Last summer, someone had sprayed graffiti on the front, and now the statue was protected by a chain link fence. She didn't want to walk near it with Tigger, didn't want any more reminders of the fire, but before she could divert him, they were in front of the square patch of land that had once been the Spray View Hotel.

It was one of the few vacant lots in town. No trees. No community garden. The field was filled with garbage and cast-offs, as if the town had taken its refuse, its hidden dark side, and dumped it here.

"They tried to build another hotel," Anne said, her voice

dropping to a sudden whisper. "But there were all sorts of zoning laws."

Tigger's mouth puckered as if he'd just sucked on something sour. They were only a block from the ocean. The air was thick with salt, moisture clung to every surface. Overhead, a jagged moon was punched into the sky, like a tooth broken off at the root.

"It was just like this," Tigger said softly. "Heavy and sort of still."

The fire.

Anne could feel the question take shape, feel it leave her mind, forming a cartoon bubble above her head. In the glow of the street lamps, his eyes appeared to glitter.

"You believe in fate?" he asked, rocking forward on the balls of his feet.

"What?"

"Fate. Destiny. Doesn't matter what we do. 'Cause it's already been planned out."

She considered the question. No, she felt just the opposite, that people made their own messes in life and usually tried to foist the blame onto someone or something else.

"If what you're saying is true, then who's pulling the strings? God?"

"No way. There is no God. But something's out there, all right, saying who shit happens to." His eyes roamed the vacant lot. "You ever wonder about people who fall asleep behind the wheel of a car? I wonder about that a lot."

In the rubble-strewn vacant lot, Anne could make out distinct shapes. Trash, mostly. Discarded soda bottles, beer cans, a broken kite.

"A guy could be driving along, see. And he's tired, he can't keep his eyes open. His head gets real heavy. He tells himself he's gonna pull over soon, grab a cup of Joe. But his head slides forward. His eyes close, just for a second."

She remembered watching the flames lick the building's wood spine, stretching all the way up to the third floor, exploding into dark plumes of fire. The whole town came out to watch.

"You listening?" Tigger asked. He swayed back and forth, put his arms out to steady himself. "This is a really good story."

The smoke was so thick that when the fire trucks first arrived, all the firemen could do was point their hoses at the windows, like little boys engaged in a halfhearted pissing contest. The fire raged on for hours while the whole town gathered to watch, clustering in the streets, on balconies and porches, peering from the safety of their homes until a necklace of people circled the building, reminding Anne of the ancient Greeks preparing a burnt offering for the gods. Flames raced through the hotel, spiraling up until they licked the sky. A hole appeared in the roof. Windows blew out, the glass seeming to shatter before the pieces hit the ground. There was fire everywhere, swallowing up the hotel in a fierce orange fist. The Spray View burned until it trembled in the air, and chunks of the building fell away. When it was over, the smell lingered for weeks, pungent and bitter. And the following morning firemen discovered the charred body of three-year-old Ruthie Klemperer, the daughter of the hotel's owners.

"So the guy closes his eyes," Tigger continued. "He can't see the tree. It comes up sudden-like, and whammo." His hands slammed together, making a popping sound. "The guy's head smacks the windshield. Blood. Bones. Glass flying. There's glass in his brain, pieces of glass from the fucking windshield." Tigger's hands clenched. " 'Cause it was too late. They didn't bother with a trial. They already convicted me. The whole damn town. Done deal."

Without warning, he crouched down, scooped up a handful of rocks, and hurled one into the darkness. It hit a pile of debris with a thud. He let another rock fly, and another, a barrage of rocks. It sounded like scattered gunshots. Faces appeared at the windows of houses adjoining the lot.

Grabbing more rocks with both hands, Tigger pitched them at the mounds of garbage. Anne heard his breath come in short, ragged gasps. His body lurched unsteadily from side to side. He was drunk. Why hadn't she noticed before?

"You happy?" he yelled at the lot. "You fucking happy now?"

"Stop it," she pleaded, yanking his arm. As he pushed her away, she stumbled slightly, losing her balance. She had just enough time to lunge to her left, so that most of her body landed on the grass bordering the sidewalk, instead of on the cement pavement.

Rocks slid from his hands, clattered onto the ground. "I'm sorry," he whispered, his face pale and vacant.

Anne checked her body for damage. Except for a tear in her stocking, there didn't seem to be any. She rose slowly to her feet and faced him, noticing his bleary eyes, the way his body shook. Even his mouth was trembling.

"I didn't do it," Tigger said. His voice was cracked and strange. "I didn't start the fire."

She heard a light scratching sound, and turned to see a cat brush against a tin can. She could make out a shadowy form in its mouth, something small that still moved. "Come on. Let's get out of here." Without looking at him, she reached toward him, felt for his hand.

Guiding Tigger through the streets of town was like leading an indifferent blind man. He stared straight ahead but appeared to have lost his sight. Once, he nearly walked into a child's overturned tricycle and veered away, bumping against Anne. When they arrived at her house, she ushered him gently up the porch steps and deposited him in the white wicker swing.

"I need a drink," he said dully.

She went into the kitchen, removed two tumblers from the pine corner cupboard. There was some fruit juice and club soda in the refrigerator, and she added some of each to the glasses. Before pouring the vodka, she hesitated. He'd already had so much to drink. She stood perfectly still, holding the neck of the bottle over the glass. Vodka splashed against the rim. What the hell, she said to herself. You can't save him.

When she came back, he was still staring at the ocean, watching it smash against the shore. He drank in one long swallow, until there was nothing left in the glass. "You'd make a lousy bartender," he told her.

"Thanks." She sat beside him on the swing.

The drink seemed to steady him somehow. He held it tenderly, like a glass rose. "Home sweet home," he said, his voice laced with anger.

In the distance, colored lights bloomed on the night sky, dissolving into darkness. The faint thud of the fireworks accompanied the sound of the waves. Anne gulped down the rest of her drink and put their two glasses side by side on the porch railing. She felt slightly giddy, straddling the line between good drunk and really looped, drunk enough so that when she closed her eyes, the porch started to spin.

She glanced at Tigger. He was staring at the beach, a strange expression on his face. "When we were kids," he said, "we had this code. Bobby, me, all the guys. We sealed it in blood, right there, under the boardwalk." He pointed halfway down the beach to a spot where the walk widened. "We'd do anything on a dare, like you said. No matter what they did to us, we'd never tell."

"Who's 'they'?"

"Parents, teachers . . ." He paused. "Cops."

In the moonlight, the leaves on the trees shined silvery black, like some alien life form. The light brushed across his face. It was like looking at two people—the handsome boy she'd once known and the alcoholic he'd become.

"The curse of adolescence," she said aloud.

"What?"

"I was just thinking about how when we were young, everything seemed out of reach. Sex. Love. Romance. It was all mixed up together in this magic potion."

"Don't knock it," he said, laughing. "I had too many sips."

"Does that make it different now that you're older?"

"Who knows? I stopped believing in love a long time ago. Love, chemistry, whatever you want to call it, is just bullshit in the end."

"What *do* you believe in?"

"Memories. Family. A sense of . . ." He hesitated,

searching for the right word. "Place. That old house is home to me. I got roots here. Deep roots. I can turn things around, if I can just get my house back."

"You'll do it," she said, smiling. "You always were the most determined person I ever knew."

"I don't know, Anne. I got a bad feeling about this. I think I'm in over my head."

"Look around you," she said, spreading her arms wide and gesturing toward the Victorian houses, the curved street lights, the wooden piers, the ocean fanning out before them. "This is probably the safest place on the entire Eastern seaboard. You know, we still don't lock our doors. There's no reason to. The crime rate's the lowest in the state."

Tigger didn't look convinced. "Old wounds run deep."

"You don't understand. I've known these people for years. They're absolutely harmless. Your coming back here just gave them something new to gossip about."

"If you could help me figure out who sent that death threat, I'd feel a lot better," he said.

"Have you asked anyone else in town for help?" Tigger shook his head. "Why me? I mean, we were in school together. But that was a long time ago. We barely know each other now."

Tigger studied her carefully. "I think you and I have a lot in common," he said slowly.

"Meaning what?" Although she knew perfectly well what he meant. She'd always known it.

"When I was a kid," Tigger said, "I used to sneak into the alley behind the bakery after dark. Press my nose against the glass and watch them bake pies. It looked so cozy inside, so clean. The smell was heavenly. But I never went in. Just kept watch outside the shop, for hours at a time. That's us, Anne. We're both outsiders, looking in. We grew up here, but we didn't belong. Not then. And not now."

It didn't make it any easier, hearing the words out loud. She felt sad and a little angry. "So I'm supposed to . . . what? Snoop around? Quiz the neighbors?"

"Hey," he said softly, putting one arm on her shoulder.

"I like you. I can't tell you why but I trust you somehow. Work with me on this one. As a favor to an old friend. Keep your eyes and ears open. Let me know what you find out."

Anne sensed her anger slipping away. She wasn't mad at Tigger. He wasn't the problem. She was mad at herself, for not leaving this gossipy town years ago and starting fresh someplace else. He removed his arm from her shoulder and on impulse, she reached out and grasped his hand. "Like I told you before," she said. "It was probably just a prank."

"Maybe. Maybe not. I'm no Boy Scout, but I believe in being prepared." He grinned at her and stood up. "Listen, I gotta get going. Thanks for dinner."

"Next time I'll cook. I make a mean spinach lasagne."

He bent down and kissed her lightly on the forehead. "You got it. 'Night now."

She waved and headed back inside the house. What she wouldn't have given for that kiss twenty years ago! God, she'd been so crazy about him back then. She used to practically hold her breath every time he spoke to her. The memory made her giggle. Puppy love was the pits. The absolute pits! She wondered how she'd ever survived it.

Upstairs, she changed into a nightshirt. All three windows in the bedroom were ajar and the ocean seeped in through the lace curtains on waves of humid, damp air. Sleep came within minutes.

She dreamed Tigger was sitting on the front porch of the Spray View, what was left of it after the fire. She wanted to warn him to get down. But despite the wreckage, he looked comfortable and relaxed, as though the hotel hadn't been damaged at all.

On his right shoulder was a huge tattoo—a long-stemmed rose in full bloom. Coiled around the flowers was a serpent, with a curved tail and pointy fangs.

He leaned forward, tossed something over the wooden railing. It landed at Anne's feet, a package for her, tied with pink ribbon. She picked the package up, undid it carefully, smoothing the brown paper wrapping, pocketing the ribbon. She peered into the box. Inside, a white lace baptism gown. Was it hers? She couldn't tell. He was standing up, the hotel looming ghostly behind him. "Put it on," he said, his voice like ripped velvet.

She unbuttoned her blouse slowly, conscious that he was watching her, unzipped her skirt, stepped out of it. She was wearing white garters over high white underwear. She picked up the dress. It was way too small, meant for a child, and the lace fell away in her hands, shredding to pieces.

She could see the flames sprouting up through the porch, like deadly flowers. The wail of sirens pierced the night air. "Get down from there," she yelled to him. But he had already vanished. She felt the flames burn her cheeks as the Spray View shuddered and burst into a thousand fiery parts. "Where are you?" she called. "Come back." But her voice was drowned out by the sharp *waaaaaahhh* of the sirens. The fire was closer now, threatening to smother her in a tower of flames. Smoke clogged her throat, poured into her ears. When she opened her mouth, her scream was torn from the heart of the sirens. *Waaaaaaahhhhh. Waaaaaaahhhhhh.*

Anne sat up in bed, jolted awake. The clock by the bed read 6:14 A.M. Outside, the blare of sirens, real sirens. From a fire engine. Something else was burning. She grabbed her windbreaker, threw on a pair of shorts and a T-shirt, and rushed out of the house. At the far end of the boardwalk, parked at a crazy angle, were three Neptune Township police cars. She broke into a run, her bare feet flying over the wooden planks. The police, in their black slickers, were clustered on the sand, talking. But there was nothing burning, no building to save, just the ocean stretching toward the horizon. The sky was an angry shade of gray. A light sprinkling of rain dusted her hair and shoulders. She ran down the steps leading to the sea. A small crowd had gathered. Even from a distance, she could see the dark shape lying at the water's edge, covered with a tarp. And suddenly, she knew who it was, knew she was running toward Tigger even before the wave of men parted to reveal the body, before she heard someone shout: "It's the Mills boy. The Mills boy is dead."

Chapter 4

*Drinking hot coffee on a
white couch is like an
accident waiting to happen.*

After, when the police cars had driven off, when the body had finally been removed, dumped into the back of an ambulance that sped away, its siren screaming like there was someone inside who still needed to be saved, Anne sat on the boardwalk staring at the ocean. It was raining, a slow, steady rain. The beach was deserted, littered with July Fourth leftovers: an abandoned picnic basket, soggy streamers, red, white, and blue miniature flags. A few feet away was the bench she'd sat on with Tigger yesterday afternoon.

Somebody wants me dead, he had told her. And now he was gone.

"Miss Hardaway?" She looked up and saw one of the cops who had been on the beach earlier. He looked to be about twenty-one years old, with a short blond crewcut and pimply skin.

"Yes?"

"I'm Officer Hefferle. Could you come with me, please? I'd like to ask you a few questions."

She got up slowly and followed him to a patrol car parked down the street. Mud stuck to her bare feet. When they got to the car, he opened the passenger door and she hunkered down on the seat, her arms folded across her chest. There was another cop sitting in the back seat. "Miss Hardaway," Officer Hefferle said. "This is Officer Ryan." Anne looked in the rearview mirror and nodded to the cop in back. Rain pelted the window of the car. The windshield was a gray blur, obscuring the view of trees, houses, things that should have been familiar. Officer Hefferle slid into the driver's seat and took a small notebook from the dashboard.

"Mr. Mills was with you last night," Officer Hefferle said.

"Yeah."

"Let's go over what happened—where you went, what time Mr. Mills left your place."

"We went out to dinner, and then we came back to my house. I'm not really sure when he left."

"Take your time. No rush. I just need some information for my report. Police procedure," the officer said, sounding as if he was explaining a difficult concept to a small, unintelligent child.

She looked away from him, toward the haze of gray rain. The Heights was too small to have its own police force. On the rare occasions when crime occurred—theft, burglary, cars stolen for a joy ride, then abandoned down the shore—a call was placed to the Neptune Township Sheriff's Office. In the rearview mirror, she could see the other cop, Ryan, who was leaning back against the seat as if he would have liked to take a nap. He didn't look much older than Hefferle. There was a photo hanging from the mirror, a picture of two kids. One wore a bunny costume and pink floppy ears. The other child was dressed as a carrot, with a hat of green sprouts. Because of their costumes, it was hard to tell whether they were boys or girls, or even how old they were. They couldn't be Hefferle's kids, Anne thought. He didn't look old enough to get a lifeguard job on the beach.

Officer Hefferle checked his notebook. "A call came in to the station at 8:32 P.M. The caller said Mr. Mills was creating a disturbance: drunk and disorderly. Vandalism. Couple of broken windows."

"We were in front of a vacant lot," Anne said hotly. "There weren't any windows."

"By the time we sent a car around, you'd already left. Where'd you go?"

"Back to my house."

"How long was Mr. Mills there?"

"I'm not sure. An hour or so, I guess."

"What time did he leave? Approximately?"

"I don't know."

"You must have *some* idea."

"It might have been around nine-thirty, ten. It might have been later."

He scribbled something in his notebook, then covered his writing with his hand, as if to prevent Anne from reading it. "How much did Mr. Mills have to drink last night?"

"We had a bottle of wine and a couple of vodka tonics."

"Did he seem upset? Did he mention harming himself in any way?"

"What are you talking about?"

"The frame of mind of the deceased."

"What does that have to do with anything?"

"Maybe you don't understand, ma'am."

Ma'am? She wasn't old enough to be his mother, for Christ's sake. "Look," she said sharply. "I've known Tigger Mills since we were kids. He's fearless, nothing shakes him. But when I talked to him last night, he was worried. He felt he was in danger."

One of Officer Hefferle's eyebrows shot up. "Is that so?"

She took a deep breath. "It sounded crazy at first. I didn't believe him."

"Miss Hardaway . . ."

"No, listen to me," she interrupted. "After Tigger left my place last night, I think somebody in this town murdered him."

"I realize you're upset, Miss Hardaway. If it makes you feel any better, no one killed your friend. His death was an accident. An accidental drowning."

For a moment, Anne was too surprised to speak. She wanted to grab the officer's shoulders and shake him, tell him to choose another career, like skateboarding. "But that's impossible," she said.

From the look Officer Hefferle gave her, Anne could see he thought she hadn't a clue—not about Tigger or police work or the complicated, messy business of dying. "Tigger was an excellent swimmer. He couldn't have drowned by accident."

"When you have five times the normal level of alcohol in your bloodstream, it's real easy."

"How would you know what was in his bloodstream?" she demanded.

"Because we tested it."

"You tested it."

"Yes."

"I don't understand. Do you normally run a blood test when a body washes up on the beach?"

"The blood alcohol analysis was authorized by Mr. Mills's father."

"Listen to me," Anne said frantically. "Tigger told me his life was in danger. His death wasn't an accident. He was murdered."

Officer Hefferle studied her carefully, as if she were some rare but ultimately inconsequential piece of physical evidence. "Look, you're not in law enforcement. So you don't know. But it's real hard to kill somebody by drowning them, unless you stick their head in some water and hold them under for five minutes."

"Maybe someone did. Tigger was lying on the beach. Maybe he never went in the ocean at all."

Hefferle glanced in the rearview mirror and exchanged a look with the cop in the backseat. "Your friend was in the water all right," he said slowly. "Matter of fact, he was about twenty-five feet from shore when we dragged him out. You know a Doris Trumbull?" Anne nodded. Mrs.

Trumbull was an eighty-five-year-old blue-haired spinster who lived four blocks away, on Peach Street. "She doesn't sleep so good anymore. Looked out her window around five-thirty this morning and saw a body in the ocean. Told us she thought it was somebody practicing to swim, doing what they teach kiddies in summer camp. You know. The dead man's float."

Anne heard a low chuckle coming from the backseat. "Does this amuse you?" she said, turning around to glare at the cop.

"Certainly not," Hefferle snapped. She could smell stale cigarettes on his breath. "You want to know what happened. Here's what happened. Your boyfriend decided to take a midnight swim in his birthday suit. Only problem was he was stinking drunk."

The image of Tigger naked in the ocean set Anne's mind reeling. "He . . . wasn't wearing any clothes at all?"

"Bingo."

Think, Anne told herself. Calm down and think. "What about the death threat?" she said. "Did you see it?"

"What death threat?"

She hurriedly repeated what Tigger had said. For the first time since she'd gotten into the car, she had Hefferle's full attention. "Because of the Klemperer girl?" he asked. Anne nodded. She could almost sense his brain working overtime, trying to process this new information. But it only lasted a moment, and then his sullen, official expression returned. "Did *you* see this death threat?" he demanded.

"No."

"Then you can't be sure it existed."

"Of course it existed. Tigger told me about it."

"From what we understand, Mr. Mills was an alcoholic. When he drank too much, he was known to stretch the truth."

"What do you mean?"

"I'm sorry, ma'am. I've told you more than I should already. You'll have to come down to the station later today to give a sworn statement. Nothing to worry about, just a formality. In the meantime, I just have a few more questions . . .''

She barely listened, responding to Hefferle's inquiries with a slight nod of her head, whether the answer was yes or no. It felt as though there was no air in the car, as though she'd suffocate if she sat here any longer. "Look," she interrupted, "I've got to go." Before Officer Hefferle could protest, she was out of the car, running back toward her house. The rain pricked her skin, like a blast of cold darts. But she was already so wet it didn't matter. When she reached the corner, she heard a siren and half turned, expecting to see the police car beside her. But the car was still parked where Hefferle left it. And she realized the siren was coming from farther away, from out by the highway where some other, more distant, emergency was unfolding.

The house was just as she'd left it. Their empty glasses rested on the railing. The bed was unmade. She removed her wet things and crawled beneath the sheets, pulling the blanket up to her chin.

When she was little, she used to try to will bad things away. The night her father left them, and moved fifteen miles away to Belmar, she sat by the window, her head pressed against the pane, watching him load up the Buick Electra, and silently commanded: *Don't go. Don't go.* For a moment, he appeared to hesitate. He leaned the cardboard box he was carrying against the trunk of the car and looked out at the ocean, his back to the house. Even now, Anne could remember how cool the glass pane felt against her forehead, how she resisted rapping on the window with her fist and crying out to him, choosing to communicate without words, the way the two of them sometimes did. So that he might reenter the house, walking past her mother, who sat stone-faced in the living room, up the winding staircase, and take Anne in his arms and tell her he loved her, that everything was going to be okay after all.

If only she'd listened to Tigger, if only she hadn't ignored his appeal for help. She pictured him on the pier that last summer in the Heights, his body slicing the air, disappearing beneath the waves. Time seemed to be playing tricks on her, the past kept getting jumbled up with the present. Her father. Tigger Mills. Herself as a teenager. She lay in bed all day, drifting in and out of sleep, until the remaining light drained from the room.

She woke up, groggy, to a series of loud bangs. Someone at the front door. The bell had broken last winter and she hadn't gotten around to fixing it.

She stumbled to the closet, put on her bathrobe, and made her way downstairs. It was still pouring outside, the rain beating a tattoo against the roof. When she opened the door, the wind swept rain against her face. "Are you Anne?" said the man standing on her front porch.

She nodded, pulling her bathrobe closer.

"I'm Jack Mills. Tigger's brother. Can I come in?"

He followed her into the living room. "Please, sit down," she said, settling into an armchair.

She hadn't seen Tigger's younger brother in years and wouldn't have recognized him if they passed on the street. Nothing about this handsome, sophisticated-looking man seemed remotely connected to the kid who used to tag after Tigger and his friends. Underneath his tan raincoat, Jack wore an expensive-looking suit and tie. His dark hair, slick from the rain, was neatly combed. His face was clean-shaven, his eyes, which darted around the room as if searching for something, were a deep penetrating blue. While Tigger had assumed the slack posture of a drifter, Jack sat upright on the chintz-covered couch, his hands on his knees, his black leather shoes tapping the floor restlessly. There was an air of authority about him, as if he was used to taking charge. Yet Anne could spot a resemblance between the brothers—the way Jack's chin jutted forward, the fullness of his lips, his don't-mess-with-me expression.

"I talked to the police," he said slowly. "They told me you were the last person to see him alive." Anne nodded. "I'm just trying to piece this whole thing together. I was planning to come down to see him this weekend. When I got here, the police were searching his room. They told me he was . . . dead."

"I'm so sorry," she said. "This has been such a terrible shock. It must be really rough on you."

He looked away from her and took a deep breath, as if struggling to contain his emotions. "Yeah. It is. Tigger and I had lost touch for many years. He was out in the midwest. I live in Manhattan. We'd only recently started to reconnect and now . . ." His expression was tense. "Tigger called me two days ago. I was out of town. When I got back, there was this weird message on my machine. He said he'd received death threats, that he was in deep trouble. He sounded frantic."

"I know. He told me about it."

"I tried to call him last night, after I got home and played back the message he left. But the desk clerk at Ravenswood told me he wasn't in. I tried again this morning. Couldn't get hold of him. So I got in my car and drove down."

"It doesn't seem real," Anne murmured.

"According to the police, Tigger was on a bender when he left here last night. He went for a dip in the ocean, swam out too far, got caught in the undertow or something. The cops are saying it was either an accident or . . ." Jack's voice trailed off.

"Or what?"

"They think he might have committed suicide. They found his clothes and his wallet lying on the beach."

Anne stared at him in disbelief. "What? That's absurd. I know he was worried—he told me so. But he didn't seem depressed."

"Did the two of you have a fight?"

"Of course not." Rain pounded the roof. A loose shutter banged against the side of the house.

"Did he tell you where he was headed?" Jack asked anxiously. "Was he on his way back to Ravenswood? Because it doesn't make sense, the whole thing doesn't make any sense. I know my brother. He wasn't stupid. There's no way he would swim out into the ocean in the middle of the night, especially if he was as drunk as they say."

Jack looked flushed and lost. Anne saw that he was holding himself in check, that his grief was just below the surface, wrapped tight.

"I'm sorry," she said softly. It felt like a lame response. A wave of fatigue washed over her. The last twenty-four hours had taken on a surreal quality. Even the house seemed different, as if Tigger's presence, and now Jack's, had altered the look of the place somehow, made it less recognizable.

"Did he say anything to you?" Jack asked. "Did he talk about his plans at all?"

"He told me your mother left him the house in her will, but your father was contesting it. Maybe your dad knows something. Have you spoken to him?"

"When I saw my father, he was working his way through a bottle of Thunderbird. He's so plastered right now, he couldn't pee straight." Jack laughed harshly. "But that's nothing new."

Anne leaned forward, twisting the ring on her finger, maneuvering it back and forth, over her knuckle. She told Jack what Tigger had said about the death threat. When she finished, Jack's face was grave. "The little girl's parents still live here, don't they?" he asked.

"Yes. Over on Beechwood Avenue."

"Do you think either of them could have sent that note to Tigger?

Anne thought for a moment. "I don't know. They're both a little . . . off. Ed Klemperer is the closest thing to a hermit that the Heights has. Hardly anyone sees him anymore. He never leaves the house."

"And Mrs. Klemperer?"

Anne frowned. "She's one of those self-righteous holy rollers, always preaching about hellfire and brimstone, how the Judgment Day is near."

"So they might have wanted revenge."

"Maybe. Neither one of them seems to have made peace with Ruthie's death."

"Did Tigger mention them by name?"

"No. He seemed to think it could have been anyone. He felt that the town never forgave him, that they saw him as a cold-blooded killer who got away with murder.''

Anne paused.

''Go on.''

''I cared about your brother. I don't believe he hurt that little girl for one minute. But I guess I'm in the minority. He told me people looked at him as if he were a monster. That they hated him.''

Jack was staring at her intently. ''Who hated him enough to kill him?''

Chapter 5

In the war against clutter, remember the 3Ds: do it, delegate it, or dump it.

The Ravenswood Inn was a sprawling white Victorian house, situated two blocks from the ocean, on Main Street. Since it was first constructed in the nineteenth century, various owners had tacked on their own additions, turning the inn into a bit of a hodgepodge, with walls and windows jutting out from every possible angle. It couldn't have been more different from the other buildings in the Heights, whose symmetrical, picturesque shapes spoke of order and clarity. Inside, the difference was even more pronounced. In the mid-1970s, the state had begun housing former mental patients from county psychiatric hospitals at the historic inn. The number of outpatients, most of them elderly, grew until they outnumbered the paying guests. Anne had been surprised to hear that Tigger was living there. And she found it more difficult to picture Jack in the dilapidated place. Still, last night, as he said goodbye, he had told her that's where he'd be staying, in Tigger's old room. He asked her to come by first thing in the morning. Actually, it was her second stop. She'd driven over to the Neptune Township Sheriff's Office, where she gave her sworn statement to the bored-looking cop on duty.

What am I doing here? she wondered, as she parked across the street from Ravenswood. A couple of days ago, Tigger Mills and his problems were as remote as a shooting star. She shouldn't be here. She didn't have time for this. Her first priority was finishing chapter five of Mary Lou's book. She had a contract and a deadline. Most of her advance check (half payable up front, the other half when she finished the book) was already spent. The house had needed new window sashes, she'd had to fix the carburetor on the Mustang. There was a stack of bills on her dining room table that were weeks overdue. She couldn't afford to be running all over town, playing detective.

She walked hurriedly up the front steps of the inn, past the row of elderly people who rocked back and forth in silence. Inside, she was greeted by a sharp musty odor. The wallpaper was torn in places. A piece of it flapped forlornly as the screen door slammed.

Behind the front desk a wizened-looking man watched a black-and-white TV. The volume was turned up so high she had to shout to be heard over it.

"Mr. Mills's room?" she yelled.

The man jerked his finger toward the stairs. "Two thirty-three."

On the second floor, she went from door to door, looking for the right one. But most of the silver numbers had worn off. At the end of the hall, a door was ajar. She'd just have to ask someone if they'd seen him. Peering into the room, she saw an elderly woman sitting on a folding chair near the window. The woman's hair was dyed a peculiar shade of yellow that was sulfurous and bright, like egg yolk. On each wrinkled cheek was a spot of rouge that hadn't been rubbed in. She wore a faded print housedress and pink fuzzy slippers with holes cut out in front. Her toes were crooked, the nails crusty and decayed. "You there," the woman shouted. "You cheap tart. You slut." Anne jumped back, startled. "Don't you be tellin' me I don't know nothing. I'm not taking guff from two-bit white trash."

Anne hesitated in the doorway, unsure whether to stand her ground or flee. "You can't fake a faker, that's what I told 'em," the old woman said, her head bobbing up and down. The woman wasn't talking to Anne at all. She appeared to be addressing a plaster statue of the Virgin that sat on the dresser.

"Come, dear," the woman said, crooking a finger at the statue. "It's time for your nap and your special medicine." A note of false gaiety had crept into the woman's voice. "Don't be a baby. Drink it all down. Every last drop."

Something brushed against Anne's shoulder, and she whirled around. "Oh, it's you," she said, relieved to see Jack Mills. He was dressed more casually this morning, in khaki pants and a black short-sleeved shirt with a shark sewn above the pocket. He looked exhausted, as if he'd barely slept.

"Come on," he told her. "I've been waiting for you."

Leading her back into the hall, he steered her to the room Tigger had lived in, right next door. It was cluttered and messy, no bigger than a walk-in closet. Though the bed was neatly made, clothes and food wrappers littered the floor; the bureau was awash in books and papers. More books were strewn on the nightstand, which also held a lamp, minus its shade and bulb. The only bright note in the room was a red geranium plant on the windowsill.

"The room looked like this when I got here. Guess they don't believe in room service."

Anne shivered. "This place gives me the creeps."

"Tell me about it. The walls are paper-thin. Someone was screaming for hours last night, so I couldn't get any sleep."

"Did you find the death threat Tigger told me about?"

"Not yet. But the sooner we find it, the sooner we can prove to the cops that Tigger's death was no accident."

Anne walked over to the bureau and began sifting through the books. "When was the last time you saw Tigger?"

"Last month. At my mother's funeral."

"Of course. I was so sorry to hear she'd passed away. I know how hard it is."

"Are your parents still living?"

"My father died ten years ago, and my mother went in '89. She had Alzheimer's."

"That's got to be tough," Jack said sympathetically.

"The worst part was at the beginning. In the seventies, when she first got sick, people didn't know much about Alzheimer's disease. Everyone thought she was off her rocker. But it's a neurological condition, an error in a gene encoding a protein." It amazed her that she was able to speak so clinically, as if Evelyn's descent into hysteria and madness could be reduced to a brief medical diagnosis.

"With my ma," Jack said, "it was relatively quick. She got sick last winter. Cancer. By the spring, there was nothing anyone could do except give her something for the pain."

"Were she and Tigger close?"

"She loved him, sure. But she hadn't seen him in years. I think she felt guilty about sending him away, after the fire." Jack's face registered disgust. "It was my father's idea to send Tigger to Indiana, to live with Ma's second cousins. Tigger hated it out there. He ran away a few times, started drinking heavily, dropped out of school. Seems like his whole life went to pieces. Ma's leaving Tigger the house was a way of making it up to him, I guess."

Anne inspected the books more closely. A copy of something called *The Layman's Guide to Law*, and what looked like a bunch of legal texts on wills and trusts. Like everything else she'd touched, they had a stale, mildewed odor. At the bottom of the pile was a book with a black cover. The New Testament. It was the last book she expected to find in Tigger's room. When she opened it, the binding came loose, and the pages slid away from the cover. A flurry of money tumbled out. "Jack," she cried out. He turned toward her and they watched, in stunned silence, as bills drifted through the air and floated down to the floor.

Jack picked some up, examined them. They were crisp

and fresh, as if newly minted. "They're Benjies," he told her.

"What?"

"One-hundred-dollar bills, with Benjamin Franklin on the front. Must be twenty or thirty of them. What are they doing in that old Bible?"

"The Bible's brand-new," Anne said, opening the book and smelling the pages.

"But the spine's broken, it's all torn up."

"Someone tore them on purpose. Take a look. It's not mildewed like the rest of the books here."

Gingerly, Jack sniffed the Bible. "Smells a little moldy to me," he said.

"Only because it's been lying underneath the other books. See the loose mold here, on this law book. It can be dusted right off," Anne ran her fingers lightly across the jacket. A layer of whitish dust hovered in the air and fell slowly toward the floor. Chapter two, Anne said to herself. *If books are mildewed, sprinkle cornstarch or talcum powder on the pages. Place a box of silica gel or activated charcoal in the bookcase to prevent future odor problems.*

"So you're telling me someone doctored the Bible and tried to camouflage it somehow?"

"Looks like," Anne said. "I think the other books smell of mildew because they've been in this musty old room for a while. The Bible must have been purchased more recently."

They picked up the money slowly. Jack counted it, then stuffed the wad of bills into his wallet. "There's three thousand bucks here. Who would give him this chunk of change?"

"I don't know," she said. "He didn't have many friends left."

"Who's still around from his old gang?" Jack asked.

"Well, P.J. McGrath lives in town. And Bobby Curley."

"All right. Let's go see Curley. Maybe he knows something."

Anne hesitated. Tigger's death was none of her concern.

What was he to her, after all? The prom date she never had? A reminder of innocence lost? A memory cherished by her teenage self? She sat down on the bed, where Tigger had slept.

"Anne," Jack said, from the doorway. "You coming?"

Still . . . he'd needed her help. And she'd failed him, refused to listen. If only she'd taken Tigger more seriously, believed his life was in danger, she wouldn't have waved good-bye so blithely, sent him off into the night, to a cold watery grave. She had to find out what really happened to him. She owed him that much at least. "Let's go," she said to Jack.

Outside, the day was just starting to turn hot. The sidewalk shimmered in the sunlight. Puddles from the rainstorm had already evaporated, and the grass, which desperately needed a cutting, looked parched. As they walked down the front steps, Anne averted her eyes from the row of people rocking in rhythm.

"You there. Mills."

Jack turned toward the porch.

"That's right, boy. I'm talking to you."

It was the woman from upstairs. She'd tied an orange scarf around her head. The red circles on her cheeks were slightly smudged. "I can keep a secret, lovie," she whispered. "I know how."

Her fingers clawed the air, like the talons of a bird. Jack walked a few steps closer, approaching with caution. "How do you know my name?" he asked.

The old woman opened her mouth and let out a screech, scaring two tourists, who hurriedly crossed the street without looking back. "Tell him, boy," she shrieked. "Tell him to go to hell. Straight to the fiery furnace."

The attendant, who had been lolling in the shade, took off his headphones and walked over to the woman's chair. He had on a white jacket with the sleeves rolled up, and white pants. "Now, sister," he told her. "Calm down."

"Apple-fed. Safety first and foremost," she recited, staring at Jack.

"What?" Jack said.

The attendant eased the rocker to a halt, and the old lady slumped forward. Anne felt a sudden rush of pity.

"They're a handful," the attendant said. "But, hey, you get used to it."

The woman raised her head a few inches. A stream of drool trickled down her chin.

"Is she . . . what's wrong with her?" Jack said.

"She's not operating at warp speed, ya know. She talks to people who aren't here. Her sister. Her kids. Her dead parrot. Like I said, you get used to it."

"She knew my name," Jack said.

"Yeah, well, if she sees you again, she'll think you're Vic Damone or Frank Sinatra's long-lost son."

"Ma'am?" Jack said. "Do you know who I am? Did you know my brother, Tigger?" But the old lady didn't appear to hear him. Her stare was frozen in place. She looked shrunken, frail. There's no one, Anne thought. She has no one to care for her. "Let's come back a little later," Jack said. "Maybe she'll feel more like talking then."

Reluctantly, Anne turned away, and they walked down the block, toward the center of town. Rows of quaint-looking storefronts lined Main Street, with identical sloping gables. The shops were painted pastel colors—rose, sky blue, apple green. Each window box overflowed with flowers. Everything in its place, Anne thought. The Heights looked so cheerful, bathed in sunshine. Too cheerful, almost, like a painting whose colors hurt her eyes. She felt a raw burning sensation in her chest. How could he be dead? How was it possible?

As if reading her mind, Jack said, "It's hard to be back here with him gone. Everything looks the same, but different somehow, like looking through the wrong side of a mirror."

They passed throngs of tourists, who wandered in and out of the shops, brandishing new purchases: T-shirts, sweatshirts, jewelry made from shells, miniature replicas of Victorian houses, pen-and-ink drawings of the Church by the Sea. On practically every corner, people were posing for pictures. So many shots to capture—the old-fashioned gazebo, the charming bed-and-breakfasts, the rows of pink geraniums lining the sidewalks. Anne got the sense that the tourists were always in a rush, as if every moment in town detracted from time spent on the beach.

The townspeople moved more slowly. Many of them stopped to offer Jack their condolences. Outwardly, they appeared sincere. Anne wondered if the kind words were genuine or hypocritical. Which of her neighbors were covering up their real feelings? She spotted Jim Walser, glad-handing tourists on the corner of Main Street and Sycamore Lane. "Hello, hello," Walser was saying, stopping to shake hands. "Have you seen our beautiful Church by the Sea? Tours of the building at the top of the hour. Hello. Have you taken a walking tour of the historic district yet? Not to be missed, believe me. There's a concert tonight. Do come. We'd love to have you with us."

"Uh oh," Jack said to Anne. "Here comes Mr. Magoo."

"They do look alike," Anne said, smiling at Walser's egg-shaped head and his thick Coke-bottle glasses.

"The meet-and-greet routine is a bit much, don't you think?"

"I don't know. The tourists eat it up. Besides, he's a really nice man."

"Hello there, Anne. Hello, Jack," said Walser, stretching out his hand in greeting, and gripping each of theirs firmly. Although Independence Day had passed, he was still dressed entirely in red, white, and blue. Under his arm was a sheaf of flyers. Anne recognized them immediately as the posters attached to the trees all over town, urging people to contribute to the restoration of the Church by the Sea. Pinned to the lapel of his shirt was a button that said: *LET'S GO, OH!*

"My deepest sympathies," he said to Jack. "I was so sorry to hear about Tigger. In fact, I was just going to see your father to find out about the funeral arrangements. To lose one's wife and son like this, it breaks my heart."

"The funeral is tomorrow at two o'clock. And *we* can check on Pop," Jack said. "I'd like to see how he's doing myself."

Anne felt a twinge of dread. Visiting Troy Mills sounded as appealing as a trip to the dentist. The old man had a vile temper. The last time she saw him he'd been drinking outside Moby's Hardware Store, railing against Tigger and life in general.

"Very well," Walser said. "But please feel free to call me if there's anything I can do, anything at all. Anne has the number. Annie, dear, have you called Harriet Tuttle yet?"

"Not yet."

"Well, take your time. There's no rush. No rush at all." He extracted two flyers from the top of the stack and handed one to each of them. "Will you be at the Gospel Musical Ministry tonight? There's a pay-what-you-wish admission charge. And we're so very, very close to meeting our goal."

"I'll try to make it," Anne said, without much enthusiasm. It seemed like the project to restore the church had been going on forever.

"Nice to see you again," Jack said to Mr. Walser.

"My pleasure. Now if you'll excuse me, I've got to put the rest of these announcements up."

Armed with his flyers, Walser strode away, down the block. Anne and Jack headed in the opposite direction, toward Embury Street. The Mills house was what was known in the Heights as a "classic box," a two-story structure, topped by a pyramidal roof, with a large front dormer window. Once the house had been painted a cheery shade of green, since faded to a chalky pea soup. At some point, Troy Mills must have covered the facade with synthetic siding, because Anne could see Victorian touches—cut shingles and wooden trim—peeking out from beneath the aluminum.

Jack tapped on the door, tried the knob. Locked. "Either Pop's sleeping it off or he's gone out."

They sat down on the front steps to wait. Everywhere Anne looked she saw signs of decay, from the rusty, dented mailbox to the half-dead flowers in the yard. The house was the only one on the block that didn't sport an American flag.

"It's getting late," Jack said. "Don't you have to be at work?"

"I work out of my house, actually. When I get home, I'll make some phone calls and do some writing."

"You're a writer? That's great. Have you written anything I might have heard of?"

"Well, let's see. Are you familiar with *Kitties on the Couch: A Guide to Cat Therapy,* by Dr. Kate Lester?"

"No."

"How about *Love Tips: Where to Find It, How to Keep It,* by Linda Wettemore Cohen, or *Raising the Rebellious Child,* by Dr. Sam Renssalaer?"

"I'm confused about something," Jack said. "If the books are by these other people, where do you come in?"

"I'm a ghostwriter, mostly of self-help books. The experts feed me information, give me their notes, advice, memoirs, whatever, and I write the books for them."

Anne wished she weren't sweating so much. It was too hot. Sunlight flooded the street, beating down on them. Droplets of moisture formed under her arms, behind her knees. Beside her, Jack looked cool. The way he sat on the steps, propped on one elbow, his legs extending languorously, he could have almost been a model for a Ralph Lauren ad. She was struck by how different the brothers' lives appeared to have been. Even Jack's sunglasses, with their reflective blue shades, looked as though they cost more than Tigger made in a week. She touched her own sunglasses; they had set her back $5 at Advance Pharmacy in town.

"Do you have any desire to write your own book, with your name in big block letters on the cover?" Jack asked.

"Sure," Anne replied. "I'm a mystery buff. I've read every Agatha Christie on the market, as well as Sue Grafton's series—you know, *A Is for Alibi, B* is for something else, and stuff by Walter Mosely and Jonathan Kellerman, all the masters. I'd love to write a mystery novel."

"Why don't you then?"

Anne shrugged. Why didn't she? Lack of time. Fear of

failure. For all her complaining about how difficult it was to work with prima donna shrinks and assorted other over-blown experts, she secretly suspected that if given the chance to write a novel herself, she'd fail miserably. It seemed better to hold on to the possibility of doing it some-day, rather than risk finding out she was a flop. "What kind of work do you do?" she said, changing the subject.

"I'm an architect. I love these turn-of-the-century build-ings," he said, gesturing toward the stately Victorian homes lining Embury Street. "They're gorgeous. Like poetry carved from wood. Someday I'd like to . . ."

A loud crash came from inside the house. Jack sprang to his feet. "Pop's home, all right, come on."

Anne followed him around to the rear of the house. The back door was locked. Jack lifted up a flower pot sitting next to the doormat. Underneath the terra-cotta pot was a key. "I should have thought of this before," he said, open-ing the door. They entered the kitchen and walked through a narrow hallway to the living room.

Troy Mills was lying in a heap next to the fireplace. "Oh, my God," Anne cried out. "He's dead!"

"No, he's not," Jack said, going over to Troy. Jack's voice sounded hardened, devoid of emotion. "I've done this dance a hundred times before."

Anne edged closer to Troy's limp body. In one hand, the old man clutched an empty bottle, the other hand was curled around a broken model ship. Above his head, on the mantel, were a half-dozen similar ships, wood models of eighteenth-century sailing vessels, with white cloth sails. A fan blew stale air through the room.

"Pop," Jack said, kneeling down and carefully prying the bottle from Troy's hand. "What happened?"

Troy opened his eyes and squinted up at them as if blinded. His face was leathery, lined with wrinkles. Al-though Anne guessed he was in his mid-sixties, he looked more like eighty. His hair was completely white, his eyes a milky blue. "My boy," he croaked, reaching up to touch Jack's sleeve. "You've come back."

"Help me move him," Jack said to Anne. Together they

half-dragged, half-carried Troy over to the Barcalounger in the corner. Anne expected the old man's body to be brittle, but his arms felt surprisingly strong and muscular. When Troy was safely deposited in the chair, Jack took a quilt that was balled up on the couch and draped it over his father's legs and chest.

"We need to talk to you, Pop. It's about Tigger's funeral."

"That sonofabitch," Troy Mill roared. "Let him rot in hell."

"Mr. Mills," Anne interjected. "Are you okay?"

Troy Mills glared up at her. He raised his hand as if to push her away. It trembled in the air. "Who the hell are you?"

"I'm Anne. Anne Hardaway."

"I know who ya are." Troy lowered his hand and clutched the quilt to his chest. "Evelyn's girl, right? The Crazy Lady's daughter."

Jack grabbed his father by the shoulders and shook him. "Pop, we need to go over the funeral arrangements. Tigger is lying in the funeral home with a tag tied around his toe. We need to give him a decent burial."

"He's no son of mine," Troy Mills yelled. "He killed that poor child. Killed her like some raggedy doll with the bad luck to get in his way. He's the devil, I tell ya. He's goin' straight to hell. He don't need no funeral. Because he ain't got a soul." A crafty look appeared in Troy Mills's eyes. "He thought he could take my house away from me? Not in this lifetime. The sonofabitch ain't gettin' his filthy paws on my house."

Troy's head lolled to one side. His eyes blinked a few times, then fluttered shut. His breathing was uneven and raspy. "We might as well leave him here," Jack said angrily. He seemed embarrassed and disgusted at the same time. "Pop'll sleep until nightfall. I know the drill, believe me."

Jack unlocked the front door, and they went back outside, onto the porch. "I'm sorry he made that remark about your mother," Jack said. He crossed his arms over his chest and stood rigid, not looking at her. "Tomorrow he won't remember you were here."

"Why does he hate Tigger so much?" Anne asked.

Jack's expression shifted. For an instant, rage flickered across his face, darkening his features. His eyes burned with anger. And then it passed, and when Jack turned to face her he was smiling. Something in the smile made her shiver.

"Tigger isn't Troy's son," Jack said slowly.

"What?"

"He and I were half-brothers."

"But the two of you look so similar."

"We both look like our mother. She married Troy when Tigger was three, after his natural father ran off. Pop always treated Tigger like dirt. He used to beat him up when he got drunk, and couldn't find anything better to do."

Anne put her hand on his shoulder. "I'm so sorry," she murmured. She wished there was something she could say that would help. She had a sudden urge to hug Jack close, to comfort him. She knew what it was like to have someone you love die, without family or friends to lean on.

Jack's eyes drifted away to someplace else, someplace she couldn't reach. After a few seconds, she removed her hand. "Did your father ever . . . did he . . . ?"

"Hurt me?" Reaching into his pocket, Jack took out his sunglasses and put them on. "No. I wished he would sometimes. I used to try to get between them, so he'd leave Tigger alone. But I wasn't strong enough or old enough to make him stop." Jack's voice dripped with bitterness. "Pop made Tigger leave. But I escaped. I won a scholarship to Princeton, and I was gone, good-bye. Away from Pop's drinking, away from Ma's crying when she thought I wasn't looking. I spent years traveling around the world. Turkey, Bali, Iceland, Nepal. I wanted to get as far away from here as I could."

"Tell me something," Anne said. "Do you think every family has secrets—bad secrets—that the rest of the world doesn't know anything about?"

Jack gazed out at Embury Street, taking in the row of

Victorian houses, the flags flapping in the breeze. "Yeah, I do," he said flatly. "You want to hear another?"

He walked down the steps and picked up a rusty shovel lying near the wilted flower beds. When he came back, he rapped the shovel against the side of the house. It sank into the wood immediately, penetrating the surface. The noise that followed was dry and hollow. "Tigger was hell-bent on keeping this place, and for what?" Jack said. "You see that?" He pointed to a large crack that had appeared in the clapboard. "It means the wood went bad, siding's buckling. The insulation is crawling with insects."

Jack knocked the shovel against the house again. "There's so much rot, it's only a question of time before the whole place comes tumbling down."

"Oh," Anne said, taken aback. "Does your father know?"

"He doesn't care. Didn't bother clueing Tigger in either, if I know Pop. He hated my brother's guts. Blood is what counts with Pop. Blood ties. Tigger was nobody, my mother's 'bastard child.' " Jack threw the shovel on the ground in disgust. "And now he's a corpse. Pop couldn't have wished for a happier ending."

Chapter 6

*Don't fight over who
does the housework.
If everybody pitches in,
it will get done a lot faster.*

Bobby Curley's business was located on the western edge of Oceanside Heights, in a strip of buildings opposite the marina. The green-and-white sign over the front door said: *Curley Consruction Co.* Then, in smaller letters: *The Restoration Specialists.*

Bobby was in the back, talking to a customer. He was a tall, stocky man, with sandy hair, a hundred-watt smile, and the easy affability of a natural-born salesman. In high school, he'd been a star football player who led the varsity squad to three consecutive championships, and the construction company was filled with sports trophies and dog-eared black-and-white photos of the team.

"I'll be with you in a sec," he called, spotting them. "Now, as I was saying," he continued, "we can sell you asphalt shingles that look just like weathered wood. But I'd go with the genuine article. You've got a historic house. Why not treat it right?"

As the customer nodded her head, Bobby whipped out

an order form and started writing up the sale.

"I heard this was a mega-bucks business," Jack whispered to Anne.

"It is," she answered. "He's got customers up and down the coast, as far away as Cape May. Delia Graustark told me he's doing some rock star's house. Bruce Springsteen or someone."

"Is she still the gossip maven around here?"

"Yup. There isn't a thing that goes on in this town that she doesn't know about."

Bobby Curley lumbered toward them. "Hi, Anne. Hiya, Jack, how ya doing?"

"Hey, Bobby," Jack said.

"I can't believe he's gone, man. I just can't believe it."

"I know."

"Seems like only yesterday we were climbing up the bell tower of the church. We caught hell for that, I remember."

The front door opened and a couple walked in. The man held a set of blueprints, the woman clutched a half-dozen paint chips.

"Elise," Bobby shouted. "Could you take care of these folks?" A young woman with towering blond hair, wearing a skintight print dress, emerged from the back room. Bobby must have a thing for hair, Anne thought to herself. Between Elise and Teri, there was enough spray action going on to lacquer Main Street. As Elise crossed the room, teetering on three-inch heels, she flashed a big smile in Bobby's direction. Anne wondered idly if Bobby could be having an affair.

"We're just trying to put the pieces together," Jack said to Bobby. "Did Tigger talk to you at all when he came back to town?"

"He stopped by. Asked me for a job."

"And you told him?"

"Look, Jack. I told him he needed to sober up, then come back and see me again. You can't tile a roof or install a bay window when you're looped. My insurance wouldn't cover an accident like that, not to mention the stink my clients would make."

"Did he want anything else?" Anne interjected. "Money, for instance?"

Bobby looked at Anne as if seeing her for the first time. "What's it to you?" he said sharply. "You and Tigger barely knew each other."

"Tigger asked for my help," Anne said. "He'd gotten a death threat and he wanted me to find out who was behind it."

"Did you give him any money, Bobby?" Jack cut in.

Bobby hesitated. "I gave him thirty bucks 'cause he looked like he could use it."

"That's all?" Jack said.

"That's all."

"We found a pile of cash in Tigger's room. You happen to know how it got there?"

Bobby shifted his weight from one foot to another. "I got no idea," he said.

"Look, we might as well be straight with you," Anne said. "Jack and I believe that Tigger was murdered."

"What?" For an instant, Bobby's good-natured face reflected a deeper emotion—anger, doubt, fear—but it vanished so quickly Anne couldn't tell what he was really thinking.

"How's that?" he said gruffly.

"Well, you know how everyone here felt about him," Anne said. "His death might be connected to what happened at the Spray View twenty years ago. To the fire."

"I'm not following."

"The little girl's parents still live here," Jack said. "They couldn't have been happy Tigger came back. And from what Anne's told me, they have a lot of friends and neighbors who weren't too pleased about it either."

Bobby glanced toward the front of the store, where Elise was poring over blueprints with the two customers. "I got to get back to work," he said abruptly. "Look, I'm sorry about what happened. But turning it into murder? No way. Tigger loved the bottle too much. In the end, that's what killed him."

"Tigger always claimed he never set that fire," Anne

said. "What if he was telling the truth? Protecting someone else?"

Bobby shook his head. "You've been watching too much TV," he said. "Besides, that's not how it was at all."

"What do you mean?" Jack said sharply. "How do you know?"

Bobby looked uncomfortable. His eyes roamed the store, as if searching for a way out. "I don't like speaking ill of the dead."

"No," Jack shot back. "You like to give 'em thirty bucks to get the hell out of your way."

"Hell, Jack. He was your brother. I guess you got a right to think he was a model citizen. But it didn't play that way."

"What exactly did happen, Bobby?" Anne said.

Bobby glanced nervously at the customers and lowered his voice. "I'm sorry to be the one telling you," Bobby said. "Especially now that he's gone. But Tigger started the fire. He told me so himself."

"That's bullshit, Curley, and you know it," Jack yelled. Everyone in the store turned toward them. Anne grabbed Jack's arm. She could feel the anger rippling through him. He looked as if he'd like to smash his fist against Bobby Curley's mouth, make Bobby stop talking.

She remembered the lost expression on Tigger's face as he gazed at the vacant lot. "No," she interjected. "I don't believe it."

"It was just a prank, just a harmless little prank," Bobby said. "Nobody was supposed to get hurt."

"What the hell are you talking about?" Jack said angrily.

Anne scanned Bobby's face. He seemed to be making up his mind about something. "Tigger did it on a dare. Fifty bucks up front and five hundred more afterward."

"Who put him up to it?" she asked.

"I don't know. He never said."

"Why would my brother do something like that?"

"There was a guy over in Belmar said he'd sell Tigger his old motorcycle if Tigger came up with the cash. That's why he wanted the money."

"What happened?" Anne said.

"I dunno. Something went wrong. Tigger told me the whole place lit up and he had to get out of there fast."

"You're lying," Jack said fiercely.

"Hey, the guy was my best buddy. I'm hurting here, too, okay? I probably shouldn't have said anything."

Anne studied him, trying to figure out what was going on. Bobby Curley was a smooth talker, a slap-your-back kind of guy with a gift for turning strangers into friends. Right now, he looked slightly ashamed of himself. "Tigger said he didn't do it," she said to him.

"It was an accident. He didn't mean for it to happen. And besides, he didn't want to go to jail for God knows how many years. Arson. Murder. You do the math."

"Why weren't you and P.J. with him that night, Bobby?" Anne said. "The three of you were always together."

Bobby scratched his head. "It's weird, you know? We were supposed to go. But my dad invited a bunch of people on board his boat that night, to watch the fireworks and all. I had to help out."

"What about McGrath?" Anne said.

"P.J. couldn't make it either."

"Why not?"

"Because of some girl. She wanted him to be with her that night. You know, high school shit."

"Jesus, Curley," Jack said. "What the hell are you doing here? How many other people have you fed this garbage to?"

Bobby looked startled. "No one else knows the truth except P.J. and me. We were the only ones he told." The front door opened, and three more people came in. "I got to get back to work," Bobby said. "I'm sorry, Jack. He never meant for anyone to get hurt. I know he didn't."

Anne glanced at Jack. His face was pale. She could hear him breathing beside her. Bobby Curley heard it, too, and began to back away, without taking his eyes off Jack's face. "Let's go," Anne said, pulling at Jack's arm with both hands. He didn't move. "I think we should go," she said again.

Jack turned to her as if hearing her for the first time. "He's lying," Jack said. His voice reverberated through the store. Across the room, the customers were staring at them openly. Elise patted her hair and studied the ceiling.

"Come on," Jack said brusquely, taking Anne's arm and striding quickly toward the door, as if he'd wanted to leave all along. Out of the corner of her eye, she could see Bobby watching them.

"You're right," Anne said, when they were back outside. "I've never seen Bobby so uncomfortable before. He's hiding something."

Jack glanced through the plate-glass window. Bobby was shaking hands with a customer. When he noticed Jack, he moved away.

For a little while, Anne and Jack walked along the docks in silence. The bay shimmered in the heat. A couple of sailboats were out on the water, but there wasn't much wind. Tied to the dock was the Curleys' Riviera motor yacht, *The Teribelle*. A few slips away was Jim Walser's boat, *Oceanside Pride*, and farther down, Troy Mills's small motor boat, *The Mariner*. "Do you think Bobby could have started the fire?" Anne said.

Jack fixed his gaze on the middle of the bay, where fishermen were casting for perch and mackerel. "Maybe," he said. "But why would Tigger take the blame for something Bobby did in the first place? If Tigger knew who did it, why didn't he just say so?"

Anne didn't have an answer.

"How many people in the Heights own a boat?" he asked suddenly.

"Probably more than half."

"The night before last, most of these boats would have been out on the Atlantic, right?"

Anne nodded. By the time Tigger left her house, the fireworks had been ending. But there must have been people out on the water—drinking, smoking, watching the night sky. Someone must have heard Tigger struggling to stay afloat. Why wasn't anyone able to save him? Why hadn't she listened instead of brushing away his concerns? *I've known these people for years,* she had told him. *They're absolutely harmless.* She pictured the ocean at night, the waves closing over his body. The sadness she'd been fighting to contain welled up, clinging to her like a second skin.

"How come nobody saw anything?" Jack asked, echoing her thoughts. "Hey," he said, catching a glimpse of her face. "You okay?"

"I feel so guilty," she said. "He asked for my help. And I tried to convince him he was perfectly safe."

"What about me? Taking my sweet time getting down here. The minute he called me, I should have gotten in my car and seen what the hell was the matter. I could have—"

"Saved him? Jack, you don't know that for sure."

"I know one thing. We're going to figure this thing out, find out what really happened to him."

"So what's our next move?"

"I need to go to the funeral home. After that, I think I'll hunt up P.J. McGrath and see if his story matches Bobby's."

"Sounds like a plan," Anne said. "In the meantime, I intend to find out as much as I can about the fire."

The library in Oceanside Heights was located in a sky blue Victorian cottage, with big white shutters and a wraparound porch. Over the years, Anne had become adept at finding research material she needed. By ghostwriting other people's books, she'd unintentionally become an instant expert on a great many subjects: divorce law, gardening, antique cars, electrical systems, potty training, cholesterol, Passover, breast cancer, direct mail campaigns, herbal medicine, split personalities, the Rolling Stones. She sometimes thought she'd make a great contestant on *Jeopardy.* The list of esoteric stuff she knew about seemed endless.

She located what she was looking for in five minutes

flat—a copy of the *Oceanside Heights Press*, dated a few days after the fire broke out.

The story on the fire was sandwiched between an article about the search for a missing cat named Thimbleberry and a piece describing a dispute among members of the Oceanside Heights Association over the policy of leasing land to homeowners. The article was accompanied by a black-and-white picture of the Spray View with its roof demolished and flames sprouting from the windows. ARSON SUSPECTED IN HOTEL FIRE, CHILD KILLED, the headline trumpeted. The item was brief:

A fire that swept through the Spray View Hotel is believed to be the result of arson, say Monmouth County fire officials. The fire broke out at 9:30 P.M., and firefighters fought the five-alarm blaze for more than three hours before getting it under control. The heavy volume of fire and swift movement of flames are signs of arson, says fire marshal Ned Taggart. Witnesses say they saw a local youth, Tigger Mills, 16, flee the hotel moments before the fire broke out. Mills has denied any involvement. The fire claimed the life of three-year-old Ruth Klemperer, who was trapped inside the burning building. Sandy Cooksey, 22, of Bradley Beach, suffered from smoke inhalation and is in stable condition at Morningside Hospital.

"As bad as it was, it could have been a lot worse," said Taggart. "Because of the holiday, most of the folks staying at the hotel weren't there. They'd gone down to the beach to watch the fireworks."

The wind-driven blaze was fought by more than 200 men from 30 fire companies in nine communities. Damage has been estimated at $750,000, according to Jim Walser, president of the Oceanside Heights Association.

Taggart says that despite some smoldering, there is little danger that fire will flare up again. Fire hoses have been left at the scene and the ruins are being carefully watched for any signs of rekindling.

Anne leafed through a week's worth of stories. It seemed that the Klemperers had been out the night of the fire, playing bridge with some friends. They had left their daughter, Ruthie, with the baby-sitter, Sandy Cooksey. Sandy told the police that right after she put the child to bed, she fell asleep on a loveseat in the office. When she woke up, the inn was on fire. She ran toward where the front door used to be and heard a noise, a loud bang. The hall staircase crumbled. She said she didn't remember anything else until she woke up in the hospital and they told her Ruthie Klemperer was dead.

Anne flipped through the stack of papers. There was a picture of Sandy, with her shoulder-length hair cut in layers. The Charlie's Angels look, they used to call it. Later accounts featured more about Tigger. He claimed he'd been walking by the hotel when it suddenly burst into flames, and he ran to escape being hurt. In grainy photographs, Tigger's face glared back at her, a portrait of rage and defiance.

Gathering the yellowed newspapers in her arms, Anne headed toward the copy machine. "Have you seen the centennial exhibit yet?" asked Delia Graustark, from her perch behind the mahogany front desk. The seventy-two-year-old woman was the library's sole full-time employee, as well as the Heights answer to Liz Smith. Sooner or later, everyone in town dropped by the library, and Delia prided herself on being in the know.

"Haven't seen it yet," Anne said. The Heights turned one hundred years old this year and the town was primed to celebrate.

"What have you got there?" asked Delia.

"Some old newspaper stories from around the time of the big fire."

"What on earth do you want with those?"

"I got another book assignment," Anne lied, "to write about the history of the Heights."

Delia's eyes widened in delight. "Then you must see the exhibit. Go on. I'll Xerox your articles for you."

"Thanks," Anne agreed. She liked Delia Graustark. De-

lia and Jim Walser were among the few people in town
who didn't associate her with her mother's illness, who
didn't act as if one day she'd suddenly turn into a crazy
person. Anne supposed it was because they'd both liked
Evelyn Hardaway and could separate Evelyn from the madness that overcame her.

The exhibit was displayed in the library's back parlor,
crammed with memorabilia: a rickety baby carriage, a rep-
lica of a stagecoach that had once brought visitors to the
Heights, a metal crimping iron that looked like an instru-
ment of torture.

Anne studied the items displayed under glass. There was
a poem written by Stephen Crane, who summered in the
Heights when he was a child because his father was a Methodist clergyman. Prayer books from camp meetings lay beside black-and-white postcards of elegantly dressed women
strolling on the boardwalk. An antiquated printing press
stood near a collection of old brochures and newsletters.
Printed in a fanciful Gothic typeface, they reminded Anne
of old Bibles she'd seen. The brochures described the ori-
gins of the Oceanside Heights Association, whose motto,
Anne read, was: "Trust in Our Future."

"Here are your copies," Delia said, handing Anne a
manila folder. "What do you think of the exhibit? Took
me months to organize."

"It's wonderful. Where did you find that picture of the
Spray View?" Anne said, pointing to a black-and-white
photo hanging on the wall.

"One of our board members donated it. But the picture
doesn't do the hotel justice. It was such a grand old place."

Anne walked over to the photo. The Spray View's sloping gables and twin turrets lent the hotel a storybook quality. She rummaged through her pocketbook and pulled out
a pen. On the back of a grocery list, she jotted down the
year the Spray View was built, along with a description of
its Victorian Gothic architecture. "What are you doing?"
Delia asked.

"Research," Anne replied. "Tell me about the people
who used to own it."

"Well, now. You know the Klemperers same as I do."

"Not really. I mean, I know she's extremely religious and he's a bit, well, strange. But I was just a teenager when the fire broke out. They must have been devastated."

"Of course they were. Ed was out of his mind with grief. Lucille took to her bed for weeks. Couldn't sleep, couldn't eat, wouldn't even go to church at first."

"Really?"

"They were getting ready to sell the place, don't you know. Lucille wanted to move down to Philly to be near her sister."

"The fire must have wiped them out financially."

"No. They were lucky that way. Ed took out an insurance policy on the Spray View a month before the fire."

"Is that right?" Anne said offhandedly. "How much was it worth?"

"Over a million dollars. But, of course," Delia added, "the money didn't mean anything to them. Not after what happened to little Ruthie."

"Did Ed ever go back to work?"

"At first, he did odd jobs for folks. But after a while, his spirits sank so low he couldn't bring himself to leave the house." Delia lowered her voice. "He was in here the other day," she said. "Needed a library card of all things. Imagine."

"Who? Mr. Klemperer?" Ed Klemperer never ventured outside his house.

"No. The Mills boy."

Anne looked up, startled. She could't picture Tigger here, amid the framed needlepoint samplers and the polished mahogany furniture. "You know what I heard?" said Delia, leaning forward conspiratorially. "I heard he broke into the Curley place. Stole a big wad of cash Bobby had locked in his desk."

"What? That's impossible."

"It most certainly is not. I happen to know on good authority it happened Sunday night. Bobby and Teri went to the charity bazaar over at the church, and when they came back, the house was a mess. Ransacked. Imagine!"

"I didn't hear anything about it in town."

"Oh, the Curleys tried to hush the whole thing up. They don't want the world to know that big old house of theirs doesn't have a decent burglar alarm. The only reason I know about it is because my niece, Darlene, answers the phone over at the sheriff's office."

Anne could practically feel her thoughts tumbling inside her head. Was it possible that Tigger stole the money in the Bible? If the money belonged to Bobby, why hadn't he told them about the theft? It didn't make sense. And something else about the story was wrong somehow. If she could only figure out what.

"So he waltzes in here the other day, cool as you please. Even asked me did I have a quarter he could borrow for the Xerox machine." Delia frowned. "I had to give him a library card, don't you know. It *is* the law."

Something about the date. She and Tigger talked to Teri on Wednesday afternoon, three days after he was supposed to have stolen the money. Yet the two of them acted like they hadn't seen each other in years. Unless Delia had gotten her facts wrong or the Curleys had fabricated the story for some reason . . .

"Stood in this very room," Delia continued, "looking at this very exhibit. Imagine! I was so nervous I was practically shaking. I even stamped his book with the wrong date. But I don't suppose it matters now."

"What book?" It seemed odd that in the middle of battling Troy Mills for the house and breaking into the Curley manse, Tigger would have time for a little light reading.

"A history book, of all things."

"Do you happen to remember the name of it?"

"Just a minute now." Delia went back to her desk and pulled out a leather-bound ledger book. Putting her spectacles on, she flipped through the pages of the ledger, searching for the right date. "One of these days, we'll switch over to computers." Her finger trailed down the line of print. "Here it is. *Vintage Victoriana: A Historical Perspective of Oceanside Heights*, by Mr. Arthur Hornsby."

"Is there another copy?"

"Sorry, dear, just the one. There wasn't much interest in it. Arthur had to publish the book himself."

"I see."

Delia put the ledger book back in her desk. "You'll be sure to mention my name, won't you? In the acknowledgments for the book *you're* writing about the Heights? It would make me so proud."

"Of course," Anne said. "don't give it a second thought."

Chapter 7

When the nursery looks like an explosion in a toy factory, make cleanup a game. Play a favorite CD or tape and see how much your child can put away before the music stops.

Anne took the long way home from the library, down Main Street for two blocks and then south on Primrose Lane, until she reached Beechwood Avenue. The houses on Beechwood were the oldest ones in town, erected back in the 1890s for the church ministers who founded the Heights. The architecture was an eclectic mix—Eastlake-style buildings next to Colonial Revivals and houses that emulated Gothic and Queen Anne buildings in England. Towering beech trees cast their shadows over the block. In winter, the pale silvery bark and bleached cream leaves lent an almost ghostly appearance to the trees. But now the leaves formed a rich, shining canopy of green.

Anne stopped in front of 26 Beechwood Avenue. Painted soot gray, with arched pediments over the windows and sloping eaves, the house was decorated with jagged gingerbread spindles that looked like frozen icicles. Enclosed by a black wrought iron gate, it was the gloomiest house on the block, made infamous over the last two decades by the man who lived there. Kids who grew up in Oceanside Heights called 26 Beechwood Avenue the "Addams Family House." They claimed the place was haunted. It was practically a childhood rite of passage—to dare your friends or be dared yourself to go up to the front door and ring the bell. You had to count to ten before you were allowed to run away, dashing down the street, howling with relief because you had knocked on the mad hermit's door and lived to tell the tale. Anne remembered hearing once that Ed Klemperer himself had appeared on the threshold, armed with a baseball bat. The children had talked of nothing else for days—how the hermit had eyes as big as plates and a long white beard, longer than Rip Van Winkle's, how his laugh had echoed down the block like a rabid dog. The old man had swung his bat in the air, roaring how he would break the children's necks, rip them in two, if any of them dared bother him again. The kids fled in terror, telling the story again and again until the recluse became every child's nightmare: the bogeyman hiding under the bed, the evil sorcerer tucked inside the pages of their comic books, the dark criminal masterminding every unsolved murder they saw on TV or read about in the papers.

Despite its fearsome tenant and overall ominous appearance, Anne noticed that the house was in mint physical condition—the exterior freshly painted, the lawn newly mowed, each pillar and railing polished to a glossy hue. That's what money could buy, she thought to herself. After the Spray View burned down, the Klemperers had moved here. Nothing but the best for Ed and Lucille. She unlatched the gate, walked up the slate pathway to the door. There didn't appear to be a doorbell. Maybe the Klemperers got tired of kids bothering them all the time and had the bell removed. She tapped on the door, tried to peer in through the long slender panes of glass on either side of the entryway. The interior was dark. Her hand rested on the polished brass doorknob. Well, Ed certainly wasn't going to invite her in. There had to be another way. She turned the knob gently and the door swung open. Anne jumped back a few steps. Nobody in Oceanside Heights locked doors during the day, but somehow she expected the Klemperers to be the exception to the rule. She took a quick look behind her and surveyed the street. Empty. This was her chance. Taking a deep breath, she slipped inside and quietly shut the door.

She was immediately hit by a blast of cold air. The house was air-conditioned and silent, save for the rhythmic muffled ticking of a clock. Gliding noiselessly through the front hallway, Anne peered into the parlor. A spacious room, decorated with period antiques: a carved camelback sofa upholstered in a rich-looking brocade, heavy mahogany chests, lamps with silk shades, Wedgwood plates on the mantel. Not your typical beach house by a long shot. Anne had heard that the Heights Association had been begging the Klemperers for years to include their home in the annual summer house tour, but Lucille always refused.

In the center of the entry hall, a curving staircase led to the second floor. Anne put one hand on the wood banister and leaned forward, straining to hear if anyone else was home. Well, of course Ed was there. Where else would the old hermit be? He never left the house. One of the floorboards groaned beneath her feet. She froze, her heart thumping against the wall of her chest. Did she dare sneak upstairs? If she was caught down here, she could always think of an excuse. But upstairs? Wouldn't that be more like breaking and entering? Retreating, she continued down the long narrow corridor, passing a library, a small parlor, a formal dining room, a pantry. Only one of the doors along the hallway was closed. Maybe that's where Ed Klemperer was hiding. "Mr. Klemperer," she whispered, tapping on the door. "Are you in there?" Not waiting for an answer, she opened the door and stepped into the room.

A little girl's bedroom, Ruthie Klemperer's room from the look of things. Along one wall was a frilly canopy bed with a flowered pink spread and a half-dozen stuffed animals reclining against pillows. A rocking horse in the corner, shelves laden with storybooks and toys. Porcelain dolls with flaxen hair and glassy blue eyes stared out at Anne from their perch on the window seat. On top of the miniature desk was a stack of colored construction paper, crayons, Elmer's Glue, and child-size scissors. It was as if Ruthie had gone outside to play and would be back any minute. Anne walked over to the closet, threw open the door. Inside, dozens of tiny shoes: sneakers and plastic flip-flops and sandals and black patent leather Mary Janes. Shelves piled high with shorts, tops, small flowered underpants. Anne reached out, ran her fingertips lightly along the row of pastel-colored dresses. Many still had price tags attached to them. She examined a pale pink dress with a velvet sash. According to the tag, the dress had been purchased at the Little Bumblebee, a children's store at the mall in Freehold, for $49.99. A chill ran up and down Anne's body. The mall had been built several years ago. Someone must have purchased this dress for Ruthie recently.

She looked around again—taking in the dolls, the stuffed animals, the new toys. There was a scrubbed, antiseptic quality to the room. The dolls stared back at her with their dead blue eyes. Carefully closing the door behind her, Anne stepped into the hallway. The house was too quiet, an eerie sort of quiet that made her shiver in a different way than the air-conditioner did. She continued down the hall, past a small study and a second, less formal parlor, until she reached the kitchen. Though the room was large, it was bare and empty-looking. A row of copper pots hung from the wall. They looked new, unused. It didn't appear as though anyone cooked meals here. At the far end of the kitchen, a door was ajar. Anne walked over and opened the door wider. A series of steps led down to the basement. "Mr. Klemperer?" she said hesitantly.

Hugging the railing, she went down the dark steps. She reached her hand along the wall, feeling for the light switch. Halfway down, she found the switch and flicked it on. For a second, she froze, staring at the scene in front of her. It looked staged somehow, like a film set for a B-movie

thriller. Other people in the Heights had converted their
basements into dens or bars or playrooms. Ed Klemperer
had made his basement into a laboratory. In the center of
the room was a large gray table, although the word that
popped into Anne's mind was *slab*. On it were things she
recognized from her high school chemistry class—racks of
test tubes, beakers filled with weird colored fluids, Bunsen
burners, vials labeled with chemical symbols. She had no
idea what some of the other stuff was: metal instruments,
electrical tubing, a gray metal object that looked like a
blowtorch. A rustling noise emanated from a corner of the
room. Anne's heart leaped into her throat. She could feel
her pulse hammering in her ears. The air smelled odd, damp
almost. She took a deep breath, inhaling the rank scent, and
edged closer to the rustling sound. It was coming from
white mice in a wire cage. The cage was divided in half.
The animals on the right side were the ones making noise.
They were hyper, scurrying manically, their paws scratching against torn bits of newspaper. The mice on the left
side of the cage seemed exceedingly tired. Some looked as
if they could barely move; others appeared to be sleeping.

Next to the cage was a gray double-walled metal storage
locker. She walked over to it, tested the doors, and found
they were unlocked. Swinging them open, she saw that each
shelf was filled with identical vials, containing liquids,
powders, and colorless solid substances that looked like
rocks. Some of the vials were stamped with a black skull
and crossbones. Anne read the labels: arsenic, strychnine,
sodium cyanide. Terrific. The mad scientist had a thing for
poison.

And a gardener to boot, she thought, catching sight of
the row of plants on the other side of the room. But Ed's
plants weren't garden-variety marigolds and tulips. They
had strange hairy leaves, bulbous roots, thick veins, and
waxy berries that looked weirdly artificial. The names of
the plants were printed neatly on small bits of cardboard:
baneberry, black hellebore, devil's trumpet, prayer bean.
Each and every one was poisonous, Anne knew. There'd
been an entire chapter devoted to lethal plants in *Green*

Thumbs: Gardening for Fun and Profit, a book she'd ghosted for Edna Rosemont of the American Horticultural Society. No wonder the Klemperers didn't want 26 Beechwood Avenue on the annual house and garden tour. All that was missing in the laboratory was a monster with screws in its neck and a jagged scar across its pasty white forehead, a monster who rose from the dead, miraculously restored to life by one of the hermit's chemical cocktails. She reached out to touch the bluish flowers on the baneberry plant.

"No!" a voice behind her called out.

Whirling around, Anne saw Lucille Klemperer standing at the top of the stairs, glaring down at her.

"Get out," Lucille commanded. Easily past sixty, Lucille was short and stocky, with gray, short-cropped hair and the erect posture and grim deportment of an elementary school gym teacher.

"I'm sorry," Anne stammered, as she walked toward the stairs. "The front door was open. I was looking for your husband."

"Ed doesn't receive visitors."

"I know. I'm sorry for the intrusion. But I wanted to speak to you and your husband. It's about Tigger Mills."

At the mention of Tigger's name, Lucille's face hardened. "Get out of my house, Anne Hardaway," she said slowly. "Right now."

Anne climbed the stairs, following Lucille into the kitchen. Lucille went to the back door, yanked it open, and walked stiffly to the sink, where she turned on the faucet. Water splashed into the white basin.

"I'm sorry for barging in here this way," Anne said. "I thought perhaps Ed ... Mr. Klemperer ... didn't hear me knock."

Lucille's back was so straight that Anne could see the outline of the older woman's spine beneath her gray dress.

"If this isn't a good time for you," Anne continued, "I can come back later. Whenever it's convenient."

Lucille looked up from the sink. "For we wrestle not against flesh and blood, but against the rulers of darkness," she intoned. "To withstand in the evil day, and having done all, to stand."

"Mrs. Klemperer . . ."

"Above all, taking the shield of faith, wherewith ye shall be able to quench all the fiery darts of the wicked."

Lucille Klemperer's eyes were far away. She rubbed her hands together under the water, pressing her palms together. Anne left through the open doorway. She could still hear the water running as she walked away.

It was slightly past noon when she got home, and the message light on her answering machine was blinking. The first message was from Jim Walser, reminding her to come to the Gospel Musical Ministry. The second was from her friend Helen Passelbessy, whose voice expressed a mixture of curiosity and concern. Then Mary Lou Popper's midwestern twang came on the line. There was no greeting, just this: "Your copy is late. I need all of chapter five by the end of the day. Or your publisher's going to hear about it. Change the remedy for getting chewing gum out of the carpet. Yes, salad oil will soften the gum but it may leave a faint oily stain. A prewash spray is better. And check your fax. I sent you four pages of notes for 'Troubleshooting Wallpaper Woes.' "

Oh, goodie, Anne thought. Can't wait.

Sometimes she questioned whether the freedom and flexibility her job afforded was worth the hassle. Of course, she *had* become an expert of sorts. She probably knew more about stain removal, race walking, time management, sexual dysfunctions, allergies, and a wealth of other scintillating subjects than anyone else on the Jersey shore.

She fixed herself a sandwich and a glass of iced tea, grabbed the cellular phone, and went out on the porch. It was her favorite spot in the house, shady and comforting. From the wicker chaise longue, she had a bird's-eye view of the beach, and the water always had a calming effect on her. When she was younger, she would sometimes awaken in the middle of the night and lie in the chaise, with a blanket wrapped around her, listening to the rhythmic pounding of the waves. The first thing she'd see in the morning was the sun climbing over the ocean, the sky smudged with pink and orange streaks.

She ate her lunch slowly. Across the street, on the boardwalk, two sandy-haired children sold shells for a penny a piece. The sun glinted silver off the water. A prop plane flew by, pulling an advertising banner for Calvin Klein, a model with her tank top raised to reveal a tiny, flat stomach.

When she had finished eating, Anne sat down at the computer and went over Mary Lou's copious, nearly indecipherable notes on buffable liquid waxes and remedies for removing rust stains from cement. She typed the first sentence, read it over a few times, then stared at the screen until the words began to blur. Who wanted Tigger dead? Who hated him enough to kill him? She stored the empty file on "Fast n' Easy Floor Care" and created a new blank document. This would only take a sec, she promised herself, as she typed out a list of names.

Ed Klemperer
Lucille Klemperer
Bobby Curley
P.J. McGrath
Sandy Cooksey
Troy Mills

The way she figured it, the people on this list either (A) had a motive for wanting Tigger dead or (B) might know how the fire got started. Is that why Tigger was interested in the history of the Heights? Because the book shed some light on what happened at the hotel? Instinct told her it did, if only she could figure out how the pieces fit together. And what was that business about Tigger stealing money from the Curleys? Could it be true? Or was it merely another lie about Tigger, like the report the cops got that he'd been breaking windows.

The phone rang, interrupting her reverie.

"Oh, good, you're finally home," said Helen Passelbessy. Helen was her closest friend. They'd met at a bake sale to benefit the restoration of the Church by the Sea. After hawking fudge brownies and sugar cookies for an hour and a half, they'd decided to take a coffee break and hadn't bothered going back. The two had had hit it off right away. Although Helen and her husband had moved to the Heights seven years ago, she was still considered a "newcomer." Helen worked at the Central Bank of New Jersey, where, she was fond of joking, people didn't care how long she'd lived there; they just wanted to know if she could approve their loan or refinance their mortgage.

"Hi," Anne said. "I'm sorry I didn't get a chance to call you back."

"Honey, don't worry about it. I know how hard this is on you. The guy was practically your crush of the century."

Anne looked at the porch railing. The glasses she and Tigger had drunk from two nights ago were still there. A fly buzzed lazily around the rims.

"Is it true what they say?" Helen continued. "Is love lovelier the second time around?"

"What do you mean?"

"Do I have to spell it out? Was it good for you? Did he just up and leave your bed in the middle of the night?"

"Helen, I don't know what you're talking about. We had a drink on my front porch and then he left."

"Get out! The buzz in town is that you slept with him."

Anne felt her face flush with anger. "What! That's ridiculous."

"Sorry, hon. Didn't mean to upset you. But that's what everyone's saying."

"Well, they're wrong."

Another plane flew over the beach, with a banner trailing behind it: *Protect Your Teeth! Call 1-800-DENTIST*. The sky was quilted with wispy clouds. "At least you got to spend some time with him," Helen said apologetically. "It would have been worse if he died and you never got to know him."

"He told me he was in trouble. He said he needed my help."

"How come Tigger came to you?"

"Because I've lived here forever and a day. Because I know how to find the answers to all sorts of arcane questions. Because he and I were alike—two outcasts in this close-knit little town of ours. Anyway, I didn't take him seriously. I shrugged the whole thing off."

"Does it matter now?"

"Yeah. It does."

Way out on the ocean, past the piers and the orange buoy, a swimmer was doing the front crawl. From a distance, Anne couldn't make out whether it was a man or a woman but the swimmer was obviously strong. The arm motion was steady, the flutter kick barely rippled the surface.

"Helen, could I call you back? I just thought of something I have to do."

"Sure, honey. If you want to talk later, I'm around."

"Thanks," Anne said before hanging up. She stared at Tigger's glass on the railing. What had he told her in front of the Spray View? Something about destiny, how the outcome was inevitable, no matter how much you tried to stop it.

From the porch, the ocean looked as it always had in the summer—deep blue, perfect. Foam spilled onto the sand. It was late afternoon, and seagulls lined up facing the wind like an organized bird army. She picked up the phone and dialed a number. "Doctor's office," said the voice on the other end.

"Hi, Katie. It's Anne Hardaway. Is he in?"

"Is there something I can help you with, Anne? Do you need an appointment?"

"No. I have a quick question for him, nothing important. It'll only take a minute."

"Hold on. I'll see if he's with a patient."

Music played on the line, Karen Carpenter singing "We've Only Just Begun," the song they'd sung at Anne's high school graduation. It had been months since she'd called David Chilton. When he first told her he wasn't leaving his wife, that he couldn't leave, despite the promises he'd made, Anne felt tricked. She said she didn't want to see him anymore, and she meant it. Their affair had been passionate, a string of clandestine trysts and late-night encounters played out away from the gossipy confines of the Heights, in no-tell motels and dimly lit restaurants. Although looking back, Anne wondered if the passion had more to do with keeping their relationship secret than it did with David Chilton himself. He was, after all, a small-town dentist whose second favorite pastime was bird watching. Driving though Bradley Beach at night a few weeks ago, she'd spotted his car parked outside Vic's restaurant, a favorite rendezvous, and she'd sensed that he'd found someone new. His number one hobby would always be cheating on his wife.

The music stopped mid-lyric. "Dr. Chilton."

"David. It's Anne."

"Anne, how've you been?" said David Chilton.

"Fine. How are you? How's Barbara, and the kids?" It was awkward, talking to him this way, as if there had never been anything between them. When she ran into him in town, it still felt uncomfortable. But she needed his help. And she didn't know who else to call.

"The kids are fine. And Barbara is . . . Well, Barbara is Barbara. We're managing." His voice was soft and buttery-sounding, a disc jockey's voice. It was one of the things she'd liked best about him. That, and his straight, white teeth. "So," he said, shifting to a professional tone. "What can I do for you?"

"I need some information for a book I'm writing. I thought you could help me even though, well, it doesn't have anything to do with dentistry."

"Anne, I'm a licensed physician." He sounded slightly annoyed. "Whatever questions you have, I'm sure I'll be able to answer them."

Her eyes skated across the ocean. Already the swimmer seemed further away, gliding just beneath the surface.

"Okay, then. I need to know about drowning."

"Drowning?"

"For a book I'm ghosting. It's . . . uh, a writer's guide to murder and mayhem."

"Doesn't sound like a terribly big market."

"Big enough. There are a lot of mystery writers who need to know about police procedure, cause of death, stuff like that."

"All right. I'm listening."

"When someone drowns, how do you know if it's accidental?"

"As opposed to?"

"Murder."

"Murder would be hard to prove. It's better if the writer arranged for the killer to shoot the victim or stab him."

"This chapter is on drowning, David," Anne said impatiently.

"It's an inefficient way to kill somebody, if it could be done at all."

"Let's start over," she said. "In an accidental drowning, what usually happens?"

"When a body drowns, it sinks to the bottom and stays there. After a while, it will start to decompose, and the tissues fill up with gas. When that happens, it becomes buoyant and floats back to the surface."

"How long does that take?"

"Depends on the water temperature. Could be days."

"What about if the water is cold?"

"In icy water, gas forms more slowly. The body could remain submerged for months."

Months. If Tigger left her house around ten-thirty, he couldn't have been in the water for more than seven hours. What was going on?

"What if the guy washed up on shore almost immediately?" Anne asked.

"If he was swimming, it probably meant he suffered a stroke or a heart attack or maybe had some kind of epileptic seizure in the water."

Anne could feel her mind racing. It didn't make any sense. Tigger was in pretty good shape. It seemed unlikely that he'd had some kind of medical problem. Unless . . .

"Could an autopsy prove anything?" she asked.

"Like what?"

"I don't know. Like the victim had been poisoned or beat up or something and then thrown in the ocean."

"Tough to prove. When a person drowns, the body always assumes a facedown position, so the arms, legs, and face may scrape against the bottom. Any abrasions and cuts could have been caused after drowning occurred as well as before."

This was getting her nowhere.

"Anne. I've got to run. My one o'clock is here."

"Okay," she said absentmindedly. "Thanks."

"There's one more thing you should probably mention."

"What's that?"

"There's a high correlation between alcohol intoxication and accidental drowning. Like that guy who washed up on the beach yesterday morning. You know who I mean? I forget his name."

Anne's gaze raked the ocean, searching for a glimpse of the lone swimmer. But all she saw were people closer to shore, splashing, wading. The swimmer was nowhere in sight.

Chapter 8

> *Homemade formula for removing smoke residue: mix ⅛ cup salt, a few squirts zinc oxide, and water into a paste. Rub on the offending spot. Rinse well with water.*

If there was one thing Anne had learned from researching books, it was that persistence paid off. She liked to think of it as a numbers game. The more inquiries you made, the more likely it was that someone would tell you what you needed to know. It took six phone calls to locate Sandy Cooksey. She hit paydirt on the next to last call, to the Monmouth County Fire Department. The man who answered had never heard of Sandy. But he did know Ned Taggart, who had retired six years ago. Yes, he had the ex-fire marshal's number. But it was against regulations to release it. Anne described her latest book project in copious detail, how it would cover the history of the Jersey shore, including an entire chapter on the fire department's growth and development, from the Victorian era right up until today. If there was any memorabilia in the firehouse—antique trucks, old uniforms, pictures of former mascots, etc.—she'd love to take a look. It so happened that there was a lot of stuff, the fireman told her. Enough to fill a museum if the state only had the dough to pay for it.

After promising to drive over and look, she was rewarded with the number. How many lies had she told lately? She was losing track.

Taggart picked up on the first ring, as though he'd been sitting by the phone, waiting for a fire alarm. Anne explained about the book and the research she was doing. "Sure, I remember the girl," Taggart said. "She was unconscious when they brought her to the hospital. Woke up, claimed she couldn't recall a blessed thing. Never did believe it myself. Always thought she was lying to save her own neck."

"Why?"

"Sandy was the one responsible for looking after that poor child. You ask me, she should have been brought up on charges."

"What's she doing now?"

"She worked in Atlantic City for a while, over at the casinos. Got busted a couple of times—drugs, prostitution. Last I heard, she was shacked up in some hole over in Landsdown Park."

"Do you have an address?"

"I might. If you tell me what in Sam Hill is going on."

"I told you. I'm researching this book."

"I know what you told me. I don't buy it is all. You a cop?"

"No."

"Private eye?"

"No." She felt oddly flattered.

"Well, whoever you are and whatever you're up to, let me give you a piece of advice about Miss Sandy Lynn Cooksey. I been with the department for thirty-eight years. And I'll tell you something: she's either stupid as all get out or she's the best damn liar I ever met."

Landsdown Park was separated from the Heights by a small, manmade lake. A footbridge spanned the short distance between the two towns. If you didn't feel like walking, you had to drive around the lake to get to Landsdown. Years ago you could reach Landsdown by merely walking north on the boardwalk. But in the 1930s the boardwalk was torn up, replaced by the Dreamland amusement park, built midway between the two towns. As Jack's red Corvette cruised toward Landsdown, Anne could see the shell of the old amusement palace, which had closed in 1965. Signs on the domed mint green pavilions heralded the Skooter Rides, Shooting Gallery, and Freak Show inside. From time to time, there had been talk of reopening the amusement park, of restoring the carved horses on the antique carousel, repairing the Shoot-the-Chutes, rebuilding the ornate arches and columns that were meant to recall an Arabian fantasy. But the park was so dilapidated that the county building superintendent had recommended it be demolished, replaced with a new convention center that would help revitalize Landsdown. The only problem: There was no money to build a convention center. Investors said you couldn't eat an apple once the worm had gotten inside.

If the Heights was a tribute to well-preserved Victoriana, Landsdown was a monument to decay. Half the storefronts were boarded up, the buildings crumbling and condemned. Graffiti was splashed on the sidewalks, obliterating the fronts of the shabby wood frame houses. Needles littered the streets. Kids collected them, stacking the syringes in piles like bones left to rot in the sun. Every so often, the cops wrote down the license numbers of expensive cars that cruised through Landsdown, cars that stopped for a minute or two, then sped away laden with powders and pills wrapped in flat white packets. After a flurry of arrests, it was back to business as usual. Nothing stopped the drug trade for long. Officials called it "relentless" and talked about the challenge of turning things around, especially at election time. The unemployment rate was the highest in the state. On street corners, groups of young men gathered, nursing bottles of beer in brown paper sacks, their radios pounding out a steady pulse of rap music. Teenage girls with baby carriages congregated on front stoops, complaining about the heat. Years earlier, the sycamores in town had succumbed to blight. They had to be chopped down, and there wasn't a single tree left. No shade. Kids had pried the covers off the fire hydrants so often that the water barely trickled out.

A hot wind blew through the car. "Did you find the history book?" Anne asked Jack.

"Yup. But I don't know what good it'll do us."

"Why's that?"

"Take a look for yourself. It's in the glove compartment." Anne flipped open the door of the compartment and removed a worn-looking library book with a crimson cover. She leafed through it quickly. The first part had to do with the Heights' numerous bylaws and regulations: building codes, historic preservation guidelines, religious injunctions against drinking in public or using the town beach before noon on Sundays. The second half of the book traced the genealogy of the town's inhabitants, dating back to 1896. There were several chapters devoted to family trees, which chronicled the assorted births, deaths, and marriages of people born in the Heights. It certainly looked like Arthur Hornsby had done a ton of research to complete his opus.

"Pretty boring stuff," Jack said.

"I don't know about that. Tigger must have thought there was something interesting in here. Otherwise he wouldn't have bothered to check the book out of the library."

Earlier, on the phone, she'd filled Jack in on much of what she'd learned so far—the newspaper accounts of the fire, the insurance money the Klemperers received, her visit to Ed's laboratory, Chilton's medical opinions. What she *didn't* tell him was that Tigger was accused of stealing money from the Curleys. She knew the accusation would only upset Jack, and she wanted to do some investigating before she hit him with more bad news. His attempt to locate Tigger's old pal, P.J. McGrath, was a bust. It seemed P.J. had suddenly quit his job at Hauser's sporting goods store in the Heights and nobody had seen him in days.

"What's your take on McGrath?" Anne said.

"The clerks at Hauser's said he inherited a ton of money from some long-lost great-aunt and he's planning to open his own gym. A boxing palace with big-time talent. I know P.J. dreamed of turning pro himself. But his hand was broken in the ring one time, and after that, his boxing career fizzled."

"Do you think the money is legit?"

"I think we need to talk to him, find out whether he hung out with Tigger during the last two weeks. He might know something."

Jack pulled the car up in front of a run-down motel called the Pink Flamingo, a squat, boxy building slapped together with cheap construction materials in the 1950s. Flakes of paint peeled off the pink stucco walls; some of the grille-work on the tiny balconies had been torn away; the rest was encased in rust. Laundry flapped on a clothesline in the yard, rows of slips and undershirts that looked permanently soiled.

"Did you know this Sandy person at all?" Jack said to Anne, as they headed up the concrete walkway.

"No. She was about five years older than me. I think I remember hearing that she went to community college. But after the fire, she dropped out."

"She must be down on her luck if she's living in this dump," Jack said, skirting a pile of dog droppings on the walkway.

"I guess. Listen, I don't mean to keep harping on this, but are you absolutely, positively sure the death threat Tigger told me about is gone?"

"Yeah. I turned the room upside down and it just isn't there. But I did come across something else that's kind of interesting." He reached into his pocket and took out a tissue folded into a small square. Unwrapping it carefully, he held up what was inside: a diamond earring, pear-shaped, perfect, with a gold clasp in back.

"Where did you find it?" Anne asked, as he handed it over. The earring sparkled in the sun.

"Between the sheets. I took the whole bed apart because I thought the note might be hidden under the mattress or something."

Anne wondered if the earring could possibly belong to Sandy Cooksey. Her room was in the back of the motel, across from a small swimming pool. There was only a little bit of water in the pool, as if the person filling it had stopped halfway through.

Jack knocked on the door. "Leave it outside," a woman's voice called out. He waited a moment, knocked again.

"Look, you can put it on my tab, okay?" The voice was harsh and raspy.

Jack turned to Anne, shrugged, and rapped on the door more loudly. There was a shuffling noise inside. The door opened a crack, then an inch wider to reveal a pair of blood-shot brown eyes. "Are you Sandy?" Jack asked.

"Who wants to know?"

"I'm Jack Mills. And this is Anne Hardaway."

"Good for you. I'm not interested—unless the Burger Barn is hiring cops to deliver a large fries and a shake."

"We're not cops."

The door swung open. "Then what do ya want?" The woman looked to be in her early forties, rail-thin, with stringy whitish-blond hair that was dark at the roots. Rheumy eyes, a chipped front tooth. She had on a short black denim skirt and a long-sleeved white midriff blouse that hung loosely on her small frame. When she turned her head, Anne could make out a faint scar that ran from her ear to her jaw.

"Could we talk to you for a minute?"

"Lookit. I'm busy."

Jack reached into his wallet and pulled out two bills. "We'd like to ask you a few questions," he said, "about the fire at the Spray View Hotel."

The woman snatched the money from his hand and tucked it inside her blouse. "Well, why dincha say so? Come on in."

The room was almost entirely brown—fake-looking

brown paneling on the walls, brown blanket covering the bed, brown indoor/outdoor carpeting on the floor, a ratty brown wood dresser and chair. "You're Sandy, right?" Jack said.

"Yeah. Have a seat." She plopped down on the bed and crossed her legs. Her thighs were milky white. Anne sat in the chair. Jack leaned against the wall, looking uncomfortable. "What'd ya say your name was?" Sandy said.

"Jack Mills. Tigger Mills was my brother."

"Tigger, huh? She took a cigarette from the bedside table and lit it. "Smoke?" she said, holding the pack out. Her nose was running. She wiped it with the back of her hand.

"No, thanks," Anne said.

"We just have a couple of questions," Jack said. "Did you see my brother on the night of the fire?"

"Nope."

"Did you see anyone or anything that looked suspicious?"

"Nope."

"How did you happen to be stuck there that night?" Anne asked. "The newspaper said everyone else had gone down to the beach to watch the fireworks."

Sandy took a deep drag on her cigarette. With her other hand, she absentmindedly scratched her leg. "I was supposed to take the kid down to the ocean to see the fireworks. I told the Klemperers I would. But I fell asleep on the couch in the office."

There was a knock on the door. "That must be the chow," said Sandy, jumping up. The delivery boy at the door was holding two large bags. "Lookit," she said, over her shoulder. "I ain't got any change. Do ya think you could spring for this?"

Jack raised his eyebrows and took out his wallet. The smell of grease and onions flooded the room. Anne felt a wave of nausea pass through her. Sandy put the bags of food on the dresser. "I can't talk too long," she said. "I got company coming." She stubbed out her cigarette, lit another.

Anne reached into her purse and extracted the earring.

"Does this belong to you, by any chance?" she said to Sandy.

"Not unless you got the other one handy. One's no good to me. Course, there are some girls that wear one ring in their nose. I think it's disgusting. Makes 'em look like whadjamacallits, those people in Australia."

"Sandy," Jack cut in. "About the fire. We could really use your help."

"I'm trying to be helpful, honey," Sandy said, resuming her place on the bed. Her skirt was hiked up so high they could see the edge of her panties.

"Come on. Talk to us," Jack said. "Do you remember anything suspicious—anything at all?"

Sandy shifted positions on the bed. She looked bored. "There was the heater. But I done told the police about that."

"What heater?" Anne asked.

"The electric heater in the office. I nearly tripped over it when I went to get Ruthie that doll she was always dragging around. See, it was July. I didn't know what anyone would want with a heater."

"Did you touch it?" Jack asked.

"Now why would I go and do a thing like that? It was hot as blazes that night."

"Did anyone else go near the heater?" Anne asked.

"Not that I seen."

"What about any unusual smells? Like gasoline?"

"Didn't notice if there was. It was Mrs. Klemperer's housecleaning day, so the whole place smelled like ammonia." She took a drag on her cigarette and exhaled a thin plume of smoke. "Sorry. That's all I know."

"Don't be so sure," Anne interjected. "Someone started that fire deliberately. We think whoever did it might have killed Tigger too."

The color drained from Sandy's face. A piece of cigarette ash dropped onto the brown coverlet. "Tigger's dead? But that can't be. I just saw . . ." Her voice trailed off.

"You saw Tigger? When?" Jack said eagerly.

"I thought I saw someone who looked like him is all—on the beach, over by Madame Mona's."

"When?" Jack persisted.

"A couple of days ago." Sandy pawed at the ashes with her finger, rubbing the remains into the blanket. "What happened to Tigger?" Her raspy voice was tinged with alarm. "You said he was killed?"

"He drowned," Anne said.

"Jesus H. Christ," Sandy said. She stubbed her cigarette out in the ashtray next to the bed and wrapped her arms across her chest. Her breath came in short whistles, like a bird that couldn't catch its breath.

Jack looked at her with suspicion. "For someone who didn't know him, you're taking this awfully hard," he said.

Instead of replying, Sandy turned to Anne. "What do ya mean someone killed him?"

"We don't think his death was an accident," Anne said. "If you know anything that could help us, anything at all . . ."

"You mean he fell off a boat or something?" Sandy said. She scratched her leg harder, leaving red marks on her skin.

"We're not sure what happened," Jack said coldly. "His body washed up on the beach yesterday morning."

"In the Heights?"

"Yeah."

"God. I'm sorry. I'm real sorry," Sandy said to Jack. She looked scared. "Lookit. I'm all talked out, okay? I don't know nothing else. And I'm expecting company. You gotta go."

"Lady, I'm not going anywhere until you tell us about my brother," Jack said.

Sandy bit down on her lower lip. "Suit yourself. But when my john shows up he's not going to like having an audience." When she took another cigarette from the pack, Anne noticed that her hand was trembling.

"Sandy, if you're in some kind of trouble, we'd like to help," Anne said.

Sandy coughed suddenly, a dry hacking cough that made

her chest heave. She scratched the back of her neck. "I'm fine."

"You don't look so fine," Jack said.

"That's cause you don't know nothing about nothing," Sandy said. She looked Jack up and down, her eyes settling on his leather loafers as if the shoes proved something she already knew.

"I know you want a fix a lot more than you want those greasy burgers," Jack said. "Look, we'll pay you for any information you can give us. Just name your price."

"You don't hear so good," Sandy said. Her nose started running again, she wiped it with her shirt. "I want you out."

"Jack," Anne said. "Maybe we should go."

"Your friend's right," Sandy said. She put the cigarette in her mouth without lighting it.

"If you manage to think of anything else," Jack said. He took a business card from his wallet. "Could you leave her your number, Anne? The desk clerk at Ravenswood isn't very reliable." Anne scribbled her name and number on the back of the card. When Sandy didn't take it, Anne dropped it on the bed.

Hurriedly, Sandy went to the door and threw it open. "Ba-bye now," she said.

Outside, the sun glinted silver off the concrete walk. The door slammed shut behind them.

Chapter 9

*If God had intended Eve
to clean the garden,
He would have given her
a lawn mower.*

Madame Mona was a Landsdown institution. For as long as anyone could remember, she'd been telling fortunes on the boardwalk, in a square white shack that was no bigger than a public rest room.

"You're awfully quiet," Jack said to Anne as they approached Madame Mona's salon. "What's up?"

"I was thinking of what Sandy said about the ammonia."

"What about it?"

"I read about the Spray View when I went to the library. It had something like twelve brick fireplaces."

"So?"

"So ammonia is one of the ingredients used to clean brick fireplaces. It could be a coincidence that Lucille Klemperer was cleaning the fireplaces the day the inn blew up. But maybe not. Also, I keep wondering why the heat detectors didn't work. Ed must have installed a sprinkler system or smoke detectors or both. But there was nothing about them in the newspapers and Taggart didn't mention anything either.''

Jack looked puzzled. ''What are you driving at?''

''There are about a dozen common fire hazards that could have caused the fire: overloaded electrical circuits, improper storage of flammable liquids, overheated sockets and wiring, insulation placed against recessed electrical fixtures, stoves vented through dirty, unlined chimneys, exposed rigid foam insulation, careless use of a portable space heater, and so on. If the fire was set deliberately, I think someone went to a lot of trouble to make it look like an accident. Hence, a space heater on the Fourth of July.''

''How do you know this stuff?'' Jack asked admiringly.

''I once ghosted a book for a guy named Ben Troutwig. He had a cable TV show called *Tools 'R' Us*. It was kind of like *This Old House*, only lower budget. Anyway, I wrote a book for him on home repair and improvement and it had a section about fire protection.''

''Too bad Sandy wasn't much help,'' Jack said. ''I bet if we showed up with some heroin, she'd be a lot more talkative.''

''She did seem pretty strung out.''

''Nothing that five minutes with her dealer won't cure. Did you catch the long-sleeved shirt? Her arms are probably marked up worse than a road map.''

Anne nodded. ''There's one thing I don't get. If she's as desperate for drugs as she looks, I'm surprised she didn't tell us more, just for some fast cash.''

''Maybe she doesn't need our money. Maybe the prostitution biz is booming these days.''

''And maybe the occult can enlighten us,'' Anne said, as they reached the entrance to Madame Mona's.

''Anything's possible,'' Jack said.

''Correct me if I'm wrong, but you don't seem like the tea leaf type.''

''Hey, I have a spiritual side.''

''I must have missed it.

"O ye of little faith," Jack said, opening the door to the fortune-teller's shack.

The salon was tiny, barely able to contain a table and three canvas chairs. A large eye was painted on one wall, with deep purple eye shadow smeared across the lid. On another wall, a sign said: *Tarot. Crystal Ball. Aura Readings. Beware of Dog.*

"Hello, hello," said Madame Mona, sweeping into the room from behind a red velvet curtain. Anne was expecting some kind of costume—flowing skirts, a turban. But Madame Mona wore a flowered print T-shirt over a pair of black leggings. Anne recognized the outfit. It was from the Limited Express, at the mall.

"What can I do for you this evening?" Madame Mona asked cordially.

"Actually," Jack said, pulling a picture of Tigger from his wallet, "we were wondering if you recognize this man."

Madame Mona took the snapshot and peered at it. "Hmm. Hard to say without first consulting the cards." She seated herself and placed the picture in the middle of the table. "Come," she said, tucking her dark hair into a bun and motioning for them to sit down. "Let us all join hands. And try to resurrect his spirit from beyond the grave."

"How do you know he's dead?" Jack demanded. "Did you see it in your crystal ball?"

"Newspapers, dear boy. I read them every morning. Now then. Close your eyes. And remember the dearly departed."

Anne shrugged and shot Jack a look that said: It's worth a shot.

"Let us all join hands," Madame Mona intoned. Anne took hold of the two hands on either side of her. Madame Mona's hand felt like dried corn husks. Jack's grip was warm and firm.

"Your brother died alone, did he not?" Madame Mona said. Her thin angular face was unreadable.

Jack squeezed Anne's hand. "The newspapers mentioned that he was my brother?"

"No. I can see for myself. You look just like him, especially around the eyes. Please think of him now, as you take twelve slow, deep breaths."

Anne tried to picture Tigger, tried to recreate his face. But once again, it was the young Tigger she recalled, the boy she used to dream about when she was sixteen. In the darkness, she saw a teenager on a red bike, hurtling down the boardwalk so fast it seemed like he was flying.

She opened her eyes. Out the window, the sun looked like a bright orange wafer floating above the ocean. The sky was streaked with tufts of pink clouds. Opening her purse, she took out a photocopy of a picture of a young Sandy Cooksey. "He might have been with this woman," Anne said. "The picture's twenty years old. Do you recognize her?"

Madame Mona studied the photo. "She comes down here at night sometimes."

"What for?" Jack asked.

"Drugs. There's a place under the boardwalk the kids call the hospital where they buy and sell all sorts of nasty things. In my day, it was liquor. Now . . ." She raised an eyebrow and smiled. "No matter. I will do a three-card spread. Three cards for the three of you." Shuffling the deck a few times, she cut it in half and placed three cards facedown around Tigger's picture. "Are you ready to gaze into the future?"

"Look," Jack said, "we just want to know if you've seen my brother recently. It's really important. Was he around here the last few days? Was he with that woman?"

Madame Mona sighed and shook her head. "The cards will tell us what we need to know." She turned over the first one. "For you," she said to Jack. The card showed a man hanging upside down from a tree. One leg was tied to the tree, the other was tucked behind his knee. Around the man's head was a halo of light.

"What does it mean?" Anne asked.

"The Hanged Man represents a break with the past," Madame Mona explained. "Centuries ago, the great mystics were suspended between reality and the unknown in their quest for enlightenment. This card is saying you must be willing to give up everything you know, cut yourself off from comforts, from your roots, and open yourself up to the mysteries of the world.''

''Terrific,'' Jack said sarcastically. ''I feel much better now.''

''Patience,'' Madame Mona cautioned. ''The next card is for the dead.'' She tapped Tigger's picture with the tip of her finger, then turned over the second tarot card: a picture of a grim-faced devil, with wings and horns, holding a torch. Chained to the devil's feet were a naked man and woman.

''Ah, this explains things. Now I see,'' Madame Mona said.

''See what?'' Jack demanded. ''In plain English.''

''Your brother gave in to temptation, did he not? He was misled by false promises—great wealth, material pleasures, castles in the air. That's what got him killed.''

''The papers didn't mention murder,'' Jack said.

''But you both know differently. That's why you've come to Madame Mona, no?''

Jack raked his hand through his dark hair. He started to speak, then stopped himself. Outside, the sky was a swirl of pink and purple.

Anne said, ''I thought that tarot cards were supposed to predict the future. Like inheriting money or falling in love—things like that.''

''They can,'' Madame Mona said softly. ''They do. The third card, my dear, is for you.'' She turned it over slowly. The card showed a skeleton wearing a suit of black armor, astride a black horse. Underneath the horse's hooves was a tangle of bodies. And underneath that, the word *Death*.

''Oh,'' Anne said. She stared at the card. The skeleton was grinning. His hollow eyes seemed to be looking right at her.

''What's going on here?'' Jack asked.

Anne felt a shiver pass through her. Was this where her future lay? In her mind's eye, she saw a cold, lifeless figure floating on the waves. Her body, her face white as moonlight, seaweed fluttering in her hair. Her lips parted, as if to speak. Her eyes snapped open, water flooded the sockets. It was cold. Tigger must have been so cold.

"Do not be alarmed," Madame Mona intoned. "There is loss, yes. But in the world of the tarot, the Death card means change."

"Let's get out of here," Jack said, grabbing Anne's arms and pulling her to her feet. "This whole setup is a scam."

"Wait," Madame Mona said. "That'll be twenty bucks."

But Jack had already pushed the glass door open and was sprinting down the boardwalk, with Anne close behind him.

"You can't hide from fate," Madame Mona called after them. "Mark my words. You can run. But there's no escape!"

At night, the ocean fanned out behind the Church by the Sea like a dark collar around a high white throat. Shadows slipped across the stained glass panels, elongating the glass lilies in the windows, flattening the images of the saints until they lost their shape entirely, transformed into eerie-looking wraiths. On the roof, a twelve-foot-high cross glowed neon, visible from thirty miles offshore. Gulls sometimes nested in the rafters, their cries echoing off the burnished oak walls.

The building itself was divided down the middle by a bright red carpet, with pews arranged in four sections located on either side of the main aisle and along the fringes of the interior, facing the center of the church. At the front was a stage containing the pulpit, a large organ console, and rows of high-backed chairs. Hanging above the stage was an electric flag whose lights blinked sequentially, making it look like the flag was waving.

Church was the last place Anne wanted to be. But she knew Lucille would be at the Gospel Musical Ministry. Tourists poured in through the main doors, clutching the paper fans they received with their tickets, fans with a picture of the church printed on both sides. It was stifling hot inside the building. The only windows were fifty-five feet above the ground, near the arched wooden ceiling. The window frames were being replaced—part of the ongoing restoration of the church—so the glass slid on a track, letting in more air. In the meantime, people made do with the paper fans or by fanning themselves with their programs. Tonight's featured attraction was called "Glory Bound," a medley of religious and inspirational songs performed by the Willis Family. Anne glanced at the program, which featured a picture of the Willises: the parents and their eight offspring, ranging in age from six to twenty-six. Each one smiled broadly. The girls had long blond hair; the boys sported crewcuts. Together, they looked like a born-again Brady Bunch.

Anne made her way up the center aisle, stopping to exchange polite chitchat with some of her neighbors. Near the stage she spotted Teri, passing out programs and good cheer. There'd be no point in confronting her now; the crowd around her was too thick.

"Anne dear, you came after all," exclaimed Jim Walser. In honor of the occasion, he had on a powder blue sport jacket and white trousers, the unofficial uniform of the men who volunteered to be ushers. His bald head glistened with sweat.

"I really can't stay too long," Anne shouted, trying to be heard above the din. "I'm looking for Lucille Klemperer. Have you seen her?"

"I believe Lucille is selling tapes and T-shirts out front, dear. But where we could really use your help is at the root beer stand. Everyone seems to be thirsty tonight!" He extended his hands beseechingly, then pulled a handkerchief from his breast pocket and mopped his brow. "We didn't expect such a crowd," he said, flustered. "We're not prepared, not prepared at all. I blame myself, really I do. I told everyone in town to be here and now . . ."

"All right. I'll see what I can do." She scanned the crowd for Jack, who had set off in search of Bobby Curley. But there was no sign of either of them.

"Have you said hello to the missus?" Walser asked.

"Not yet." Jim Walser's wife, Carolyn, had multiple sclerosis. Anne could just make out her crown of gray curls next to the front pew where the people in wheelchairs congregated.

Organ notes fill the air, followed by a flurry of flutes and violins. Now that the orchestra was warming up, the program would start soon. She'd better hurry. Outside, late arrivals were busily purchasing last-minute tickets. The sky was clear, except for the moon, hovering over the water. It was cooler out here. The breeze felt like a gift after the oppressive heat in the church. By the front entrance, volunteers were selling audiotapes and T-shirts. On each shirt was a picture of the Willis Family, smiling for eternity.

"Is Lucille around?" Anne said to Mrs. Carberry, a horse-faced woman standing behind a stack of T-shirts.

The woman jerked her thumb toward the array of tents clustered around the church.

"Which one is hers?" Anne asked.

"The green one with the big sign out front. You can't miss Lucille's. It's all lit up."

"Thanks."

Every summer since the Heights was founded, camp meetings had been held near the Church by the Sea. In keeping with a time-honored tradition, more than a hundred tents lined the streets around the church. When she was young, Anne used to count the number of days until mid-May, when people from all across the country started setting up their tents and moving in. Neat and compact, the tents seemed to her like fairy tale houses, complete with plank floors, bathrooms, kitchens, and curtains at the windows. No two were the same. Some had striped awnings out front or pots of hanging geraniums. Others were crammed with wicker porch furniture or decorated with flags.

Like many of the townspeople, Lucille Klemperer reserved a tent each summer. Anne realized she'd passed by many times, without knowing whom it belonged to. Strung up outside were white light bulbs that spelled *Jesus*. The glow from the bulbs was momentarily blinding. Colored spots danced in the air before Anne's eyes.

From inside the screen door came a familiar sound: a woman's voice raised in prayer. Anne peered through the mesh screen. The living area was nearly devoid of furniture. An armchair, a table, an oval rag rug. In the center of the room was a large black trunk trimmed with brass hardware. Lucille Klemperer knelt before the trunk, which had been set up to serve as an altar. A picture of a youthful bearded Jesus was in a large gold frame, surrounded by candles and an array of wooden crosses festooned with jewels. "If I have wounded any soul today," Lucille recited. "If I have caused one foot to go astray. If I have walked in my own willful way. Dear Lord, forgive me." Lucille Klemperer looked up. For an instant, her dark eyes were trained on Anne. Then she lowered them again and resumed gazing at the picture of Jesus. "Forgive the sins I have confessed to Thee. Forgive my secret sins I do not see. Help me. Guide me. And my keeper be. Amen."

Rising to her feet, she turned her back to Anne and walked out of the room. "Come in," she called, from the back of the tent. "Shut the door so the bugs don't follow."

As she entered the tent, Anne was aware of a strong odor—incense of some sort, a musky smell, sickly sweet. Hanging from one wall was a poster of a little girl in a frilly red dress. For a three-year-old, Ruthie Klemperer had a serious, almost adult expression on her tiny, round face. The photographer must have told her to stay very, very still, because instead of smiling, she appeared to be holding her breath. Her hands were folded neatly in her lap; her eyes stared directly into the camera. The photo was grainy, the colors somewhat blurred, as if it had been blown up from a wallet-size photograph. Anne noticed that the gold frame on Ruthie's portrait matched the frame on the picture of Jesus.

"Beautiful, isn't she?" Lucille said. She came back into the room carrying a bowl of rose petals, which she placed on a table beneath the picture. "Such an angelic child. Never cried. Never gave me an inch of sorrow." There was a severe, pinched quality to Lucille's appearance. Although it was a warm night, a sweater was draped over her beige long-sleeved dress, fastened at the waist with a thick belt. Her tan shoes were the flat crepe-soled sort favored by nurses in hospitals. She stood very straight, as if an invisible string existed between the top of her head and the ceiling. Beneath her wrinkled skin, the deep lines carved on her face, Anne could glimpse high cheekbones and a regal profile—traces of the attractive young woman she must once have been.

"She's lovely. Listen, Mrs. Klemperer, I came by to apologize again for this afternoon. I'm terribly sorry. I thought you were home and you just didn't hear me knocking." Lucille nodded warily. "Do you have time to talk for a minute?"

"Time? What is time? A bird that has flown away, a vapor appearing for an instant, then vanishing into the mists."

"Yes, well . . ."

"Your mother was a good woman, at heart. I believe she was. Yes, I do."

"Mrs. Klemperer . . ."

"She was led astray by a force too powerful to tame. By her own unchecked desires. If she had testified, God could have saved her. God is merciful to those who trust in His infinite wisdom."

Anne wasn't about to discuss her mother with this woman. Evelyn had had a word for people like Lucille Klemperer: *holy-bullies*. They talked *at* you all day long, her mother had said. Badgering you, preaching, until they broke your spirit in two.

"Mrs. Klemperer, I'm here about Tigger Mills."

A faraway look came into Lucille's eyes. "The Judgment Day was upon him. He knocked on heaven's gate and the Lord called him to account for his sins. Jesus forgives those who lift up their voices in prayer to Him, who lay their souls bare, opening their sinful hearts to His mercy and goodness. I walk in the light of the Lord."

"I don't think his death was an accident, Mrs. Klemperer."

"An accident? No. It was a prophecy from above. The Lord walks beside me in my darkest hour, leading me down the path of righteousness."

"I believe he was murdered."

Lucille Klemperer stared at the picture of her daughter. "He was a murderer from the beginning," she recited, "and abode not in the truth, because there is no truth in him. When he speaketh a lie, he speaketh of his own: for he is a liar, and the father of it."

Lucille's voice sounded hollow. Her eyes were fastened on Ruthie's picture, as if she were talking to the dead girl. Watching her, Anne got the sense that the child had been transformed into a religious icon, an emblem of suffering and loss.

The sweetish odor in the room had grown stronger. The air smelled like spoiled candy. It must have been coming from the candles; wax dripped onto the altar, forming crusty golden puddles.

"About Tigger Mills . . ." Anne began.

"It's a blessing," Lucille said softly, "a blessing for you that he's dead."

"What do you mean?"

"She was the sweetest little thing," Lucille said, still gazing at Ruthie. "An angel sent from God."

The smell in the room had become unbearable. It felt as though the odor was sucking up all the air. "Tigger Mills told me he didn't set that fire," Anne said. "I believe him."

"He sweet-talked lots of gals in this town. Watch and pray, that ye enter not into temptation: The spirit is willing but the flesh is weak."

"What if it wasn't him?" Anne persisted.

"He fled from the flames like Lucifer before our King. O treacherous viper, who hath warned you to flee from the wrath to come."

"I'm telling you he may not have started the fire. And if that's true, the person responsible for Ruthie's death is still walking around free." There was a trancelike emptiness in Lucille's expression, the face of a sleepwalker who couldn't wake. "Before he was killed, Tigger received a threatening letter. Do you know anything about that?"

Tearing her gaze away from Ruthie, Lucille focused her attention on Anne. Her eyes burned with the power of her conviction. "He must have suffered out there. He must have suffered, same as my baby girl."

The words slipped out before Anne could stop them. "Did you kill him?"

Lucille flicked her tongue over her lips. The gesture was almost obscene. "Through envy of the devil came death into the world."

Behind her, candle wax fell silently onto the altar.

Chapter 10

> *To remove dark "mystery" spots on sealed floors, dampen fine steel wool with odorless mineral spirits. Wash area with vinegar, wait three minutes, then wipe with mineral spirits. Sand with fine sandpaper, stain, rewax, and repolish.*

When Anne returned to the church, the concert had already begun. Peering in through one of the doors, she saw the Willis Family assembled on stage. The boys wore navy blazers over white slacks; the girls were dressed in matching pink outfits. They sang a hymn Anne remembered from childhood: *"On a hill far away stood the old rugged cross. An emblem of suffering and shame. But I love that old cross the dearest and best. For a world of lost sinners was slain."*

Behind her, Anne heard shouts. Two men, arguing. The voices were coming from the white Victorian gazebo, a half-block away from the church. Anne recognized Jack's baritone filling the night air with a stream of staccato questions. The other angry voice belonged to Bobby Curley. Turning, she half-walked, half-ran toward the gazebo.

"You come into my place of business. You make a scene. And now you want my help?" Bobby was saying. He stood on one side of the small octagonal gazebo. Jack was on the other side, his back to the gingerbread railing.

"I want the truth."

"No. You want to hear what a stand-up guy Tigger was, a regular model citizen. Sorry, Jack. It didn't play that way."

The lights on the outside of the church illuminated the beams crosshatching the gazebo's roof. Light played across Bobby's face.

"Why do I get the feeling you're not telling us the whole story," Anne said, as she mounted the steps leading to the gazebo.

Bobby turned toward her. "I don't know," he said. "You tell me. The guy was my best friend. Why would I want to spread lies about him, huh? Especially now that he's not here to defend himself."

"Tigger told me you had a code," Anne said. "You and P.J. and him—a code of honor."

Bobby's lips parted in a half-smile. "That's right. We did. We signed it in blood. God, it seems like a million years ago."

"So you protected one another, right?"

"I think what she's trying to say," Jack interrupted, "is that you could have been there that night. Maybe my brother lied to protect your sorry hide."

"Go ahead, Jack. Think whatever you want. If it helps you deal with the pain of his death, blame me for the fire. But it won't bring that little girl back to life. It won't change the past."

Music floated through the gazebo, a song about salvation and loss. "The two of you were always together," Jack said. "I never saw one of you without the other. So how come you weren't with him that night, Bobby?"

"I told you where I was. Out on my father's boat with

a shitload of his friends. Check it out for yourself, if you don't believe me. There are dozens of people in this town who'll swear to it.''

"We'll do that," Anne said.

Bobby glared at them. "I tried to help him," he said angrily. "I offered to give him some money. Hell, I told him I'd find him a job just as soon as he cleaned up his act. And you know how he repaid me?" Bobby's voice throbbed with anger. "He trashed my whole house."

"What the hell are you talking about?" Jack demanded.

"You haven't heard? I guess not. That's another favor I did him. I said I wouldn't spread it around town. The last thing he needed was more bad publicity."

Anne felt a surge of regret. She wished she'd been straight with Jack from the beginning. She hadn't wanted him to hear about the money this way. Not from Bobby Curley.

"You want to know what my 'best friend' did for me?" Bobby said angrily. "He broke into my house, turned it upside down, and made off with $3,500 in cash. How's that for friendship, huh? How's that for loyalty?"

"What are you trying to do here, Curley?" Jack said. "You know, I used to look up to you. I used to think you hung the moon."

"You didn't know him, Jack. You thought you did. So did I. But we were both wrong. Last Sunday night, your brother broke into my house and robbed me. The place looked like a tornado hit it. The living room, den, bedrooms—all ransacked. Clothes, books, strewn all over. You got any idea what that feels like?"

"How do you know it was Tigger?" Jack said quickly.

"He came over to my place, drunk as a skunk, hollering about how he needed money. Teri told him to get the hell out. A few hours later, while we were over at the church bazaar, he broke into the house and helped himself to what he could find. You know, Jack, I would have given him the money myself, if he'd told me how desperate he was. He didn't have to trash the place."

"You can't be sure it was him," Jack said.

"Damn straight I'm sure. I would have told you this morning only I was trying to spare you. You're the one who found the money he stole from me. You said so yourself. I betcha it wasn't just lying out in the open, was it? He must have hidden it somewhere, right?"

"That still doesn't explain what happened twenty years ago," Anne said. "We're just trying to get at the truth here."

"Wake up, Anne. There is no secret 'truth.' Tigger set the fire. And then he lied to save his skin. I'd have done the same." Bobby shrugged, then walked across the gazebo. Halfway down the steps, he turned. "If it makes you feel any better, Jack, he never meant to hurt anyone. I'm sure of it."

They watched him as he walked away, heading back toward the church. "Do you think Tigger stole the money we found in the Bible?" Jack said softly. Anne heard frustration in his voice and something else, something that sounded like uncertainty.

"I don't know," she said, going over to stand beside him. "Something about Bobby's story doesn't sit right with me." Hymns streamed from the church. The night was alive with stars, a thousand pinpricks of light forming a glittery white pattern against the sky. "Speaking of Bibles, I just came from talking to Lucille Klemperer."

"And?"

"She's looney tunes. Every other word out of her mouth is a quote from the Good Book. She thinks Tigger was the devil incarnate."

"So she could have written the threatening note?"

"In a heartbeat."

"Where is that damn thing?"

"I'm guessing whoever wrote the note removed it from Tigger's room after he was killed."

"Where does that leave us? We're obviously not going to get anything more out of Curley except bad news about Tigger."

Anne thought for a moment. "Last night, you mentioned

that the police found Tigger's wallet on the beach. Did you get a look at it?''

"No. The cops gave it to Pop, along with Tigger's clothes."

"I think we should track it down. Just in case there's anything inside that could help us."

"We could go get it now. Pop's either asleep or out cold."

"Okay."

Jack's car was parked on the side of the church. The doors of the building were thrown open, to help dispel the heat. Inside, the crowd was on its feet, swaying back and forth to the music. There must have been close to a thousand people, clapping their hands, singing. Anne watched the ushers move swiftly down the aisles, passing the metal collection plates across the pews. Money was stuffed into the boxes. Even children dropped something in, one or two spare coins. She could feel the fervor mounting in the church. The clapping was like a heartbeat, a rhythmic palpitation. Up on stage, members of the Willis Family pounded their tambourines. The youngest child had her eyes closed, her lips pressed to the microphone. The burning. That's what Anne's mother used to call it. Old-time religion, she'd say. A chance for healing and togetherness. Only when Evelyn got sick, her friends from church stopped coming around. Where were charity and compassion then? Anne wondered. Where were hope and kindness and all those lovely words in the hymns?

She got into the Corvette. As they drove away, a chorus of hallelujahs followed them down the block. Anne flicked on the radio, and the gospel music went away. The Heights was deserted. Jim Walser was right. It looked like the whole town had gone to the concert. "Let's swing by P.J.'s place first," Anne suggested.

"Good idea." Jack made a right turn onto Grove Street and drove five blocks, slowing down in front of a small putty-colored house with black shutters. The house was dark, the driveway empty. "I guess he's still not home," Jack said, continuing past the house. "I left a message on his answering machine, telling him what time the funeral starts tomorrow. I also said I wanted to talk to him.''

"Maybe that scared him off.''

"Nah. P.J. doesn't scare easy.''

"How well do you know him?''

"He and Tigger used to be pretty tight. I thought he was such a cool guy when I was a kid. Never lost a fight. His hands moved so fast, you know?''

Anne nodded. She'd seen boys who'd been pummeled by P.J. McGrath's fists. It was not a pretty sight. "Is the new gym he's building going to be here in town?''

"No. They told me at the sporting goods store that P.J. rented out space on Route 35. It's going to be a big complex, real state-of-the-art.''

"If Tigger needed cash, you think he went to P.J?''

"Up until last week, the well was bone-dry. I'm sure P.J. didn't have much money until he came into that inheritance.''

Jack stopped the car in front of Troy Mills's house on Embury Street. "Do you mind if I wait for you out here?'' Anne asked.

"No problem. This shouldn't take long. I think I know where to look.''

Anne rolled down the window. The night was humid, the sky blanketed with stars. On Embury Street, nothing stirred. The old Victorian houses loomed silent and ghostly. They looked fake somehow, placed there for effect. After about ten minutes, Jack came back out. He got in the car and tossed a black wallet in Anne's lap. The leather was cracked and worn, the wallet nearly empty. A ten-dollar bill, Tigger's driver's license, his temporary library card, and the business card of a lawyer named Marvin Childs, whose office was in Sea Girt. Anne turned the business card over. "Switch on the light for a second,'' she said. "There's something written on the back.''

When the light came on, Anne peered at the card. Scrawled on the back were two words: *Cloister Black*. She handed the card to Jack. "What do you make of this?''

"You got me. Maybe it's the name of a restaurant or a store around here."

"Maybe. *Cloister* sounds cutesy enough to be the name of an inn."

"We can call Childs tomorrow. Maybe he knows something."

Anne twirled the card with her fingers. "Maybe."

"You sound skeptical," Jack said.

Above the Heights, the stars gleamed white, a multitude of lights swallowing the night sky. "I was just thinking," Anne said slowly. "What if Cloister Black is a she?"

After Jack dropped her off at home, Anne got out the phone book. Cloister Black wasn't listed, but there were eight C. Blacks and one B. Cloister living in Monmouth County. In the business directory, she found Cloister Owner Corporation, Cloister's Café, and Cloister Construction Company. Not a whole lot to go on. And it was too late to call anyone at this hour.

She drank a cup of tea, got into her pajamas, and lay in bed, sorting through the day's events. Each time she was on the verge of drifting off to sleep, another thought jolted her awake. Her mind felt like a machine she couldn't switch off, a blur of recurring images: the diamond earring, the history book, the money in the Bible, the anonymous threatening note, the senile old woman at Ravenswood who thought Jack was Tigger. Were they all connected somehow?

After what seemed like hours, she got up, threw a blanket around her shoulders, and padded out onto the porch. She settled back on the chaise and stared at the darkened ocean. The waves made a gentle shushing sound. There was something she'd overlooked, a thread that would tie all the loose ends together. Her mother was always telling her to pay attention. *Open your eyes, Anne*, she would say. *Wake up*.

Which was ironic, in a sad sort of way. Evelyn was the one who became delusional, confusing dates, times, places, people. Spinning out paranoid fantasies of neighbors poisoning her with casseroles, stealing her jewelry. Anne thought back to all the nights she sat on the porch with the door locked from the outside, guarding her mother, preventing Evelyn's night wandering. All the measures Anne took to fight the disease—labeling the kitchen appliances, keeping all the lights on during the day so Evelyn would remember it was daytime, taking Evelyn's cigarettes away so there wouldn't be any more fires. Anne sat up suddenly. *Fire*. The night the Spray View burned down, Anne couldn't find Evelyn. She'd searched the neighborhood, visiting all her mother's usual haunts, but there was no sign of her. In a panic, Anne had run in the direction of the fire, intending to ask someone there for help—a fireman, a cop, anyone who looked official. When she got to the Spray View, flames were shooting through the roof. Heat seared the air, moving in thick waves so that Evelyn seemed to appear out of nowhere. One minute she wasn't there, the next minute she was, leaning against a tree near where a crowd had gathered to watch the blaze. Just for an instant, before Anne locked the thought away in that place she kept things that were too terrifying for words, she wondered if Evelyn had something to do with the fire. Her mother was always leaving lit cigarettes around the house. She remembered how tongues of flame bit through the Spray View's porch, devouring the wood. It was impossible, really. One little cigarette couldn't have caused so much damage. And then the thought was gone, banished, and Anne concentrated on what was real—on getting Evelyn back home, back to the house, where they sat together in the kitchen, listening to talk radio. Evelyn was frightened that night, frightened of sirens and smoke; the radio soothed her.

She couldn't have been responsible, Anne thought now. It was merely the bright flames that drew her mother to the scene of the fire. There was no reason for Evelyn to be inside the Spray View that night. No reason for Tigger to be there either, despite what Bobby Curley had said. She leaned back, closed her eyes. When she opened them again, dawn was breaking over the water. It arrived in stages—an eerie blue light that gave way to a series of pink ribbons on the horizon. She got up, dressed, downed a bowl of cereal and a cup of coffee. Today was Saturday. She had to get some work done on Mary Lou's book, at least start chapter five. She sat down at the computer with a sheaf of notes. "Fast 'n' Easy Floor Care." Right. Where to begin? Anne skimmed through Mary Lou's notes again: Maintaining Penetrated Sealed Finishes, Removing Scuff Marks, Wax Facts, How to Clean Vinyl Tile. The notes were so sloppy and disorganized that Anne wondered how "America's Number One Homemaker" got anything done around the house. She shuffled through the garbled scrawl again. Ah, here was something interesting—*Recipes for Ridding Floors of Dark "Mystery" Spots.*

"The problem with deep dark mysteries," Anne typed on the screen, "is that too many clues are missing."

With a sigh, she shoved the sheaf of papers aside. It wasn't like her to blow a deadline. She felt guilty, but it was just so hard to concentrate. How would she ever finish this cleaning tome anyway? The longer she waited, the more pressure there'd be. Chapter six was due on Tuesday—"Dust Musts." Oh, well. If Mary Lou could speed clean, Anne could certainly speed write. Later.

Going over to the phone, she found the numbers she had copied down the night before and started dialing. Four of the C. Blacks were at home this morning, but there wasn't a Cloister in the bunch. There was no answer at two of the numbers and she reached a machine at two others, leaving a brief message explaining who she was and what she wanted to know: whether anyone in the family was named Cloister. Anne wasn't sure why Cloister Black should be a woman, as opposed to a grotto or a code of some sort, but given Tigger's history, it was worth a shot.

She went into the living room and picked up the history book on the Heights that Jack had taken from Tigger's room. Now what could Tigger have found so fascinating about *Vintage Victoriana*? There was lots of information here about buildings and architecture, the types of houses common to Oceanside Heights—Colonial Revival, Victorian Eclectic, Eastlake, Queen Anne. There was even material about building permits, new construction applications,

leasing agreements between homeowners and the Oceanside Heights Association, rules concerning the historic district designation, blah, blah, blah. She flipped through the
latter part of the book. This stuff was more interesting. Arthur Hornsby must have spent months poring over old court
documents, birth certificates, and marriage certificates to
trace these elaborate family trees. She looked up the Hard-
aways. It was all here, her whole lineage recorded in black
and white. Her mother and father, her grandma Kate, aunts,
uncles, and at the top of the page, her great-great grandfather Nathan Hardaway, who settled in the Heights back
in the late 1880s. Her own name was on the very bottom.

Family trees were such intricate structures. It amazed her
that the complicated paths of hundreds of lives could be
collected in one volume. She went over to her desk and
took out her list of suspects, looking up the names one at
a time in *Vintage Victoriana*. She ran down Bobby Curley's
family tree, and then turned to the McGraths, noting that
P.J.'s great-great grandfather had been one of the town's
founding fathers, meriting an entire page in the index.
Sandy Cooksey's family wasn't listed. Probably Sandy
grew up nearby, in Bradley Beach or Neptune City. Anne
looked at the last name on her list. Troy Mills. Sure enough,
Troy was in the Ms, alongside his wife, Ellen, with an
asterisk beside Ellen's name to signify she wasn't born in
the Heights. Two kids—Theodore and Jack. Theodore! She
grinned. No wonder he preferred Tigger. Anne's eye
skipped down the page and stopped. In smaller type was
another name, connected to Troy's by a dotted black line,
the mark Arthur Hornsby used to signify marriages. Anne
stared at the name: Katherine Davenport. Mmm. Jack said
his mother had been married to someone else before she
married Troy. But he never mentioned that his father had
been married before, too. She turned the pages of the book
slowly. There was no doubt about it. The dotted black line
between two names meant the two people were married.
She was just about to look up Teri Curley when the phone
rang.

Putting the book down, she walked into the kitchen to answer it. "Hello?" she said.

"Hey, it's Jack."

"Hi. I was just looking through the book you gave me. You didn't tell me your dad had been married before he met your mother."

"What are you talking about?"

"Katherine Davenport."

There was a pause on the other end of the line. "Who's she?"

"According to Arthur Hornsby, she's your father's first wife."

"What!"

"He listed her on your family tree."

"That's ridiculous."

"Arthur Hornsby didn't seem to think so."

"Well, he must have been senile. If Pop had another wife, we'd have heard about it. Forget the book for a second. I think I might have something on this end."

Anne sat down at the kitchen table. "Okay."

"I called some companies in the phone book whose first names begin with Cloister. And I think I hit pay dirt. Cloister Construction Company is in Sea Girt, a couple of blocks away from that lawyer Tigger went to see. I'm going to drive over there and talk to the guy, then drop by the construction company."

"That sounds like a good idea. But I can't shake the feeling that Cloister Black is a person."

"You got to admit it's a weird name."

"I know. It sounds made-up for effect, the kind of name a gypsy or a fortune-teller might use."

Jack sighed. "You're not thinking of asking our friend Madame Mona? I wouldn't trust a word she says."

Anne hesitated before answering. "I guess you're right."

"You want to come to Sea Girt with me?"

"No, there's something I want to check out here. How about I meet you back at Ravenswood at twelve-thirty?"

"You got it."

After she hung up the phone, Anne went back to the

living room and picked up the history book. She flipped to the front, skimming the acknowledgments and Hornsby's foreword. Was there any connection between *Vintage Victoriana* and the big fire? What had Tigger detected in here? The Heights had its share of twisted histories and stunted family trees, secrets as tarnished as old sterling silver. Had Tigger spotted something in this book that someone wanted to keep buried—permanently?

Chapter 11

*Never use liquid or spray
products containing
silicone on genuine
antiques. Try paste wax
instead. It will give your
heirloom Louis XIV chair or
the cherished mahogany
table that once belonged
to your great-grandma
a more durable,
longer-lasting finish.*

Bobby and Teri Curley lived in a rambling Queen
Anne–style house a few blocks from the marina.
Built at the turn of the century for a wealthy railroad magnate, it was the fanciest house in town. Towers
and balconies sprang from the facade, as if lifted from the
pages of a storybook castle. White gingerbread decorating
brackets and moldings clambered up the railing of the
wraparound porch like lace trim on a wedding gown. But
the most striking thing about the house was its color—
painted four shades of pink, ranging from dusty rose to
deep salmon.

Surrounding the house were dozens of rose bushes, including some varieties that dated back to the Victorian era. Each bush was labeled with its original name: Blaze. Marie Lambert. American Pillar. Mon Cheri. Teri was known for having the most beautiful garden in the Heights. Her roses were still flourishing in late September, long after everyone else's had faded and died.

She answered the door dressed in a flowered skirt and a short-sleeved white silk blouse. Her long dark hair was pulled back from her face with a velvet headband.

"Oh, it's you," Teri said to Anne. She looked annoyed.

"Hi, Teri. I was out for a walk and I stopped to admire your flowers. They're gorgeous."

"Actually, now isn't the best time. I'm right in the middle of my morning baking."

"This'll only take a sec. I'm on the steering committee of the Philadelphia Flower Show this year and I wanted to talk to you about entering. There's going to be a whole section devoted to Victorian gardens."

"Really?" Anne could almost hear the click of Teri's smile as it locked into place. "Come on in."

Anne had never been inside the Curley manse. The house was hushed, silent, the living room done entirely in ballet slipper pink, stuffed with pricey-looking furniture. A crystal chandelier hung above a high-backed sofa, overflowing with needlepoint pillows. Instead of a coffee table, there was a large tufted ottoman, sprouting fringe and tassels. The whole room looked as if it should have been preserved behind red velvet ropes in a museum. Every surface was gilded or lacquered or painted to the hilt. Even the floor was decorated, with a trellis of stenciled roses and peonies that formed a diamond pattern. Anne wondered if Teri hired someone to do the work or designed the space herself, decoupaging and gilding like mad, the Jersey shore's own Martha Stewart.

"Where are the girls?" Anne asked.

"Bobby drove them over to Red Bank," Teri said, arranging herself on the sofa. "Ballet lessons." She took a leather photo album from an end table and opened it up on her lap. The album was filled with glossy pictures of roses. "Don't these shots look professional?" she said proudly. "I took them myself."

Anne plunked herself down in a pink wing chair. "Actually, Teri. I didn't come here to talk about the flower show."

Teri's face registered annoyance. "Then why *are* you here?"

"Tigger Mills. You told the police he broke into your house last Sunday night."

"That's right."

"What happened?"

"What do you think? He came to hit my husband up for money. Drunk out of his gourd, as usual. I told him to leave and I thought that was the end of it. Bobby and I went out later that same night, to the charity bazaar. When we came back, the house had been ransacked. Tigger broke into Bobby's desk and stole $3,500."

"Do you always keep that much cash lying around the house?"

"It's mad money. We wouldn't have been so upset if only he hadn't turned the house upside down. You should have seen the mess he made."

"How do you know it was Tigger?"

Teri glared at her. Her upper lip curled into a sneer. "Of course it was him. He left his muddy boot tracks all over the place."

"So you immediately reported the theft to the police?"

"Yes," Teri snapped. "They searched his room. But they didn't find the money. You did though, didn't you? Bobby told me about it. By the way, we'd like the cash back as soon as possible. Just put it in an envelope and slide it under the front door."

"There's no proof that money belongs to you."

"Fine. Keep it if you like. You can show yourself out." Teri waved her hand dismissively.

"There's just one more thing I can't figure out," Anne said, rising. Teri looked up impatiently. "You say Tigger broke in here Sunday night. But when you saw him on the beach on Wednesday, you acted all chummy.''

A flush spread over Teri's cheeks. ''Anne, I really don't have time to review the social graces.''

''Were you and Tigger having an affair? Is that why he was over here?''

''That's absurd,'' Teri sputtered.

Reaching into her pocket, Anne took out the diamond earring. ''I thought this might belong to you.''

Teri's laugh was scornful. ''I wouldn't be caught dead in junk jewelry.''

''Isn't this yours?''

''It's cubic zirconium, and not fourteen-karat gold. But I bet I know whose it is. Why don't you ask Heather Vance?''

Heather Vance? Joe Vance's daughter was the last person Anne would associate with Tigger. She'd never seen them exchange two words.

''You look perplexed,'' Teri said with a laugh. ''If you're going to play Nancy Drew, you really should brush up on your sleuthing skills.''

''How do you know this belongs to Heather?'' Anne said, struggling to keep her temper. Teri Curley liked having the upper hand and she was starting to piss Anne off.

''I've seen her wearing them,'' Teri said. ''The little tramp is dating P.J. McGrath, so I'm forced to socialize with her.''

''I heard they're engaged.''

''So what? She's been sleeping with Tigger since high school. Never could keep their hands off each other for more than five minutes at a time. As soon as he came home, they were back to their old tricks.''

''Does P.J. know?''

Teri shrugged. ''Maybe. He's Bobby's friend, not mine. All I can say is, I wouldn't want to be around when the S hits the fan.''

''What do you mean?''

''P.J.'s got a rotten temper. Figure it out for yourself.''

Teri got up. "Now if you'll excuse me, I have a million things to do."

Anne crossed her arms over her chest. She didn't feel like leaving. Not yet. "You know, none of this explains why you acted so nice to Tigger on the beach. You never mentioned the money. You didn't even seem mad."

Teri pondered this a moment, as if the thought had never occurred to her. "I knew I'd never see that money again," she said slowly. "The police told us as much. So there was no use confronting him about it. Besides, he did have something else I wanted. His varsity letter from the swim team. I'm collecting stuff for the reunion."

"That was very kind of you—to forgive him like that, I mean."

Teri smiled again, the self-satisfied smile of a tabby cat who's polished off an especially tasty mouse. Her irony meter was still stuck on zero, Anne thought.

"Just one more question," Anne said sweetly, "and then I'll let you get back to your baking."

"What is it?" Teri said crossly.

"I was wondering if you were with Tigger the night of the fire. You and he were tight back then. So I'm thinking maybe you know what really happened the night the Spray View burned down. Was there some big secret the four of you shared—you and Tigger and P.J. and Bobby? A secret that got Tigger killed?"

Teri's eyes flickered with anger. "You're insane," she said, spitting out the words. "Stark raving mad, just like your mother. I was miles away from here that night. Tigger set the fire. Everyone knows it, everyone but you. So stop going around town spreading crazy stories, stirring up trouble. Tigger slept with *you*. He used *you*. Oh, don't look so shocked. Everyone in town knows you were his final one-night stand."

"Then everyone has their facts wrong," Anne said angrily.

"Oh, get real," Teri shouted. "*You* were the last person to see him alive. For all anyone knows, you murdered him and dragged his body out to the ocean. Now get out. Get out of my house before I—'' Teri's arms flailed wildly at her sides.

"Before you what?'' Anne said coolly. "Call the cops again? Accuse me of pilfering your prize rose bushes? Save it for someone who believes you.''

Teri's mouth dropped open. She looked stunned. Before she could recover, Anne turned on her heel and walked out of the room, through the long foyer that led to the front door. Well, Anne thought to herself, the S is plastered all over the fan now.

The Fourth of July specials were still on at Advance Pharmacy, proclaimed in red, white, and blue signs tacked on the walls: Scope mouthwash just 99 cents! Two bottles of Advil for the price of one! The ads contrasted with the otherwise old-fashioned flavor of the drugstore, which featured a long Formica counter and a row of stools upholstered in crimson-colored vinyl. Anne supposed that the specials scrawled on the sandwich board looked much the same as they had back in 1954, when Joe Vance bought the place. The blue plate special—a dish of macaroni and cheese, a cherry Coke, and a bowl of Jell-O—cost $2.99, plus tax. In an interview earlier in the summer with the features editor of the *Oceanside Heights Press*, Joe Vance had said he refused to raise his prices over the years lest his customers take offense. He also let it be known that Advance made the finest egg cream soda on the Jersey shore. When it was pointed out that his establishment was the only place for miles around that still offered the drink, he promptly fixed the editor an egg cream and winked. A picture of a paunchy Joe standing next to the soda fountain made the front page of the *Press,* and the story was picked up in newspapers around the state, making Advance Drugs a hot spot for a couple of weeks until the fuss blew over.

The teenager minding the cash register said that Heather was out sick. Anne looked around for Mr. Vance and spotted him in the back of the store behind the counter where prescriptions were prepared. She waited while the druggist discussed the vagaries of infant eczema with an anxious young mother—a tourist Anne didn't recognize—and then waited some more while Joe Vance reviewed possible remedies for arthritis of the toes with Mrs. Kelly, who worked as a cashier at the Mini-Mart. When the customers were gone, Anne approached the counter.

"Hello, hello," said Joe Vance, looking up. Over his clothes he wore a white lab coat, a blue tag on the lapel said: *Dr. Joe*. "What can I get you, Anne?" he said cheerfully.

"Nothing, thanks. I was wondering if we could talk in private."

Joe Vance looked at her closely and nodded his head. The skin on his face hung in loose folds, his chin spilled over into two sections, his cheeks were as droopy as a basset hound's. Putting the *Back in a Jiffy* sign on the counter, he unlatched the door separating the dispensary from the rest of the store and beckoned her to follow him. She trailed him into the back, passing shelves stocked with various medicines, until they reached his office.

"Now, then," he said, shutting the door and crossing to his desk. When he sat down, his chair emitted a loud squeak. "Make yourself comfortable," he said, pointing to a metal folding chair across from the desk. Anne slipped into the chair. "Well," Joe Vance said, rubbing his hands together. "Female troubles, if I'm not mistaken."

Anne stared at him. "Pardon?"

"Don't you worry. Anything you tell me stays in this room."

"I'm not sure I understand," Anne said slowly.

"Don't worry, dear," Joe Vance said, tugging at the lower fold of his chin. "Over the years, I've had women come into this office and tell me things they wouldn't tell their own mothers." Joe cleared his throat. "Menstrual cramps. Irregular cycles. Spotting. Fertility tests. We can even discuss methods of birth control, if you like."

Anne felt herself flush. "I think you misunderstood. I'm not here about a medical problem. I'm here because, well . . ." Anne paused. The druggist looked at her with a half-smile on his face, as though he'd heard it all before.

Years of female troubles, the smile seemed to say. Nothing new to report there. Nothing she could reveal would surprise him. She dropped her gaze, focusing on a pile of magazines spread out on the desk. ''We've known each other a long time,'' she said.

''Of course we have. I remember when you were no higher than my knee, Anne. ''Carrot-top'' I called you, remember? Because you wore your hair pulled back in a ponytail. When your mother came in here she'd walk out with her medicine and a lollipop for you. Poor woman. What a time you've had. There are some things even science can't cure.''

Joe Vance rested the tips of his fingers together, forming a bridge with this hands. Anne said, ''Tigger Mills told me he ran into you and your wife the other night on the boardwalk. He said you were pretty angry.''

The druggist's smile was peculiar. Sinister, almost. Like an old man on the brink of flashing open his raincoat and exposing his nakedness to a room full of schoolchildren. Anne dropped her eyes to the desk. There was a scissors next to the magazine and a pot of Elmer's Glue.

''Mary's high-strung,'' Joe Vance said. ''And I won't pretend I was happy to have that fella back here.''

''The fire happened a long time ago. Nothing was ever proven.''

''Does that make it right? A murderer walking our streets, with easy access to our wives and daughters? They weren't safe.''

Next to the glue and the scissors was a glass bowl, half-full. Anne could barely make out what the bowl contained. It looked like bits of colored paper.

''What do you mean?'' she asked Vance.

The druggist patted the breast pocket of his white lab coat, as if the answer was concealed there. ''I'm not two-faced. I speak my mind, even when folks don't like what I have to say. Maybe it's my profession. When a lady walks in here complaining of pains in her chest, nine times out of ten she's not having a heart attack. More like heartburn. So I'm not going to prescribe a whole bunch of pills. Or send her to some doctor over at the medical center. Or tell her she needs a stress test or an herbal massage or children who are better behaved. Best cure for heartburn is still bicarbonate of soda, if you catch my drift.''

''I'm not sure I do.''

''Tigger Mills was a bad seed. Born bad. Used to steal candy and magazines from the store, before he upped the ante to arson and killing innocent little girls. And another thing. Ed Klemperer used to be a friend of mine, back in the days when he had a beautiful daughter and a bright future. That man had his heart ripped out when Ruthie died. He's so torn up about it he can't bring himself to live in the world with the rest of us. So I'm not going to tell you I'm sorry the bastard's dead. What goes around, comes around. He got what was coming to him in the end.''

''You sound like a man who's out for revenge.''

Joe Vance snorted. ''I leave vengeance to those who have time for it. Myself, I'm too busy with my store and my family to go poking my nose where it doesn't belong.''

Anne scanned his face. His expression was neutral, the face of a small-town druggist dispensing prescriptions and free advice. ''Are you referring to me?''

''You'll wear yourself out running all over town asking questions.''

''I don't mind. Tracking down the facts has become kind of a hobby of mine. By the way, I like your handiwork,'' Anne said, gesturing to the bowl filled with paper. ''Only it looks like it takes a while to cut all the letters from the pages of the magazines.''

Vance shrugged. ''It's no trouble. Spruces up the specials out front. Makes them look more colorful, instead of me printing out the sales by hand.''

Anne leaned over the desk, scrutinizing a pile of different-size letters Vance had cut from the magazines. ''What are these for?''

The druggist spread the letters out on a piece of construction paper. ''Johnson & Johnson Baby Shampoo,'' he said. ''On sale starting Monday for $1.49.'' Anne noticed that all the O's were pink. The B in the word *baby* formed a curlicue.

"You know," Anne said, "Tigger told me he got a death threat with the letters cut out of some magazine."

Vance raised his eyebrows and smiled. This time he seemed genuinely amused. "Is that right? And here I thought I was so original. I guess a lot of folks must know this old trick. It all comes down to marketing, Annie," he said, with a wink. "I got a nice place here. Real homey, fair amount of charm. But you still got to advertise so folks'll pay attention."

"I never noticed it before," Anne said slowly. "The way you construct the signs. I wonder if that means the ads are working or not."

"Hard to say. I tell you what though. Stop by first thing Monday morning for the shampoo. The bottle says it's for babies. But the ladies all tell me it makes their hair real shiny-like."

"I wouldn't know," Anne said, studying him. His smile was exaggerated, like the plastic grin on a Halloween mask. "Anyway, the other reason I stopped by was to see Heather. I have something of hers I need to return."

"Heather called in sick this morning. I think she's laid up with the flu bug that's been going around."

"I'm sorry to hear it."

"Tell you what. If you stop by and visit with Heather, bring her some of this chicken soup her mama made for her this morning. You can have your penicillin. Nothing kills the flu like a hearty bowl of soup."

"All right," Anne said.

She checked her watch. Eleven o'clock, not too early to make a house call.

Chapter 12

*An unmade bed is an
eyesore. Take two minutes
to tuck in the sheets
and throw on a comforter
and you'll feel better
all day long.*

Heather Vance lived in the Bay Crest Arms, the only apartment building in the Heights. Built in the mid-1970s, shortly before the town gained its historic status, the Bay Crest was a modern condominium complex designed to look old. Painted a cheery lilac with deep purple trim, the building was covered in fancy-cut shingles. Spooled columns flanked the double front doors; the facade fairly dripped with all sorts of embellishments: intricate moldings, spindle work, curved balustrades, a flurry of finials. If they could have done it, Anne thought, they would have tacked on a couple of turrets for good measure.

Heather lived in apartment 3C, which for some reason was actually on the fourth floor. The doorbell played a tune that sounded like ''Midnight at the Oasis.''

''Just a sec,'' Heather called. When she opened the door,

she looked puzzled. "Oh," she said, taking a step backward. "Hey, Anne."

"Hi, Heather."

Heather Vance had always reminded Anne of a pin-up girl in a dime-store calendar. Everything about her was overblown, from her voluminous chest to her billowy blond hair. But today she looked worn out. No makeup. No elaborate hairdo. Her eyes were puffy and red-rimmed. She looked like she needed about a week's worth of sleep.

"I was in the drugstore this morning and your dad mentioned you have the flu," Anne said. "I told him I wouldn't mind dropping off some medicine for you on my way home." Anne handed Heather a white paper bag.

"Soup?" Heather said, examining the contents. "Ugh! It's way too hot. Leave it to Daddy to overreact. I take a sick day and he turns it into the flu."

Anne took a good look at Heather. She wore a lacy white tank top, a pair of gray cotton shorts, and flip-flops. Apart from the lack of makeup and the swelling around her eyes, she didn't look especially sick.

" 'Scuse my manners," Heather said, opening the door wider. "Come on in."

The living room was small and L-shaped, with a butcher block dining table and four chairs arranged against the short wall. Around the corner was a chintz loveseat and matching armchair, upholstered with crimson and lavender peonies. The drapes were in the same peony fabric. On the glass coffee table was a pile of glossy decorating magazines, tagged with yellow Post-it notes. A box of Kleenex sat on the table, surrounded by balled-up tissues. "Do you want some coffee?" Heather said. "I just made a fresh pot."

"No thanks."

"I'm gonna have some," Heather said, scooping the crumpled tissues off the table. There was a bruise on her forearm, a greenish-purple circle. "Have a seat." Anne sat in the armchair and surveyed the room. It was scrupulously neat, the way a hotel room looked before the guests arrive. Anne noticed there were no personal touches—no photographs, no tchotchkes, no paintings on the wall. The place barely seemed lived in.

When Heather came back, she was carrying two steaming mugs and two coasters. "Here," she said. "I fixed you a cup anyway." Anne took a sip. It was too hot and tasted like walnuts.

"Your apartment is nice," Anne said.

"Thanks. I'm thinking about redecorating. I bought all this furniture in the eighties. But I want a whole different look. Chintz is out now."

"It seems to have held up pretty well," Anne said, patting the arm of her chair. "Oh, before I forget. I believe I have something that belongs to you." She reached into the zipper compartment of her pocketbook, took out the earring, and passed it to Heather.

"Wow. I've been looking all over for this," Heather said. "Where'd you find it?"

"It was in Tigger Mills's room," Anne said slowly. She paused and fastened her gaze on Heather. "In his bed."

Heather looked embarrassed. "Oh, Jesus. I should have gotten the catch fixed. It pops open all the time." She put the earring on the coffee table and twirled it around like a top. "I went to visit Tigger once at that horrible place. You know, Ravenswood? Weirdwood is more like it. The nut jobs in that dump belong in a mental institution." Heather looked away. She crossed her legs, uncrossed them, and began fiddling with a pillow on the couch. "Not that there's anything wrong with mental institutions," she blurted out. "I mean, I'm sure they help people."

"Are you referring to my mother?" Anne said evenly.

"Um, I guess. She was in an institution, wasn't she?"

"In Red Bank there's a hospital with a special wing for people with Alzheimer's. I don't recommend visiting unless you have to."

"I didn't mean anything," Heather stammered. "It's just that Ravenswood creeps me out."

"I know. I don't like it, either."

Heather's puffy eyelids opened a little wider. "I heard you were with him the night he died."

"We had dinner together," Anne explained. "I'm trying to figure out what happened to him after he left my place."

"I thought he drowned," Heather said. She sipped her coffee noisily, making slurping sounds. Another black and blue mark stained the inside of her thigh, just below the hem of her shorts.

"That's what the police think."

"Did you and him . . . ?" Heather began. She clasped her fingers together and rubbed them back and forth. "You know?" For an instant, Anne could see Tigger and Heather sprawled on his bed at Ravenswood, his hands stroking her tousled blond hair, his mouth pressed against her kewpie-doll lips.

Color rose to Anne's cheeks. "We were just friends."

"He liked women. I mean, he liked being around women. Some guys don't."

"You sound like you knew Tigger pretty well," Anne said, reaching for her mug and taking another sip. Coffee scalded the roof of her mouth.

"We go back a ways."

"To high school?"

"Yeah," Heather said, smiling.

Anne wondered how they'd managed to keep the relationship quiet. It was hard to hide anything in a small town like the Heights. As if reading Anne's mind, Heather said: "Back then, Tigger and I didn't want anyone to know we were going out. He had these official-type girlfriends. And then he had me."

"What was the big deal if people knew?" Anne asked.

"It was more fun sneaking around. Not a helluva lot else to do in this joint. Might as well have a few secrets."

"So you've been together all this time."

"No," Heather said testily. "It was over between us ages ago. We kept in touch is all, over the years."

"Kind of like pen pals?"

"Uh huh."

"It's funny where the earring ended up. Tigger's brother, Jack, found it between the sheets."

Heather frowned. "So? Tigger wasn't exactly a neat

freak. When I dropped by to visit, he hadn't made the bed.''

"I'm curious, Heather. Why did you go see him?"

"To find out what he was up to, I guess. It'd been a while since his last letter. And I wanted to tell him how sorry I was about his mom. She went real quick. Ovarian cancer. Isn't that horrible? I can really relate, you know. I found a lump in my breast right after New Year's and I thought I was toast. The doctor cut it out. Benign, thank God. 'Cept now I have this big red scar. It looks real ugly.''

"You must have been frantic before the biopsy."

"You don't know the half of it. Hey, by the way, how'd you know the earring was mine?"

"Teri Curley told me it might belong to you."

"That dip," Heather said, rolling her eyes. "She makes me puke. What a Twinkie!"

Anne couldn't resist smiling. A Twinkie. Now that was an apt description of Teri—puffed up on the outside, oozing sugary stickiness. Heather Vance was beginning to grow on her.

"Wait a sec," Heather said suddenly. "What'd Teri tell you about me and Tigger?"

"That you two were close."

"Christ," Heather said angrily, "I should have known she was behind this whole mess! She told you we were sleeping together, right?" Anne nodded. "And I bet you're not the only one she told."

"What do you mean?"

"Don't you see what she's gone and done? She must have told P.J. the same thing. We've been going together for a year and a half, until he up and dumped me last week. Just like that." She snapped her fingers. "For the life of me, I can't figure out why. I mean, we were talking about going to New York this weekend. Stay at some fancy hotel, see a Broadway show, watch the fireworks from the Statue of Liberty. And then, out of the blue, he tells me it's over. Bye-bye baby."

"Did you try to talk to him about it?"

"Are you kidding? I did everything but get down on my knees and beg. At first, I was so stunned, you know. I could barely believe it. And then I kept wanting him to tell me what was wrong so I could fix it. But he was so cold. Like he'd never cared a fig about me. We had fights before, but nothing like this. I kept thinking he'd met someone else. But he said no. It wasn't that. Finally, I told him I'd just camp out on his doorstep until he told me what was wrong. Know what he said?'' Anne shook her head. ''He said the attraction wore off. I almost fainted from shock. I mean, can you believe the nerve of this guy? We screw so much I'm always sore down there. And he claims he's not attracted to me anymore. Bullshit. Even when he was telling me, he had this look in his eye, like he wanted to do me right there on the kitchen floor. I knew it was bogus. But what could I say? I told him if he didn't like the way I looked, I could change. I'd cut my hair or lose weight. Whatever. But he said it wouldn't help. Once you lose your attraction for somebody, it doesn't come back. Not ever.''

Heather paused and took a breath. ''Now he won't even return my calls, you know. He acts like I'm something he scraped off the bottom of his shoe.'' Heather's eyes started to water. She brushed a tear away with the back of her hand. ''Love stinks,'' she said, reaching for the Kleenex box.

''I heard the two of you were engaged.''

Heather blew her nose. ''Engaged to be engaged is more like it. He was talking about getting me a ring. I'd already picked out the one I want. Pear-shaped, fourteen karat.'' Tears spilled down her cheeks. She dabbed at her eyes. ''Sorry,'' she sniffled. ''Once I get started, I can't stop.'' Her hand strayed to the bruise on her leg and she pulled her shorts lower, covering it up.

''Did P.J. do that to you?''

Heather looked away. ''You mean 'cause of what I said before, about us screwing so much? No. I hurt myself when I banged into a door. When I get up in the morning and my contacts aren't in, I can't see straight.''

It could have happened that way but Anne didn't think it had. She looked at the bruise on Heather's arm. There was another one on her lower leg. And a cut on her hand.

All in all, Heather was pretty banged up. Would P.J. have gone after Tigger, too, if he discovered his old buddy was sleeping with his fiancée? "Listen, Heather," Anne said, "were Tigger and P.J. still such good friends?"

"They had a couple of beers together when Tigger got back to town. I think Tigger hit P.J. up for some dough."

"Speaking of money, did you ever meet P.J.'s aunt? I heard she left him a fortune in her will."

Heather shook her head. "No. He never even mentioned her and then boom—he gets this big fat inheritance check. I thought we could finally get married. And now..." Heather picked at the damp tissue, shredding it to pieces. "We just celebrated his birthday together, you know. We had the best time. I got him one of those camcorders and this really nice shirt. By Ralph Lauren. He looked so good in it. We were laughing, making plans. I even baked him a strawberry shortcake. And now everything's ruined." Heather was on the verge of tears again.

"When did you visit Tigger at Ravenswood?" Anne asked.

Heather thought for a moment. "I guess it must have been the day before he died."

"How would Teri know you were there?"

"I have no idea," Heather wailed. "That mean little bitch. I'm gonna make her pay, if it's the last thing I do."

"When you saw Tigger, how did he seem?"

"Great. Real upbeat and all."

"Did he mention anyone named Cloister Black?"

Heather frowned. "Is that like a monastery or something?"

"Never mind. What *did* Tigger talk about?"

"Oh, he was telling me about some new business venture he had in the works."

"What kind of business venture?"

"He didn't say. But I know he was fixing to get an awful lot of money from it. He kept talking about how rich he was gonna be, how everybody in town was finally gonna show him some respect." A worried look crossed Heather's face. "Don't mention what Teri said about Tigger and me to anybody else, okay? It's bad enough P.J. thinks it's true. I wouldn't want Teri's lies to get back to my father.''

"Don't worry. I won't say anything.''

"Thanks. Daddy's very protective of me. He wouldn't like it if he knew Tigger and I were friends. Even if it's all ancient history.''

"I know what you mean. Your father doesn't seem sorry Tigger's dead.''

"Name me one person in this town who *is* sorry.''

"Are you?''

"Of course,'' Heather sniffed. "Tigger was a good guy. A good friend to me. Nobody understood him is all.''

"Did he mention that he received a death threat?''

Heather plucked another tissue from the box, and stared at it as if she was unsure what it was for. "What?'' she said, crumpling the tissue up in her hand.

"He told me he got a death threat. Somebody cut up a bunch of magazines and pasted the letters together. Basically they spelled *Drop dead.*''

"That's awful,'' Heather said quickly. "I had no idea.'' She pressed the tissue between her palms. Her expression was not so much horrified as panicked. She's lying, Anne thought. She knows something.

"The note seems to have vanished into thin air,'' Anne said. "I thought of it again when I was at the drugstore. I noticed your father cuts letters out of magazines, to advertise stuff that's on sale.''

"So?'' Heather said. She looked scared.

"So what's the deal with Tigger and your parents? Your mother spit at Tigger on the boardwalk the night he died. And your father seems to have taken what happened to heart. The fire. Ruthie's death. Like it happened to him personally.''

"Did he say something to you?'' Heather said anxiously.

"He said Tigger was a murderer. A bad seed. And then he said something else that struck me as peculiar.'' Heather waited expectantly. "He said Tigger had 'easy access' to women. Something about endangering wives and daughters.''

"Well, that's Daddy for you," Heather said uneasily. "He's like the sheriff in an old Western. Round up the women and children and stick 'em in a corral. Like I told you, he's overprotective."

"I was just wondering if there was more to the story."

"I don't think so. More coffee?" Heather said, picking up her mug.

"No, I'm fine. Listen, when you were with Tigger, did he talk to you about the fire?"

"Not really. He didn't like to talk about it much."

"Do you think he was responsible?"

Heather shrugged. "What's done is done. Accidents happen all the time. You just have to pick up your life and move on—that's what I say."

"Were you with him that night?"

Heather looked startled. "Me?"

"Yeah."

She ran her tongue over her lips. "What difference does it make?"

Anne scanned Heather's face. "I'm not sure. But something happened that night. And I can't shake the feeling that whatever it was got Tigger killed. If you *were* with him, I was just wondering if you noticed anything suspicious at the Spray View. Like someone hanging around who shouldn't have been there. Or something—a smell, a noise—that struck you as odd."

Heather averted her eyes, fixing her gaze on the coffee mug. "Oh," she said. "I don't know. I mean, I wasn't there." She set the mug down again. "You know what? I'm not feeling all that great actually. Serves me right. I play hooky from work, and I start feeling sick."

"Well, I should get going. I hope I haven't upset you."

"No, no. It's just that Tigger's death was such a shock. First the lump in my breast. Then P.J. walks out on me. And now this. It just makes you think how fucked up life is. One day everything's peachy, and the next, you're . . . gone. Even the weather is screwy. I mean, it's beyond hot. It's so humid outside I can barely breathe."

"I know what you mean. The heat's been deadly this summer."

On her way out, Anne noticed another stack of decorating magazines on the hall table. "Are you thinking of hiring a decorator to redo your apartment," she asked, "or are you planning to do it yourself?"

"I don't know what I'm gonna do," Heather said. "I might sell the apartment. Daddy wants me to move back home."

"What do *you* want?"

Heather hesitated, there was a faraway look in her eyes. "I want P.J. back," she said dreamily. "I'd crawl through glass for that guy. Honest I would."

Chapter 13

To reduce the amount of dust on your furniture, mix 4 parts water with 1 part liquid fabric softener, moisten a rag with the solution, and wipe clean.

For as long as Anne could remember, Saturday afternoons had meant storytime at the library. In the summer, because of the heat, the storytelling sessions were held outside, under the shade of the big maple tree. When Anne walked by, there were about a dozen kids sitting cross-legged in a circle, underneath the tree. She knelt on the grass, next to a pile of books. All her old favorites were here—*Alice's Adventures in Wonderland, Charlotte's Web, Black Beauty.* She wondered if she could write a children's book, some wonderful fable about enchanted kingdoms and magic potions. Did kids still enjoy that sort of stuff? She couldn't remember what it was like to be so young. Her memories of her own childhood were fuzzy, distant. It seemed as if it had happened to someone else.

"Joining us for story hour?" Delia asked with a smile,

as she crossed the lawn, holding the worn three-legged stool she always sat on during storytelling sessions.

"Only if you're reading a Dana Girls mystery."

"My, how you used to love Louise and Jean Dana. Do you remember the *Clue of the Black Flower*?"

"I couldn't recite the whole plot, but I bet the sleuths saved the day."

Delia placed the stool in the center of the circle. "You told me you liked the book so much that some day you were going to go to Hawaii and dance the hula."

"How come you have such a great memory?"

"Born with it, I suppose. Now what can I do for you? Are you here to do more research on the Heights?"

"I wanted to let you know I have that book Tigger Mills borrowed from the library, the *Vintage Victoriana* book."

"Good. I hate for books to stray."

"Is it all right if I keep it awhile longer?"

"Certainly," Delia said. She took an embroidered handkerchief from the pocket of her dress and delicately wiped her face. "Is it hot enough for you? I heard on the radio we might see one hundred degrees today. What do you think of that, children?" She regarded the faces looking up at her. "Would you like to have story hour on the beach?"

The children clapped their hands in delight. "Do you know what I think?" Delia said to them. "I think it might be cooler right here, underneath this big old shade tree. When we're through, we can visit the Good Humor man and have ourselves a nice treat."

"Delia," Anne said, rising to her feet, "where can I find Arthur Hornsby?"

"Over in Harvest Home cemetery."

"You mean he's dead?"

"Last time I checked." Delia smoothed the folds of her cotton dress. "That man knew more about this town than anyone else. Even me."

"How long ago did he die?"

"Let's see. I believe it was either in '77 or '78. Had a heart attack, died in his sleep. But at least he finished his book before he passed on. He worked on it for years. Why, he spent so much time looking through old records at town hall that Darcy Busmiller, the clerk who used to work over there, started to think he was sweet on her. Can you imagine such foolishness!''

Anne glanced at the kids, who were beginning to fidget. The old town hall, a nineteenth-century red brick building on Main Street, had been converted into a home and garden shop a few years ago. "Where would those records be now, Delia?"

"Right here, in the basement of the library. I sorted through some of the boxes when we were getting the centennial exhibit ready."

"Would you mind if I took a look?"

"I guess not, if you can stand the dust. Is this more research for your book?"

"Uh huh." Some of the children were plucking blades of grass from the lawn and chewing on them. It struck Anne that the concept of story hour was one more quaint Heights tradition. Wouldn't these kids rather be indoors, playing computer games?

"Do you know anyone around here named Cloister Black?" she said to Delia.

"Cloister who? What kind of a name is that?"

"I'm not sure. How about a woman named Katherine Davenport? Does she live around here?"

"There've been Davenports in the Heights since I was a little girl," Delia said. "I don't know any named Katherine, but that doesn't mean she didn't live in these parts at one time."

"When can I look through those old records?"

"Any time you like. We're open till five today."

"I'm not sure I can get to it this afternoon. Would tomorrow be all right?"

"I don't see why not. Library's closed on Sundays, but you have a key." Delia shifted her attention to the circle of children. "Now, Tommy," she said, addressing a tow-headed boy in a striped shirt. "Don't you go pulling Becky's hair." Delia turned back to Anne. "They're getting a little antsy from the heat."

"I'm sorry to delay story hour. There's just one more thing I wanted to ask you."

"What's that, dear?"

"It's about Heather Vance."

Delia walked toward the library steps. "I'll be back in a minute, children," she called over her shoulder, "and then we'll get started." She beckoned Anne to follow her. "Now what's this about Heather?" Delia said, when they were safely out of earshot.

"I was just wondering what you thought of her."

Delia adjusted her spectacles. "Nice enough girl. A little rough around the edges. She's had her share of bad breaks."

"Like what?"

"Oh, she got into some trouble when she was a teenager. Ran away from home. Her father had a fit, don't you know."

Anne vaguely remembered hearing something about it. But at the time she was too wrapped up in her mother's illness to pay much attention. "What happened?"

"She fell for the wrong fella, I guess. Joe dragged her back here kicking and screaming."

"Who was the guy?"

"Nobody knows. I heard it was a fella she met in a bar. But he dropped out of the picture pretty darn fast once Joe Vance got wind of it."

"You mean Joe threatened him?"

"Joe doesn't stand for any nonsense, Anne. And Heather's the apple of his eye."

"She seems a little afraid of him."

"He can be a bear now and then. But he means well."

"Do you think Tigger Mills could have been the guy Heather ran off with?"

Delia looked at Anne in surprise. "The Mills boy? I don't think so. He was too busy getting his own self into trouble. Lord, I hope we never see the likes of that fire again. Sometimes I worry about these old wood buildings. You know half the folks staying in the hotels smoke? Doesn't matter what the signs say. They do it anyway. Of course, it's not the same thing. They're not stirring up mischief. I always said if Troy and Ellen had disciplined that boy properly, little Ruthie would still be alive today!''

Anne started to argue, then stopped herself. What would be the point, she thought. She had absolutely no proof Tigger wasn't involved.

"Anne, dear, I really musn't keep the children waiting any longer.''

"I won't keep you then,'' Anne said. "I only asked about Heather because I heard she and P.J. McGrath broke up.''

Delia pursed her lips. "That girl is better off without him, though she probably doesn't know it. P.J.'s not the marrying kind, if you know what I mean.''

"Do you know why he broke it off?''

"He probably got tired of her. Plain and simple. She was gallivanting around town announcing their engagement, but I'd bet my life savings he never gave her a ring or made her a promise she could take to the bank. Some gals eat hope for breakfast, if you catch my drift.'' Delia fanned herself with one of the books. "My goodness. We're late. I've got to get started,'' she exclaimed, hurrying over to the children and seating herself on the stool. "Today,'' she announced, "we're going to hear all about *Charlotte's Web,* a wonderful story about a pig and a spider who become fast friends.''

Anne glanced at her watch. Ten past twelve. There wasn't time to look through the records now. She was supposed to meet Jack in twenty minutes. She waved goodbye to Delia and the children and walked the six blocks to Ravenswood. The inn was quiet this afternoon, forlorn and deserted. Half the rocking chairs on the front porch were empty.

"Is Mr. Mills in his room?'' Anne asked the man behind the front desk.

"Dunno,'' he replied, without looking up from his newspaper.

Anne slipped up the stairs and knocked on the door of Jack's room. No answer. She started to walk away, intending to wait for him downstairs in the lobby, then retraced her steps. Hesitantly, she turned the knob and the door swung open. The room was neater than the last time she was here. All the bottles and food wrappers had disappeared. But the place still had an institutional quality; it looked bare and impersonal, like a cell or a hospital room. The geranium plant on the windowsill drooped from lack of water.

Anne sat down on the edge of the bed. Through the open window she could see a corner of the boardwalk and beyond that a slice of ocean. The beach was probably packed today with tourists streaming toward the water, eager for a little relief from the heat. She looked around the room, trying to imagine Tigger living here. There was something haunted about him, a smoldering anger she knew about because she recognized it in herself. Life was unfair. She'd accepted that fact early on. But what if the blame was wrong, misplaced. If Tigger was telling the truth all along, it meant his life was rigged somehow. He'd been hounded out of town, punished for a crime he didn't commit. She thought of her mother's friends, dropping away one by one like petals yanked from a daisy, until no one came around anymore. People fled when they saw Evelyn Hardaway approaching. They thought she would hurt them. Crazy Evelyn. Always talking to herself, rooting through garbage cans, parading around on her front porch with no panties. The town had shunned Evelyn. And when Evelyn was alive, they shunned Anne, too, as if madness were catching.

"Where is he?" The old woman from next door was standing in the doorway, leaning on a cane. "He back yet?"

Anne got up and went over to the woman. But the old lady waved her away. Moving gingerly, she settled herself in a chair, holding the cane out in front of her, like a scepter. "He tell you where it's hidden yet?" she said excitedly.

"Where what's hidden?"

"The money," she whispered, rubbing her fingers together. Her milky eyes darted around the room. "He don't know I know."

"The money in the Bible? Is that what you mean?

The old woman shook her head impatiently. "I seen it through the wall," she said. "The angel came. And then I seen the key."

Anne stared at the wall behind the old woman's chair. Rising, she moved closer, searching for small holes, places an eye could peer through. Nothing. The old woman laughed, a shrill birdlike cry that punctuated the stillness. Anne felt goose bumps form on her arms. It seemed like she'd had this conversation before. The specifics were different, but the tone was the same. Her mother used to talk this way, in garbled riddles, a secret language only Evelyn understood.

"Show me," Anne said gently. "Show me the key."

"When he gets back," the old woman said, with a sly wink. "Safety first and foremost." Using the cane to steady herself, she rose to her feet and shuffled slowly down the hall.

Anne looked around the room. First the letter disappeared and now there's supposed to be a mysterious key. The place was way too small for secret hiding places. She went over to the wall again, running her hands from the baseboard up to the ceiling. The old woman seemed so sure. But there was no peephole. She walked over to the bureau and opened the drawers. Two of them were empty. Sliding her fingers around to the back, she probed the wood for a hidden compartment. Nothing doing. Opening the third drawer, she felt around the edges, skirting Jack's clothes.

She used the same technique in the closet, running her hands over every surface. She checked the baseboards and the floor, hoping to spot a loose board, a secret nook or cranny. Nothing. Sweat streamed down her face. Her bare knees were raw from crawling on the floor, her hair brushed against dust bunnies. Where could the damn thing be? For some reason she couldn't explain, she believed the old woman's story, if only because she so wanted to find a magic key that would unlock the mystery of Tigger's death.

Frustrated, she sank down on the bed and stared into

space. Once, when she was little, her parents had taken her on a trip to Virginia to see a bunch of eighteenth-century homes and gardens. It was a boring vacation. Anne had begged to go to Disneyland instead. But her parents insisted the house tour was better. In the backyard of a big white Colonial house they visited was an elaborate maze designed especially for children, patterned after a garden in England. The maze was constructed of large boxy topiary that flared up toward the sky like leafy towers. Her parents had guided her to the front of the maze and then walked around the outside to wait for her at the exit. Anne could hear their voices, tantalizingly close, but she couldn't see them. As she walked deeper and deeper into the heart of the maze, she felt as if she were lost in a dream where nothing was real, nothing was what it seemed, until the voices of her parents sounded foreign, unfamiliar, and the towering clusters of leaves threatened to swallow her up. These last couple of days had been like reentering that maze; it was as though her field of vision had become unreliable.

Being in Ravenswood didn't help. Further down the hall, she heard an incoherent stream of words, nonsense syllables really, the ramblings of an aged tenant. Even the inn itself was constructed oddly. All of the additions over the years had created a series of right angles, with portions of the building jutting out awkwardly from the facade. From where she sat, she could look out the window, and see part of the room next door, where the senile old woman was lying on a bed. Anne picked up the phone on the night stand and dialed Helen Passelbessy's number. Her hand left a streak of dirt on the receiver.

"Hiya," Helen said. "I just finished making gazpacho."

"Could you do me a favor?"

"Sure, honey."

"Could you use the computer at the bank to access P.J. McGrath's account?"

"Could I what!" Helen said in amazement.

"He's been going around town telling everyone he inherited all this money from his aunt. I just wanted to make sure it's true."

"Anne, I'm a loan officer. I'm not supposed to go into our customers' private files."

"Yeah, I know. But could you just see who signed the check? Maybe there was an estate trust set up for him or it might have come from his aunt's lawyers. The check would have been for a really large amount, about twenty grand, deposited in his account over the last week and a half."

"Do you even know for sure that P.J. is one of our customers?" Helen sounded skeptical.

"Well, most people in town use the Central Bank of New Jersey. I figure he does, too."

"Anne, what's going on?"

"I'm not really sure. But I need to know if P.J.'s being straight about where he got that money. Nobody will mind if you do a little snooping."

Helen sighed. "I was going to go to work for a couple of hours this afternoon, to clear up some paperwork."

"Great. Then you'll help me?"

"Anne, I don't know. I could get in big trouble if anyone finds out."

"Please, Helen. It's really important."

"All right. But you owe me one—big time." Anne smiled and hung up. She glanced out the window. The old lady next door was taking a nap.

Picking up the phone again, Anne dialed into her answering machine. There were three messages. Mary Lou Popper had checked in, complaining that Anne was running way behind schedule. The second call was from one of the Blacks, whose first name was Christine, not Cloister. The last call crackled with static, a bad connection. Anne heard a woman's voice, but the words were drowned out by a roaring noise. A computerized operator interrupted the call and then the line went dead.

Anne looked out the window, watched the old woman's chest rise up and down. The phone slipped from her fingers. If she was close enough to see the old woman breathing in the room next door, did that mean the old woman could see everything in here? Removing her shoes, Anne dragged the chair over to the window sill and climbed onto it. From this angle, she had a bird's eye view of the adjoining room. It was identical to this one, with a bed, dresser, table and chair. The old woman's breath came in slow heaves. Later, Anne couldn't remember which came first—whether the bee that flew in through the window caused her to lose her balance or whether the chair gave way of its own accord. As she fell, her foot kicked out, struggling to find a toehold. The geranium plant on the sill tilted over and crashed to the floor. And then she was lying facedown on the floor, next to the broken chair and the smashed terra-cotta pot. The roots of the geranium poked through the soil and next to it, something small and silver—a dirty silver key.

Chapter 14

My husband once told me he'd clean the house over my dead body. I said, "Suit yourself. But who's going to cook dinner when I'm gone?"

The service for Tigger Mills at the Whitehall Funeral Home was attended by exactly eleven people: a couple of little old ladies who liked coming to funerals in the summertime because the chapel was air-conditioned, two men Anne had never seen before, Bobby Curley, Jim Walser, Troy Mills, Jack, and Heather Vance. Heather was wearing a sleeveless black dress and a black hat with a clump of fake cherries attached to the band. Her blond hair cascaded down her shoulders. In the last pew, seated near the door, was Lucille Klemperer, her hands folded in her lap, a beatific smile on her face. Anne wondered what she was thinking, whether Tigger's death brought her joy or relief, whether anything could offset the pain of losing a child. An eye for an eye, a life for a life, the Bible said. But when the enemy was finally punished, were old hatreds buried beside him? Closed up, sealed off?

If not, it must have been even worse, no place to put the rage, nobody to blame for Ruthie's senseless death.

Anne sat in the front row, next to Jack. On Jack's other side was Troy Mills. His hair was disheveled. He smelled like he hadn't showered in days. Jack told her it had taken forty minutes to get Troy dressed and ready, and another half-hour to coax him out of the house and into the car.

"Pop's going to make a scene, I can feel it," Jack said to Anne, not bothering to lower his voice. "He's been drinking nonstop."

Jack looked like he could use a stiff drink himself. His handsome face was drawn, his lower lip trembled. When Anne looked at his hands, she saw they were shaking and she slipped one hand into his, hoping to steady him. He couldn't take his eyes off the pine box near the altar, where Tigger lay.

Earlier, Anne had forced herself to peer into the coffin for one last good-bye. She'd seen dead bodies before—including those of her mother and father—and she always wondered how people could describe them as lifelike. There was nothing natural about a dead body in a silk-lined box. Looking at Tigger was no different. The mortician had added a hint of color to his cheeks and lips, and applied foundation to his face and hands, in a futile attempt to disguise the chalky countenance of death. Barely visible on Tigger's left cheek was a jagged pink cut; the outline of another cut grazed his forehead near his hairline. Underneath his nostrils, Anne could make out faint abrasions.

She'd been dreading the funeral. One image kept playing over and over in her mind: Tigger diving off the pier when they were younger. She could't make him stop falling, couldn't stop visualizing him beneath the waves.

"Let us pray," the minister intoned, as taped organ music filled the air. Light streamed in through the stained glass windows. Beside her, she could feel Jack tense up.

"For He is the resurrection and the light," said the minister, "leading us through the valley of death."

Out of the corner of her eye, she saw Troy Mills stand up. "Fiddlesticks," Troy bellowed.

"Pop," Jack said, tugging on Troy's sleeve.

"Rotten loser," Troy yelled out. His eyes were glued to the coffin. "Don't you run away from me."

From his podium, the minister hesitated, unsure how to proceed.

"Pop, sit down," Jack pleaded.

"Come here and take your lumps like a man." Troy weaved unsteadily on his feet. His whole body shook.

"Pop, shut up. Now," Jack commanded, yanking his father back down to the pew.

"Leggo me, Jacky," Troy shouted. "He knows what he done."

"Tigger's dead, Pop. Don't you get it? He's dead."

For a moment, Troy looked confused. His face went blank, his eyes lost their focus. Then he threw his head back and howled with laughter.

Jack let go of Troy's arm. "Jesus," Jack said. He brought one hand to his mouth. When he spoke again, his voice was muffled. "Jesus."

"Mr. Mills . . ." Anne began.

But the funeral director was already at Troy's elbow. He seemed only mildly concerned, as if this kind of thing happened all the time.

"I think your father might be more comfortable in the other room," he said pleasantly.

Jack nodded. The funeral director took one of Troy's arms. An usher in a gray suit took the other arm. Together, they lifted him up and escorted him down the center aisle, toward the back of the chapel. Anne turned around. Troy's feet weren't touching the floor. She caught Jim Walser's eye. His expression was grim. In the last row, Lucille Klemperer was smiling.

"Well, now," the minister said doubtfully. "Where were we?"

Anne touched Jack's arm, but he didn't appear to notice. His head rested in his hands.

"Christ being raised from the dead dieth no more," the minister said. "Death hath no more dominion over him.

For in that he died, he died unto sin once: but in that he liveth, he liveth unto God.''

The minister talked of God and forgiveness, the miraculous way God forgave his wayward children. How very generous, Anne thought, to forgive the dead. Beside her, Jack remained motionless. She looked at the coffin, then looked away, picturing Tigger's waxen face. He was going to be cremated, his ashes scattered in the ocean.

After the service ended and the mourners filed out, she and Jack went to collect Troy. They found him slumped in a chair, mumbling to himself. It took three men to carry him to Jack's car and deposit him in the backseat.

When they pulled up in front of the house on Embury Street, Anne stayed in the Corvette. The top of the convertible was rolled back, and the sun beat down on her. The light was so bright it was almost blinding, the air dense with humidity. It must have been at least one hundred degrees, a perfect ten on the beach meter. It seemed sacrilegious for the day to be so gorgeous. After a few minutes, Jack came back out. He climbed in without a word, his eyes shielded behind his sunglasses. His hands gripped the steering wheel tightly, but he made no move to start the car.

"I'm sorry," Anne said.

"I shouldn't have brought him," Jack said tonelessly. "Guess I'll never learn."

"Is he sleeping?"

"Curled up tight with his bottle."

"It's been a rough day. Maybe we should take it easy this afternoon. I could go home, do some work."

"No," Jack said sharply. "I mean, I think we should keep going, see this thing through."

"If you want to talk, I'm here."

"I know." He looked over at her, his eyes hidden behind the sunglasses. "Thanks." He tried to force a smile, but it wouldn't come.

She wanted to hug him close, tell him everything would be all right. But she couldn't. She had no idea if things would ever be back to normal again. She didn't even know what normal was anymore.

"Let's get going," Jack said, turning the key in the ignition.

The car cruised down Embury Street and made a left onto Ocean Avenue. The beach was jammed with tourists basking in the sun.

"Tell me about Sea Girt," Anne said.

"I talked to Marvin Childs, Tigger's lawyer. Childs said Tigger gave him a $500 retainer. That would account for the rest of the money Bobby said Tigger stole. Great, huh? Childs said he was working on getting the will to stand up in court. My ma wrote it out on a notepad and got two neighbors to sign it, but the will was never properly notarized. When Childs called my father to discuss the negotiations, Pop cursed him out and hung up on him."

"Did Childs know anything about a Cloister Black?"

"No. I dropped by Cloister Construction Company afterward. They never heard of Tigger. But they do know Bobby." Jack's laugh was rueful. "Seems Curley Construction doesn't have a sterling reputation around here."

"What do you mean?"

"The owner told me Bobby underbids on jobs, then goes way over budget. Plus, Bobby doesn't like using union workers and that pisses a lot of people off. I hear he's not above offering a bribe or two to get what he wants."

"Interesting."

Jack's car stopped at a light. A family of four crossed the street, lugging beach chairs, a picnic hamper, tote bags, and a plastic raft. On the corner, a group of boys were breaking eggs on the sidewalk.

"When I got back," Jack said, "I asked around to see if anyone knew where Bobby Curley was the night of the fire. Seems Bobby's story checks out. A few people confirmed he was out on his dad's boat, like he told us."

"Another theory down the drain."

"I also swung by Madame Mona's. I thought you might have tried to talk to her again, and I didn't want you to go alone. The place was locked. So I went over to the Pink

Flamingo to talk to Sandy. She's gone. The manager told me she checked out yesterday an hour after we left.''

A sigh of exasperation escaped Anne's lips. Sandy Cooksey was connected to Tigger's death somehow. Anne was sure of it. Taggart had said Sandy had connections in Atlantic City. It would be hard to locate her now. "Okay," Anne said, "let's concentrate on the key."

When she had first showed Jack what she found in the geranium pot, he thought it was the key to a diary. But Anne knew it wasn't. She'd recognized what the key was for immediately. It had three numbers carved into the surface—317—just like the key her mother had used to open the family's safe deposit box.

"The question is, where's the box?" Jack said.

"I guess the first place we could look is the Central Bank of New Jersey. My friend Helen can check to see if Tigger was using the vault in one of the branches." The light flashed green and the car turned up Main Street. On the porch of Ravenswood several elderly people rocked in silence. The old woman was not among them. She'd mentioned something about an angel and something else . . . some weird phrase. *Safety first and foremost.* The phrase brought to mind a jingle. *La da da da dum.* Anne had an image of a tree in the middle of a forest. Lightning pierced the sky. *Da da dum.* The lightning flashed and disappeared, narrowly missing the tree. The camera focused in on the shiny red fruit, healthy, delicious.

She turned to Jack. "Of course," she said excitedly. "It's from that commercial. The one with the fruit. Apple Federated."

"Huh?"

"Apple Federated Bank. Haven't you seen the commercials on TV? It's one-stop shopping. You bank there, but they'll also do all your financial planning for you, sell you home insurance, anything you want." She started to sing. "Your money's safe with us. Da da dum. Relax. Coast. Da dum. Safety first and foremost."

"How would the old lady know about the bank?"

"Maybe she overheard Tigger talking about it. You said yourself the walls were paper-thin."

"But how would she know about the key?"

"She must have seen him hide it. Ravenswood is built oddly. Her room juts out a little bit, so she has a bird's eye view of Tigger's room. I went in there after I found the key and looked out her window. You can see everything—Tigger's bed, the dresser, the geranium plant, everything."

Jack swung the car onto Route 35. "It's Saturday. The bank'll be closed."

"Apple Federated is open till three on Saturdays. At least that's what they say in the commercials."

"You mean we just walk into the bank and access the safe deposit box?"

"No. The only way they'll let you open the box is if Tigger gave you power of attorney."

"Are you sure?"

"Yeah. I know about this stuff because of my mother. When she got sick, all the financial responsibility was transferred to me. I had what's known as 'durable power of attorney.' I could write checks, pay bills, access her safety deposit box, whatever."

"Then basically we're sunk."

"Not necessarily. They won't let *you* open the box, but Tigger should be able to do it."

The Apple Federated Bank was in a strip mall on the outskirts of the neighboring town of Bradley Beach. A guard led them down a flight of stairs to the vault, where another older guard sat behind a bullet-proof window. A portable radio rested by his elbow playing "all Sinatra, all the time." Anne hoped the guards stuck to easy listening music. Tigger's death was old news—it'd been two days since his body washed up on the beach. Still, it might have occurred to someone in the bank that a ghost shouldn't be able to cruise right in. The guard shoved a clipboard through a slot in the glass. Jack signed Tigger's name, pushed the clipboard back. No alarms went off, no police officer appeared to arrest them. A buzzer sounded and they followed the younger guard through two sets of heavy steel doors into a big gray room lined with metal boxes.

The guard walked over to one of the boxes. Removing a key from a manila envelope, he placed it in the lock and turned it to the right. Jack put Tigger's key into another keyhole in the same box. Anne heard a slight click. The guard slid the box out of the wall and led Anne and Tigger to a tiny anteroom with a desk and two chairs. "Press the buzzer when you're through," the guard said, pointing to a small black knob on the wall before shutting the door behind him.

"Here goes nothing," Jack announced as he slid back the metal cover. He reached inside the box and pulled out a piece of paper the color of old parchment. "This is all there is," Jack said, unfolding the paper carefully. "A letter."

He began reading what was written on the page. "It's the death threat, isn't it?" Anne said excitedly. "We couldn't find it in Tigger's room because he put it here for safekeeping." She watched the expression on Jack's face shift from curiosity to concern to fear.

"What is it?" Anne whispered. Without uttering a word, he handed her the piece of paper. His face was ashen. Anne scanned the paper quickly. It was an anonymous note, all right, but one that was dated twenty years ago. The paper on which it was printed was faded with age. Instead of being handwritten, the message itself was composed in fanciful, old-fashioned Gothic type, like a printed handbill:

Dear Tigger:

I am writing to you because I have a business proposition. On the night of July 4, I would like you to come to the back entrance of the Spray View Hotel at precisely nine o'clock. Look in the green garbage can next to the back stairwell. There you will find a paper bag containing a firecracker and a book of matches. The kitchen door will be unlocked. Enter the hotel and proceed to the back parlor. Light the firecrackers in the parlor, then leave the same way you came. The hotel itself will be empty, so there is no chance of anyone getting hurt.

Enclosed is $50. If you agree to carry out this plan, you'll find another $500 taped beneath the fourth bench on the north side of Fisherman's Pier. The money will be there by daybreak on the fifth of July. If you show this note to anyone or share its contents in any way, the deal is off.

You always seem ready for adventure and I hope you'll go along with this harmless little prank.

From,
A Friend

Anne read the letter twice. When she finished, she folded it up again and handed it back to Jack. "Could this be for real?" he asked softly. He sounds tired. The dark suit he had worn to the funeral gave him a somber air.

"It looks authentic, like it was written around the time of the fire." There was something else about the letter, something familiar about it, although she didn't know what.

"You read the newspaper clippings," Jack said, staring at the letter as if it were alive. "What caused the fire?"

"There was some sort of explosion," Anne said.

"An explosion," Jack repeated.

"It sounds like whoever wrote the letter was pretty familiar with the Spray View."

"I bet Ed Klemperer knew the hotel inside and out," Jack said. "Maybe he sent Tigger the letter and left him the firecrackers. That way, old Ed could collect on the insurance policy."

"What about Ruthie?"

"You heard what Sandy Cooksey said. Ruthie wasn't supposed to be anywhere near the Spray View. Nobody was." He stopped, turning the letter over in his hands. "Either way, this looks pretty bad."

"It doesn't prove Tigger set off a firecracker. If the letter is genuine, all it means is that someone other than Tigger wanted to damage the hotel."

Jack ran his hands through his hair. "Why wouldn't Tigger have turned this over to the cops? Why'd he hold on to it for so long?"

"The police believed he was guilty and so did everyone else in town. This letter just proves them right. But your second question is the one that bothers me. Tigger felt the letter was valuable enough to lock up in a vault. I wonder why he kept it all these years."

"I don't know anything anymore, Anne. What if Bobby was right and Tigger did start the fire after all?" It took a moment for Anne to let this possibility sink in. Could it be that she and Jack had been wrestling with shadows, twisting history to fit their own needs when the truth was somewhere else entirely? "Let me see it again," she said, taking the letter and rereading it. *You always seem ready for adventure and I hope you'll go along with this harmless little prank.*

"That's the phrase Bobby Curley used," Anne said suddenly.

"What?"

"When we were talking to him during the concert. He told us Tigger set the fire as a 'harmless little prank.' "

"You think it's a coincidence?"

"I'm not sure." She sat down at the desk. She was wearing her good black dress and black high-heeled shoes. Her feet ached. She slipped the shoes off and buried her bare toes in the thick pile carpet.

"I'm all mixed up, Anne. If this letter is authentic, it means Tigger lied about not being there that night. Maybe Bobby *was* telling the truth. About the fire, about the missing money. Teri was positive that Tigger broke into their house, right?"

"Yeah. She seemed pretty indignant about the whole thing. In fact, she wants us to give the money back. But that still doesn't explain why she acted so chummy to Tigger when we saw her on the beach the other day. I know Teri. She's not the forgiving type.''

''How'd she explain it?''

''Oh, she said she was being nice because she wanted to borrow Tigger's varsity letter from the swim team.''

A puzzled expression appeared on Jack's face. ''His what?''

''His varsity letter—to include with some other stuff she's been collecting for our reunion next year.''

''Tigger never got a varsity letter,'' Jack said slowly. ''The school doesn't award them until senior year and Tigger left the summer before his senior year started.''

Anne thought back to the other afternoon on the beach. ''But he said he had it. Teri offered to buy it from him, and Tigger told her you can't put a price on memories.''

''I don't understand.''

''Neither do I. Teri isn't nice to anyone unless there's something in it for her. She must have wanted something from him.''

''That doesn't explain my brother's friendliness. I mean, she and Bobby accused him of breaking and entering, messing up their house, robbing them. Why didn't he tell her to go to hell?''

Anne's head ached. Each new bit of information they unearthed only led to more questions. ''Let's get out of here,'' she said. Jack put the letter in the breast pocket of his jacket and rang the buzzer for the guard.

Outside the bank, it was still sweltering hot. Heat rose from the pavement in waves. There was no breeze at all and the air was heavy. Anne felt like it was an effort to move, as if the heat was pressing down on her. The leather on the seat of Jack's car scorched her bare legs. They drove down Route 35, stopping at Jean's Sandwich Shack for cheese steaks and Diet Cokes. Anne took two bites of hers and pushed it away. It was too hot to eat. Grease from the sandwiches stained the wax paper wrapping.

She watched Jack pick at his cheese steak and was struck by how cool he looked, how untouched by the heat. He'd removed his suit jacket, and his white cotton shirt was crisp and fresh, his cuffs neatly pressed. Although he didn't seem to realize it, his presence in Jean's Sandwich Shack had not gone unnoticed. Two teenage girls at the next table were mooning over him, giggling and staring so much they'd barely touched their food. When the waitress brought the check she leaned into him, brushing his arm with her wrist. "Will there be anything else?" she said hopefully.

"Want any coffee, Anne?" Jack said.

"No thanks."

"Then I think we're finished," he said, taking out his wallet.

After the waitress moved away, he scraped back his chair, then stopped. "I feel like I'm losing it," he said abruptly.

She looked at him. "You're allowed to lose it once in a while."

"Not in my family. If you let your guard down for a second, you're through."

"What do you mean?"

"Living with an alcoholic, you're always holding your breath. Waiting for something bad to happen." His eyes were trained on her face. "Usually, you don't have to wait too long."

"Jack, this has been a nightmare for you. Give yourself a break."

He leaned back in his chair. "I can't."

"Why?"

"Because I feel like it's my fault."

"What are you talking about?"

"If I were here, I could have saved him."

"You don't know that."

He got up and dumped the remainder of their meal in the trash. Anne followed him outside to the Corvette. When he reached the car, he walked around to the passenger side and held the door open for her. But instead of getting in, she reached up and put her arms around him. "We're going to get through this," she said softly.

He hugged her close. She could feel his heart beating

against her chest. "I hope to God you're right," he said, releasing her. He put his sunglasses on. She couldn't tell what he was thinking. "How about I drop you off at home?" He walked around to the driver's side. "I want to go back to Ravenswood and change out of this suit."

She felt lightheaded from the contact. Her body was trembling.

"Sure," she said, trying to sound calm. "Would you mind if we run an errand on the way? My friend Helen lives over on Crestwood. Could you go by her house? I want to see if she's home yet."

"All right."

It was a short trip back to town. The traffic leading out of the Heights was bumper to bumper. Everyone seemed to be leaving the beach at the exact same time. But the road was completely clear in the opposite direction, and the Corvette cruised down Main Street, past the line of cars snaking away from the ocean.

Helen Passelbessy was in her front yard, watering her impatiens. "Hey." She waved when she spotted Anne in the passenger seat. She walked over to the car, the hose trailing behind her.

"Did you find out anything?" Anne said.

"Yup," Helen answered, pushing her prematurely gray hair behind her ear. "You must be Jack," she said.

"Hi there," he said.

"I was sorry to hear about your brother," Helen said.

"Thanks."

Helen leaned in close to the car, bending her tall frame toward them. She lowered her voice. "I looked up those checks in the computer like you wanted," she said to Anne.

"And . . . ?"

"P.J. McGrath received two payments in the last week. One check in the amount of $10,000. The other for $15,000."

"From his aunt?" Jack asked.

Helen shook her head. "You're going to be surprised. I know I was." She paused, simulated a drum roll on the side of the car. "The checks," she announced, "were made out to P.J. from Mrs. Robert Curley."

Chapter 15

To clean your TV screen, moisten a sheet with rubbing alcohol and wipe the surface. Never use spray! The oil and water could go into parts where they shouldn't be.

In the summertime, darkness settled over Oceanside Heights in stages. The sky turned dusky pink, then blue-violet, until the remaining light bleached away entirely, folding into the ocean. Anne and Jack watched the light disappear just as the street lamps went on outside P.J. McGrath's house. They'd been sitting in Jack's car for hours with the headlights off, waiting for P.J. to come home.

The house was up on a hill. From the car, Anne could see the entire square-mile town, spread out before her like a Victorian postcard—the nineteenth-century cottages, the quaint shops on Main Street, the curved wrought-iron street lamps, the white cross atop the Church by the Sea.

"What if he doesn't show?" Jacks said, glancing at the clock on the dashboard, which blinked 9:04 P.M.

160

"He has to come home sometime."

Cold air streamed from the air-conditioner, blowing on Anne's face and neck. It felt good against her skin. She could sit in this car all night, insulated from the town and the people in it. From here, the Heights looked so much smaller, insignificant almost. She could be anywhere.

"Let's go over it again," Jack said.

They'd been trading theories about P.J.'s riches ever since Helen told them Teri had written the checks. "She just doesn't strike me as the silent partner type," Anne said, "unless we're talking about some upscale women's clothing shop or a trendy little antique store." Stretching her legs, Anne smoothed out the folds of her green cotton sun dress. She'd never done undercover work before. If she'd known there'd be so much sitting involved, she would have worn something wrinkle-proof.

"So you don't see Teri investing in a sweaty, smelly boxing gym," Jack said with a grin.

"Absolutely not."

"What about Bobby?"

"If Bobby was backing the gym, why wasn't *his* name on the checks? For that matter, with Bobby's money behind him, P.J. wouldn't have had to make up a phony story about inheriting money from a long-lost aunt."

Jack's eyes were fastened on Anne. "Maybe P.J. didn't want the gym to be associated with Bobby. That guy at Cloister Construction had me convinced there's something shady about Bobby's business."

"Maybe so. But as far as we know, Bobby hasn't done anything illegal. He and P.J. are friends. It's perfectly natural they'd be partners."

"And if that were the case, Bobby would have written the checks, like you said. We're back to square one."

"How about square two?"

"Aahhh. The blackmail theory?" Jack's teeth gleamed in the darkness as he smiled. In his faded blue jeans and white T-shirt, he looked more relaxed than Anne had seen him all day. He smelled nice, like fresh pine needles.

"It's the only thing that makes sense, if you think about

it," she told him. "P.J. lied about the money because he has something to hide—and what he's hiding is that Teri gave him the money in the first place."

"Now for the $25,000 question—why?"

"My guess is it has something to do with Tigger. Teri and P.J. have lived in this town all their lives, but he waits till Tigger comes back to hit her up for money. Whatever P.J.'s got on her, he couldn't have had it for very long."

Jack drummed his fingers against the steering wheel. "Maybe when we find out what he's holding over her head it'll help explain why Tigger died."

Anne recalled the bruises on Heather Vance's body. Could P.J. have turned his fists on Tigger as easily as he did on Heather? Anne suspected P.J. was the type of man to start swinging first and ask questions later.

She heard Jack take a deep breath and exhale through his mouth. "Are you okay?" she said, not bothering to keep the concern out of her voice.

Jack turned toward her. When his hand gripped her forearm she felt a tingling sensation shoot through her body. "I just need to know the truth, Anne. About the fire. About the letter we found in the vault. About why Tigger drowned. About everything." He looked at her closely. "Are you cold? I've got a jacket in the back."

"No. I'm fine." Her cheeks were flushed. She had suddenly become conscious of how close they were sitting to each other, aware of the snug fit of his jeans. For the past few days, she'd thought of Jack as her partner in a murder investigation. Now she realized she was becoming attracted to him. He was so sure of himself, so unlike most men in the Heights, whose lives seemed narrow and sheltered. He'd traveled all over the world, seen unusual things. She glanced at his profile, at his high cheekbones, the fullness of his lips. He was good-looking in a casual, offhand way; he acted like he didn't even know how handsome he was. One kiss from those lips could probably inspire a woman to think she was in love with him. Oh, snap out of it, she told herself. This wasn't about her and Jack. It was about finding out what happened to Tigger.

She cleared her throat. "Tell me how you got interested in architecture."

"You really want to know?"

"Sure." In a few days he would be gone and her life would be back to normal.

"It started with pick-up sticks."

"Huh?"

"That game everyone played when we were kids, remember? You had to pick up the colored plastic sticks without toppling the whole pile."

"Oh, yeah. I remember."

"I loved those sticks," Jack said, smiling at the memory. "I used to play with them for hours at a time. I guess it got me thinking about how buildings are constructed, the parts you don't see from the outside. At Princeton, there were all these wonderful buildings on campus—churches and old-fashioned-looking dormitories and big brick houses with white pillars and ivy skirting the walls. I wanted to know who built them, why they looked the way they did. Architecture kind of grabbed hold of me like nothing had before. When I look at a historic old building, it's like looking at a map of the past."

"You make it sound like a mystery."

"I guess it is, in a way," Jack said. "The frame of a building, the way the ceiling and floors are constructed, is kind of like a skeleton, and the bones are what make the exterior beautiful."

"That's what I love best about the Heights," Anne said. She gazed out the window at the Victorian houses, with their turrets and gingerbread trim. At night, the town took on even more of a storybook quality; it looked like an enchanted village in a fairy tale. "The houses are so pretty, almost like big dollhouses sitting on the edge of the ocean. Sometimes I think it's the most beautiful place in the world."

"I know what you mean. It's ironic that we have some of the most stunning architecture on the entire East Coast and I leave it behind for New York City, modernism central. Although there is something to be said for urban—"

Jack stopped talking abruptly. A black jeep was pulling into the driveway of P.J. McGrath's house. A man got out of the jeep. He was wearing a black leather jacket and black jeans and carrying a large gym bag. He went up the front walk, bobbing slightly on the balls of his feet. In high school, Anne remembered, the movement was known as the "hood walk." P.J. McGrath still moved as if he were playing a bit part in a Jimmy Cagney movie. She watched as P.J. checked his mail, unlocked the front door, and went inside the house.

"Let's give him ten minutes," Jack said, "so he doesn't suspect we were staking the place out."

"All right." When the clock on the dashboard hit 9:28 P.M., they got out of the car. There was a small garden on P.J.'s front lawn filled with hydrangeas and roses. Window boxes brimmed with petunias and geraniums. Anne would never have thought he'd be interested in gardening. He didn't seem like the type.

"Jack Mills," P.J. exclaimed when he saw who was on his doorstep. He was short and stocky, with a massive chest and huge biceps that always reminded Anne of Popeye, post-spinach. He had taken off his jacket and wore a red T-shirt with *P.J.'s Boxing Palace* in big black letters on the front. "Long time no see," he said to Jack.

"Hey, P.J. You haven't returned my calls."

"I been busy, man. Hiya, Anne," he said. "Whaddya guys want?"

"I heard about your gym," Jack said, pointing to P.J.'s shirt. "Can we come in for a few minutes?"

P.J. leaned against the door. "I was watching the ball game. Jesus, the Phils stink! They got no pitching whatsoever."

"Who they playing tonight? The Mets?" Jack asked.

"Nah. The Cardinals."

"Well, this'll only take a minute," Jack said, with a smile.

"Sure, sure. Come on in," P.J. said, walking back inside. "You want a beer or something?"

"Okay," Jack called. He and Anne went into the living

room where the baseball game was playing on television. Like Anne, P.J. had lived in the Heights his entire life. She'd heard he inherited the house from his parents when they retired to Florida a few years ago. The living room, with its plaid couch and kidney-shaped cocktail table looked like it hadn't been redecorated since the 1950s. Fake wood paneling covered the walls. The shag carpeting on the floor was the same golden tan color as the furniture.

When P.J. returned he was carrying two cans of Budweiser. "Help yourself to some chips," he told them, sprawling out in a reclining chair.

"Thanks," Jack said. He sat down on the sofa, opposite the television set. Anne sat next to him, putting the Budweiser on the table. The top of the aluminum can was covered with a grimy film of dirt.

"Sorry I couldn't make the funeral," P.J. said to Jack. "I was down in Atlantic City today, finalizing a couple of things for the gym. It's gonna be awesome when it's finished. We're gonna get some real big names to train here, major talent."

On the TV screen, the Astroturf covering the baseball diamond was purplish-brown. The picture was so blurred it looks like there were two pitchers on the mound and two men standing behind the plate. "P.J.," Jack began, "you saw Tigger when he came back to town."

"Sure. We had a couple of beers, talked about old times."

"He hit you up for money?"

P.J. tilted his head back and chugged at his beer. Anne could see his Adam's apple moving up and down. When they were in school together, P.J. was one of her biggest tormentors. He used to follow her down the hall, spewing a string of nasty words describing various parts of her mother's anatomy.

"Nah. He had enough cash. He was doing all right, except for the booze."

"You must have been pretty mad at him, no?" Jack said.

P.J. looked up. On TV, the man behind the plate swung and missed. "Whaddya mean?"

"When you found out about him and Heather," Jack said.

P.J.'s eyes narrowed. "Heather's a tramp," he said. "I should've thanked Tigger for clueing me in to what the bitch was up to."

"He *told* you they were having an affair?"

P.J. hesitated. "Not exactly. But Heather's not good at hiding things from me. Her mouth is as big as her cunt. Excuse my French," he said, with a nod in Anne's direction.

She smiled weakly. P.J. reminded her of a ferret that her fourth-grade science class kept as a pet. The animal was slippery and mean-looking, with sharp, pointy teeth. But he allowed the kids to stroke him, tolerating their attention and fumbling caresses. Their teacher, Mrs. Adler, kept insisting that ferrets got a bad rap; they were just as lovable as mice or rabbits, Mrs. Adler used to say, until the day she took the ferret out of its cage, and he bit her on the wrist, drawing blood.

"Heather's really upset that the two of you broke up," Anne said. "I think she'd like to get back together."

"That's life," P.J. said, turning his attention back to the game. "Jesus, the Phils can't buy a break."

"We might as well tell him the *real* reason we're here," Anne said to Jack.

"Sure," Jack replied, shooting her a puzzled look. "Go ahead."

"P.J.," Anne said, "Teri Curley is a close friend of mine."

P.J. stared at the television set, where two infielders were diving for a ground ball. "That so?"

"Yes. She wanted to come herself tonight, but she wasn't sure how you'd react."

"React to what?"

"To what she asked me to tell you. This is difficult for Teri. She's not used to being put in this position."

P.J. scratched his stomach. "I don't catch your drift."

"Teri is very . . . upset with how things are going."

"Upset?" P.J. echoed.

"Yes."

"In fact, she's had just about enough." Anne took a deep breath and plunged ahead. "She told me to tell you she's not giving you one more dime."

P.J. looked at Anne. His eyes were hooded. His body seemed to have tightened. The muscles in his arms flexed and contracted. "Is that right?" he said mockingly.

"That's what she sent me here to say. Yes."

P.J.'s lips parted in a half-smile. "I don't think Teri's calling the shots. If she's got a problem, you tell her to come talk to me herself."

"That's just it," Anne persisted. "She's through talking. She gave you the twenty-five grand, and that's it. If you don't stop harassing her, she's going straight to the police."

P.J. hit the mute button on the TV. "Now why would she want to go and do a thing like that?" he said. His voice had an edge to it.

"Because she's tired of being blackmailed," Anne said quietly.

"Who said anything about blackmail?" P.J. retorted.

"If you'd gotten the money in cash, it'd be one thing," Anne continued. "But the two checks can be traced. There are bank records."

P.J. sprang to his feet. He was fast, Anne thought. In a boxing ring, fast would be useful.

"I think Teri's forgetting something," P.J. said. He walked over to the fake wood entertainment center that housed the TV set. Opening a cabinet door, he pulled out a black videotape and waved it in the air. "Don't think this is the only one. I made copies."

So that was what P.J. had on Teri. What could it contain? The answer rushed back at Anne with such force and clarity, she knew she should have seen it before. Sex. That's what P.J. had captured on tape. Teri and Tigger making passionate love to each other, as adults this time, maybe in Teri's house. Yes, it would have had to have been there, on pink satin sheets, or pink high-pile carpet, or against the pink tile floor, everything pink, their bodies rosy with desire.

P.J. smacked the tape against his thigh. "Teri's a bitch, but she's not stupid," he said. "Am I right, Jack?"

Jack glanced at Anne. His look betrayed what he was thinking. Whatever was on that tape, it must have been damaging enough to make Teri scramble for her checkbook. "Teri's upset," Jack said carefully. "I think she means business about the police."

P.J.'s jaw was set. He ran his finger along the edge of the tape, caressing the plastic.

"Teri is thinking about telling Bobby," Anne said suddenly. She tried to make her voice sound authoritative. "They say confession is good for the soul."

"The princess doesn't own a soul," P.J. said.

"She realized how angry Bobby would be if he knew you were blackmailing her," Anne continued. "So she asked us to speak to you first. Before this goes any further."

"Like I told you before," P.J. said harshly, "Teri's not the one giving orders here."

Anne made one last stab at convincing him. "Teri's an influential person in this town," she said hurriedly. "She's got friends on the force, and they've assured her they'll press charges against you. Blackmail is a federal offense, punishable by fifteen to twenty years in prison."

"She thinks she can threaten me?" P.J. yelled. He slammed the tape angrily into the VCR. "Tell her to think again."

On the television set, the baseball game disappeared. Anne tensed, dreading what she was about to watch. But instead of Teri and Tigger's writhing nude bodies, what appeared on the screen was P.J. McGrath, P.J. here in this room, on the ratty plaid couch. The camera pulled back slightly. She heard Jack gasp. Sitting next to P.J. on the couch was Tigger, dressed as he was when she first talked to him on the boardwalk, in a white T-shirt and jeans. P.J. had on a gray undershirt and a pair of sweatpants. A bunch of bottles littered the wood coffee table in front of the couch. Wine, beer, Jack Daniel's, a bottle of something dark. From the way the men were moving, sloppily, frenetic, gesturing wildly with their hands, she could tell they were drunk. P.J. grabbed the remote control and Tigger's voice floated through the room.

"... didn't know what to do," Tigger was saying.

"Oh, man," the onscreen P.J. said. "Man, I wish I'd been there."

"I told her I couldn't go through with it," Tigger said. "But she wouldn't listen." His voice was unsteady, his speech slightly slurred. Anne glanced at Jack. But Jack's eyes were riveted to the screen.

"Why didn't you tell her to get the hell out of there?" P.J. said to Tigger.

"I tried. I wanted to. She wouldn't go." Hearing Tigger's voice sent goose bumps up and down Anne's arms. "She grabbed it and lit it up before I could stop her," Tigger said. "There were all these sparks. I remember. Red sparks. The firecracker. Flared up so fast." His voice hurried to get the words out. "She grabbed my hand and we ran. We ran and ran and then there was this big ..." Tigger's hands flew up. "Whoosh. A noise like something popped. And bright light. There was so much fire. Everywhere."

"It was Teri all along," P.J. said excitedly. "Teri started the fire."

Tigger wagged his head. "She begged me not to tell. She had no idea the kid was inside ..."

Anne watched P.J. smile on the screen. Even then, he must have realized how much this tape was worth, how much Teri would pay to keep the past quiet.

P.J. flicked the remote and Tigger vanished. After a second, the baseball game reappeared. "There's more," P.J. said. "But you get the gist. Teri was a bad girl. And now, she's got to pay for her sins."

"I don't think that tape's going to hold up in court," Anne said.

"Wrong," P.J. retorted. "I got me a lawyer friend, and he told me the statute of limitations hasn't expired on the little kid's death. So Teri's looking at involuntary manslaughter. You tell her to check it out herself if she doesn't believe me. If her next payment is even one day late, I'm dropping this baby off at the sheriff's office.''

''Did my brother know you were taping him?'' Jack said suddenly. His voice sounded hollow.

''Hell, no,'' P.J. said. ''The videocam was a birthday present from Heather. I was just testing it out to see if it worked. I figured me and Tigger could laugh about it later on. But the laugh's on Teri, don't ya think?'' P.J. smiled, baring his teeth. Anne thought of the ferret again. Some of the kids cried when they took the animal away. Mrs. Adler had to get a tetanus shot. ''You tell Teri no more checks. I want the whole amount in cash first thing Monday. Got it?''

On TV, the man behind the plate swung at strike three. The inning was over.

''My mother could've hit that out of the park,'' P.J. complained, settling back in his chair. ''I don't know why the hell I bother. The Phillies suck.''

Chapter 16

*Nobody ever died
from a little bit of dust.*

Jack's car careened through the Heights. He was in such a hurry to get to the Curleys that he barely braked at stop signs. "Deep down, I knew it," Jack said triumphantly. "I knew Tigger didn't do it—and now we have proof."

"You mean P.J. has proof." Anne was still focusing on the tape. Teri lit the firecracker! Whether she intended to or not, the preppy prom queen had destroyed an entire family, not to mention the price Tigger had to pay. All these years, Teri had sat back and watched everyone in town blame her high school sweetheart for a crime she knew she'd committed.

"Remind me never to play poker with you," Jack joked.

"Are you kidding? At first, P.J. and I weren't even in the same game. I thought he'd caught her cheating on Bobby."

"What!"

"It was the video camera. I figured he snuck into Teri's house, planted it somewhere, and captured her rolling around in the sheets with someone who wasn't Bobby." Like your brother, she added silently.

"You've got a great imagination."

"I'm just glad P.J. didn't know I was bluffing. I kept expecting him to get up and call Teri. That would have ruined everything!"

The Corvette pulled up in front of Teri and Bobby's house. All the lights were out, the driveway was empty. "Where are they?" Jack said, staring at the darkened house. "Oh, God. Do you think P.J. called her just now and tipped her off? She could be miles away from here."

"It takes Teri more than five minutes to pack," Anne said ruefully. "No. He looked pretty smug when we left. He thinks he's got Teri right where he wants her."

"But if she knows *we* know about the fire . . ."

"She won't be a happy camper," Anne finished.

"You know what I don't understand?"

"What?"

"Why Tigger never told the cops she did it in the first place."

"They had this code of honor back then. Maybe he felt he had to protect her." She thought back to the nights she looked out her bedroom window and saw Teri and Tigger making out under the glow of the street lamps. "I think he was probably in love with her."

"But his whole life went down the toilet after that night. He never got over it."

"I know." In her mind, Anne pictured the scene on the beach the other day, when Teri came over to where she and Tigger were sitting. He didn't seem angry or upset with her, like a man who'd been nursing a grudge for twenty years. He was pleasant, cordial even. She recreated Tigger's easy manner, the relaxed tone of his voice. It seemed like he was in control.

"Jack, are you positive that Tigger never received a varsity letter for being on the swim team?"

"Yeah. He was upset about it, too. Especially since he was the strongest swimmer on the squad."

"But when Teri asked him about it," Anne said slowly, "Tigger made it seem like he had the letter, but didn't want to part with it. It's like they were talking in code, for my benefit.''

''What do you mean?''

Anne went over it again in her head. She and Jack still hadn't found the death threat Tigger said he'd received. Could it have come from Teri? It didn't seem like her style. And if she *did* send it, why in the world would she tell him she did and ask him to give it back? Anne's mind wandered back to that afternoon on the beach.

You have something I want, Teri had said.

Is that right?

You remember that old letter you were awarded, the varsity one, from when you were on the swim team?

She could see Teri, in her revealing white bathing suit, her lips parted slightly. The cat who ate the canary. Or was it the other way around?

You have something I want.

Of course. What else could it be?

''The 'letter' she wanted wasn't from the swim team,'' Anne said excitedly. ''It was a *real* letter. The one we found in the vault.''

Jack looked puzzled. ''I'm not following you.''

''I think the reason Tigger put the letter from 'A Friend' in a safe deposit box is that he hadn't had it very long. My guess is he stole it from Teri when he broke into her house last Sunday night. When she came up to us on the beach, it was to let him know she wanted it back. She even offered to pay him for the letter, but he wasn't interested.''

''But why would the letter have been valuable? And what was Teri doing with it?''

''For one thing,'' Anne said, ''it's addressed to Tigger, not to Teri. So if Tigger ever decided to come forward and tell the police his ex-girlfriend was the one who set off the firecracker, the letter might be helpful to her. It proves that Tigger was the one who was hired to damage the Spray View. She wasn't even supposed to be there.''

''That still doesn't explain how she got hold of it.''

''But it does explain the whole burglary business. Teri kept saying that Tigger turned their house upside down when he broke in. I think he made a mess because he was searching for the letter.''

''Why would he wait so long to get it back?''

''I don't know.''

Jack scanned Anne's face. ''And what about the $3,000 in the Bible? Did Tigger pocket the money while he was searching the house? Did she plant the money in his room so he'd look bad? What?''

''I have a feeling when Teri shows up we're going to get some answers.''

''You know, when we took the letter out of the vault, I wished I'd never set eyes on it. But now I'm glad we found it, especially if it'll make Teri squirm.''

''Just think. If the old lady next door hadn't seen Tigger hide the key, we'd never even know the letter existed. Secrets upon secrets.''

They sat in silence for a moment. The street lamps cast shadows on the roses in Teri's garden. From inside the car, they looked like bony fingers clawing at the ground.

''Could Teri have killed him?'' Jack said suddenly.

''Well, she's got a boat. And she was probably out on the ocean the night of July Fourth, with half the other people in town.'' Anne reached for the knob on the air conditioner and turned the setting up a little higher. ''I know Teri. I grew up with her. She doesn't like it when her plans are disturbed. Tigger's return must have shaken her up pretty badly.''

A full moon had risen over the Heights, a milky oval face pasted against the black sky. It reminded Anne of a storybook moon, larger than life, perfect.

''I wonder how much Bobby knows,'' Jack said. ''He's been acting weird, like he's hiding something, too.''

''Maybe he knew Teri set the fire all along.''

''Then why is he in the dark about P.J.'s blackmailing scheme?''

Questions upon questions. The more they found out, the more there was to uncover. She looked out the window to see a woman emerging from the house next door to the Curleys, holding a leash attached to a large St. Bernard.

Anne rolled down her window. "Mrs. Granville," she called.

The gray-haired woman stopped, then limped toward the car. "Who's there?" she said.

"It's Anne Hardaway."

The gray-haired woman wrinkled her nose. "Oh," she said, peering into the car. "You startled me."

"I dropped by to visit Teri. But she's not home. Do you know where she went?"

"It's awful late," Eleanor Granville said. She jerked on the dog's leash and the animal let out a mournful yelp. "I was watching your car from my window. Couldn't figure out what you were up to."

"I'm on one of the committees for the Philadelphia Flower Show," Anne explained. "And Teri wanted me to drop by and look at some pictures she'd taken of her roses."

"Who's that with you?" Mrs. Granville said suspiciously.

"Hello, ma'am," Jack called out. "I'm Jack Mills. Troy's son."

"Teri's not home now." The St. Bernard lifted his leg and peed against Jack's front tire. Mrs. Granville didn't appear to notice.

"Do you have any idea when she'll be back?" Anne said sweetly. "I really need to talk to her about the flower show. There's a deadline for submissions."

"They'll be home tomorrow, I guess."

"Is there any way I could get in touch with her by phone?"

"I don't see how. Not unless you know which hotel they're staying in. They took the girls down to Atlantic City to see Barry Manilow at the Sands. I guess they decided to stay overnight."

"All right," Anne said. "I'll swing by tomorrow then."

Mrs. Granville peered into the car again. "Why don't you leave a note next time, instead of sitting out here with your motor running? We have a neighborhood watch on this block. In another minute, I'd have called the police."

"A neighborhood watch?" Jack repeated.

"Because of the young hooligans from Landsdown. I thought that's who you were—making some sort of drug deal. We can't take any chances around here."

"I'm sorry we scared you," Anne said. "Have a good night." She rolled up the window. Jack started the car.

"She's a strange old bat," he said.

In the rearview mirror, Anne could see Mrs. Granville standing in the middle of the street, watching the car drive away. "I'm surprised she didn't go ahead and call the cops. She doesn't like me much."

"Why's that?"

"Oh, a lot of people in the Heights seem to feel I'm a little . . . touched."

"Touched?"

"That's their word for crazy. Like mother, like daughter, if you know what I mean."

"Nice," Jack said sarcastically.

"Not everybody's like that. Helen certainly isn't. Neither is Delia Graustark. Or Jim Walser."

"What do the others think? That you're going to develop Alzheimer's, too? For one thing, you're too young. Plus, your mother's disease has absolutely nothing to do with you."

"Some people don't see it that way," Anne said quietly.

"Then they're stupid. Where to next?" he said, changing the subject.

"Well, we could drive down to Atlantic City, check out the Sands."

"I know a quicker way." He picked up his car phone, called information, and dialed the number of the Sands. After a quick conversation, he hung up. "They're not registered there," he said to Anne. "You want to try some of the other big hotels?"

Anne got on the phone and started calling around. She checked the Taj Mahal, Bally's, Caesars, the Claridge, and a half-dozen other resorts, but no luck. The Curleys weren't staying at any of them.

Jack said, "I guess we're going to have to wait until tomorrow to confront her."

"What if P.J. beats us to the punch and leaves a message on her answering machine?"

"Saying what? *Head for the hills. I've held a private screening of the tape and you're cooked*? Nope. She's got to come home sooner or later. In fact, if P.J. does leave a message, it'll probably bring her back pronto, to chew you out."

Anne thought about that for a moment. It made sense. When Teri found out what Anne had done she'd be furious.

"In the meantime, how about if we grab something to eat," Jack said. "I'm starving."

"Sounds good. But we'll have to go to Bradley Beach. All the restaurants in town should be closing soon."

"Is the Blue Marlin still in business? They have the best Jamaican jerk chicken I've ever tasted."

"Sounds great." She settled back against the leather seat. "Could I check my messages from here?"

"Sure."

Anne picked up the car phone, dialed her number, and punched in the code. Mary Lou Popper's flat nasal whine filled the car. The Queen of Clean sounded like she was reading a prepared speech, a litany of complains about Anne's work habits—her tardiness, her arguments, her gall in challenging the opinion of a renowned expert. Anne jabbed at the buttons, trying to turn off the speaker phone. "If you don't fax me chapter five by Monday, I'm calling Triple Star and having you removed from this project," Mary Lou intoned. "There are lots of writers out there who would kill to work with me."

"Like fun," Anne muttered.

After the beep, there was a raspy voice. "Anne Hardaway? Are you home?" It was noisy on the other end of the line, horns honking, a steady roar. "This is Sandy. I have something for you and your friend, something Tigger gave me." The background noise swelled. It sounded like waves smacking the shoreline. "Meet me on Fisherman's Pier at ten o'clock tonight. And bring money. It'll cost you five hundred bucks, if you're interested.'' There was a click, then the low hum of a dial tone. Sandy must have called from a pay phone.

Jack made a quick U-turn. The clock on the dashboard read 10:35. ''It's five minutes fast,'' he said. ''Maybe she waited.''

''What about the money?'' Anne said.

''Let's hope she accepts checks.''

The Corvette speeded back toward Landsdown, along Ocean Avenue. The beach was deserted. Unlike other towns along the Jersey shore, the wooden gates separating the boardwalk from the sand were locked every evening at seven-thirty. The rule was designed to keep the beach free from ''unsupervised activities''—volleyball, swimming, toasting marshmallows. Anne knew if she was driving by the ocean in any other shore town on a Saturday night, she'd see people lounging on blankets and beach chairs by the water's edge, trying to keep cool. But not here.

She spotted Fisherman's Pier up ahead. The oldest of the town's three piers, it was situated near the footbridge separating the Heights from Landsdown. It had almost been destroyed several times, most recently during last winter's blizzard, when sixteen-foot waves lashed the wood pilings and tumbled over the benches lining the rails. But the pier had survived, a testament to its nineteenth-century builders who wanted a place where gentlemen could fish undisturbed.

Jack parked next to the boardwalk. Because of its proximity to Landsdown's notorious drug hangouts, just over the bridge, Fisherman's Pier was usually empty after dark. Tonight, a solitary couple occupied one of the benches beneath the curved wrought-iron lamps. Entwined in each other's arms, their mouths plastered together, the couple were still as statues, oblivious to everything but each other. Probably high school kids, Anne thought. When love was new it was so pure and clean. So trusting. As Anne walked past them, she could almost smell their pleasure, a mixture of sea air, beach grass, and salt, which for her would always be associated with sex and summer nights.

From the pier, she had a great view of the deserted Dreamland amusement park and in the distance, the ramshackle houses of Landsdown. The lights on the shoreline glistened. Gulls circled overhead, wheeling and keening. "We're too late," Jack said. "Sandy's gone."

They had almost reached the end of the pier, near the small wooden shack where fishermen kept poles and tackle boxes.

"Maybe she's waiting for us in there," Anne said. She went up to the door of the shack, pushed it open. It was dark inside and smelled of fish. Fishing equipment was strewn all around—nets, poles, jars of old bait.

"It's empty," she said, pulling the door shut.

Jack walked over to the wooden railing and looked out over the water. The moon hung in the sky like a jeweled pendant, illuminating the boats, the white foam on the waves. "We used to sit out here and fish off the pier," Jack said slowly. "He would tell me stories about all the wonderful things ahead of us." Anne went over to the railing. She pictured Jack and Tigger as boys, sitting at the end of the pier, swinging their legs and dangling their fishing poles in the ocean.

"He had so many plans, so many schemes about what he'd do when we were finally grown up," Jack continued. "Sometimes we'd sit out here and count the whitecaps on the waves. God, he had so many dreams. He was going to dive in the Olympics and sail to Timbuktu." Jack laughed. "We didn't know where Timbuktu was. But it sure sounded good."

"Hey, Jack, how come everyone called him Tigger? In your family tree, it says his real name was Theodore."

"Yup. He hated it. So Ma nicknamed him Tigger after the tiger in *Winnie the Pooh*. He was always getting into scrapes, just like the character in the book."

Jack fell silent. He looked out over the ocean, at the moon shining on the black water. There was a brooding, thoughtful expression on his face. The only sound was the slap of the waves against the rocks below and the high-pitched cry of the gulls.

"Jack," she said hesitantly.

"Yeah."

"How long did it take to put everything behind you?"

"What do you mean?" he said, turning. His eyes were a deep steely blue.

"After you moved away from here. Was it like you were never here at all?"

He leaned his arms against the railing. "For a while, I guess. New York is such a big anonymous place. People don't care where you're from or who you were before you got there. After about ten minutes, you're as much a New Yorker as the next guy."

Anne tried to imagine what that would be like, to reinvent herself in one stroke, severing the past, like a dead limb that had lost all feeling. Nobody would know her as the Crazy Lady's daughter. Nobody would know anything about her at all, unless she chose to tell them. The thought made her giddy with longing.

"Are you thinking about leaving?" Jack asked.

From the pier, she could see all the way down Ocean Avenue. The big yellow house stood at the other end of town, silent and dark. "I don't know if I can. I made a promise . . ."

The wind had picked up. Her long red hair whipped forward. Jack reached down and brushed the strands away from her face. She looked at him questioningly. He let go of her hair. His arms slid around her waist, pulling her closer. His body was hard and lean. Stroking the back of her neck, he kissed her lightly on the mouth.

"I've been wanting to do that since I met you," he whispered.

Had she been wanting it, too? She didn't know. "You're the only one around here who understands," he said quietly. She rested her cheek on his shoulder. Behind him, the ocean was a flat dark carpet. A gull lighted on the railing, close enough for Anne to see the black ring circling its bill. It flew to the ground, near the edge of the shack.

"Talk to me," Jack said into her ear. His hardness pressed into her dress.

She felt herself responding, her nipples stiffening in the darkness, a warm sensation between her thighs.

She watched the gull hop across the wood planks. The bird was pecking at something white that stuck out from behind the shack. Something white and strange-looking, twisted in a heap.

Anne's scream pierced the night as she realized what it was. She pulled away from Jack and rushed forward. Sandy Cooksey was sprawled like a stuffed doll against the rear wall of the shack, her legs spread open, her eyes staring off into the night. She looked startled, as if death had come as a surprise.

Chapter 17

*Housework is like sex.
It might take a little time
to learn the ropes, but in
the end, it's definitely
worth the effort.*

The Neptune Township Sheriff's Office was quiet as a crypt on Saturday night. The desk clerk didn't even glance up when Anne and Jack walked in with Officer Hefferle and another young cop who arrived at the pier after they called to report Sandy's death. Hefferle led them into a dingy room in the back, which smelled of smoke and air freshener. It took ten minutes for him to question them about Sandy. "If this happened in Landsdown no one would pay any attention, but since she died in the Heights, there's going to be a real big stink," Hefferle said, flipping his notebook shut.

His dark blue uniform looked too small, the sleeves barely covering his wrists. Anne again wondered how old he was. Twenty-two? Twenty-three? He should have been out drinking beer with his buddies, she thought, not investigating crime scenes.

"The coroner's office will do an autopsy," Hefferle said. "But it's pretty clear what we got."

They looked at him expectantly.

"Sometimes dealers cut the heroin to dilute it, keep the drug pure for themselves. She must have got hold of some bad stuff."

"What makes you think it's heroin?" Anne said.

"Track marks. A fresh injection on her arm. My guess is she shot up right before you found her. We'll canvass the waterfront in Landsdown, try to get the word out that there's some bad shit going around. But between you and me, these addicts don't care. They're gonna ride the white horse no matter what."

"About that autopsy," Anne said. "Will it reveal what time Sandy died?"

"Within a range of hours. It probably happened fast."

"Why do you think the heroin was bad?"

"Position of the body. The victim's neck and face were stiff. Her back was arched, probably from spasms produced by the drug."

"You mean that wouldn't have happened if she overdosed on pure heroin?"

Officer Hefferle looked at her closely. "You got a lot of questions."

Anne gazed back at him. "I'm a writer," she said, by way of explanation. "Right now, I'm working on a procedural guide to crime."

"Huh?"

"A how-to book for mystery writers. What kind of handguns criminals use. What the inside of a morgue looks like. How you identify the remains of a body."

"Why would anyone bother with a book like that?"

"Mystery writers need to get their facts straight. Most of them aren't cops or detectives, so they have to get their information somewhere else." As she finished talking, she realized it was actually a good idea. A writer's guide to murder. There could be an entire chapter on drugs.

But Hefferle wasn't buying. "I got work to do," he muttered brusquely, moving away.

"Wait a minute," Jack demanded, grabbing hold of Hefferle's arm. "Didn't anything we said register with you?

Don't you think it's peculiar that Sandy calls and asks us to meet her on the pier and a half-hour later, she's dead?''

"Junkies aren't good at waiting," Hefferle said. "They got better things to do." He laughed to himself, appreciating the joke.

"Officer Hefferle," Anne interjected, "please forgive us for taking up so much of your time. I know you're really busy. It's just that it was really upsetting, finding her on the pier like that. I've never seen a dead body before," she lied. "And well, sometimes I guess it helps to know why things happen the way they do. It's . . . comforting, in a way."

Jack shot her a sideways glance. But Hefferle seemed to like this explanation better. "That's all right. You're not in law enforcement," he said, absentmindedly scratching at a pimple on the side of his neck. "We've seen things that'll make your blood freeze up."

"I can imagine," Anne said sympathetically. "Anyway, did those teenagers on the pier happen to mention if they'd noticed anything suspicious. A dealer? A pusher? I never saw those kids before. Are they from the Heights?"

"You shouldn't have gone through the druggie's purse," Hefferle said. His face registered disappointment, as if he was personally offended.

"I know. Police procedure, right?" Anne said. "But it's like we told you before. Sandy said on the phone that she had something belonging to Jack's brother."

"And you expected her to be telling the truth? Drugged-out hookers aren't the most reliable source of information. She was probably so desperate for a fix she'd say anything to get her hands on some money."

"Did you question those teenagers or not?" Jack cut in impatiently. "They told us they didn't see anything, but they might be more forthcoming with the police."

Hefferle put his hands on his hips and smiled. "You know, I think you two missed your true calling. You both should have been cops. That way, you could do our jobs for us and I could be home watching *Homicide*."

"Look," Anne said, "when we talked to Sandy yesterday afternoon, she said she didn't even know Jack's brother. Obviously, she was lying. They must have seen each other before Tigger died. I think he gave her something that was dangerous or damaging to someone else. It might have even been what got him killed in the first place."

"In other words," Jack cut in, "we don't think these 'accidents' are what they seem."

"Last time I checked, *I* was the police officer," Hefferle said, still smiling. His tone was patronizing. "Now why don't you both call it a night? I tell you what," he said, when Anne and Jack made no move to leave, "you can call here first thing Monday morning and find out the result of the autopsy tests. Better yet, you can read all about it in the papers. This place will be crawling with reporters soon, not to mention what the community watch groups and the Heights Association will have to say about it. There'll probably be boardwalk patrols to keep the druggies and hookers in Landsdown—where they belong."

"Thanks for the help, Officer," Jack said, with a forced smile. He turned to Anne. "It's getting late," he said. "Let's go."

Outside, invisible crickets were singing in the trees. Wispy gray clouds glided across the surface of the moon. The air was muggy, promising rain.

They climbed into the Corvette. Jack turned on the radio and music floated through the car, a song from the sixties about love gone wrong.

"You still want to go to the Blue Marlin?" Jack asked, as the car headed back toward the Heights.

"I'm not hungry anymore."

"I know what you mean. Seeing her lying there like that was so . . . horrible. I keep thinking if we'd only gotten there a few minutes earlier, we could have done something."

"I know." She'd laid it on thick for the cop, but ever since Anne first spotted Sandy leaning against the wall of the shack, she'd been feeling afraid. Sandy's body had been strangely contorted, her back arched, her limbs askew. The dead woman's mouth was twisted into a grimace, her eyes open too wide, as if her skin was being pulled in opposite directions. It was the face of a clown in a funhouse mirror, everything exaggerated, horrifying yet comic. A vulnerable look of surprise. The seagull had pecked at Sandy's legs as if Sandy were carrion and the bird was a vulture tearing at her flesh. Anne's stomach lurched slightly. She flicked off the air-conditioner and rolled her window down all the way. "I need some fresh air," she said to Jack.

"Should I pull over?" he asked, rolling down his window.

"No. I just want to go home."

"Sure thing." He turned into the entrance to the Heights, with its big wrought-iron gate. *Enter Into the Kingdom of Heaven on Earth*, the sign said. Anne had passed it thousands of times before, but tonight the message seemed ominous. Something bad was going on in the Heights. There was something wrong here; she could feel it spreading like a cancerous growth, invisible and deadly.

They drove down Main Street, heading south on Seaside Avenue. Anne's house was at the opposite end of the beach from the pier dividing Landsdown and the Heights. She looked behind her; Fisherman's Pier was dark. The police cars had all left by now. "Do you want to come in? I could make us a pot of coffee," Anne said, as the car pulled into her driveway.

"Sure. I'm never going to fall asleep tonight anyway. I can't get Sandy off my mind."

The rain appeared without warning. As they walked up the path leading to the house, the sky opened up, and it began to pour. They ran the last few feet to the porch, but by the time they reached shelter, they were both thoroughly soaked. Once inside, Anne went upstairs to her bedroom and changed out of her wet things, putting on a pair of jeans and a sweatshirt. She came downstairs carrying a pair of navy sweatpants and an oversize T-shirt she got for completing a three-mile "Fun Run" on the boardwalk earlier in the summer. "Here," she said, tossing Jack the clothes. "I hope these fit."

When she returned to the living room carrying two

steaming mugs of coffee, she found him on the sofa, study-ing the *Vintage Victoriana* book. The sweatpants were too small; his thighs strained against the cotton fabric. "I can't believe this dumb book says Pop was married to somebody named Katherine Davenport," he said.

"Did you ask him about it?"

"Yup. He laughed in my face. Then he went back to his bottle."

"We could go to the library tomorrow and try to look her name up in the records from town hall. Maybe there's a marriage license or something."

"Tomorrow's Sunday."

Anne sat next to him on the couch, curling her legs be-neath her. "Delia gave me a spare key a while back. It comes in handy when I have to research my books."

"Speaking of which, are you really going to write that murder book for mystery writers, like you told Officer Know-Nothing?"

"Maybe," Anne said with a laugh. "Who knows? It could come in handy."

"There are tons of publishing companies in New York," Jack said offhandedly. "If you decided to move, I mean."

"I know. It's just that I made my mother a promise I would never sell the house." She looked around the room at the pine furniture, the antique quilts, the grandfather clock in its old-fashioned case. "The past can be comfort-ing sometimes."

"Or it can be a big steel trap, waiting to spring shut and hurt you." She gave him a curious look. "I was thinking about Tigger," he explained. "How he could never shake loose from the past."

Outside, rain lashed against the house. The wind howled noisily, causing the shutters to flap. Only two nights earlier Jack had first showed up on her doorstep, asking about Tigger; only yesterday afternoon they'd seen Sandy Cook-sey alive. Somehow it felt like months had passed between then and now.

"We need to know what really happened to Sandy," Jack said quietly, as if reading her mind.

Anne nodded. "Hefferle's right about one thing. It didn't look like anyone forced bad drugs into her system. If they had, she would have screamed or put up some kind of a struggle. Somebody would have heard her."

"Just like somebody would have heard Tigger?" Jack said. "This town's gotten pretty good at turning a deaf ear."

"I know."

Jack took a sip of his coffee. "Let's backtrack for a minute. What if Tigger gave Sandy the threatening note we can't find, for safekeeping? Maybe she figured out who wrote it and that person killed her."

"Maybe. Only why would Tigger have given her the note or anything else, for that matter? They barely knew each other. In fact, up until an hour or so ago, I didn't think they knew each other at all."

"Do you think Sandy saw Teri set off the firecracker?"

"It's possible, I guess. But that fire inspector I talked to, Inspector Taggart, he seemed to think Sandy wasn't even in the house when the fire broke out."

Jack groaned and set his mug on the coffee table. "We keep going round and round in circles."

In her mind, Anne saw Sandy's face, her stringy blond hair, the way her legs jutted out at an angle, as though even in death she were offering herself up. "She must have died almost as soon as she got the injection."

"I don't get it. Why would she be shooting up when the only reason she was on the pier in the first place was to meet us?"

"You think her death and Tigger's are connected somehow, don't you?"

"Yes. I just don't know how we'll be able to prove it."

"Maybe the autopsy will show something."

"If that jerk Hefferle even lets us know what's in the report. He looks like a kid himself. I bet the only crime he's solved since he's been on the force is which cat ate Mrs. Granville's petunias."

Jack picked up a piece of paper from the end table next to the sofa. He unfolded it slowly. Anne could see it was the letter they had retrieved from the vault. "I carry this around with me because I don't have a safe place to put it," Jack said. "Tigger seemed to think it should be protected."

"You can leave it here if you want. There's a wall safe behind that picture." Anne pointed to a framed portrait of a young woman with red hair, hanging on the wall opposite the sofa.

"Is that your mother?"

"Uh huh. It was painted when she was a teenager."

Jack studied the picture of Evelyn. In the portrait, her eyes were a luminous sea green. Her red hair cascaded past her shoulders. "She was really beautiful."

"I think so, too," Anne said softly.

"You know, you look just like her."

"No, I don't."

"Yeah, you do. You both have the same smile."

"Thanks," Anne said, blushing.

She took the letter from him and read it again. She still had the feeling that there was something familiar about it, like she'd seen the letter before. But she knew that was impossible. The letter was over twenty years old. Anne glanced at the signature: "A Friend." Who in the world would send this to a teenager? Who would want to destroy the Spray View?

"What's wrong?" Jack asked.

"I get such a sense of déjà vu when I look at this letter. It's really strange."

"Well, maybe things will clear up once Teri gets back. I wonder how she'll try to talk her way out of this one."

"I'm sure she'll think of something," Anne said sarcastically.

"The two of you aren't exactly close, are you?"

"Not exactly."

"I never understood what Tigger saw in her. She always seemed so vacant. Like nobody's home."

"Don't underestimate her. Teri's smart. She's good at getting what she wants."

"I guess she hit the jackpot when she married Bobby."

"I don't want to talk about Teri." Anne smiled. "Maybe we should take a break from this stuff for a little while. My brain is on overload."

"I know what you mean. I don't know how I'm ever going to sleep tonight."

"You don't have to go, do you?"

"I'm in no hurry to get back to Ravenswood. That place is like a haunted house, especially at night. How about if I just hang out here for a while?"

"Sure." Anne got up and went over to her mother's portrait. Pulling at the frame, she swung the picture forward, revealing a metal safe embedded in the wall. She punched in a series of numbers on the combination lock, opened the safe, and stuck the letter inside, next to her mother's pearl necklace and the deed to the house. "It's official," she announced, as the safe swung shut. "No more talk of death tonight."

"I'll drink to that," Jack said, swallowing the last of his coffee.

"Can I get you anything? A sandwich? A glass of wine."

"No thanks. I'm fine." She walked back to the sofa and sat down again. "So," he said, "tell me more about you. What would you be doing right now if this whole mess hadn't happened?".

"Actually, I'd much rather hear about you. About your travels."

"To which country?"

"Whichever is the most exotic."

"That would be Tibet," Jack said, launching into a story about the months he spent in that part of the world. As he talked, Anne could envision the Buddhist monks in their saffron-colored robes, the woven baskets, the wood masks arrayed in the marketplace, the monkeys perched on the roof of the great temple.

"There's a custom I heard about in the capital city that I'll never forget," Jack said. "Every six years, the king holds a contest. All the little girls from the surrounding villages gather in Katmandu. And he chooses one of them to be his 'living goddess.' "

"What's that?"

"It's a ceremonial title. The girl lives in the palace for six years. She doesn't leave. Nobody's permitted to speak to her, not even the king's servants. She can't be seen, except once a year on the feast day, when she comes to the window. Everybody in the city gathers around the palace, and they all cheer and wave when they catch sight of her. The summer I was there, I saw one little girl, that year's living goddess. I remember she was wearing lots of thick bracelets and she kept waving and smiling. Everyone applauded."

"What a strange custom."

"It's considered an honor, actually. All the girls want to be chosen. But when the living goddess is released and sent back to her village, she's considered unlucky. None of the young men will marry her. I heard all kinds of stories about the bad luck surrounding her. Crops rotting, cattle dying."

"How awful," Anne said, shuddering. She pictured the children, shut in for years with no one to talk to, no mother to care for them. "Those poor little girls. They must be so lonely."

"Don't look so sad," Jack said, smiling. "It's a different culture, that's all."

"I know. It just sounds so . . . barbaric."

"The world is a curious place. That's what I discovered in my wanderings."

Thunder rumbled in the distance. Through the window Anne could see jagged streaks of lightning flickering in the sky above the ocean. She shivered suddenly, hugging her arms across her chest.

"Are you cold?" Jack asked.

"A little."

He reached for the crocheted afghan draped over the arm of the sofa. "Here," he said, pulling it around her. His hand lingered on her shoulders.

"Thanks," she said. His eyes were the color of the hyacinths in her garden.

"Anne, I . . ."

"What?" she said gently.

"We haven't talked about what happened between us on the pier."

"I know."

He brushed her hair away from her face, letting one finger glide down her cheek. "I feel so close to you," he whispered.

Her heart flopped wildly in her chest. "Me, too."

Bending forward, he brushed his lips against her mouth. His arms slid around her as he kissed her more deeply, his tongue exploring the inside of her mouth. She closed her eyes. He pulled back slightly, and she felt his lips stroke her cheek, her eyelids, the base of her throat. His hand slid underneath her sweatshirt, caressing her bare breasts. "Anne," he said. "Anne."

He repeated her name slowly, again and again, as they lay back on the sofa, and his arms enfolded her, holding her close. Kissing him was like awakening from a dark, hazy dream. Their bodies pressed together, as they explored each other with their hands and lips, until their limbs were so entwined that it seemed he was part of her, an extension of her body. The rain drummed against the house, a steady patter that mingled with the beating of her heart. And for a while, there was no such place as the Heights, no such thing as death and drowning.

Only this.

Chapter 18

Clutter can be hazardous to your health. In 1947, police entered the New York brownstone of the Collyer brothers, crammed with forty years' worth of newspapers, magazines, and mail. They found the body of sixty-five-year-old Homer first. He'd died of a heart attack. But it took the cops weeks to find sixty-one-year-old Langley, who had been crushed to death by a toppling pile of junk.

When Anne woke up the next morning, the rain had stopped. But the sky was still overcast, the ocean a sulky shade of gray. Jack lay beside her on his stomach, with one arm stretched out, as if reaching for her in his sleep. He didn't stir as she climbed out of bed and padded noiselessly downstairs. She was ravenously hungry. Spying some leftover spaghetti in the back of the refriger-

ator, she spooned it directly from the bowl, not bothering
to heat it up. She caught herself smiling, thinking about
Jack, how good it felt to be with him. He was a tender
lover, gentle and caring, mindful of her needs. Afterward,
he had held her for a long time, and they'd talked for hours,
until they moved upstairs to the bedroom and made love a
second time.

She polished off the spaghetti with some chocolate chip
cookies and a glass of iced tea. Back in her bedroom, Jack
was still sleeping. For a moment she was tempted to slip
beneath the sheets and go back to sleep herself. But she
had a better idea. Tiptoeing from the room, she climbed
the short flight of stairs to the attic. Tucked beneath the
eaves of the house, the attic was crammed with treasures
from the past—a black steamer trunk containing toys and
books, cartons filled with old *National Geographic* magazines and dog-eared copies of *McCall's*, oil paintings of
sailboats and steamships stacked against the wall, and in
the middle of the room, a dressmaker's dummy in a ruffled
red taffeta dress, her mother's favorite party dress, which
Evelyn had worn on special occasions.

Anne walked over to a cardboard box marked *School* and
rummaged through it until she found her high school yearbook. Sitting cross-legged on the plank floor, she flipped
the pages, stopping when she came to her graduation picture. In the photograph, she was wearing a striped turtle-
neck sweater and a gold chain with her name written in
script. Her red hair was long and straight, parted in the
middle. Underneath her picture was the quote she'd selected, a verse from a Walt Whitman poem. She chose it
because she loved Whitman's poetry, loved the beauty of
his images and the longing his words instilled in her. She
liked that the poem wasn't inspirational, like so many other
quotes in the yearbook. It didn't convey anything porten-
tous or monumental about life. What did she know of life
back then anyway? She was only seventeen. She could remember how happy she felt when the photographer
snapped the shutter, how relieved that high school was finally coming to an end and she would soon be making her

escape. She'd planned to go to college in California, which was about as far away as she could get in the continental United States. Only it hadn't happened. Her mother had gotten sicker, money for school had slipped away.

Anne turned the pages of the yearbook. The pictures were culled from four years in the life of the graduating class, spanning ninth through twelfth grades. She flipped back to the section from when they were juniors. There was Teri, surrounded by a flock of cheerleaders, and a few pages away, a picture of Bobby, Tigger, and P.J., posed on the bleachers of the football field. Tigger was in the middle, with his arms around his friends' shoulders. It must have been taken in winter—the winter before the fire—because the boys were wearing ski jackets. Bobby was facing the others, laughing, his head thrown back, captured in the middle of some private joke. P.J. looked past the camera, into the distance, while Tigger stared straight ahead, smiling, his lips parted in a broad grin. The three of them were always together—at school, on the boardwalk, on the beach. Her mind skipped ahead, to the summer after the photo was taken. She had a sudden vision of the three boys on a hot summer night, lighting a bunch of firecrackers. She combed her memory for when it must have been. A couple of days before the Fourth of July. She remembered the thin flashes of color bursting out of the darkness, heard the sharp pop that sound like scattered gunshots. Each summer, kids bought illegal firecrackers and set them off on the beach. No big deal. No one ever got hurt.

She turned to Bobby's graduation picture. Underneath his photo was the quote he'd selected, a couple of lines from a Neil Young song about hope and the death of innocence. Did Bobby know the truth about the fire? Anne wondered. Was he covering for Teri all these years?

"Hey." She looked up. Jack was standing in the doorway, bare-chested, wearing the sweatpants she lent him. "How long have you been up?"

"About an hour."

"Whatcha doing?"

"I was hoping to find a clue in here," she said, holding up the yearbook.

"Clue?"

"About the Three Musketeers." She was surprised to find she felt shy around Jack.

"Did you?"

"No. But these pictures are pretty awful. I don't know why fashion designers are dredging up the seventies again. We all looked like ragamuffins."

He walked over and sat down beside her. "Let's see," he said, picking up the yearbook. "Bellbottoms, clogs, cut-offs, halters. You're right. What goes around, comes around." He kissed her lightly on the lips. "Last night was wonderful."

"I know."

"Are you hungry? I make a mean omelet."

"Actually, I'm starved." So much for spaghetti al dente, she thought. She was hungry enough for a three-course breakfast.

"Great." Jack peered around the room. "This is a really cool attic. What's in the boxes?"

"All kinds of stuff. Books. Clothes. Memories, mostly."

"I guess it'll be tough to move," Jack said, smiling. His hair was rumpled. He looked half-asleep.

"You don't strike me as a morning person."

"And you're changing the subject. Last night it sounded like you were thinking about leaving."

She took the yearbook, put it back in the cardboard box. She still hadn't called the real estate agent about selling the house. "I couldn't just up and move."

"Why not?"

"I don't know." Through the small windowpane, she could see the ocean, a smooth metallic band set against the pale gray sky. She would miss the ocean most of all if she left. Over the years, she had grown accustomed to its moods, the sudden shifts of color and texture that varied from day to day, hour to hour, and sometimes minute to minute. She watched the sea as carefully as a painter studied a canvas. She listened to it the way other people listened to a symphony. Even last night, the pounding of the waves had accompanied their lovemaking, like a metronome marking their passion.

"Well, think about it," Jack said. "One of my friends owns a real estate agency. He could help you find an apartment."

Anne got up and went over to the dressmaker's dummy. "I don't think all this stuff would fit in an apartment." Her fingertips brushed against the dark red taffeta. When she was a child, she had played dress-up in this gown. She remembered the way its train swished noisily when she walked, remembered the promise she made to her mother about never selling the house.

"I see I have my work cut out for me," Jack said, with a grin. He rose to his feet and went over to her. Clasping her around the waist, he kissed her lightly on the lips, stared into her eyes. "You are so beautiful," he murmured. "Your eyes. Your hair. God, I love your hair. It's the most gorgeous shade of red."

Anne felt herself blush. The sound of bells filled the air, chiming nine times in succession. "It must be time for the first church service," she said.

"I take it we're not going."

"I'd rather have that omelet."

"Done," Jack said, sweeping her up into his arms and carrying her downstairs to the kitchen.

After breakfast, they got dressed and left the house. It had gotten slightly cooler, and the breeze felt welcome. The sky had faded to an eggshell white. They walked down Main Street, past rows of darkened shops. In other shore towns, stores stayed open on Sundays. But here in the Heights, it was the Lord's day, the day of rest.

When they reached the Curleys' house it was as silent and deserted as it had been the night before. "Guess they're not back from Atlantic City yet," Jack said.

"Well, they have to come home sometime."

They cut over to the marina and walked the few blocks to the library, which was dark and shuttered, like the rest of the town. Anne took out the spare key Delia had given her and opened the massive oak front door. "Where are the records from town hall?" Jack asked, as they walked through the front hallway.

"In here, I think," she said, flicking on the lights and leading him to a small anteroom that served as the Heights' unofficial Hall of Records. The walls were lined with dark mahogany bookshelves. But instead of books, they contained hundreds of stacked shoe boxes, stretching from floor to ceiling. Anne peered at the dates on the boxes. They ranged from the turn of the century all the way up to the 1990s.

"What is this? Shoe Town?" Jack said with a laugh. "Let's see. I'd like a pair of black loafers, size ten."

"I don't think efficiency was Darcy Busmiller's strong suit," Anne said, sighing.

"Who's Darcy Busmiller?"

"The clerk in the old town hall. She was about a hundred years old and she always smelled like breath mints."

"I hope Darcy had a system. Otherwise, it's going to take days to sort through this stuff."

"Let's divide it up into walls. You take that one," Anne said, pointing to the shelves on the left, "and I'll tackle these."

"What, exactly, are we looking for?"

"Two names. Cloister Black and Katherine Davenport. I'll start with the marriage licenses."

"And I'll tackle the birth certificates. You know, this could be a giant wild goose chase."

Anne pulled her hair into a ponytail and rolled up the sleeves of her shirt. "Maybe. Maybe not."

"All right. Let's get to it."

For an hour, they worked steadily, poring over the contents of the shoe boxes. Though each box contained marriage licenses from a specific year, Anne discovered that they weren't filed in any particular order, merely dumped inside randomly.

"Couldn't these people have had more uncommon last names?" Jack burst out. "Do you know how many Blacks and Davenports were born in the Heights?"

"Dozens?"

"More like hundreds," Jack groaned. "I need a break. Is there a soda machine in this place?"

"There's a water fountain down the hall."

"Great. I'll be right back."

Anne scrutinized the contents of the shoe box in her lap, containing marriage licenses from 1962. She'd been working her way through the late 1950s and early 1960s. Jack told her Troy Mills had married his mother in '63, and it was reasonable to assume he was a young man when he married the mysterious Katherine Davenport. *If* he married Katherine Davenport, that is. Jack's right, she thought, as she sorted through a sheaf of documents. This was a huge waste of time, like sifting through grains of sand for buried treasure. All the names on the licenses were starting to blur together.

Besides, *Vintage Victoriana* must have traced the lives of thousands of families living in the Heights. Any one of the family ties outlined in the history book could have attracted Tigger's attention. As for Cloister Black, she couldn't even be sure it was the name of a person.

Her skin itched. It felt like she was inhaling dust with every breath. She put the shoe box back on the shelf. So much for 1962. This whole process would have been a snap, if only the town would enter the modern age. But by the time the Heights Association invested in computers, the machines would probably become obsolete, replaced by newer technology. She got up and stretched her legs. Come to think of it, she was thirsty, too. The omelet Jack cooked her had been flecked with onions and peppers. She wandered out into the hall, and gulped down some water from the drinking fountain.

"Jack," she called out.

"In here." She followed the sound of his voice to the back parlor where the centennial exhibit on the Heights was housed. "This stuff is amazing!" Jack exclaimed, admiring the carved wood on the old stagecoach.

"I saw it the other day. Delia told me she spent months organizing everything."

"Look at this," Jack said excitedly, pointing to a series of postcards showing the Heights at the turn-of-the-century. "It's like walking into a time capsule or something. Look at the clothes people wore to the beach."

"I know. Ladies' 'bathing costumes' were pretty bulky, weren't they? It's a wonder they could swim in those funny old things."

She wandered over to a roped-off area containing clothing and shoes from the late 1800s. One of the dresses was fashioned from black silk, with big puffy sleeves and a bustle. Women were so short back then, Anne thought. The collar of the dress barely reached her chest. She examined a silk parasol and a pair of black leather shoes with hooks and laces. The shoes would have extended up over a woman's ankles. Actually, they were kind of funky-looking.

"Do you remember Mrs. Wagner's homemade pies?" Jack asked.

"Sure. Other kids had the Good Humor truck. We had the pie lady."

"Here's a picture of her by the pie wagon. Remember the lemon chiffon ones? Man, those were good."

"My favorite was raspberry. I think she grew the fruit herself, and they had to be one hundred percent ripe before she put them in the pies."

Anne studied the signs hanging on the wall: *No Parking on Sundays. No Construction on Sundays. No Ball Playing, Bike Riding, or Roller Skating on Sundays.* "It's a wonder we were allowed to breathe on Sundays when we were kids," she said. The signs had a quaint, old-fashioned flavor to them. Sure, some things had changed. Kids living in the Heights today had it a little easier. But the respectful, hushed atmosphere on Sundays remained exactly the same.

"Anne, come here." Jack's voice sounded peculiar. She walked over to where he was standing, next to the antique printing press. "Read what it says." On a white card attached to the wall was a description of the way camp meeting pamphlets and brochures used to be printed in the Heights. *This metal printing press was brought to New Jer-*

sey from Germany in the early 1800s, Anne read. *Its type-face is a black letter-type, which is still widely used in Germany and other European countries today. The closely set letters, with their curved, heavy strokes, were used to print the Gutenberg Bible. The Nazis adopted the black letter typeface in the 1930s because they considered it na-tionalistic. Rooted in Germany's past, it was therefore anti-modern.*

Anne glanced at Jack. "So? It doesn't surprise me that the Nazis used this style of lettering. It's formal, impos-ing—the perfect way to convey the Heights' 101 stric-tures."

"Keep reading," Jack said.

Anne turned back to the description of the press. *In the Heights, however, the ornate alphabet was prized for its charm and beauty. Religious leaders in our town have used the type on brochures since 1896. The practice was stopped in the mid-1970s, when the board of the Oceanside Heights Association deemed it more efficient to prepare pamphlets and tracts on typewriters. Although the type is commonly referred to as Gothic, its correct name is . . .*

Anne stopped. "I don't believe it," she said.

"Go on," Jack said, smiling.

Anne read the last sentence out loud. "Although the type is commonly referred to as Gothic, its correct name is Cloister Black."

Chapter 19

*When two people get
married, they should sign a
blood oath. One of them
agrees to do the vacuuming
for the next forty years and
the other one doesn't point
out how much dust has
accumulated.*

"That's why the letter from 'A Friend' looked so
familiar!" Anne exclaimed. "Whoever printed it
used this old press. I must have recognized the
typeface from when I was in here on Friday."

"My brother made the same connection. I can't believe
we thought Cloister Black was a woman."

"It's my fault. I guess Madame Mona got to me with
her fortune telling. The name was so dark and mysterious,
I kept thinking it had to be someone associated with tarot
and crystal balls."

Jack peered at the index card. "It says here that the press
still works. It was lent to the exhibit by the estate of Miss
Lavinia Osborn. Who's she? Her name sounds familiar."

"Lavinia Osborn used to sponsor a lot of cultural events

in the Heights. Choir programs, gospel sings, ballroom dancing, that sort of stuff.''

''Let's go talk to her.''

''We can't. She died about ten years ago. There was a big concert in the Church by the Sea commemorating her life and everything she's given to the town.''

''Do you think she could have sent Tigger the letter?''

''Miss Lavinia destroy the Spray View? No way! She would rather have marched through town naked than harm one shingle on any of the old houses in town. She was a big Victorian architecture buff. She even got the Heights listed on the National Register of Historic Places.''

''Another dead end.''

''Not necessarily. Look at these pamphlets.''

Jack bent down and examined the material in the case. Along with printed sermons, there were newsletters about house tours, quilt shows, and preservation awards. Some of the booklets described the rules governing homeowners in the Heights—what construction permits were needed, how to apply to the architectural review board, the process regulating how homes were bought and sold.

''Don't you see?'' Anne said excitedly. ''These were all printed by the Oceanside Heights Association. If you worked at the Association, you probably knew how to operate the press.''

''The association is a pretty small operation, isn't it?''

''Yes. The question is who would have been involved back then?''

''Here's your answer,'' Jack said, glancing at the bottom of one of the printed pamphlets. ''Jim Walser was president. Ed Klemperer was vice president, Joe Vance was treasurer, Pop was assistant treasurer, and the secretary was Miss Lavinia.''

''Your father's not involved anymore,'' Anne mused. ''Neither is Klemperer. Joe Vance is vice president now, and Mr. Walser is still president.''

Jack frowned. ''My money's on Klemperer. He's the only one who benefited financially from the fire. How much did you say the insurance payoff was?''

"Delia told me Ed and Lucille got more than one million dollars."

"I rest my case."

Anne gave him a skeptical look. "It doesn't make sense, Jack. The man's not going to get his own daughter killed."

"Sandy said the kid wasn't supposed to be there, remember?"

Here we go again, Anne thought. Round and round, but still no closer to solving the mystery of Tigger's death.

"I have an idea," Jack said. "Let's go talk to Walser. He should be able to tell us which people in that office knew how to work the press."

"What about Katherine Davenport?"

"Anne, I swear I can't look through one more dusty shoe box."

"Sure you can. Besides, we're batting .500. Let's go back and give it one more shot. Maybe we'll get lucky."

Jack sighed. "All right. But Pop was pretty adamant that he'd never heard of Katherine. He can be out of it sometimes, but you'd think he'd remember if he married someone besides my mother."

"Maybe he doesn't want anyone else to know."

"Maybe," Jack said uncertainly.

"Half the people in this town seems to be hiding something. Troy could have a wife stashed away somewhere."

"Anne, the man's a lush. He's not Bluebeard."

"I'm sorry," she said quickly. "I only meant that I used to think everyone here was so honest. Plainspoken, God-fearing folk. You might not like what they have to say, but at least they're giving it to you straight."

Jack nodded. His face was troubled. "I guess deep down I don't want to believe my father had anything to do with Tigger's death. I mean, I know Pop couldn't stand Tigger. And odds are Pop *was* out on his boat the night of July Fourth. Hurrah for the U.S. of A., right? Let's toast the country till the bottle runs dry. But I can't imagine him . . . holding Tigger's head under water or something. I guess that sounds weird, huh, after what I told you about the way he used to beat Tigger up."

"Of course not," Anne said gently. "He's your father." But inwardly, she wasn't ready to cross Troy Mills off her list of suspects. Troy had a motive, and he had the means.

"Good old Pop," Jack said. "A bad-ass drunk in God's square mile. I thought I'd accepted what he is. I thought I'd learned to live with it. But I come back here, and he pushes all my buttons. He gets me so mad I can't see straight. It's like all the years in between get erased. I'm right back where I started. The old man gets smashed, tears things up, and there's not a thing I can do about it."

"I know what you mean." Anne thought of her mother crouched in a corner of the kitchen, screaming so loudly the neighbors called the cops. Later, having to explain it was nothing, really. A mouse. A nightmare. Not telling them the real reason: Evelyn was convinced Anne had poisoned the drinking water. Or stolen her memory. Or chopped off half her hair in the night. "I know," Anne repeated. "It's hard to watch someone you love self-destruct."

Jack took her hand in his. "But we go on, right?"

"Right."

He forced a smile. "How about we get back to work?"

"Sure. There are plenty of shoe boxes left."

"Who knew you could be such a slave driver?" Jack said lightly.

"There's a lot you don't know about me," Anne said, as they walked back to the small anteroom. Thinking of Evelyn had stirred up all the old feelings of loss. What was the point of hanging on to the past? She'd call the real estate agent first thing tomorrow morning.

"Oh, yeah? What don't I know?" Jack asked.

"Let's see," Anne said, stalling. It would take years to explain what growing up with Evelyn was like, how it had changed her. "I'm allergic to chocolate. I'm a horrible swimmer. I love music from the forties and fifties—Frank Sinatra, Tony Bennett. Oh, and I tend to roam around the house when I brush my teeth."

Jack paused at the threshold of the room containing the town records, blocking the doorway with his arms. "What about your deep dark secrets? You said everyone in the Heights is hiding something. 'Fess up or risk the consequences.''

"When I was nine, and we all went trick-or-treating for UNICEF, on Halloween, I kept the money people gave me.''

Jack groaned in mock horror. "Absolutely shocking! That must have added up to what? A hefty $5.99?''

"About $7.00. Mostly in pennies. I meant to turn the money in at school, but I kept forgetting. And then I just wound up keeping it.''

"I don't know, Miss Hardaway. This changes everything. I'm not sure if I can associate with a known criminal. Even if she is incredibly sexy.'' Gathering Anne up in his arms, he kissed her firmly on the mouth. His hand strayed to her ponytail. With a gentle tug, he pulled off the cloth band, and her hair tumbled down her shoulders. Her body tingled. She felt his kisses all the way down to her toes.

"Jack,'' she said weakly. "The records.''

"I must be losing my touch,'' he joked.

"Absolutely not.'' Her face felt flushed.

"How about we take a break and go back to your place?''

In the dim light of the library, his eyes were a deep royal blue, like the ocean on a clear morning. It would be so nice to forget about everything and lose herself in his arms. But they had work to do.

With an effort, she straightened up and took a step back. "One hour,'' she told him. "If we don't find Katherine Davenport in one hour, we'll get out of here.''

"Why don't I believe you?''

"Because you've probably figured out I don't give up easily.''

"Anne,'' he said, touching her arm.

Her heart skipped a beat. "Yes?''

"Why is this so important to you? Finding out what happened to him, I mean.''

She hesitated, feeling the guilt wash over her, remembering what Tigger had said. *I got a bad feeling about this.*

I think I'm in over my head. "He asked for my help, Jack. And I didn't listen to him. All I kept telling him was how safe this town is. A few hours later, he's dead."

"But it's not your—"

"You know what I dreamed last night? I dreamed he was at the bottom of the ocean. His eyes were hollow." She shuddered. "Water was flowing through the sockets. I thought the sea had driven him blind."

"Anne."

"I'm the one who's been blind. Because he should be here now." Her voice caught in her throat. "It wasn't his time to die."

"I know," Jack said. "I let him down, too. My own brother. If only I'd gotten here sooner . . ." He took a deep breath, then grabbed Anne's arm, leading her down the hall to where the records were kept. "Let's get to work."

After an hour and a half, they still hadn't found a trace of Katherine Davenport. "I think old Hornsby was wrong about my family tree," Jack said. "We may be dysfunctional, but we're all accounted for."

Anne sighed. She'd just finished sifting through the marriage licenses dating from the 1950s through the 1970s and come up with nothing. Zilch. Zero. "I guess there's always the possibility that the record was lost or destroyed," she said.

"Even if what the book claims is true, so what? How does Pop's marriage to this Katherine person tie into Tigger's death?"

Anne shook her head. "I wish I knew. But Tigger must have had his reasons for holding on to that book."

Jack looked at his watch. "It's a little before one. How about we take a break?"

"Let's each look in one more box. Then we'll go grab a sandwich, I promise."

"All right." He closed his eyes, ran his hand across the bookshelf. "Eeenie. Meenie. Minie. Moe," he said, pulling out one of the boxes. "Birth certificates from '33. That's the year Pop was born. Maybe Katie D. was born then, too.

Maybe they were classmates or something.''

Scanning the bookshelves, Anne couldn't decide which files to take out next. She closed her eyes and trailed her hand across the top shelf. "I suppose it's as good a method as any," she said to Jack. "Catch a tiger by the toe. My mother says . . . to . . . pick . . . you." When she opened her eyes, her hand was resting on top of a box of birth certificates labeled 1935. She blew a layer of dust off the lid, then sat down to sort through the contents.

"Here's Pop's birth certificate," Jack called out. "Born Troy Edward Mills at 12:37 P.M. on November 25, 1933, at Cedar Hills Hospital in Landsdown. Mother—Eileen Figelhorn. Age 21. Father—Robert Preston Mills. Occupation—Bookkeeper. Age 24. Address—14 Embury Street. My grandparents lived in our house for fifty years. It was my grandmother's house, actually, which is why it got passed on to my mother and not to Pop."

"The stuff in my box is a mess," Anne said.

"Darcy Busmiller again. Maybe she was nipping gin when she should have been filing these forms away."

"That's how vicious rumors get started," Anne joked. "Hey," she said, turning serious. "Are your grandparents still alive?"

"No."

"I thought maybe they could shed some light on Troy's other marriage."

"They died in a car accident when I was away at college."

"I'm sorry."

"I didn't know them all that well. They didn't get along too well with Pop."

"I didn't know my grandparents all that well either," Anne said. "They died when I was young and . . ." Her voice trailed away. She stared down at the piece of paper she was holding. "Jack. I found her," she said excitedly.

"What?"

"I found Katherine Davenport." In an instant, he was by her side. She handed him the small square of paper. "Katherine Lucille Davenport," he read aloud. "Born

June 2, 1935. Mother—Lindsay Anne Turner. Father—
James Davenport. Address—26 Beechwood Avenue.'' He
stopped reading and looked at Anne. "But that's . . ."

". . . the Klemperers' house. Right?"

Jack looked puzzled. "I don't get it."

"Lucille must not be using her birth name," Anne said
slowly. "That's why Delia didn't recognize it when I asked
her. Everyone knew her as Lucille Davenport."

"Until she married Ed Klemperer and dropped her
maiden name," Jack said, catching on.

"Uh huh. If *Vintage Victoriana* is right, your father and
Ed Klemperer were both married to Lucille."

"But Anne, it can't be. This town is too small to hide
something like that. If they'd gotten married, everyone
would have known."

"Not if they eloped."

"You're grasping at straws, don't you think?"

"If they didn't want anybody to know about it, they
probably would have run off and gotten married someplace
else. That would explain why we can't find the marriage
certificate."

"This is nuts, Anne. Up until the fire, Pop was best
friends with Ed Klemperer. They've been neighbors for
years. Hell, they used to go bowling together every Friday
night when I was a kid."

Anne got up and puts the box back on the shelf. "What
exactly did your father say when you asked him about
Katherine Davenport?"

"He told me he never heard of her. He said Hornsby
was an old fool who was just trying to stir up trouble."

"Now that we've figured out who she is, Troy might be
more forthcoming."

"Don't bet on it," Jack said sarcastically.

He put the shoe box back and they left the library, making sure to lock the door and replace the key. Outside, the
wind had picked up. The sky was overcast, swollen with
clouds. Main Street was more crowded now. The second
service of the day had just ended and worshipers streamed
out of the Church by the Sea, dressed in their finest Sunday

clothes. Boys in short pants and jackets, and girls with frilly dresses the pale color of after-dinner mints and white party socks, walked quietly next to their parents. If her neighbors had parasols and longer skirts, Anne thought, the scene would look just like the pictures from one hundred years ago that they saw in the exhibit. She spotted Lucille Klemperer up ahead, weaving among the parishioners like a shepherdess guiding her flock. "Let's go talk to her," Anne said to Jack.

"It's worth a shot. Thou shalt not lie tops the Ten Commandments hit parade."

Quickening their steps, they caught up to the older woman. "Mrs. Klemperer, hi," Anne said. "Could we speak to you for a minute?"

"A minute is all I have," Lucille Klemperer snapped. "I left one of my prayer books at home, and I'm late for Bible study." In her high-necked white blouse, adorned with a cameo, and her long navy skirt, Lucille reminded Anne of a schoolmarm out of *Little House on the Prairie*. Her silvery gray hair was combed back from her face in short, wispy ringlets.

"You know Jack Mills, don't you?" Anne asked.

"Certainly," Lucille answered.

"Nice to see you, ma'am," Jack said, extending his hand.

"You may have heard," Anne continued, "that I'm working on a history of the Heights."

"An excellent plan," Lucille said. "Particularly if you're intending to focus on the architectural richness of our town."

"One of my reference materials is *Vintage Victoriana* by Arthur Hornsby."

"I'm not familiar with it."

"He wrote about architecture, history, town bylaws, stuff like that. He also researched an entire section on genealogy, which I intend to do, too."

"You should be studying theology. The Lord is an exceptional tutor."

"I'm sure," Anne said. "But getting back to Mr. Hornsby, he wrote rather an extraordinary thing himself. According to him, you were once married to Troy Mills."

Lucille Klemperer looked startled. "What?" she said, her dark eyes widening slightly. "Why, that is utterly ridiculous."

"Mr. Hornsby didn't think so. You're listed on our family tree," Jack said. "Or rather your given name, Katherine Davenport, is listed. It says you and my dad were married."

Lucille drew in her breath sharply. She gave her head a shake. The gray ringlets jiggled slightly. Anne saw that her lips were trembling. "For in the resurrection they neither marry nor are given in marriage," Lucille recited. Turning to Jack, she says: "Your mother was a saint, God rest her soul. You must honor her memory."

"I loved my mother very much," Jack said quietly. "But I need to know the truth. Were you married to my father at one time?"

"Married to Troy?" For an instant, a stricken expression crossed her face. But the next moment, it was gone, replaced by Lucille's normally stern countenance. "Heaven forbid. Now, if you'll excuse me, I really must be going. May the good Lord bless and keep you." Crossing the street, she hurried away in the direction of the tents.

"That wasn't especially enlightening," Jack said.

"I wonder."

Anne looked out over the ocean, which was rough today, flecked with whitecaps. On the boardwalk, groups of tourists were lining up to buy beach passes. Others poured onto the sand, like lemmings rushing over cliffs into the sea.

"You think she's lying?" Jack asked.

"The thought crossed my mind."

"We'll never be able to prove it. And I doubt if we'll be able to get anything out of Pop, assuming he's sober enough to give us a straight answer. But I'm game. If we can get a quick lunch first."

They ordered two hot dogs, a big bag of potato chips, and two cans of Diet Coke from a vendor on the boardwalk.

"It looks like another storm's coming," Jack said, as they sat down to eat. The waves were several feet high, striking the shoreline hard. All up and down the beach, lifeguards were planting red flags in the sand, warning people to stay out of the water.

"I guess I'm really not a beach person, at heart," Jack continued. "I can't sit still long enough to enjoy getting a tan. Tigger was just the opposite. Even when we were kids, he used to swim out a little farther each time. It was like a game to him."

Anne scanned the shoreline. The ocean was a swirling gray void, completely free of swimmers. The image of Tigger came without warning—Tigger alone, in the dark, swallowed by the vast, indifferent waves.

Chapter 20

*You deodorize the
refrigerator, you steam
clean the carpet, and six
months later you have to
start all over again.*

At the other end of town, the marina was bustling,
too. Gusty winds had lured boaters out onto the
bay. Fishermen hunched forward in their motor-
boats, staring at their lines as if willing the fish to bite.
Sailboats skittered rapidly across the bay. Instead of being
a deterrent, the weather appeared to have spurred Anne's
neighbors toward the open water. Many of the small pleasure boats were gone from their slips, although she noticed
that *The Teribelle* was still moored to the dock.

They found Troy Mills bent over the outboard motor on
his boat, an old wooden Chris-Craft scarred by nicks and
gashes. The rough water of the bay made the boat lurch
back and forth. Troy had to struggle to keep his balance.

"Goddamn," Troy scowled, looking up at them. He
rummaged through his toolbox and picked up a wrench.
"She's a bitch to fix."

Troy looked more alert today, Anne thought. His eyes

213

were less rheumy, his movements quicker. "We went by the house first," Jack said. "When you weren't home, I figured you might be down here."

"Yup. If I can ever get this dang motor to work, I'm gonna take her out for a spin," Troy said. He cranked the head of the wrench against a metal cylinder.

"I need to talk to you, Pop."

Troy wiped his hands on his trousers. "So talk."

"We found out about you and Katherine Davenport."

A half-smile played on Troy's lips. "What's that?"

"When I asked you before, you denied it. But now I know Katherine Davenport and Lucille Klemperer are one and the same. The two of you were married once, weren't you?"

Troy chuckled. "What if we were?"

"Then there's no point in hiding the truth," Anne said.

"You know, missy," Troy said, "you and my son been spending an awful lot of time together. First you was with Tigger. And now Jack." The corners of his mouth bunched up. He pursed his lips and let fly a stream of saliva, which landed in the bay. "Seems to me you're sticking your nose into everybody's business but your own."

"Anne's a friend of mine, Pop. She's been a big help these last few days."

"Is that right?" Troy stared at Anne. His eyes were mocking. She wondered what Troy knew, who he'd been talking to. She'd always assumed people like Troy, people who drank too much and passed out and drank some more, were not paying attention, hurtling through life with blinders on. Now she wasn't not so sure.

"Were you married to Lucille Klemperer?" Jack said slowly, enunciating each word.

Troy peered at the sky. "Looks like rain," he said. "I got to get back to work."

"*Were* you?" Jack persisted.

"My boat's broke."

"Tell me the truth," Jack said fiercely. His expression was pained. "Tell me, damn it. You owe me that much."

Troy considered this last statement. He looked Jack up

and down slowly, as if seeing him for the first time. "All right," he said suddenly. "I suppose you got a right to know. We were married years ago. It's ancient history. End of story."

"When?"

"Before I started courting your mother. Lucille and I were kids back then. We didn't know any better." He spit again, over the side of the boat. "Didn't last long. Four, five months."

"Why didn't you tell me about this when I asked you before?"

"I dunno. Like I said, it was a long time ago. Didn't seem important."

"Did Mom know?"

Troy laughed. "Lord have mercy. Nobody knew. Best-kept secret in the Heights."

"Arthur Hornsby knew," Anne said quietly.

"Hornsby, huh? Meddlesome fool. So he's who I got to thank for spilling the beans. If he weren't six feet under, I'd punch his tomfool lights out."

"I don't get it," Jack said. "How do you hide a marriage?"

"We eloped. Run off to Pennsylvania. Got hitched. Came back here, pretended like nothing happened. Lucille was living with her folks at the time. And I was living at home too, with Gramps and Gramma Mills. Lucy wanted to wait before she sprung it on her parents. But then she up and changed her mind, had the marriage annulled. Can't say as I blame her. I was a pretty ornery young fella back then."

"What about Ed Klemperer?" Jack demanded. "Did he know?"

"Old Ed doesn't know his ear from his elbow on a good day. And that's before he went off the deep end."

"Why keep it a secret at all?" Anne asked.

Troy scanned her face. "Now, missy, you above anyone should know how important it is that some things stay hid. You think folks in this town know all the things your mama did when she was alive?" Anne felt her cheeks burning. It always came back to this in the end: Her mother's shame clung to her like a second skin.

"This isn't about Anne's mother," Jack cut in. "It's about you and Lucille Klemperer. And Tigger."

Troy Mills raised his shaggy eyebrows. "Tigger?"

"He figured out there was something between you and Lucille, didn't he?"

"What if he did? It ain't a crime to be married twice."

"Why would it be a crime, Mr. Mills?" Anne said.

Troy shook his head impatiently. Leaning over the steering wheel, he turned the key in the ignition. The engine sputtered and died. Troy jerked the key again. With a loud cough, the engine turned over and the outboard began to shake. Troy loosened the rope attaching the Chris-Craft to the dock and the boat took off toward the middle of the bay. A plume of blue smoke hovered above the transom.

"Unbelievable," Jack said, staring at the boat as it receded into the distance. "I always fall for his lies. Even now."

Anne turned to him, waiting.

"He looked me straight in the eye the other day and swore he never heard of Katherine Davenport," Jack said, his voice thick with anger. "When will I ever learn?"

"It's not your fault, Jack. He had the whole town fooled for decades."

"What does it mean anyway? Why would he bother to keep it a secret?"

"I don't know. But at least he told us the truth. Lucille's still pretending the marriage never existed. I wonder if she's afraid Ed will find out."

"Everything always leads straight back to Klemperer, doesn't it?"

Anne gazed out at the bay where Troy was anchoring the Chris-Craft. She watched as he baited his hook and cast the rod into the water. "Has your father always been handy around boats?"

"Sure," Jack said. "He grew up on the water. He's a good mechanic. Never met an engine he couldn't fix. Even stone drunk."

"Was he out on his boat the night of the fire?"

Jack turned to her, his eyes troubled. "I guess so," he said uncertainly. "Pop always liked fireworks."

"Did you see them?"

"Sure. They were spectacular, especially that part at the end with the stars."

Anne nodded, remembering the red, white, and blue stars tearing across the sky, exploding in a dark burst of noise. She'd been watching from the beach, right across the street from her house so she'd know her mother was safe. But when she got back, Evelyn was gone.

"What's wrong?" Jack said, staring. "You look upset."

"It's nothing. I was just thinking about that night. You remember how hot it was? Like there was no air at all. I was watching the fire and . . . and it was hard to breathe."

"Speaking of the fire, let's swing by Teri's again. She's got to come home sometime."

"Okay."

They walked along the dock, past the boats bobbing in the wind and the row of darkened stores. Curley Construction was closed, the shades drawn. The day was cooler now, almost like autumn. The sky had turned a deeper shade of gray. It looked like dusk was falling, although it was only two o'clock in the afternoon.

When they reached the Curleys, nobody was home. The car was still gone. As they walked by, Anne spotted Mrs. Granville peeking out from behind a curtain in the house next door. When Anne waved, Mrs. Granville's head bobbed out of sight.

"Right neighborly," Jack said, noticing.

"She's probably waiting for Teri to come back so she can run right over there and tell her we were snooping around."

"Where to next?"

"Let's go talk to Jim Walser like you suggested," Anne said. "He was tight with your dad back then. Maybe he knows something."

The Oceanside Heights Association was housed on the second floor of a mauve-colored Victorian-style building,

sandwiched between Bea's Kite Shop and the Enchanted
Florist. It had once been Jim Walser's real estate office.
But after he retired, he leased the space to the association
in exchange for the sum of $1 a year. The office consisted
of two rooms—a waiting area and a larger cluttered space,
furnished with antiques and nautical memorabilia. Walser
was seated behind a large mahogany partner's desk in the
back, talking on the telephone. He was wearing a short-
sleeved powder blue shirt and navy slacks. Behind him on
the wall hung a calendar featuring various color photographs of Oceanside Heights. The picture for the month of
July was of the Church by the Sea, shot at night, with its
eight-foot-high cross lit up in white neon.

"Doesn't have to be marshmallows," Walser said into
the receiver. "States right here in the bylaws, any food at
all is legal. Now that would include pork products, don't
you think?" He looked up, motioned them into two leather
chairs across from his desk. "Well, I know it's an animal.
But it's not alive now, is it?" He paused, tapping a pencil
against the desk. "There's nothing in the bylaws about hot
dogs. I know. I agree with you. I think franks and beans
would be a better choice myself. But there's nothing stip-
ulating they have to cook 'em. Nothing about hamburgers
either, for that matter. All it says is 'food.' That's all. Food.
In black and white." He rolled his eyes. "Yes, Doris. I
will. I'll look into it." He hung up and threw his hands in
the air. "Doesn't that beat all? You know who that was on
the phone? Mrs. Halpern. Fit to be tied because the Boy
Scouts were roasting a pig on Seaview Pathway. I tell you,
people get the strangest notions into their heads."

Anne murmured something she hoped sounded sympathetic. She wasn't quite sure what the association staff did
on a daily basis, only that this was where you came if you
needed a building permit or your gutters were clogged or
you wanted to change the type of windows you had in your
living room.

"I shouldn't even be here today for Pete's sake," Walser
continued. "But if I wasn't, you know what would happen?
The phone in my kitchen would ring off the hook. Folks

got all sorts of questions and problems on Sundays, same as every other day. If this office is closed, they just come knocking on my front door.''

"Sounds like you need an assistant," Jack said.

"You got that right, son. There's not enough hours in the day to do this job."

"Well, I'm certainly glad you're here," Anne said, smiling. "Without your help, I would never have found that oak molding for my mantel."

"I know a fellow down in Sea Bright who's got an architectural salvage business," Walser said to Jack. "He specializes in vintage hardwoods. If you're ever in the market for an oak-paneled door or a handcarved banister, let me know."

"I'll be sure and do that."

"Lovely service yesterday," Walser said. "The reverend's eulogy was quite moving." He coughed delicately into the palm of his hand. "I hope your father's feeling better. He seemed quite . . . distraught."

"Actually, that's partly what we came to talk to you about," Jack said.

Walser leaned forward in his chair expectantly. He had a look on his face that Anne had seen plenty of times before—the half-curious, half-eager expression of someone who was about to be spoon-fed a juicy morsel of gossip.

"You see," Anne explained. "We stumbled across a few things at the library that we found kind of curious. Apparently, Jack's father was once married to Lucille Klemperer." She studied Jim Walser's face. He didn't seem surprised. Apparently, Arthur Hornsby wasn't the only one who knew about the marriage.

"We thought since you and Pop go back a ways," Jack added, "you might be able to shed some light on what went on."

"What'd Troy say?" Walser asked slowly.

"Not much. He told us he and Lucille were secretly married for a couple of months when they were young. Until she broke it off."

"You talk to Lucille about this?"

"Yes. She denied it ever happened."

Walser nodded. "It's best to let sleeping dogs lay by the outhouse."

"If you know something, sir, I wish you'd share it with us," Jack said.

Walser picked up a pink conch shell lying on his desk and turned it over in his hands. Clearing his throat, he shifted his weight in the chair and studied a fly that was crawling on the windowsill. "It's none of my business," he said.

"No one has to know you breathed a word to us," Anne said.

Walser held the shell up to his ear. "From Florida," he said, putting the conch back on the desk. "People think they can stroll down our beach and find 'em right here."

"Please, sir," Jack said. "If there's anything you can tell us."

Behind his thick glasses, Walser's eyes were thoughtful. "I suppose it's all right," he said finally. "It was years ago, when all of us old geezers were fresh out of high school. Troy fell for Lucille like a ton of bricks. In the beginning, we thought his crush was a big joke. Lucy was a beauty back then. Everyone was after her. When she crooked her little finger, all the fellows came running. Oh, she was loads of fun. A real party girl, not spitting fire and brimstone like now. She resisted Troy at first. But after a while, he plumb wore her down. She came around and started loving him back. Well, they didn't tell a soul they'd eloped. There was always bad blood between the Davenports and the Mills clan. Lucille knew her parents would never approve. So she decided they didn't have to know. Not at first, anyway."

"What happened?" Jack asked.

"Lucille fell out of love with your father right quick. She decided she made a mistake and got the marriage annulled."

"Pop must not have liked that very much."

"You're darn tooting," Walser said ruefully. "Saying no to Troy is like barking at the moon. Doesn't do you any good. See, he was after Lucille for years, even after she took up with Ed and he married Ellen. Don't get me wrong, Jack. He never cheated on your mother. He just couldn't get Lucille off his mind. She was like a fever dream that took hold of him and wouldn't let go for all the doctoring in the world."

"But the Klemperers were friends with Ma and Pop."

"Sure they were. We've all known one another since we were in diapers together. Sure they were friends, until the night of the fire. Lucille blamed Troy for raising Tigger wrong. The apple doesn't fall far from the tree, she used to say. And Ed. Well, he's never been the same after poor Ruthie died. He's not in his right mind anymore."

Jack threw Anne a quick look, which Walser seemed to pick up on. "You mind telling me why you're interested in all this?"

"Sure," Jack said. "You might as well know what's going on. We don't think my brother's death was an accident."

"What?" Walser exclaimed. He studied their faces. "You suspect foul play?"

"Yes," Anne said.

"Oh dear, I was afraid this would happen," Walser said.

"What do you mean?" Jack asked.

"This whole to-do about the bridge to Landsdown. I'm afraid folks are right, after all. We're going to have to lock it at night. Too many teenagers coming into the Heights, high on Lord knows what." Walser's face crinkled with worry.

"Actually," Anne said, "we think the murderer might live right here in town."

"Good gracious," Walser said excitedly. "Is that why you're asking about Troy? I know there was bad blood between him and Tigger, but Troy's no murderer. I'd stake my life on it!"

"We're not insinuating that Mr. Mills had anything to do with Tigger's death," Anne said. "We're just trying to piece things together."

"Why don't you tell me the whole story," Walser said

eagerly. "That way, I'll have a better idea of how I can help you."

Taking turns, Anne and Jack filled him in on everything that had happened since Tigger's body washed up on the beach. Walser listened attentively, asking an occasional question. When they were finished, he leaned back in his chair and stared at the ceiling. "Well, I'll be," he said. "I always thought there was something odd about that fire. The hotel went up so sudden-like. To think Teri Curley caused that poor child's death! How can she stand to live with herself?"

"As soon as she gets back from Atlantic City, that's just what we intend to ask her."

"Who knew how to work the printing press?" Anne asked.

"Everyone who worked at the association. It wasn't hard to operate. Do you have the letter with you? Maybe if I took a look at it, I could figure out who printed it up."

"The letter's locked up in my safe, at home," Anne said. "Who would you say used the press the most?"

"Joe did, I suppose. As our treasurer, he was the one in charge of printing all the pamphlets we issued to try and make the association some extra money. House tours, quilting bees, church socials, things of that nature. But we could all get that press up and running. Nothing to it."

Anne recalled the scissors and paste, the glass bowl filled with scraps of paper that the druggist had cut from magazines. Letters used to spell out a message like the death threat Tigger received.

"About Mr. Vance," she said. "It's strange. But I get the feeling he hated Tigger with a passion."

"He had a right, don't you think?" Walser said. Then, addressing Jack, "With all due respect to the dearly departed."

"What do you mean?" Anne said, puzzled.

"Can't say as I blame Joe. Abortion is a mortal sin."

"I'm sorry, sir. We're not following you," Jack said.

"All I'm saying is your brother should have stood by Heather Vance. She didn't need to go to some back-alley doctor who fixed it so she couldn't have any more children.''

''Tigger got Heather pregnant,'' Anne said, beginning to put things together.

''He had his own troubles, Lord knows,'' Walser continued. ''But he could have married her. She didn't have to run off the way she did.''

Anne's mind was racing. Delia had said that when Heather was a teenager, she'd run away and her father had dragged her back home, kicking and screaming. No wonder Joe Vance hated Tigger. Abortion was more than a mortal sin in the Heights. It was a crime against the church, an abomination. Anne thought of Mary Vance, working with Korean orphans. She'd never have grandchildren now. And what about Heather? What were Heather's real feelings toward Tigger Mills? Did she secretly despise him, harvesting her resentment all these years, saving it up for one final act of revenge?

''What do the police think about all this?'' Walser asked suddenly.

''The men in blue believe Tigger's death was an accident,'' Anne said. ''And Sandy Cooksey died of a drug overdose. Case closed.''

''You think Teri Curley killed both of them, don't you?'' Walser said.

''It's a definite possibility,'' Jack said. ''On the other hand, I can't see Teri forcibly drowning my brother or peddling drugs to a hooker.''

''Well, I got to tell you I think you're barking up the wrong tree.'' Walser rubbed his hand across his mouth. He appeared uncomfortable, as if the conversation suddenly pained him. ''Ed Klemperer's the one you should be talking to,'' he said brusquely.

''Ed's little girl died,'' Anne said. ''He wouldn't have risked her life, no matter what.''

''No,'' Walser agreed. ''Of course not. But Ruthie wasn't supposed to be there. I know for a fact because we were with him. Sunday nights the four of us—he and Lucille and me and Carolyn—always played bridge.'' Walser's eyes were dreamy, as though he was traveling back in time. A thoughtful expression appeared on his face. "We played cards that night, same as always. My Carolyn said if you seen one fireworks show, you seen 'em all. It was hard for her to get around in the wheelchair, anyway, especially in crowds. I think that was the real reason she didn't want to go. And I gave in. Joe was our treasurer, he was running the whole shebang. So we stayed home and played bridge with the Klemperers."

"Why didn't they want to see the fireworks?" Jack interrupted. "It was a pretty big deal."

"I couldn't say. They came over at eight o'clock, same as always. But right from the start, Ed seemed real nervous. He called the baby-sitter—Sandy that would be—a couple of times, to make sure she was taking Ruthie to the fireworks show. I thought it was strange at the time. Ruthie was a little bit of a thing. I remember thinking she should have been home in bed, asleep."

"Did you mention it to the police?" Anne asked.

"I can't remember. It didn't seem important at the time. What with Ruthie dead and the hotel a pile of cinders."

"I think Klemperer's involved in this, too," Jack said. "Thanks. You've been a big help."

Walser started to say something, then stopped.

"What is it?" Anne asked.

"Be careful around Ed," Jim Walser said slowly. "He's not right in the head anymore. And he's got a gun. I've seen it."

Chapter 21

*Cleaning is one of the few
things in life that doesn't
require a whole lot of
money. You could
hire a maid. But chances
are you'd do a better
job yourself.*

One of Teri's daughters was in the front yard, picking flowers, the next time Anne and Jack stopped by the big pink Victorian house. The little girl looked like a miniature Teri, with long black hair and pear-shaped brown eyes. Anne noticed that she even moved like Teri, with a confident air and theatrical gestures that made it seem as though she was starring in a movie based on her life. Girl cutting the stem of a rose—take one. The child couldn't be more than eight years old. She looked like she was wearing makeup.

"Is your mother home?" Anne asked. It was three in the afternoon. The black Volvo was parked in the driveway. But Anne couldn't shake the feeling that Teri had fled, left her children behind, turned her back on the fairy tale house with its twin turrets, its pastel pink rooms, and taken off for God knows where.

"Mommy's inside," the child said, tossing her head and lifting her dark hair away from her face. Uh oh, Anne thought. This kid even had the hair mannerism down pat. The child watched them climb the porch steps, then turned away, indifferent. They heard the click of her shears as she snipped at the stems. It seemed like it took a long time for someone to come to the door.

"Hi," Jack said, when Bobby Curley appeared on the threshold. "Can we come in for a minute?"

Bobby glared at them. There was a splotchy red patch on each of his cheeks. "This stops now," he said angrily. "Do you hear me? I will not have my family harassed."

"We need to get a few things straightened out," Jack said. Without answering, Bobby wheeled around and went back inside the house. They followed him into the hall where another dark-haired daughter was sitting on the staircase, her arms wrapped around her knees. "Taylor, go to your room," Bobby commanded.

"But, Daddy," the girl whined. "I want to go skating. You promised we could practice."

"Upstairs," he snapped. "Now."

Bobby walked into the living room and sat down on the pale pink sofa, resting his hands on his knees. His large frame looked awkward and out of place against the fussy, luxurious furnishings.

"Where's Teri?" Anne said casually.

"Upstairs. Look, I've had just about enough of these interrogations. My neighbor told me you've been lurking around the house all weekend."

"We were waiting for you to get back from Atlantic City," Jack said.

"I'm sorry about your brother, Jack. I really am. But hounding Teri and me night and day isn't going to bring him back. If the cops thought Tigger was murdered, they'd be conducting an investigation. But they're not. You wanna know why? Because this whole murder mystery plot you've cooked up is a fantasy. I know it's been rough on you. I grew up here, too, remember? I know what the two of you went through. Hell, Tigger was so black and blue some days it looked like he'd banged into the side of a truck. His life was messed up. And he took care of himself the best way he knew how—with a bottle of something wet to ease the pain.''

"Someone else was killed last night," Anne said quietly.

"What?" Bobby's eyes were alert, his body suddenly tense.

"A woman named Sandy Cooksey. She was Ruthie Klemperer's baby-sitter the night of the fire."

"What happened?" Bobby asked.

Ignoring the question, Anne said, "We need to talk to Teri."

"She's upstairs lying down. She has a terrible migraine headache."

"I'll bet she does," Jack said ruefully.

"Look, Bobby," Anne said. "We know Teri set off the firecracker that night. You and Tigger kept quiet about it for a long time. But your secret's out now. Tigger spilled the whole story about how the fire really started. It's all recorded on videotape."

"I don't believe you," Bobby said hotly. "Tigger would never—" He stopped talking abruptly and glared at them, not bothering to hide his emotions. The hatred showed on his face, violent and ugly, and underneath, something else, a thin sliver of fear.

"You better get your wife," Jack said.

Scowling, Bobby rose from the couch and left the room. They heard him walking up the stairs, heard the murmur of voices, then the sound of a door slamming shut.

"You think she offed Sandy?" Jack said, keeping his voice low.

"I think Teri hires other people to take care of unpleasant chores. Besides, being with Bobby and her kids in Atlantic City is an awfully good alibi."

"Hire who? P.J?"

Anne shrugged. "Boxers have access to drugs. I wrote a book once on sports medicine and learned about all the drugs some athletes take to stay competitive. Steroids, uppers, painkillers, you name it."

She gazed around the room, taking in the tassels and fringe, the gold filigree outlining the chairs, the ornate marble mantel, the flowered trellis painted on the floor. She tried to imagine what it would be like to live in this house, surrounded by so many shiny things. Once you got accustomed to wealth, you probably wouldn't want to live without it. There was more at stake when you had money, more things that could be taken away.

After a time, they heard footsteps on the stairs. Bobby came back into the living room, followed by Teri. She was wearing a powder blue dress with a white sweater draped over her shoulders. She sat down on the other end of the sofa, away from where Bobby was, with her legs crossed. She looked younger than usual. She could have been the older sister of the two girls they had seen before, not their mother.

"We watched the video," Jack said abruptly.

Teri stared down at her hands.

"P.J. said something about showing it to the police," Jack continued.

"He's not going to do a damn thing with that tape," Bobby interjected. "Not when I get through with him."

"So you didn't know P.J. was blackmailing your wife," Jack said.

"If I'd known about it, he'd be hurting right now. The man's my best friend. I never figured he'd stab us in the back like this."

Anne looked at him closely. "You and P.J. have always known the truth about that night, haven't you, Bobby?"

His face was flushed and angry. "Sure we knew. Tigger told us. And then he made us promise not to tell a living soul. We took a blood oath, down on the beach. Stuck pins in our fingers, recited our code of honor—the whole nine yards." He glared at them, his teeth clenched. "But tricking Tigger into saying it on videotape twenty years later, now that's real honorable, don't you think?"

"Boxing gyms cost money," Jack said. "P.J. must have thought it was a good way to finance his dream."

"What I don't understand," Anne said, "is why Tigger

waited all these years. He knew he was innocent. His best friends knew it. Why did he wait so long to come back here and clear his name?''

"Money," Teri said. Her voice was strained. "It always comes down to money in the end." The three of them turned to look at her. Her skin was pale and waxen, like a porcelain doll. "He needed money to pay some lawyer a retainer. If I didn't give it to him, he said he'd go straight to the police."

Jack cut in, "Why didn't he tell the police the truth twenty years ago?''

"He was in love with her," Bobby said bitterly. "Couldn't you tell? He was so in love with her he couldn't see straight." Bobby stared at Teri. After a moment, she looked away.

"How much did he want?" Anne said to Teri.

"Thirty-five hundred dollars."

"And you gave it to him?"

Teri nodded. "What else could I do?" Her voice was plaintive. "I thought the whole thing was over with. And then Tigger comes back here and digs it all up again." She stopped, her hands fluttering in the air. When she spoke again, the words came tumbling out fast. "I didn't know anyone else was in the hotel. Honest, I didn't. At the last minute, Tigger didn't want to go through with it. I was teasing him for being a chicken. The hotel was dark. I remember the dark and the stillness. And the smell, an ammonia smell. I wanted to get out of there. And then the fire started up so fast. There wasn't time. I had to run. I was running and running. I thought I was going to die." She paused to catch her breath. "God, I wish I'd never gone with him that night."

Anne glanced at Bobby. He was hunched forward, watching his wife explain how things were. The look in his eyes was one of pure longing, as if despite everything, he wanted to grab her, hold her down, and have sex with her right there on the pink velvet couch. He couldn't have been having an affair with Elise. He was too much in love with his wife. He knew what she'd done. The fire. The cover-up. But he'd married her anyway and backed her up all the way.

"What about the instructions from 'A Friend'?" Anne said to Teri. "Where does the letter fit in?"

"I took the letter from Tigger's room the next day. He was over at the sheriff's office. I don't know where you were, Jack. Nobody was home. I walked right in and took it."

"You were afraid he'd turn you in, is that why?" Anne said. "The letter was an insurance policy?"

"It was addressed to Tigger. It proved he was in the Spray View. It even proved he had the firecracker."

"Did my brother know you'd taken it?" Jack asked hotly.

"Not till last week. When he came here asking for money, I was worried I'd never hear the end of it. That's when I showed him the letter. I held on to it all these years, just in case."

"Then Tigger hadn't seen the letter in twenty years?" Anne said.

"No. I told him if he tried to make trouble for me, I'd take the letter straight to the cops. But he outsmarted me. When Bobby and I were at the charity bazaar, he broke in here and stole the letter back."

Anne said, "Only you told the cops it was money he stole—$3,500."

"I was hoping they'd search his room and find the letter. That way, no one would believe him if he said I started the fire."

"How do you live with yourself?" Jack broke in angrily. "You killed a little girl. Destroyed her parents. Ruined my brother's life."

"I never meant for it to happen," Teri cried. "It was an accident. A terrible, terrible accident."

"Like Tigger's death," Anne said slowly.

"What do you mean?" Bobby interjected.

"Where were the two of you the night of July Fourth?"

"Out on our boat."

"And you didn't happen to see my brother?" Jack said

sarcastically. "You like telling everyone what a big lush he was, Bobby. Maybe he was having a few drinks with his best buddy, until you got him wasted and tossed him overboard."

"You're nuts," Bobby said angrily.

"What about the baby-sitter?" Jack continued. "What'd she happen to see that night, huh, Teri? Did you bump her off because she was on to you?"

"I never killed anybody," Teri protested.

"Except Ruthie Klemperer," Jack said. "At least she's the only death you're owning up to *this* week. What do you think is going to happen to you when your friend P.J. turns that video over to the cops?"

"He wouldn't," Teri said weakly.

"That's not what he told us. In fact, the way things stand now I'm surprised old P.J. is still alive and kicking. Oh, that's right," Jack added, "P.J. said he had a copy of the tape. If he gets into an *accident*, the tape gets delivered to the sheriff's office before you can say *life in prison*."

"That's enough," Bobby said. "Teri's had twenty years to regret causing the fire. She still has nightmares about it."

"Is that right?" Jack said. "Imagine what Ed and Lucille Klemperer must be dreaming about."

"Teri," Anne cut in, "did P.J. contact you last night?"

"He left a message on our answering machine early this morning. Telling Bobby he needed some advice about the new gym. That was our code for me to call him."

Bobby's jaw was set. His expression was pained.

"What'd P.J. say?" Anne asked.

"He told me how you and Jack stopped by to see him. Then he warned me to get you off his back. He said he wanted another $10,000 tomorrow. Or else he'd go straight to the cops."

"You're not giving him one more dime," Bobby yelled.

"I have to," Teri said fearfully. "He'll tell. I know he will." It was the first time they'd spoken to each other since they'd entered the room. "What are you going to do?" Teri said to Anne. "Are you going to the police?"

"Yes," Anne said slowly. "As soon as we find out who killed Tigger and Sandy." She stood up. "Let's go, Jack."

"Anne," Teri began.

"What?"

"We were friends once." The pleading tone was back in her voice. Her dark hair fanned out from her face in waves.

"That was a long time ago," Anne said, realizing as she said it how much had changed. She'd moved beyond envying Teri, beyond the frightened teenager hovering in Teri's shadow. All she felt for Teri Curley was disgust.

On their way out, Anne turned and looked behind her. Teri was sitting motionless on the couch, staring at the wall. Beside her, Bobby stretched out one hand to touch her wrist. She stiffened at his touch, brushed him off, as if shooing away an insect. His body sagged slightly, his face registering defeat. In that instant, Anne glimpsed the nature of their relationship. Bobby Curley loved his wife. But she didn't love him back.

In the car, on the way to Red Bank, Anne kept changing her mind about Teri. A woman who was clever and desperate enough to cover up arson and murder for two decades would probably do just about anything to keep the truth buried. Tigger was merely an inconvenience who needed to be removed. Because he was dangerous, he became expendable. On the other hand, she knew Teri Curley. They'd grown up together, shared childhood secrets. Teri was the most self-centered, controlling woman Anne knew. Anne couldn't picture her deliberately setting out to murder someone—not without being sure the plan had succeeded. She couldn't visualize the ice princess throwing Tigger off a boat. Or hiring a thug to sell bad heroin to Sandy Cooksey. It was too . . . Anne searched for the right word. Too . . . haphazard. Too much lag time between the action and the end result. If Teri were going to kill someone, she'd stick around to make sure the job was done right. A bullet to the heart. A knife in the ribs. A pinch of arsenic in a pink Wedgwood cup. Teri would be right there to make sure her victims were dead.

"Can we trust this guy?" Jack asked, interrupting her reverie. Anne turned down the volume on the radio. An oldies station, the Drifters crooning "This Magic Moment."

"I think so. Taggart's been haunted by the case for twenty years. He retired from the fire department without ever solving it."

"Why couldn't he tell us what we needed to know on the phone?"

"I think he wants to make sure we're on the level. I told him I was writing a book about the history of the Heights, but he isn't buying it. If he sees you're Tigger's brother, he might open up."

They drove by a railroad station and the car turned onto the main commercial shopping street. Anne hadn't been in Red Bank for years and she was struck by how much it had changed. What was once a blue collar town had been transformed into yuppie heaven. Barnlike wood plank buildings advertised hundreds of antique stalls, crammed together under the same roof. There were clothing stores, art dealers, book shops, a couple of ice cream parlors. It seemed every other corner had a coffee bar. Anne ticked off the names: House of Coffee, Ordinary Joe, the Dublin Bar. How caffeinated could Red Bank get?

"Take a good look," Jack remarked. "This is what the Heights is going to become in another couple of summers."

"Never," Anne said. "The Heights Association won't allow it. They tried to open a Gap store on Main Street last year, but it was voted down."

"America's become one giant shopping mall. You think a historic district is immune? No way. Do I make a left at the traffic circle?"

Anne glanced at the directions in her lap. "No. It's the next light. There should be a Fannie Farmer store there. Then straight for another mile and a half."

When they got to the light, Anne saw that the Fannie Farmer candy shop, with its wonderful chocolate drops and lemon creams, was gone, replaced by Starbucks Coffee.

"Starbucks, huh?" Jack said. "I might as well be back in Manhattan."

The Corvette turned left and they passed a strip of housing developments filled with clusters of identical homes. Red brick "villas" gave way to gray stucco buildings, each with the same slate roof and putty-colored trim. Then the landscape opened up and a golf course hugged the side of the road. The people on the greens looked fairly young, in their twenties and thirties. Anne was slightly surprised; she'd always thought golf was an old folks' game.

Ned Taggart's house was a block from the course, a two-story white saltbox enclosed by a green picket fence. A navy blue Cadillac rested on four gray blocks in the gravel driveway. The ex-fire marshal was sitting in an Adirondack chair under a shade tree near the car. Curled up at his feet was a gray cat, fast asleep. A pitcher of lemonade and some cookies were arranged on a folding table, next to two chairs.

"Miss Hardaway, I presume," he called out, as Anne and Jack walked across the neatly cropped lawn, bordered by red and white petunias.

"Yes," Anne said. "Pleased to meet you. This is my friend, Jack Mills."

"Nice to know you," Taggart said, shaking Jack's hand. He was a tall, wiry man in his late sixties, with thick white hair, a beaked nose, and a bushy mustache. His face was deeply tanned, his clear gray eyes seemed to take stock of them, sizing up the situation. "This is Cinder," he said, reaching down to stroke the cat. "Help yourself to a snack. I baked the gingerbread snaps myself."

"Thanks," Anne said, pulling up a chair.

"Nice car," Jack said, pointing to the Cadillac.

"Restoring old cars is a hobby of mine. Got to do something to keep busy when you're retired. Otherwise, you go mad with boredom." Taggart poured three glasses of lemonade into paper cups. "Now what's all this about?" he asked. "You said on the phone it was urgent."

"Sandy Cooksey died last night," Anne said. "Officially, the cause of death was an overdose. But we think she was murdered.''

Taggart frowned. His shaggy eyebrows knitted together. ''Because she knew something about the fire?''

''Exactly,'' Jack said. ''Turns out my brother paid her a visit last week, a couple of days before he drowned. He gave her something that she was going to pass along to us. Next thing you know, she turns up dead. We don't think it's a coincidence.''

''I'll bite,'' Taggart said. ''What have you got?''

Taking turns, Anne and Jack told him everything they'd learned so far, right up until their conversation with Teri and Bobby.

When they finished, Anne said, ''What we want to know is whether that videotape could send Teri Curley to jail. Is there a statute of limitations on arson and/or murder that runs out after twenty years? How much trouble is Teri in here? If she faces a prison term, it gives her a pretty strong motive for getting Tigger and Sandy out of the way.''

Taggart shook his head. He reached for a ginger cookie, snapped it in two, and put one half in his mouth. ''Mrs. Curley doesn't have a blessed thing to worry about,'' he said, chewing. ''She didn't cause that fire.''

''But we just told you—'' Jack began.

''I heard what you said. I got ears. Only the blaze wasn't caused by any firecracker.''

Anne could feel her heart skipping in her chest. ''What do you mean?''

''Oh, a firecracker could have done some damage, sure. Hotel was made of wood. Lots of rugs, wood furniture. But a blast of that size had to be caused by a concentrated explosive. Plastic, most likely. Guess you'd call it a home-made bomb.''

''How can you be sure?'' Jack said excitedly.

''The fire radiated outward in all directions. Lots of shattering, lots of tiny fragments. A firecracker is more of a low-level explosive. The damage would have been much more contained.''

Anne's head was spinning. "If a bomb exploded, how did Sandy get out?"

"My guess is she didn't."

"What!"

"Here's how I think it must have been: Somebody sneaks into the house the back way, plants the bomb in a supply closet off the kitchen. That's where we think the fire started." Taggart paused and looked at Jack. "I always figured it was your brother, Mr. Mills. Only I thought he messed up the timing mechanism because the bomb went off while he was still on the property. He hadn't made a clean getaway. The little girl got killed, of course. But our Sandy was fine except for a few scratches. She wasn't hurt much because she wasn't inside the house."

"Then where was she?" Jack demanded.

"Probably close by. Necking with a boyfriend in the bushes or smoking a joint outside so nobody would smell it in the hotel. She had a gash on her forehead meaning something hit her, probably some type of fragment from the explosion. Knocked her right out. Sandy knew she was supposed to have been looking after little Ruthie. Once she invented her cover story, we couldn't get her to budge come hell or high water."

"You're absolutely sure about the explosives?" Anne said.

Taggart let out a wheeze of exasperation. "I was with the fire department thirty-five years. I know more about arson than anyone in Jersey."

"Inspector," Anne said, "I looked over the newspaper accounts. None of the articles mentioned a bomb."

"That's right. We don't tell the press what they got no business knowing."

"When you questioned my brother about an 'explosive device,' could he have thought you were talking about a firecracker?" Jack asked.

Taggart scratched his head. "Could be. He was so intent on proving he wasn't anywhere near the joint, I don't think he was paying attention to specifics. Of course, he was focusing all his energy on lying through his pearly whites.

Not that we believed him. Too many witnesses put him smack dab at the scene.''

''So where does this leave us?'' Jack said impatiently.

Leaning forward in his chair, Taggart lowered his voice to a stage whisper.. ''With one question: Who went to a whole mess of trouble to make sure your brother was in the wrong place at the right time?''

Chapter 22

*Common household items
that are potentially
poisonous include
bleaches, dishwashing
detergent, drain cleaners,
oil furniture polishes,
oven cleaners, and rust
removers. Make sure to
store these cleansers
in a safe place—for the
protection of children
and pets.*

It was six o'clock by the time they got back to the
Heights, and Officer Hefferle was just going off
duty.

"Hi there," Jack said, catching up to him in the parking
lot of the sheriff's office. "Do you have a minute? We
dropped by to ask you about Sandy's autopsy report."

Officer Hefferle shot them an annoyed look. He'd exchanged his uniform for a pair of black jeans and a Hootie
and the Blowfish T-shirt. Without his uniform, he seemed
even younger. The gun tucked into his waistband looked

like a toy. "Don't you two have anything better to do than play detective?" Hefferle asked.

"Nope," Jack said.

Anne added, "We were the ones who found her body. We'd like to know how she died."

"You can read all about it in tomorrow's *Oceanside Heights Press*. There's a big story on how the cops aren't doing enough to protect people from drugs and pushers." Hefferle shook his head in disgust. "Like we're supposed to clean up Landsdown when our budget's been sliced and diced. They got some nerve."

"We'd rather not wait until tomorrow," Anne said. "Besides, if the article is focusing on the sheriff's department, they probably won't spend too much time going over the details of Sandy's death."

"You're damn right they won't. These reporters are out to kick ass, maybe get some of us fired. They act like they're working for the *Philadelphia Inquirer*, instead of some pissant small-town rag."

"That's rough," Anne said, trying to sound sympathetic. Personally, she'd like nothing better than for Officer Hefferle to get into another line of work. Like selling magazine subscriptions. Or collecting fares on the Jersey Turnpike. A job where he wasn't paid to think. "But back to Sandy," she said, "do you know how she died?"

Hefferle sighed. "You don't give up, do you?" Anne shook her head. "Okay then. This'll make your day: According to the coroner, the cause of death was asphyxiation. It's just like I told you last night. She got hold of some bad junk. Heroin laced with strychnine."

"In other words, she was murdered," Jack said.

"In other words," Hefferle repeated, "junkies aren't particular about what they shove in their veins. It's not like this stuff comes in a package with a love note from the FDA. This is street dope. You take your chances."

"Did she die instantly?" Anne asked.

"Coroner said she probably bought the farm about ten minutes after she gave herself the injection. She had some spasming, too. Death throes, they call it. That's why her back was arched and her legs were stuck out funny. Rigor mortis set in right away. Her face and neck were stiff as a board.''

"Don't you think the timing is peculiar?'' Jack asked. "She calls up, tells us she's got something of my brother's, and the next thing you know she's mainlining poison. Where's the logic in that? If she wanted money from us, why get high before the transaction?''

Hefferle shrugged. "You ever seen that beer commercial. Why ask why?''

"Isn't it possible,'' Jack said, "that someone gave her the injection deliberately, against her will?''

Hefferle looked skeptical. "She didn't exactly run screaming off that pier now, did she?''

"Maybe someone was holding her down. Or somebody sold her bad drugs deliberately, to shut her up.''

"You mean a pimp? A dissatisfied customer?'' Hefferle laughed. "One of these days, I got to go out to Hollywood. I could make a mint writing BS for the tube. Ever watch *Homicide*? Or *NYPD Blue*? That stuff is so bogus. Those TV guys should come down the shore, ride around with me awhile. I'd show 'em how a beat cop does his job. Handing out parking tickets, dragging deadbeats off to the morgue . . .''

"Thanks, Officer,'' Anne interrupted. "We don't want to take up any more of your time. Thanks again for the info.''

"Hey, no problem,'' Hefferle said, smiling. "Just trying to help. You have a good night, now.'' He turned and walked toward his car, a 1977 white Dodge that looked like it had seen better days.

"Do you believe this guy?'' Jack said to Anne, after Hefferle drove away. "He can't tell a crime from a day at the beach.''

"At least he told us what we needed to know—how Sandy died.''

Anne gazed past the fence separating the parking lot from the highway. Day trippers were crowding Route 35, heading west, away from the shore. She watched the cars crawl along, trapped in bumper-to-bumper traffic. Overhead, the pale ghost of the sun glimmered behind a mass of gray clouds, as if mocking sunbathers for abandoning the beach. Strychnine. Now there was a poison you don't find lying around the house. Who would have access to strychnine? A druggist would. She pictured the white shelves in the back of Advance Pharmacy, with their tidy rows of pills and potions. Even if strychnine wasn't dispensed with the same regularity as Prozac and Zantac, Joe Vance could probably order it, no questions asked. A thought teased at the corners of Anne's mind. Where had she read about strychnine lately? In a magazine. No. Anne closed her eyes. It had something to do with gardening. Protecting flowers and plants. Her eyes snapped open. Mary Lou Popper. In Mary Lou's notes for the gardening chapter, the Queen of Clean had mentioned toxic substances used in the latest crop of household pesticides. Teri's roses thrived in the heat of July all the way through the end of September. Teri probably relied on all sorts of chemicals to keep the flowers free from harm. Anne imagined Teri standing in her pink kitchen, unscrewing a bottle of powder with a skull and crossbones stamped on the label. Skull and crossbones . . .

"Oh," Anne exclaimed suddenly.

"What is it?" Jack said. "What's wrong? You look like you're miles away."

"I was just remembering the stuff I saw in Ed Klemperer's laboratory. There were all these little vials of poison lying around, like he was using them in his experiments or something."

"Klemperer again! Do you realize he's been lurking in the shadows all along? Who's got poison in his basement? Ed Klemperer. Who knows how to operate an old printing press to send my brother a set of phony instructions? Ed again. Who can assemble an explosive? Ed Klemperer, the eccentric inventor! And who's got a motive to destroy the Spray View? Mr. Ed Klemperer. The man who happens to collect a big fat insurance check if anything happens to his hotel."

Anne looked at Jack. His eyes flashed with determination. "What are we waiting for?" she said. "Let's go."

They parked down the street from the Klemperers' house, approaching it stealthily, as if they'd already broken in and were trying to avoid getting caught. The wrought-iron gate looked forbidding, a warning to trespassers: *Keep Out.* When they were directly across the street from the Gothic-style house, they stopped, taking cover behind a large weeping willow tree.

"Okay," Jack said. "What's the plan?"

"I don't know. We can't just walk up and ring the bell. And I don't think Lucille would leave the door unlocked again, not after I waltzed right in the other day."

"You think she's home?"

Anne glanced at her watch. Five past seven. "Tonight's Sunday. She's probably at Vespers."

"That doesn't give us much time."

"It does if we work fast," Anne said, stepping out from behind the tree.

She crossed the street. Jack hurried after her. The porch lights were on at the Klemperers. A cloud of insects hovered around the front door. Swatting them away, Anne turned the doorknob. Locked. Lucille was no fool. The back door was probably locked, too. Bugs crashed into the electric zapper on the porch ceiling, disintegrating in a burst of blue sparks. Anne hated the crackling sound of their dying. It made her think of cooked flesh. There was a rumor in the Heights about Ed Klemperer: He ate little boys who strayed onto his property, cooked them like steaks sizzling on a grill.

She left the porch and veered to her left, heading around the side of the house. Luckily, because of the fence and the shade trees on the lawn, the house was partially hidden from the street. Otherwise, somebody would be sure to notice them. She saw that Jack had ducked down, half-walking, half-crouching, and she did the same. Above her, the house loomed gray and foreboding. There had to be a way to get in. "What about the windows?" Jack said under his breath.

"It's worth a try." They went over to a small window about four feet from the ground. Anne peered inside. It was dark. She could make out a desk and some tall bookshelves. This must be the library she'd seen on her last visit.

"Ready?" Jack asked. She nodded. Gripping the sash, they tugged at the windowpane. It didn't budge. "No go," Jack said. "Let's try another."

Heading toward the back of the house, they approached each window in turn, with the same result. "It's got to be awfully hot in there," Jack said.

"Actually, it's freezing. I think they've got central air-conditioning."

"Must cost a mint," Jack said, rolling his eyes. "What does Ed care? He can afford it."

Anne studied the house. It looked silent, deserted. But Klemperer had to be in there. He almost never went out. Was he watching them? Calling the cops? Anne pictured Hefferle driving up in his Dodge and arresting her and Jack: Off-duty cop catches would-be burglars. She couldn't imagine how she'd talk her way out of a breaking and entering charge.

They reached the back door. Jack jiggled the knob. No luck. Lucille must have locked it before she went off to pray. Working quickly, they tried the windows on the other side of the house. All of them were securely fastened. "I've got an idea," Jack said. "You game?"

"Shoot."

He pointed to a beech tree next to the house. One branch of the tree led directly to the roof, the leaves brushing against a dormer window. "You mean climb up there?" Anne said, incredulous. "Forget it!"

"It's the only way."

"How do we know the window isn't locked?"

"We don't. But it's our only chance to get to Klemperer."

Anne stared at the tree. The trunk split off in two directions like a wishbone. A tangle of branches extended toward the roof. Her eye measured the distance between the ground and the roof line. The roof was what? Thirty, forty feet high? If she fell, she might not be killed. She could wind up a quadriplegic. A paraplegic, if she landed just the right way.

"You go first," she said to Jack.

"All right." Jack walked over to the base of the tree. "Follow me. Watch where I put my feet."

With the ease of an acrobat, Jack nimbly scaled the trunk and started his ascent. In no time, he had disappeared. Although the leaves trembled, his body remained hidden in a canopy of green.

"Anne," she heard him call. "Come on."

Reluctantly, she went toward the tree. Don't think, she said to herself. Just do it. Grasping the trunk with both hands, she pulled herself up so she was standing on the spot where the tree started to fork. There, that wasn't so bad. She craned her neck. Five branches above, to her right, was Jack. He seemed to be moving easily, hoisting himself higher the way children climbed a jungle gym, one rung at a time.

"Keep going," he urged. "You can do it."

"Yeah, right," she said. "I've never climbed a tree in my life."

Treading gingerly, she reached for the closest branch, first locating a foothold, then using her arms to propel her higher. The branches weren't completely smooth. Some had funny bumps and knots. If she took one wrong step . . . She swallowed and kept climbing. The tree felt rough against her skin, leaves slapped at her face. Don't look down, she told herself. Thrusting her hand out, she grabbed hold of the next branch, willing her feet not to slip. Without warning, the tree shuddered, a sudden jolt that caused her to tighten her grip. She peered toward the house and saw that Jack had landed on the roof.

"You're almost home," he encouraged her.

"Great," she muttered under her breath.

She climbed a little higher, resisting the temptation to look down, to glance across the street and find one of her neighbors gaping at her, wondering why on earth Anne Hardaway was stuck in a tree like a stray cat. Cautiously, she inched closer to the house. The branch that she was standing on was parallel to the hipped roof. Between the beech and the roof's edge was a gap of about two feet. If there were a wooden plank, she could lay one end of it on the branch and the other end on the roof and walk straight across. Without it, she'd have to jump, like Jack did. The thought made her dizzy.

"Come on," Jack said, stretching out his arms. "I'll catch you."

"I can't." She rested her cheek against the rough surface of the branch. It was true. She couldn't move. Her limbs felt like jelly.

"It's not far," Jack urged.

"You go on," Anne said weakly. "See if the window's locked."

She heard Jack rattle the sash. "It's open," he said excitedly. "We're home free."

"Go ahead. I'm just gonna rest here awhile."

"Anne, you can't stay on that branch all night."

"Why not?"

Jack leaned back against the roof, digging his heels in for balance. "How do you plan on getting down?"

"Same way I got up." She glanced down. Big mistake. The ground looked like it was miles away. Her legs felt wobbly. Great! She was stuck! There was no way she would be able to climb down. She clutched the branch with both hands. Maybe if Jack called the fire department, they'd send a truck with a ladder and—

"Anne, come on. We can't stay up here. Somebody's going to spot us and call the cops."

She looked at the ground again. Terra firma was an awful long way off. She'd slip for sure if she tried to climb down. She imagined herself plummeting, crashing into branches, the crunch of her bones against grass. "Promise you'll catch me?" she whispered to Jack.

"Yes."

"Okay. One . . . two . . . three." Taking a deep breath,

she pushed off and lunged toward the house. For an instant, she was sailing through the air, and then Jack was grabbing her arms, her legs scraping against the slate roof. He pulled her up beside him, and she realized that the roof was flat enough to sit on. A wave of relief washed over her. She had made it. Safe.

"You in one piece?" Jack asked.

"I think so."

"Good. Let's go." Grabbing her hand, he led her over to the dormer window. Anne crawled through first and found herself in a small guest room, furnished with twin beds, a bureau, and a rocking chair. She opened the window wider so Jack could get in. Trying to be as quiet as possible, they made a quick tour of the second floor. No sign of Klemperer. They walked down the curving staircase, treading lightly so the floorboards didn't creak. Everything looked as it had on Anne's first visit, dark and still. When they reached Ruthie's old room, Anne motioned Jack inside. She noticed the stuffed animals had been moved. Instead of lying against the cushions on the bed, they were lined up on the window seat.

"Wow," Jack said, in astonishment. "It's like a mausoleum in here."

"Or a shrine. Her clothes are in the closet. Her toys are on the shelves."

A low whistle escaped Jack's lips. "It's like Ruthie's going to walk in here any minute."

"Exactly. Come on. I'll show you the laboratory."

Back in the hallway, Anne guided Jack toward the kitchen. In the dining area, she stopped short. "Listen," she whispered. The noise was faint—a humming sound, like a distant swarm of bees. "It's coming from the lab," Anne said. "Maybe he's down there."

Edging forward, she reached the door that led to the basement. A faint light glowed underneath. Anne turned the knob and the door swung open. Slowly, she and Jack crept down the stairs. There was a damp smell in the basement, a scent that Anne associated with mold. A quarter of the way down, she caught sight of Klemperer and stopped. The man couldn't be more than sixty-five years old, but he looked ancient. His shoulders were stooped, his hair completely white, his face the color of powdered chalk. He was wearing a tattered maroon bathrobe over a pair of baggy trousers. With his long, ragged beard and wire-rimmed spectacles, he looked like Santa Claus gone to seed. Set before him on the big steel table was a row of glass test tubes containing brightly colored liquids. The liquids bubbled and frothed, like miniature fountains. A beaker filled with a dark substance sat atop a Bunsen burner, its flame glowing blue. Next to the beaker was a machine that resembled a small vacuum cleaner with a hose attached. The machine vibrated slightly, making a steady humming sound.

Using a pair of metal tongs, Klemperer picked up the beaker and poured its content into one of the test tubes. There was a crackling noise, a sudden burst of smoke, and the liquid in the beaker turned vermilion red. Klemperer waved the smoke away; it drifted up toward the ceiling in a swirling cloud. Anne felt Jack move past her. He bounded down the steps until he was directly in front of the inventor, as though he'd been conjured up as part of the experiment.

"What on earth!" Klemperer exclaimed, taking a step backward.

"I want answers," Jack said, "about my brother's death."

"Who are you?" Klemperer said. "What are you doing here?" His voice sounded hoarse and scratchy, as if unaccustomed to speech.

"I'm Jack Mills. Tigger Mills was my brother."

Anne hurried down the steps. "And I'm Anne Hardaway," she said to Klemperer. "We need to ask you a few questions."

The hermit's eyes widened in surprise. "Stay away," he yelled. Holding the tongs out like a weapon, he backed up until he was standing near the metal cabinet on the far side of the room. Anne recognized the cabinet from the other day; it contained the vials of poison she'd seen. Next to it were rows of plants. She suspected the damp smell was coming from them.

"We're not leaving until we get some answers," Jack said firmly.

"Stay away," Klemperer repeated, brandishing the tongs. His breath came in short gasps.

"You hated Tigger, didn't you?" Jack said. "All these years, you blamed him for Ruthie's death. When he came back to town, you decided to get revenge."

"What?" Klemperer wheezed. His expression was distraught. His hands shook. He looked like a cornered animal, snared in a trap. Despite herself, Anne felt sorry for him.

"Mr. Klemperer," she said softly. "We're here to find out what happened the night of the fire."

Klemperer let out a low moan. His body sagged. For a moment, Anne thought he was going to collapse. "I knew you'd come," he croaked. "I've been waiting."

"Tell us about the fire," Anne said. "Why did you want Tigger to destroy the inn?"

Klemperer appeared to be struggling to take in air. "Lucille says the wicked must be punished," he gasped.

"Like you punished my brother?" Jack said angrily. Anne put her hand on Jack's arm. Badgering Klemperer wasn't going to get them anywhere. The old man looked disoriented, frightened. She was reminded of her mother—her mother cowering in the garden, terrified of her own shadow.

"Why did you send Tigger the note?" Anne asked gently. "To frame him for the fire? So he could take the fall for you?"

"Note?" Klemperer said uncertainly.

"On the printing press. Instructing Tigger to go to the Spray View, telling him where the firecrackers were hidden."

Klemperer looked confused. Was it possible that he'd become mentally deranged, hiding from the world because his mind was unbalanced?

"An accident," Klemperer rasped. "Didn't mean it."

"What was an accident?" Jack shouted. "Tigger's death?

Were you out on the ocean that night? Did you poison him? Drown him? Tell us the truth."

Klemperer dropped the tongs. He pressed his palms against his face. "My baby," he moaned. "My poor baby girl." He lifted his head. His eyes burned with the weight of his grief. "I loved her so."

"Enough to murder the man you blamed for killing her?" Jack persisted.

Klemperer blinked. His face crumpled. "I killed Ruthie," he said slowly. "I killed my baby. And now I've got to pay."

Chapter 23

To remove dust from plants, you could flick them with a feather duster. Or you could stick them under a shower or leave them out in the rain.

There was stunned silence in the laboratory. Anne stared at Klemperer. The old man was trembling, his face the color of faded plaster. As she moved toward him and took his arm, he emitted a weak, mewling cry, like a kitten that had lost its mother. "Why don't you sit down?" she said kindly, guiding him over to a high stool on the other side of the table.

He sank onto the stool, breathing heavily. Anne wondered if he has asthma or some kind of heart condition. On the table beside him, the test tubes bubbled merrily. "My medicine," he said weakly, pointing to a bottle of pills on a shelf. Jack went to get the pills. "Is there water down here?" Anne asked Klemperer.

"Over there," Klemperer said, indicating a steel sink next to the row of plants.

Jack filled a glass of water from the tap. When Klemperer reached to take it, Anne saw that his hand was shaking. He swallowed two of the pills and then stared at Anne and Jack unsteadily. "Do you want us to help you upstairs?" Anne said.

Klemperer shook his head. "I'll be all right."

"We didn't mean to upset you," Anne said. "We're only trying to get at the truth."

"The truth," Klemperer echoed. His gray eyes were watery. "The truth is I killed my little angel. She was my heart, my life."

"Back up a minute," Jack said. "You planted the bomb at the Spray View?"

"There were explosive materials in the basement. Dangerous toxins. Chemicals for my experiments. I should have known better than to store them at the inn. I was a fool."

"But you thought Tigger was responsible, right?" Jack said. "He was the one accused of setting off the firecracker that caused the explosion."

"I blame myself. For being arrogant. For gambling with my daughter's life."

"Looks like you got the same setup right here," Jack said, gesturing toward the test tubes and the Bunsen burner.

"There's nothing inflammatory in this lab, no dangerous substances," Klemperer said. "But as an extra precaution, the whole house is installed with an indoor sprinkler system. History won't repeat itself."

"No dangerous substances, huh?" Jack said sarcastically. "How about poison?" He pointed to the metal cabinet against the wall, which was partially open. "You've got enough toxins in here to poison the entire town."

"None of them are flammable, I assure you," Klemperer said. "You're perfectly safe." All of a sudden, he started to wheeze. Reaching into the pocket of his bathrobe, he pulled out an inhaler and brought it to his mouth. After a few moments his breathing returned to normal. "Asthma," he explained. "Pollen count is high this summer."

"Let's go back to the night of the fire," Anne said. "You called the baby-sitter, didn't you? You called Sandy and told her to take Ruthie to see the fireworks show."

For an instant, a faint smile played upon Klemperer's lips. "Ruthie loved bright things. Colors. Flowers. The lights on the ships at night. Fairy lights, she called them."

"So you did speak to Sandy?" Jack interrupted.

"Yes. The girl promised she'd take Ruthie down to the beach. But . . ." Klemperer's voice trails away.

"But she didn't," Jack finished.

"No," he whispered. "Because of my carelessness, my precious Ruthie is dead."

"Why didn't you come forward at the time?" Jack demanded.

Klemperer's expression was dazed, as if he was reliving the experience in his mind. "I was in shock. Nothing made sense. I knew I was responsible, but . . ."

"You let the whole town go on believing that Tigger murdered your daughter," Jack cut in. "Why?"

"I don't know," Klemperer said slowly. "Maybe because I couldn't bear what I'd done. At first, I tried to tell myself your brother was responsible. Lucille believed he was. She wouldn't listen to me. She kept telling me it was all his fault."

"My brother nearly got sent to jail," Jack said coldly. "His whole life fell apart after the fire."

"If he'd been arrested, I'd have come forward. But the police let the matter drop." Klemperer raised one hand to his mouth. "Only I can't forget." His voice sounded muffled. "Sometimes I think I hear her calling me. I walk into a room and it's like she's just left. She's hiding from me, playing a game."

Again, Anne felt herself pitying the man. Klemperer looked so forlorn, so utterly lost. She glanced at Jack, expecting a similar response. But Jack's expression didn't waver. His face had taken on a stony cast.

"What about the insurance money?" he said abruptly.

Klemperer's hand dropped. "What?"

"The million bucks you got when the Spray View went up in smoke."

"I don't know what you mean," Klemperer faltered.

"A month before the inn blew up you took out an insurance policy on the property. Seems kind of peculiar since word was you were looking to sell the place.''

''My old policy had lapsed. I needed another for the flood insurance. *Farmer's Almanac* predicted bad storms that summer. We couldn't sell if the building got damaged.'' A horrified look appeared on Klemperer's face. ''Are you saying I set the fire deliberately? For the money!'' His eyes blazed. ''You think I'd kill my baby for a lousy check. Why, we couldn't even give her a decent burial. There wasn't anything left of her, poor thing. Her body was burned beyond recognition.''

''We're sorry for your loss,'' Anne said gently. ''But the fact is there have been two more mysterious deaths. Tigger. And Sandy Cooksey.''

''Lucille would tell you it's the Lord's will.''

''She has made her feelings quite clear on that point,'' Anne said.

''She smiled all the way through Tigger's funeral,'' Jack added, ''like she nailed the coffin shut herself.''

''Lucy's changed,'' Klemperer said sadly. ''She used to be so full of life. God, she was beautiful.''

''Did you know she was once married to my father?'' Jack cut in.

Klemperer laughed harshly. ''Of course I know. In the beginning, I think they might have been fooling around on the sly. Can you believe it? These days, Lucille gets up in arms if one of the church biddies wears her skirt too short. Modesty in the eyes of the Lord and such.''

''You and Pop were good friends once,'' Jack said.

''Things change. My wife used to be a fine, loving woman. Not anymore. Something snapped inside her the day our Ruthie died. Drove her straight over the edge. In the beginning, I was glad she took comfort in God. But then I figured out just who she thinks is up there. I had a dog once, came down with rabies. Started frothing at the mouth, went mean around the eyes. That's Lucille's God. Vengeful and ornery. Fire-and-brimstone Christians, some folks call it. I call it a shame.''

"Did Tigger come here last week?" Anne said. "Did he try to talk to you?"

"No. I haven't seen him in twenty years, not since that night at the sheriff's office when we were both being questioned."

"What about Sandy? Had she tried to contact you?"

Klemperer shook his head. "I don't have many visitors," he said with a wry smile. "Speaking of which, how'd the two of you get in the house?"

"The back door was open," Anne lied. Jack walked over to the metal cabinet along the wall. "See now, this is interesting," Jack said coolly. He ran his hand over the row of glass vials. Inspecting the labels, he picked up one of them. From where she was standing, Anne could see the familiar skull and crossbones. "Strychnine," Jack announced. "The same stuff that killed poor Sandy Cooksey."

"For my experiments," Klemperer said. "My mice."

"You find it amusing to poison small animals?" Jack asked.

"Of course not," Klemperer retorted. "It's for the plants."

"I don't understand," Anne said. She'd almost forgotten about the plants. In the short time they'd been in the lab, she'd become accustomed to the damp jungle smell they gave off. The scent was almost soothing.

"I'm working on a cure," Klemperer said.

"A cure?" Anne repeated.

"For asthma. It's my life's work. Look here." He walked over to a plant with pale purple flowers and purplish black berries. "This is belladonna. Also known as black nightshade. When you grind up the leaves and roots, you get a powder that helps relieve asthma symptoms."

"Where do the mice fit in?" Jack said sarcastically.

"These plants are cuttings. I grow hybrids in the garden. Mixing and matching rare plants, if you will. To refine my cure. Deer and rabbits are a constant nuisance. I needed to develop a pesticide of sorts to keep them away. In tiny doses, strychnine is quite effective. I use the mice as my guinea pigs, to determine what's safe to eat."

"So you're poisoning the town's wildlife," Jack said grimly. "What about people? People like Sandy Cooksey, the baby-sitter who caused all your problems in the—"

He was interrupted suddenly by a shrill cry. "Get out!" Lucille Klemperer was standing on the stairs, livid with rage. "Get out of my house this instant."

"Now, Lucy," Klemperer said, stretching out his arm in a gesture of appeasement.

"You," Lucille said, pointing to Anne. "You're the one responsible. You need to be taught a lesson."

Anne stared at Lucille Klemperer. She was wearing a white cape over a white dress, her arms cloaked in long white gloves. Her gray hair was disheveled, her eyes burned with hatred. In the half-light, she looked like an avenging ghost.

"Look, lady," Jack said. "We're just having a friendly chat with your husband."

"See that ye walk circumspectly. Not as fools. Redeeming the time, because the days are evil," Lucille fixed her eyes on Anne. "Lead us not into temptation, but deliver us from evil: For thine is the kingdom, and the power, and the glory, for ever and ever."

"Skip the Scripture," Jack said. "We're not interested."

"Lucille, I can explain," Klemperer said. There was a pleading note in his voice. Anne glanced at him. His hands had started to shake again. He seemed afraid of her.

"Mrs. Klemperer," Anne said. "We're not going to stop until we find out the truth."

"If you don't go," Lucille threatened, "you'll be sorry."

Anne nodded. "Just so you know where we stand." She moved toward the stairs, with Jack close behind her. Lucille didn't budge. Anne climbed the stairs, brushing against Lucille's rigid form on the way out. She could feel the venom rising from the older woman, like steam swirling above a boiling pot.

"We were just leaving," Jack muttered.

* * *

Dusk settled over the Heights. Over the ocean, the sky was a deep inky blue. Anne imagined this was the way it looked on summer nights in Scandinavia, when the sun didn't set until well after midnight. The clouds drifted by so quickly she could chart their progress as they skimmed the horizon. She gazed up at the sky, listening to Jack talk. For the past half-hour, they'd been going over what Ed Klemperer said. The boardwalk was practically deserted. Now that the holiday was over, the town had regained its usual quiet, at least until next weekend, when another wave of tourists began checking into the hotels.

This was where it all began, Anne thought. Four days ago, she had sat on the boardwalk with Tigger. It felt like another lifetime.

"I can't believe Klemperer snowed you," Jack was saying. "He's deranged. Just think about Ruthie's room—her stuff waiting for her like she's out playing hopscotch and she'll be back any second. And that creepy lab. It's like something out of a B-movie. *Nightmare on Beechwood Avenue.* He's definitely mixed up in Tigger's death."

"Did you see how upset he was?" Anne said. "Klemperer's been holed up in that house for twenty years because he's convinced he killed his daughter. I don't think so, Jack. Did you see the metal storage locker he has? There's a ground connector attached to it. That means it's vented to the outdoors."

"So?"

"So grounding drains off static electricity, making the entire basement less of a fire hazard." Jack raised his eyebrows quizzically. "It's true. I researched it when I was writing the home improvement book."

"The guy is a nut job," Jack said. "You think he's playing with a full deck? He's experimenting with poison, for God's sake! Doesn't that tell you something?"

"It tells me he wants to make amends. By finding a cure for asthma, he can erase some of the guilt he feels about causing Ruthie's death."

"Spare me the dime-store psychology. I had no idea you were this gullible."

"I just don't think he's putting on an act. I can't see Ed Klemperer stealing a boat, luring Tigger aboard, poisoning his drink and heaving him over the side. Can you?"

"It makes sense."

"The man's a recluse. If he's out on a boat in the middle of the ocean on July Fourth, don't you think half the town would notice?"

"It all fits," Jack said, shooing away her objections. "If Tigger was poisoned, drugged, whatever, it explains why he couldn't swim to shore. And it explains Sandy's death, too. You heard what Hefferle said: Someone laced the heroin she bought with strychnine."

Anne looked at him skeptically. "So you think Ed's a drug pusher, too?"

"Who else stockpiles strychnine like it's candy?"

"I don't buy it." The wind was blowing away from the ocean. The tide was low, seaweed ringed the water's edge like a slick green collar. "And there's something else," Anne mused. "Klemperer admitted a lot of things back there, but he didn't seem to know anything about that letter we found in the vault."

Jack threw his hands in the air. "He's not going to admit he set Tigger up to take the fall for the fire."

"Assuming you're right, assuming Klemperer is 'A Friend,' why use the printing press? He's one of a handful of people who knows how to operate the press. If the police discover the note, they're sure to trace it back to him. As soon as they find out about the insurance money, he's their number one arson suspect. Don't you see? It's too *obvious*. It's almost as if the person who sent Tigger that letter wanted to get caught."

"Maybe he did, okay? Klemperer's obviously psychotic. Maybe subconsciously, he wanted to be punished for his crime."

Anne looked at Jack. His face had the same hardened expression she'd noticed in the lab. It was clear he thought Ed Klemperer was guilty. For an instant, she wondered what Jack would do next. The thought worried her. So many of the people she'd spoken to in the last few days seemed hell-bent on getting revenge for real and imagined sins. She had never considered what Jack might do to avenge his brother's death. "We don't have a shred of proof that Klemperer was involved in Tigger's death or Sandy's," she told him.

Jack sprang to his feet. "But we do have proof. The strychnine. It should be enough to have the old man hauled in for questioning, don't you think? I'm going back to the sheriff's office. I bet Klemperer would confess what he did if the cops had a crack at him. You want to come?"

Anne shook her head. The light was fading, the sky bleeding into the ocean.

"No, thanks. I've had all I can stand of Hefferle and company. I still think you're wrong about Klemperer. Didn't you see his face, Jack? The man is a wreck."

But Jack had already turned away and was jogging down the boardwalk in the direction of his car.

Chapter 24

Don't clean surface-sealed floors with water. It can get between the cracks, eventually causing the floor to warp and give way.

In just a few short minutes, a velvety darkness had covered the beach like a shroud. From the boardwalk, the sand looked like a flat, black stone set against the ocean. Clouds blanketed the sky, obscuring the stars and the sickle of a moon behind a grayish curtain. A thin layer of fog rolled silently over the beach.

From where she was sitting, Anne couldn't see the water at all. The fog was playing tricks, altering her perspective. Kind of like life, she thought. These last few days had wrenched her out of her safe, comfortable existence and deposited her in an unfamiliar world. Everything seemed different since Tigger's death, wrong somehow, off-kilter. Her hometown, her neighbors, people and places she'd known all her life had taken on a strange aspect—as though she were seeing them through the wrong end of a magnifying glass that distorted the image, threw it back to her hazy and misshapen. Even her own emotions were blurred;

she didn't know what she was feeling or what she wanted from one moment to the next.

Anne stared at the water, listening to the sound of the waves. She loved watching the ocean. It was a constant presence in her life, yet it was always changing, always in motion. After dark, when the sky was overcast, the water seemed to disappear, turning into a shapeless black mass, an unseen force that lapped the sand gently or howled and crackled with rage, depending on the weather.

Her earliest memories were of the beach. She used to play by the water for hours, building sand castles, filling her yellow pail to the brim. Sometimes her father would lift her up onto his shoulders and walk out into the ocean. She remembered how important she felt, held aloft, high above the rest of the world. She gripped his neck tight, holding on, eyes fixed on the horizon. Sometimes she saw the wave curling toward them. Other times, she closed her eyes so it would come as a surprise. Even now, she remembered the thrill of being swept off his shoulders, buffeted by the force of the ocean. The water closed over her head as she let the wave lift her up and away from him. She felt the sea crash into her, rushing past in a blur of noise and foam. She couldn't see, couldn't breathe. There was nothing except the pounding in her ears, the taste of salt on her lips. She flailed her arms, kicking out with both legs. She was drowning, almost. Little girl lost. And then he was there, her father, cradling her in his arms, lifting her up, out of the sea, and she knew she was safe. He would carry her back to shore, wrap her in a big fluffy towel, and buy two Italian ices from the Good Humor man, lemon for him, grape for her. They played that game until the summer she turned ten, when he left them and moved away. She remembered watching his car disappearing around the corner, remembered the bewildered expression in her mother's eyes.

Her mother's ashes were buried out in the ocean somewhere, tiny gray bits that floated on the surface and disappeared before Anne had time to cry, before she had time to realize, *My mother is drifting to the bottom of the sea.*

She recalled the dream she had had the other night—Tigger's bones bleached white, fish wriggling through the sockets of his eyes.

She looked at her watch. Nine-thirty. She'd been sitting here for nearly forty-five minutes. She got up slowly, her joints stiff, and walked the three blocks to her house. The Heights was quiet, the only noise she heard was the low murmur emanating from her neighbors' television sets. She imagined the way the town looked from above—quaint, tidy, a patchwork of faith and serenity.

On her porch, she paused, noticing something white tucked halfway underneath her front door. She stooped to pick it up—a piece of paper. She opened the door, flicked on the light in the living room. The note was short, scrawled by hand on one of those freebie notepads placed in hotel rooms by the phone. At the top in small print, it said: *Harrah's, Atlantic City.*

Dear Miss H:

My friend Sandy said I was to give you something if anything was to happen to her. Meet me inside Dreamland at ten tonight. Bring the letter Sandy hid in the bank, and some $$$ for my trouble.

Yours,
Susie Jenks

Anne read the note twice. What was Sandy Cooksey's real connection to Tigger? Sandy knew something—probably more than Taggart or anyone else suspected at the time. Somewhere along the line, Sandy had stumbled on the truth. It sounded like Sandy even had some kind of proof. Otherwise, why did Susie Jenks think Sandy put the letter from "A Friend" in the bank vault? Working quickly, Anne opened the safe in the living room and removed the letter to Tigger. She examined the contents of her wallet. There was a grand total of $37.50, along with

a blank check. It would have to do. Grabbing a flashlight
from the toolbox in the closet, she locked up the house and
headed for her car.

According to the clock on the dashboard, it was 9:47
P.M. She had time to stop off at Ravenswood. Maybe Jack
was back from the sheriff's office. But when she pulled up
in front of the inn, there was no sign of the red Corvette;
it wasn't in the lot or parked on the street. Jack's window
was dark.

She turned the car around and headed north on Ocean
Avenue. It still felt like rain. The wind had picked up, the
air was damp. Gulls perched atop the telephone poles lining
the road, their heads tucked into their breasts. Anne
couldn't tell whether they were asleep or shielding themselves from the approaching storm. Way out over the ocean,
a jagged lightning bolt flashed once and disappeared. The
storm might not even hit there, Anne thought. She'd seen
it before. Miles away, storm clouds gathered, yet the
Heights remained untouched. Or the reverse happened. The
town was deluged with rain, while over the water a patch
of sky opened to reveal a rainbow.

Ahead, the towers of Dreamland were ablaze in sparkling
lights. During the day, the hulking shell of the old amusement park looked tawdry and run-down. But at night, with
hundreds of electric bulbs glimmering on its facade, the old
glamour of Dreamland was restored. Twin towers sprang
from the roof of the pavilion, flanking gold minarets and
colonnades. A bulbous white onion dome towered over the
colossal building like the crown on an Arabian palace.
Anne parked beside the chain link fence enclosing the
amusement park. There weren't any other cars on the
Heights side of the pavilion. But Dreamland was huge,
about the size of two football stadiums. Susie Jenks might
have parked on the Landsdown side.

Anne surveyed the fence, searching for a way in. It was
about eight feet high, with metal spikes on top, to deter
trespassers from making the climb. Walking toward the
ocean, she skirted the perimeter of the fence, trying to discover an opening she could slip through. It was an odd

choice for a rendezvous. Just how was she supposed to get inside? And how had this Susie person managed to get in?

Anne trained her flashlight on the fence. Behind it rose the mint-colored walls of the pavilion, decorated with painted advertisements for the Dreamland Museum. *Living Wonders of the World,* a sign promised. *Freaks of Wax. Spook House—Come One, Come All!* Some of the attractions were painted on the exterior. There was the Turtle Girl, showing a woman's face emerging from a green spotted shell, and the Four-Legged Woman, the Fat Lady, the Mermaid (a buxom Venus reclining on a clamshell), and the Penguin Girl, with her flippers and flip hairdo from the 1950s. Nice, Anne thought. A real girlie show. Weren't any of the freaks men? Her flashlight passed over a drawing of a female vampire with blood-stained lips, fangs like ice picks, and the outstretched wings of a bat. She stopped, staring straight ahead. There, by the vampire lady, was a chain link door that was part of the fence. A heavy metal padlock was lying on the ground, next to a long steel chain. Anne walked closer. The door was ajar. She pushed against it, and the door swung open with a groan.

Moving cautiously, she approached the pavilion. Far off, in the distance, lightning pricked the sky and was gone, followed by the low grumble of thunder. The entrance to Dreamland was under an archway. Carved into the building on either side were life-size statues of women, or at least what was left of the statues. Over the years, vandals had hacked away at the sculptures, smearing them with graffiti, cutting off arms, hair, parts of the torsos, until what was left was unrecognizable. Anne walked toward the massive double doors, decorated with gold-colored floral medallions. She reached out, touching one of the twin knobs gingerly. The door fell back, revealing the pitch-dark, cavernous interior.

On the threshold, Anne hesitated. There was something airless and oppressive about the building. A rank smell emanated from inside, a fetid, decaying odor, like spoiled meat. She had an uneasy feeling. The amusement park had been closed for thirty years. Why was it suddenly so easy

to walk right in? Anne checked her watch. It was 10:02
P.M. Time for her meeting with the mysterious Susie. She
couldn't back out now. Summoning her resolve, she
stepped inside the building, and the door swung shut.

Instantly, the darkness enveloped her, a deep opaque
black, thick and impenetrable as fog. It took a few moments
for her eyes to adjust. She held the flashlight straight out
in front of her, moving it up and down, back and forth, like
a knife slicing the air. Gradually, she began to make out
dim shapes, the faint outlines of objects. She moved forward slowly, taking small precise steps, her left arm flung
sideways, in an effort to keep her balance. Her footsteps
reverberated against the floor. Even her breathing sounded
overly loud, she could almost hear her heart thumping in
her chest.

To her right was an old-fashioned carousel, its carved
wooden horses still intact. Brass poles pierced the horses'
backs and reemerged underneath their bellies. Their manes,
saddles, and legs were milky white, covered by a filmy
layer of dust like ghost horses whose riders had forsaken
them. She swung the flashlight to the left, illuminating a
dozen wooden barrels arranged on a platform. The platform
itself was broken up into a series of paths, separated from
one another by ropes. A sign on the front of the contraption
said: *The Tickler*. Anne's mother had told her about the
ride. The barrels were on movable casters. You climbed in
and rolled down a wooden incline, bumping into other people in barrels along the way. Her mother said it was loads
of fun. Dreamland was in full swing back then. During the
mid-1950s, when Anne's mother and father were dating,
they used to come here and ride the Shoot-the-Chutes and
the Steeplechase.

Evelyn told her about all the wonderful attractions: The
railway that rattled through enchanted grottos. The motorized bumper cars. The Space Ship that vibrated so furiously
that couples were thrown against one another, their knees
and shoulders colliding, providing the only fumbling contact that teenagers living in the Heights were permitted. The
donkey rides up and down the boardwalk, and the red-and-

white striped bathing tents that looked like jellyfish with curtains. The mouthwatering food—deviled clams, plum pudding, sausages, saltwater taffy. The three-hundred-foot-tall observation tower, with a genuine steam engine that took people to the top. The giant seesaw. The painted carts pulled by goats. The pavilion after dark, defined by strings of light bulbs causing every bulge and spike on the exterior to look as if it were sketched in flame. The mineral cures. The flea circus. And best of all, the amazing Dreamland Museum, peopled by freaks of nature so beautiful and terrible to behold that Evelyn told Anne it made her insides weak and gave her nightmares and made her somehow ashamed of being normal, ashamed and strangely terrified to wake from a dream and discover she'd turned into the Turtle Girl, with scaly arms and a hard, spotted shell.

Anne peered around her. Along the wall were large glass cases and metal cages with bars, the kinds of cages she'd seen at the zoo. She realized that she was standing in the heart of Dreamland, smack in the middle of the most elaborate freak show on the Jersey shore. A rat as big as her fist dashed out from one of the cages. Anne drew back, shuddering. There were probably all sorts of rodents and bugs in this creepy place. She shined her flashlight up toward the ceiling. No bats, thank heavens. Just rafters thick with cobwebs and jagged holes punched in the roof. She paused by the cage where she had seen the rat. The cage was about ten feet tall and fifteen feet wide. The bottom and the rear wall were lined with torn red velvet. Anne peered between the bars. There was a tall three-legged stool inside the cage, next to thick coils of rope and what looked like a silver sword. She swept the flashlight over the length of the cage. On the ground, toward the back, was a sign painted on a piece of driftwood showing a woman with her head tilted back, swallowing a fiery sword. Underneath the picture it said: *The Lady Flame*. So the freak show included a female fire eater. Anne wondered if the woman—if all the women here for that matter—was coerced into performing for the crowds who flocked to Dreamland. Did the women willingly display their deformities and show off their bizarre tricks for a paycheck, punching in from nine to five? Or were they captives, helpless prisoners of the amusement park, who, when the park closed down in 1965, simply ceased to exist?

From somewhere off to her left, she heard a faint scratching sound.

"Susie," she called. Her voice echoed back to her— *Susie . . . Susie . . . Susie*—growing fainter each time.

Anne tried again. "Susie," she called into the darkness. "Are you there? It's Anne Hardaway." *Anne Hardaway . . . Anne Hardaway . . . Anne Hardaway.*

Her voice sounded thin and queer, as if it belonged to someone else. She guided the flashlight to her watch. 10:18 P.M. These last few minutes had seemed like an eternity. She inched forward. What if Susie's corpse was sprawled in a cage, her throat slit from ear to ear? Susie could be strangled or poisoned. Stone cold dead. Just up ahead, Anne heard a faint *plink,* like a stone hitting a well. She felt the blood pulsing in her neck. The bars of the cages loomed against the walls, great towering shadows that gave Dreamland the look of a prison. And that smell was getting stronger—the odor of rot and decay. It smelled like death. Without warning, she was shoved from behind, her pocketbook wrenched from her shoulder. She half-turned, her hands pinwheeling in front of her. The flashlight dropped. It was pitch dark. A scream escaped her lips. She staggered back, scrambling wildly, but the floor had dropped away, and she was falling, down, down into the darkness until her head hit bottom, and she blacked out.

Chapter 25

Housework can kill you—
but sometimes it's worth it.

Something warm and wet was trickling down her face. Her eyes fluttered open. Dark. All around her the deep cool dark of a cave. Is that where she was, in a cave? She struggled back to consciousness as if awakening from a dream. Images floated in and out, borne by the darkness. Bursts of color appeared and disintegrated like shooting stars. Somewhere above, a white light. Was she dead? No. Her head wouldn't ache so much if she were dead. She felt like it was about to burst open. She touched her hand to her forehead. It came away wet. She smelled the coppery scent of blood. Slowly, she pulled herself up to a sitting position. Her left ankle throbbed. She groped for it in the darkness and touched solid rock. No, not a cave. A hole in the floor. A small, narrow hole where the foundation had given way.

The smell was unbearable. The death smell. It was coming from here, in the hole. She pressed her hands to her head, trying to make the dizziness go away. Her knee brushed against something small. Reaching out, she touched it, her fingers gliding over matted fur, smooth cold

267

bones. She jerked her hand away. An animal. A dead animal. Dozens of them, scattered all around her. The hole was a graveyard for animals that fell in by accident and got trapped. Or a lair for a large animal to store its food. She shuddered.

Above her, she heard a string of muttered curses. A white light crisscrossed the opening above the hole. "Help," Anne yelled, at the top of her lungs. "Somebody help me."

Instantly, the light was trained on the hole, blinding her. She squinted, beckoning to the person holding the flashlight. It was *her* flashlight, the one she'd dropped. "Help," she yelled again. "Help me."

"Stop your caterwauling," a voice said. "Nobody can hear you." A man's voice, a man she knew.

"What?" she gasped.

The light shifted to the right of Anne, so it wasn't shining directly in her face. She could see a little better now. The hole was about twenty feet deep and three feet wide. Awash in mud and dirt and heaps of dead animals, some half-rotted, others stripped to glistening piles of bones. She stared at them, horrified.

"The letter," the voice said. "Give it to me."

She glimpsed the man's arm, the sleeve of his shirt. The sleeve was blue.

"I don't know what you mean," she mumbled. But she did know. The letter from "A Friend" wasn't in her handbag. When she left the house, she'd tucked it into the pocket of her jeans.

"Where is it, Anne?" the voice asked. Firmly, this time, as if he meant business. The voice of a man used to being in charge.

And all of a sudden she realized who it was, who stood above her wielding the light. He knew how to operate the printing press. He sent the letter framing Tigger for arson. And now he wanted it back.

"Why, Jim? Why'd you plant the bomb in the Spray View?"

"The letter," he repeated.

"I'll give you the letter if you give me some answers. I'm not going anywhere."

The flashlight wavered a bit, and then climbed the rock wall of the hole. Anne looked up. Directly above her was Jim Walser's flushed, perspiring face, his egg-shaped bald head.

"What have you done with Susie Jenks?" she demanded.

He laughed. "Susie doesn't exist. I needed a way to get you here."

Her heart thudded against her chest. She ran her tongue over her lips and tasted blood. "Why destroy the Spray View?" she persisted. If she kept him talking, someone would find her. She wouldn't be left in this hole to die.

Jim Walser let out a sigh. "Ed was going to change the rules."

"What rules?"

"The association rules. He was fixing to sell the hotel. Greedy bastard wanted the full purchase price. He didn't want the town to get its cut."

Anne's mind was racing. The four percent commission on property bought and sold was meant for improvement projects—preventing beach erosion, beautifying Main Street, renovating the Church by the Sea. But they'd been working on restoring the church for more than thirty years. The work never seemed to get finished. "You've been pocketing the real estate commissions."

Jim Walser smiled. "As association president, I don't get paid a salary."

"But you owned your own real estate firm all those years."

"Real estate's a tricky business, Anne. Lots of lean times, when the market's so bad a body can't give houses away. Besides, I got to cover Carolyn's medical bills. Insurance money ran out years ago."

Carolyn Walser. She'd developed multiple sclerosis before Anne was born. The Walsers' house was equipped with all sorts of devices to make her life easier: a motorized lift, custom-built fixtures in each bathroom, brick ramps leading up to the front and back porch. Carolyn even had a live-in nurse to look after her.

"How did you learn to build a bomb?"

"Korean War. I worked in a munitions unit. We lobbed all kinds of explosives at the Chinese."

"You almost got Tigger and Teri killed."

Walser folded his arms across his chest. "Timer went off too soon. He was supposed to have lit the damn fire-cracker fifteen minutes before the bomb went off. Ruthie shouldn't have been there. I heard Ed on the phone. He specifically told Sandy to take the girl down to the beach."

"Tigger figured the whole thing out when he came back here. He knew you were behind the fire, that you tried to frame him."

"He found some stupid book in the library, started putting two and two together. Guess he wasn't as dumb as he looked."

Of course. Why hadn't she seen it before? Tigger didn't care about tracing his family tree in *Vintage Victoriana*. He was interested in the other half of the book, the part that described the Heights Association's rules and regulations in copious detail. After Tigger realized that the letter was composed on the association's printing press, he must have narrowed down the list of suspects. Walser had the strongest motive—solid, old-fashioned greed.

"You used the press deliberately, didn't you? If the police got hold of the letter, they'd think Ed Klemperer set the fire himself to collect the insurance money."

Suddenly, Anne was blinded by the flashlight. She threw her hand up, shielding her face.

"The letter. Give it to me," Walser said icily.

"Why?"

"Mills used it to get to me. You would have, too. I couldn't have you running to the police with your theories and suspicions. When you stopped by my office this afternoon, I was surprised by how much you already knew."

"Could you get that light out of my eyes?" Anne said. Walser lowered the flashlight. Colored spots danced in front of Anne's face. Reaching into her pocket she removed the letter from "A Friend." "Here it is," she said, waving the yellowed sheet of paper. "Come on down."

Walser squatted above the hole, his eyes fixed on the letter. "Crumple it into a ball and throw it up here," he said.

Anne stared at him. Her ankle hurt so much it felt like it was on fire. "First, I want some answers. Tell me how Tigger died."

"He drowned," Walser said with a grin.

"Somehow I don't think so."

"It's the God's honest truth. He got hold of that letter and came to see me. Told me he was going to turn me over to the police. I said I had a better idea."

"How much did you offer him?"

"Sixty grand."

She remembered how confident Tigger had seemed that night. He was going to win his court case, get his house back. Hell, he acted like he could just about shoot the moon. And why not—with $60,000 in the bank. "What'd you do to him?"

"He came aboard my boat, and we went for a little ride. The ocean was nice and quiet. Most of the folks watching the fireworks had gone home. Tigger was still celebrating though. Helping himself to my liquor. Lord, how that man could drink. He was standing out on deck, probably counting the things he was gonna do with the money. I came up behind him and hit him on the head with my tackle box."

"Then you pulled off his clothes," Anne said, with disgust.

"That's right. Your friend was drunk as a skunk. I wanted it to look like he'd gone for a dip in the ocean, swam out too far, and underestimated the power of the booze. When I pushed him over the side of the boat, I thought it'd be weeks before they found him. But the son of a bitch must have regained consciousness. Guess he was too plastered to make it all the way back."

Anne shivered. She looked at the bones scattered next to her, imagined Tigger swimming toward shore. He must have struggled to remain afloat for hours. "And Sandy

Cooksey? Did Sandy know you planted the bomb at the Spray View?"

"Nope. She didn't know anything except how to shoot dope through her veins. What's the phrase the kids use? Clueless. If she had half a brain, she'd have been dangerous. Tigger tracked her down, told her all about what I'd done. See, he had some crazy idea she'd seen me sneak into the inn that night. He was hoping she'd back him up. That was when he was fixing to turn me over to the cops. Before he got greedy. He even gave her a copy of that damn letter you're holding."

"She was going to show it to us, wasn't she? She was going to tell us you were responsible for Ruthie's death. Why didn't she run from you the minute she saw you on the pier?"

"Because I had something she was dying to get hold of."

"What'd you do? Make her a deal? Her silence for a dime bag of heroin?"

Walser rose to his feet. "I did the Heights a favor," he scowled. "We don't need hookers parading up and down our beach."

"Where'd you get the strychnine?"

"From Ed's lab. I paid him a visit on Saturday, and helped myself when he wasn't looking. Just in case the police got to thinking about who keeps poison lying around the house. Now, I don't know about you, but I've done enough talking. I want that letter," he said, his eyes narrowing. "And I want it now."

"So you can leave me here to die? Nothing doing."

Walser reached behind him and pulled out a handgun. Steadying the flashlight beam, he pointed the gun at her chest. "Sorry, Annie. You should have let things be."

Anne heard the click of the safety. Her heart thumped wildly. "Wait," she cried out. "It won't look like an accident." Walser hesitated. "It's supposed to, right? I've been telling people I'm researching a book on the Heights. I decide to poke around Dreamland, only I fall down a hole and break my neck."

"Something like that. You know, Annie, you're too smart for your own good."

"When they find my body, they'll find the letter, too. Don't you see? They'll figure it out."

Walser lowered the gun, stepped away from the hole. Darkness enveloped her. She hugged her arms to her chest, shaking with relief. He wasn't going to kill her. All she had to do was wait. Someone would find her. She rested her head on her knees. No, they wouldn't. Nobody lived near Dreamland. They'd built it out here on purpose, so the noise wouldn't disturb people living in Landsdown or the Heights. As a member of the planning committee to restore the amusement park, Walser was one of the few people in Monmouth County with a key. And he sure as hell wasn't sending reinforcements. "Help," she screamed, knowing no one could hear. "Help me." The stench from the animals was unbearable. And then she smelled something else, something bright and deadly. Her heart flip-flopped. Looking up, she saw a faint orange glow just beyond the rim of the hole.

She struggled to her feet, howling in pain when she stepped on her ankle. "Jim, wait," she cried out. "Please, you can't."

He appeared above her, his face damp with sweat. "Bye, Anne."

"You can't just leave me to die like the others. You *know* me. We're friends."

Behind the thick frames of his glasses, his eyes looked like black marbles. "You know too much."

Her mouth was dry with fear. She opened it to speak, but before she could utter a sound she heard someone say his name.

Walser froze, hearing it too. He wheeled around. "You," he said, to someone Anne couldn't see. "What are you doing here?"

He reached for his gun. A shot rang out, followed by another. Walser pitched sideways. He hit the ground with a thud, his hand dangling near the edge of the hole.

"Help," Anne yelled. "Help. I'm down here."

She heard footsteps. A face peered down at her, a pale face with shaggy hair and a long white beard. "Miss Hardaway," said Ed Klemperer. "You all right?" One of his hands hung limply at his side, the other clutched a pistol.

"My ankle's sprained."

"I'll go for help."

"There's no time," she said. "The fire's spreading fast." As she spoke, she heard a loud crackling noise, followed by a crash. "What's happening?"

"The carousel. It's burning."

"Listen," Anne said quickly. "I saw some rope in one of those cages against the wall. Get it. Hurry."

Klemperer stumbled away. Already the air was tinged with smoke. The fire gave off a fierce light, illuminating her prison: the rock walls, the mud, the dead animals with their empty, glittering eyes. If she died down here, she'd end up like them, a heap of rotten flesh, bones crumbling to dust. After what seemed like forever, Klemperer came back with the rope.

"Is there anything you can tie it to?" she called up to him.

He looked around. "There's a post over there. Don't know how sturdy it is."

"Try it."

He disappeared again. Anne craned her head, trying to gauge how far the fire had spread. The smell of smoke was stronger now. Jim Walser lay motionless where he fell, his hand outstretched. He wore a big gold ring with a black onyx stone in the center. The sight of it made Anne's blood run cold. Would Jim Walser's pinkie ring be the last thing she saw before succumbing to smoke inhalation? She wondered if her death would be like Tigger's—a slow struggle against the forces of nature—the flames consuming her, tearing her flesh to ashes. Panic welled up in her throat. The air was as hot and dry as an oven.

"Here," Ed Klemperer called, tossing down the rope.

Anne struggled to her feet. A spear of pain shot through her left ankle. Reaching up, she grasped the rope with both hands and swung herself off the ground, flailing her legs wildly. The walls of the hole were uneven, with crevices on either side. She wedged her feet into the narrow opening and let out a scream.

"What?" Ed cried. "What's the matter?"

"My ankle," she gasped, "I think it's broken."

She propelled herself higher, working her way up the rope a couple of inches at a time. Above her, the air shimmered. Her hands were burning, raw from the rope. Swinging from side to side, she shoved her feet into crevices in the rock wall, trying to ignore the pain searing her ankle each time she put pressure on her left foot. Her arms ached. The muscles in her legs felt like they were turning to jelly.

"Come on," Klemperer yelled. "You're almost there."

I can't hold on, she thought. *I can't. Can't.* Everything hurt—her hands, her head. Her ankle throbbed so badly her eyes watered. She strained against the rope, willing herself not to give in to the pain. The opening of the hole was just above her. Reaching out, she curled one arm over the edge, a few feet away from where Walser lay. Letting go of the rope, she hugged the ground with both arms, her feet dangling beneath her. She felt Klemperer reach out and grab her by the shoulders. With all her remaining strength, she swung her good leg over the top of the hole and rolled on her back, panting.

"Hurry," Klemperer urged. "We don't have much time."

All around them, the amusement park was ablaze. The fire was spreading fast. Flames scrambled up the Shoot-the-Chutes, devouring the ring-toss booth and the wooden barrels on the Tickler ride. The giant Wheel of Fortune had crumbled to the ground.

"Is he dead?" Anne shouted, pointing to Jim Walser.

"I . . . I don't know," Klemperer stammered.

Anne limped over to where Walser was lying. His eyes were wide open. There was a hole in his neck the size of a quarter. "Come on," Anne said to Klemperer. "Let's get out of here."

The old man put his arm around her waist. "Lean against me," he said.

Anne looked around, trying to find the way out. Smoke burned her eyes. To the left, the carousel was engulfed by flames, the wooden horses crackled and fell.

"Straight ahead," Klemperer said. "Through the museum."

They hurried past the metal cages, which seemed impervious to the flames. For the moment, Dreamland's freak show was still intact, unscathed by the fire gathering force behind them. When they reached the entrance, Anne tried the big gold knobs on the wooden door. "It's locked," she cried out.

"What'll we do?" Klemperer said, his eyes bulging in terror.

"Didn't you come through here?"

"No. The door was locked from the outside. I broke a window near the bumper cars. But we can't go back that way. We'll be caught in the fire."

"We have to break it down," Anne said, coughing. She couldn't breathe, it felt like her lungs were clogged with smoke.

She backed up a few paces, hurled herself against the door. It held fast. "Now you," she yelled to Klemperer, as she hugged her aching shoulder.

The old man threw himself against the door and immediately staggered back. "I can't," he cried out. "We're trapped."

"No," she said. She backed up a little further and started to run, her ankle throbbing with every step. When she hit the door, she heard a groan, felt the wood give way. She pitched forward, falling to the ground as the door swung open.

Outside, it was raining hard. She was soaking wet in an instant. But the rain was cool against her skin. She stumbled to her feet, with Klemperer trailing behind her. Limping past the metal fence, she headed toward where she'd parked.

Sirens wailed in the distance. She looked toward the Heights and saw three fire trucks speeding down Ocean Avenue. At the car, she reached in her pocket for her keys and realized they were inside her handbag, the bag Jim Walser took from her. Her fingers brushed against the letter from "A Friend." She started to take it out, then shoved it back inside the pocket of her jeans, so the rain wouldn't smear the print. Beside her, Ed Klemperer was staring at the fire, tears streaming from his eyes.

"Ruthie," he whispered. "My poor sweet baby."

"It's okay," she said gently. "It's over." The pain in her ankle shot straight up her leg. She sat down gingerly by the side of the road. Behind her, Dreamland was ablaze with light. The ruined amusement park glowed orange against the night sky.

"What I don't understand," Jack said, "is how Klemperer knew you were at the amusement park."

"Apparently, he followed me," Anne said. "He told me he was thinking about what we'd accused him of—hiring Tigger to destroy the Spray View. It didn't make sense to him. He drove over to my house to ask me more about it just as I was leaving for Dreamland."

They were sitting in the wicker swing on Anne's front porch the following morning, eating French toast and strawberries.

"Will he have to go to jail?" Jack asked.

"No. Officer Hefferle said it sounded like Klemperer shot Jim Walser in self-defense."

"How much do you think Walser's made over the years, sucking the town dry?"

"Millions, probably. The price of real estate keeps going up and that means bigger and bigger commissions on each property bought and sold."

She wiggled the toes on her left foot. Her cast itched. The doctor said it would take about six weeks for her ankle to heal.

"You think Walser was behind the death threat Tigger got?"

"No. I think we can thank Joe Vance for that one."

"The druggist?"

"Uh huh. Those words he cut out from magazines looked a lot like what Tigger described."

"So he broke into Ravenswood and destroyed his handiwork after Tigger died?"

Anne reached for the syrup. "I think Heather took the death threat. I've thought so ever since I went to see her. She looked so scared when I asked her about it. Tigger probably showed it to her when she was in his room."

"And she guessed her father was behind it?"

"Sure. She knew Joe hated Tigger and blamed him for the abortion. It would have been easy for her to swipe it when he wasn't looking. She probably ripped it up and hoped that her father wouldn't carry out his threats."

A boy on a bicycle rode by the house and tossed a newspaper on the porch steps. "I'll get it," Jack said, retrieving a copy of the *Oceanside Heights Press*. "Let's see what's going on in the world." He removed the rubber band, unfurled the paper and read the headlines. FIREFIGHTERS BATTLE BLAZE IN AMUSEMENT PARK, HEIGHTS ASSOCIATION PRESIDENT KILLED. I suspect you've had your fill of that story. Here's another one that should interest you: COPS INEFFECTIVE IN WAR ON DRUGS, COMMISSIONER CALLS FOR DEPARTMENT REVIEW."

"You mean Hefferle could really lose his job?" Anne said.

"It's about time. Maybe the police force should hire *you*."

"Thanks," she said ruefully, touching the bandage on her forehead. "But I think I'll stick to writing."

"Speaking of cops, I feel like turning P.J. in to the police. He didn't exactly help Tigger all these years. Not to mention his blackmail scheme."

Anne smiled. "That's kaput, now that Teri's in the clear. She should be relieved to learn she didn't kill anyone that night."

"Jim Walser turned so many lives upside down. Not just my brother's."

"All these years, I thought he was being so nice to me and my mother," Anne said, taking a sip of orange juice.

"What he really wanted was to get her out of town. He even helped us locate a nursing home in Red Bank."

"Why?"

"Because she was an eyesore. You can't sell beachfront property when there's a crazy lady loose in the neighborhood. I'm ashamed to admit it, but for a couple of minutes there, I actually thought my mother started the fire in the Spray View."

Jack stared at her. "You're kidding."

"She used to be fascinated by fire—matches, the burners on the stove. It got so bad I had to take her cigarettes away. I remember worrying she was going to burn our house down. Thank God she didn't."

"You really love this old place, don't you?"

"Yeah. I guess I do. Look out there."

Jack followed her gaze. The ocean was a sultry shade of turquoise, glinting in the sunlight. "Then you're not going to sell the house?"

She turned toward him. "I don't think so. It's not just that my mother was attached to this place. I'm pretty attached, too. The house, this town—it's home. Besides, I couldn't bear not living by the water. It's hard to explain, but the ocean is a part of me."

Jack reached out and touched her hand. "Anne . . ." he began. She turned toward him. "I could kick myself for racing off like that last night. If anything had happened to you . . ." His expression was gentle, his blue eyes filled with concern. "Anyway, I want to thank you for getting to the bottom of this thing. Nothing can bring Tigger back. But I'm glad we finally know what happened to him. After all these years, his name is cleared. It's like he can finally rest in peace."

Anne stared out at the ocean, which was calm and still as glass. "Tigger was the town scapegoat," she said. "He was ostracized. People blamed him for things that weren't his fault. And I guess I identified with him, you know? Because growing up here, I was blamed, too. For being my mother's daughter, for the things she did. Does that make any sense?"

"Absolutely." He leaned over and kissed her firmly on the mouth. "Just so you know how wrong they were about you. How great you are. These last few days, you've become very important to me. I don't want to lose you."

She smiled. "You won't."

"Even if I'm miles away in New York?"

"It's only an hour and a half by car. I can come visit. And you can stay with me on weekends. Summer's just beginning. There's going to be lots of beautiful beach days." She glanced down at her cast. "Even if I can't go in the water."

"I don't care what we do, as long as we're together." He scooped her up in his arms and carried her down the front steps of the porch.

"Hey," she said, laughing, as the wind whipped through her hair. "Where are we going?"

"To the beach," he grinned. "You might not be able to swim, but we can sit on the sand and count clouds for a while."

"There aren't any clouds," Anne said, glancing skyward. He looked up. Above them, the sky was a powdery blue dome arching over the turquoise ribbon of the sea.

BETH SHERMAN is a writer and editor based in New York City. She writes a biweekly column, "Design and Décor," for *Newsday* that gives decorating tips and home-related advice. Her work has also appeared in the *New York Times*, the *New York Post, Cosmopolitan, Ladies' Home Journal, Harper's Bazaar, Martha Stewart Living, Bride's, Fitness, Working Woman, House Beautiful, American Health, Parents*, and many other publications. *Dead Man's Float* is her first mystery.